PETER ROSE is a graduate of the George Washington University and the Yale Law School. He first practiced law in Washington DC. It was during a posting in Hong Kong with Goldman Sachs as its Asian Head of Public Affairs that he started to visit Macao – an hour's ferry-ride across the Pearl River delta from Hong Kong – and became fascinated with the story of this incongruous piece of Portugal on the edge of China.

T0258660

The Good War
of Consul Reeves

Peter Rose

BLACKSMITH BOOKS

For Alicia, Erica, Alexis and Evan

_____

The Good War of Consul Reeves

ISBN 978-988-76748-7-0

Published by Blacksmith Books
Unit 26, 19/F, Block B, Wah Lok Industrial Centre,
37-41 Shan Mei Street, Fo Tan, Hong Kong
Tel: (+852) 2877 7899
www.blacksmithbooks.com

Cover images:
Upper: Japanese soldiers. Photograph by Malcolm Rosholt.
Image courtesy of Mei-Fei Elrick and Special Collections,
University of Bristol Library (www.hpcbristol.net).
Lower: Junk in Macao harbor. Photograph by Henry Rue. Image
courtesy of SOAS Library, document reference HR01-092.
Many thanks to University of Bristol Library and SOAS Library.

Contents

Cidade Do Nome De Deus: Não Há Outra Mais Leal

"The City of the Name of God: There is None More Loyal"

The motto of the Portuguese colony of Macao

Prologue

The day the Japanese consul in Macao was shot was beautiful, not unusual in February, which was by far the most pleasant month in this little Portuguese colony on the coast of southern China. When Mr. Fukui – that was the name of the Japanese consul – left his consulate on the *Calcada do Gaio* for his morning walk that day, a few minutes before 7:00am, he was reminded of a spring day in Japan when warm sunlight would flicker through thick clouds of white and pink blossoms floating on the cherry trees. Mr. Taki, the secretary to the consulate, accompanied him on his walk. Mr. Fukui and Mr. Taki were dressed in dark suits with shirts and knotted ties; Mr. Fukui had placed a Homburg hat precisely level on his head.

It was 1945, and Mr. Fukui on his walks would think only of how badly the war was going for Japan. He thought back often about how the Army and Navy had launched a war against China over a dozen years ago – quite against the advice of the Foreign Ministry, but they never listened. Then just four years ago, the Army and Navy had struck boldly at the Americans at Pearl Harbor and the British in Hong Kong and gone on to conquer much of Asia. But those victories now seemed many years ago and they had been followed by the many defeats and losses he had read about in the secret papers from the Foreign Ministry. Now the massive fleets of the American Navy were close enough to Japan to launch aircraft to bomb its cities; those same fleets had destroyed almost all of the Japanese Navy; and the Japanese Army, in retreat elsewhere, was mired in an interminable war in China, where there was little chance of victory.

The end was near, thought Mr. Fukui; it was simply a question of time before Japan was defeated. But there would be a world after the war.

Then the Foreign Ministry would resume its rightful position as Japan's sole representative to the world, the Army and Navy would be shamed, and he would play his part – in Europe, he hoped, because he spoke English. He would be part of building a new world, a world held together by diplomacy and men like him. He was sure, at least most of the time, that the Foreign Ministry would remember who he was when they were looking for people for these roles.

He did not mind waiting in Macao. The Foreign Ministry in a rare victory had prevailed with the Cabinet in Tokyo to order the Army not to seize Macao when it had conquered Hong Kong, just thirty-five miles away to the east. Portugal was neutral in this war and the Army had reluctantly submitted to the command to respect Macao's neutrality. Macao became a tiny island of peace surrounded by a vast storm-ravaged ocean of a brutal war. Here at least, Mr. Fukui could fulfill his proper role as consul and as the most senior Japanese representative. Besides, Mr. Fukui from his first day here thought that this small city looked exactly like the pictures he had seen in books and magazines of towns on the shores of the Mediterranean. This Mediterranean town, however, ten thousand miles from Europe, clung to a small peninsula in Canton Province in China where the Pearl River met the South China Sea. Although he did not know it that morning, Macao would be the closest he would ever come to Europe.

Closing the gate in the low stone wall surrounding the consulate, he came out onto the street, and, as was his habit, turned around for a brief look. There were the Chinese shops, now shuttered, under the arcades of the *Rua do Henrique de Macedo*. There was the Japanese consulate still in shadow, its Italianate architecture in outline. There was the British consulate next door, also built in the Italian style and nearly identical to his own. Over four years ago, six months after war was declared between Japan and Great Britain, the British consul, Mr. Reeves, had moved away to a big white house on Penha Hill. At the time Mr. Fukui had thought that Consul Reeves must have found it awkward to live next to the representative of a country with which Great Britain was at war.

Mr. Fukui still missed the brief conversations the two had had before the declaration of war.

Consul Reeves was the only senior representative of any of the nations fighting Japan within a radius of thousands of miles. Mr. Fukui had often wondered if his was a lonely existence. Perhaps once the war was over, they would meet again in Europe, when their two nations could work together on the great project of rebuilding a devastated world. This is what diplomats do. They do not go to war. He and Consul Reeves had no part in the fighting.

Mr. Fukui turned to face the road that led up Guia Hill; Mr. Taki fell in alongside him, but still slightly behind, too polite to talk to Mr. Fukui without being spoken to first. At the foot of the hill, the road narrowed and began to climb steeply. This side of the hill was still in shade and chilly; Mr. Fukui and Mr. Taki had no issue with keeping their coats buttoned. But then the road rounded a curve and suddenly the two men, breathing heavily, were in full sunshine and warmth at the summit of Guia Hill.

The city of Macao on its western slopes had just caught the light. Mr. Fukui saw the ancient forts and castles on hills and the city walls twisting over ridges; he saw a score of spires and towers of churches and cathedrals; he saw the merchants' and officials' houses painted in pinks, lemon-yellow, peppermint, blue, magenta and ochre. Their balconies were still in shade, but he saw a few people sitting in wicker chairs enjoying the cooler weather.

He looked over the water to the north and there were, very close he thought, the long low gray hills, half-hidden in the morning mist, that marked the coast. Behind those hills was all of China, and Mr. Fukui thought of the one million Japanese soldiers in their thirteenth year of the war without end in that country. Mr. Fukui turned again and started down the hill to return to the consulate and Mr. Taki fell in, just behind him.

"We will go down that street," Mr. Fukui said, pointing at the *Calçada dos Parses*, "and then through the park." Mr. Fukui had trouble pronouncing the Portuguese names of the streets and did not often say them. There were blue-and-white tiles on walls with the names of the streets in both Portuguese and Chinese and he could sometimes make out the Chinese characters because they were similar to those used in Japanese. But the Portuguese names of the streets were almost always different from the Chinese names, so that was of little help.

Mr. Fukui looked at the houses with affection: some had deeply shaded porches and verandahs that ran the length of both stories, others had curved wrought-iron balconies made of fantastical curlicues. He loved the colors of the houses, the yellows, reds, blues and greens, like a painting. There were gardens hidden behind tall walls. From the street you could see the trees above the walls – tall pines or royal palms, or the tops of orange and lemon trees, some of which had just started to blossom.

He had been invited to parties in some of the gardens. The walls kept out the noise of the city and there was a quiet that always surprised him. The trees provided shade and their leaves caught almost any breeze with a soft whisper of a rustle. Even in the heat of summer, he felt cool in the garden. People talked happily; there were drinks with ice. Macao was a tiny kingdom of its own and it was as though the whole tumultuous bloody war-torn world outside did not exist.

He and Mr. Taki continued down the street to Vasco da Gama Park and walked through it to come out on the *Rua de Henrique de Macedo,* almost back at the consulate to begin the day's work.

On one side of the street was the long arcade with the shops behind it that Mr. Fukui could see from the consulate. Some of the shopkeepers, already up, were removing the tall shutters that had covered the fronts of the shops when they closed for the night. In front of the stores on the pavement were small shrines, each with a squatting clay god grinning broadly at the passers-by. At the base of these shrines, a few sticks of incense, the white ash at their tips smoldering, had been pushed into tin cans filled with dirt. The wisps of smoke drifted in the air and Mr. Fukui caught the occasional scent of the incense. He thought of the temples in his home town in Japan, the burning incense in them, and wondered if he too was under the protection of these gods.

At first he did not see the two Chinese men, gaunt, pale – almost skeletons, barefoot and dressed only in ragged pajama pants and dirty singlets, the skin of the faces paper-thin and stretched tightly so that the bones of the jaw and cheeks could be seen in outline. They lay barely covered, propped against the arcade facing the street, their eyes looking off to the side and their chests heaving up and down in shallow breaths the only sign of life. These were some of the tens of thousands of refugees who had fled the fighting in China and swarmed into Macao, many only to die on the streets. Mr. Fukui thought of all the death he had seen. He had been sent out by the Embassy in Nanking to help document the slaughter of the Chinese population of that city by the army – the civilian diplomats at the Embassy made a strong protest to Tokyo of this violation of the norms of war, but their protests were ignored and the massacre continued unimpeded. He had seen so many dead on the streets of Nanking that now he did not sometimes notice a dead or dying refugee on the streets of Macao. He sometimes felt ashamed of this.

Mr. Fukui had taken a few steps on the other side of the street before stopping. Looking across to the arcade, he saw a person, mostly hidden by a column and the rest of him deep in the shadows. All Mr. Fukui could see clearly was an arm in the sunshine, extended towards him. The hand at the end of the arm was holding a large long-barreled pistol, with a black metal box under the barrel. The gun looked heavy, a little like Colonel Sawa's pistol. In Mr. Fukui's mind at that moment, time had stopped and he thought only about Colonel Sawa.

Colonel Sawa commanded a unit of the Kempeitai, the Japanese military police, that the Japanese army had moved into Macao. This was a clear violation of Portugal's neutrality and the Foreign Ministry had protested to the Prime Minister and the Cabinet in Tokyo. But the Foreign Ministry rarely won an argument with the Army, and Colonel Sawa's military police unit stayed in Macao. The Portuguese authorities were silent about this violation of neutrality, perhaps realizing they could do nothing about it. There were 1,500 Portuguese troops in Macao and 60,000 Japanese soldiers just across Macao's northern border in China. Some things you pretended did not exist.

Colonel Sawa would often just appear at the consulate without an appointment and walk into Mr. Fukui's office to berate him for one thing or another. Colonel Sawa saw Mr. Fukui as the embodiment of the political interference that had stopped the Japanese army from invading and occupying Macao, as it had done in so much of the rest of Asia. Mr. Fukui had never seen any fighting as Colonel Sawa had. Instead he was sitting out the war in some comfortable office trying to interfere in the Imperial Japanese Army's plans to conquer all of Asia, even Macao.

Even on the hottest days, Mr. Fukui and his staff would wear their jackets with their ties knotted; Colonel Sawa would arrive in the consulate dressed in his field uniform of rough stained khaki, with his shirt open to the third button. He wore high riding boots but the leather was dull and rough, unlike the high gloss on Mr. Fukui's shoes. Mr. Fukui tried not to look at the fat sagging muscles on Colonel Sawa's chest while the Colonel was yelling about things he did not like in Macao which he expected Mr. Fukui to fix. But then, if Mr. Fukui looked directly at him, he saw Colonel Sawa's unshaven face, the spittle on his lips and chin, and his look that was sometimes a smirk and sometimes a sneer. Colonel Sawa had the rough manners of a rural farmer, which he had been before the war; Mr. Fukui was a graduate of the University of Tokyo. Colonel Sawa had risen through the ranks of the Kempeitai because he was a big brutal man who had no compunction about using his strength against any unfortunate Chinese who offended him; Mr. Fukui had been selected for the Foreign Affairs Ministry by competitive examination. What did this uncouth farmer know about the importance of diplomatic norms and how offensive his presence was in Macao? Was he part of the slaughter of the Chinese in Nanking?

In that instant, those thoughts about Colonel Sawa had flashed through Mr. Fukui's mind.

The hand holding the gun moved slightly to the left and fired twice, the shots first sharp and then echoing amongst the arches. Mr. Taki, standing next to Mr. Fukui, gave a little high-pitched scream, more like a squeal, and his hand went up to his left shoulder, grasping the cloth of his jacket tightly. He made no effort to turn or run, but stayed standing next to Mr. Fukui.

The hand holding the gun then moved a little to the right and down slightly. Three more quick shots were fired and Mr. Fukui felt a dull pain in his stomach. He sat down abruptly on the pavement, keeping his upper body upright, with his hat still level on his head, and his hands clasped low in front of him, pushing on his stomach. He could feel the damp wetness of blood. A red stain slowly spread on his clean white shirt above and below where his jacket was still buttoned. He leaned slightly to the side and his right hand went out to the pavement to keep him from falling over. Mr. Taki, gripping his jacket at his left shoulder, still stood next to Mr. Fukui, who was still looking, uncomprehending, at the hand that held the gun in the shadows of the arcade.

The arm holding the gun lowered and then it was lost in the shadows of the arcade. The shadows shimmered, a shape flickered along the arcade towards the end of the street and then it was gone. The two shopkeepers, still holding the tall shutters that they had been removing from their store fronts, came to the edge of the arcade, staring without expression at the two Japanese, but they did not move to help them.

Mr. Fukui and Mr. Taki were taken by ambulance to the *Hospital Conde de S. Januario*, a large lemon-yellow and white building with long verandahs, tall windows, and an immense portico, two stories high with yellow columns. If you walked out on one of the balconies on either side of the portico, you could look out over the gardens to the South China Sea. Mr. Fukui thought for a moment that he was actually in Europe.

The stretcher-bearers took Mr. Fukui into a big hall between an opened pair of polished and varnished doors. The hall was cool and dark. Mr. Fukui could see several people standing around as though they had been expecting his arrival. At the back of the hall was a series of windows looking into a brightly lit room, which, as Mr. Fukui was carried into it on the stretcher, his Homburg hat placed next to him, he saw was an operating theater with three doctors and several nurses.

Mr. Taki was taken to one of the chairs in the main hall and left to himself in the darkness. It would be hours before the bullet was removed from his shoulder in a doctor's office and he was sent back to the consulate.

The people standing around in the hall moved to the windows of the operating theater, which stretched from the ceiling to the floor to provide a full view of everything that went on inside.

Mr. Fukui was lifted onto the starched white sheets of the operating table and then the two stretcher-bearers left, with Mr. Fukui's Homburg hat still on the stretcher. A surgeon unbuttoned Mr. Fukui's jacket and pushed it to either side to expose all of his blood-soaked shirt. He called for a pair of scissors and began to cut away the shirt to expose Mr. Fukui's stomach.

The doctors looked at the blood and the wounds and then at each other. One doctor leaned down to Mr. Fukui and explained in English that they needed to operate to find any bullets that might still be in him and to staunch any further bleeding. They would need to give him ether. But the doctor's Portuguese accent was strong and his voice was muffled by his surgeon's mask and Mr. Fukui, by now very weak, did not understand any of what was said.

While a doctor and a nurse were fitting a mask to a tube connected to a tank of ether, Mr. Fukui turned his head towards the windows looking into the operating theater. At the last window Mr. Fukui saw Colonel Sawa, his face expressionless, looking directly at him. He saw that he was standing at ease, his hands clasped behind his back. He saw that he was in his rough stained field uniform and that his shirt was half-unbuttoned as usual. He saw the offending sweat stains under each of his arms. He did not want to die and have this crude man live. Mr. Fukui had been respectful to his superiors in the Foreign Ministry; he in his small way had tried to make the world a better place; his parents were dead, he had no brothers or sisters and perhaps no one would remember him but he had done his duty, he had done his duty.

These were Mr. Fukui's last thoughts before the mask was placed over his face, the ether turned on, and he slipped into unconsciousness.

Over the next several hours, the doctors worked diligently, probing for any bullets or fragments that might have lodged in Mr. Fukui's stomach, clamping arteries and otherwise attempting to repair the damage from the shooting.

But it was to no avail and Mr. Fukui died in the late afternoon on what was still a beautiful day, his dreams of being part of the new world that would follow the war unfulfilled. Colonel Sawa, when the surgeons came out and told the people waiting that Mr. Fukui had died on the operating table, went away quickly to find Mr. Taki and learn exactly what Mr. Taki had seen. He was eager to do this as quickly as he could.

Chapter 1

Mr. Reeves, the British consul in Macao, had arrived in the colony to take up his post in June, 1941, a few months before the December declaration of war with Japan by the British and Americans and their allies. He had followed over the years from this little part of Portugal on the southern coast of China the Japanese victories and the long retreat of the British and Allied forces to Australia and India. Then, as fortunes of war reversed, he watched, still from afar, the Allied victories in Burma and the American Navy's triumphs in the Pacific until the present moment in early 1945 when the American army seemed ready to invade Japan itself and secure a final victory.

He took pleasure and a certain amount of pride in what he was doing in Macao. He believed he was doing useful things, unlike in his previous posts in China. He thought his actions might be recognized and he might be promoted to a more important post but he had no illusions that he was a participant in the great events of history. To those, he was a spectator, not a player in the arena, and he watched them take place at a great distance. Other people were fighting the war. He had friends, or at least people he knew, from his university in the Army, Navy and the RAF. They had landed in France on D-Day to storm beachheads in the face of fierce fire, were fighting in the jungles of Burma, and had flown fighter planes in the Battle of Britain. They had led men and shown bravery. Some had been killed and died heroically, honored with posthumous medals. Often, their smiling photos from their bright college days when they were just boys were at the top of the obituaries in the newspapers that were, several months later, delivered to the consulate in Macao. Two of the dead men were on his university rowing crew. He remembered them at college parties, beers in their hands, cigarettes in the other, pretty girls surrounding them and looking up with wide admiring eyes. He never knew to whom to write to express his condolences and even when he did, he wondered if, by now, it was too late. In the end, he did nothing.

He had two uncles on his mother's side who were admirals and he had applied in his last year of university to the Navy. He was rejected for his poor eyesight and even today, he wrestled with the guilt of suspecting he had been secretly relieved at his rejection. He wondered how he would have behaved in the face of danger and death. He never really felt himself in danger in Macao in the four years he had spent here since 1941. The assassination of the Japanese consul in 1945 was so shocking because it was such a contrast to the quiet peaceful life he had come to enjoy in Macao. But even after that singular violent act, Reeves continued to think that his bodyguards and the little pistol the British Embassy in Chungking had sent him were more part of some theatrical performance than a real necessity.

Sometimes, but not often, he wondered what his parents thought of him. When his parents' friends told them of their sons in the Armed Forces, were his parents secretly ashamed of him for not serving? Did they in their own minds compare him unfavorably to his uncles, the admirals? Did they respond by saying Reeves was "in essential war work"?

He had heard his parents use the expression of people who had, by pure luck or happenstance, been far from the fighting during the last war: that "they had had a good war." There was no opprobrium attached to that; far from it, just a recognition that by some random chance a person had had the good fortune to miss the worst of the war. There was even a little envy in their voices when they used the phrase, or perhaps a wry acknowledgement of the vagaries of fate, especially if they or their close ones had been in the bitterest combat. Perhaps people would say of him later that he had had a good war, with a tip of their hat to his good luck.

There was no way of telling his parents what he was doing in any way except in the broadest generalities. All his letters home, like those of all the China consuls, were read and censored in the British Embassy in

Chungking and his mother's letters – his father rarely wrote and then only usually to pass on some cuttings from the newspapers which he thought might be of interest – were infrequent, and then only contained brief superficial news of their comings and goings. She always hoped he was well, that he needed to take care in "those foreign parts" but that was really all. Reeves thought how difficult it must have been for her to try to stay in touch over the ten thousand miles that separated them.

Reeves was an only child whom his parents had had late in life, and they looked on him as he was growing up with a mixture of wonder and incomprehension. He spent some of his childhood alone with his nurse or staying with aunts and uncles and their many children – "we want you to have someone to play with" – before he was old enough to go away to school. His parents visited him there without fail on the prescribed days. They appeared eager to come but the conversations were sometimes halting and awkward. He could see they were trying; the little jokes that did not quite succeed; the questions about his studies and games that trailed off after a while; the packet of sweets and the half-crown his father slipped to him; the awkward hug from his mother and the handshake from his father when they left, always some of the first to depart. Reeves had wished at the time he could have done something to please them more, but it was difficult for him to see what they really wanted of him.

At Cambridge, Reeves had rowed for the university and had studied modern languages. That was not a popular field of study and Reeves sometimes thought that his fellow students in the department were all the outcasts and misfits of Cambridge. After his rejection by the Navy, his father had once started a conversation with him on what he might like to think about as a career. At its end, his father, who was a partner in a large importing business in London, suggested, before glancing at his son with rheumy eyes, that Reeves could perhaps find a suitable position as a traveler for a British company with interests overseas. He did, after all, speak some foreign languages. Reeves thought how rarely his father gave him advice. The last time he remembered was when he was eight and going off to school. "Keep your head down at first," said his father, "and don't be a show-off."

Reeves thought of living overseas and, equally suddenly, thought of joining the Diplomatic Service. He imagined that he would like representing the British Government in different cities, living in Europe or somewhere in the Americas, or even the Middle East. He could negotiate treaties, prevent wars, solve disputes. There would be dinners and drinks parties. He would retire, an honored man, perhaps with a knighthood or at least a medal of some sort. He did not mention this to his father, unsure of how his father might react to even the idea of his son working for the government.

Reeves went to see his tutor at Cambridge, who had friends in Whitehall and often recommended his students for positions in the government. It was one of the last days of term; spring had finally come and the courtyards and quadrangles of Cambridge were flooded with a golden light. It flowed through the gothic tracery of the windows of his tutor's rooms, enveloping the tutor in a bold pattern of shadows and light. Voices Reeves did not recognize and of people he would never know could be heard outside.

Reeves sat entirely in shadows. A glass of sherry was untouched on the small side table next to the tutor. Reeves had finished his glass. He would not be offered another. Reeves, somewhat tentatively, raised the possibility of his applying to the Diplomatic Service. His tutor pursed his fat lips and paused before replying.

"I would not recommend applying to the Diplomatic Service. They are looking for a particular type of man from a certain type of family." He put a slight emphasis on the word "type" as though he thought that was all he had to do to convey the meaning he intended. He paused for a moment and looked over at Reeves to see the effect his words were having. But the tutor's round face was in the sunlight and that of Reeves was in the shadows and he could not see Reeves's expression. The tutor continued, as though Reeves might have missed his point. "Diplomats must be comfortable around kings, lords and heads of governments.

Men from some of our finer families are more used to such interactions than others and thus the Foreign Office prefers to appoint them to the Diplomatic Service."

Reeves's silence disconcerted the tutor and he worried that he might have caused some offense. He went on hastily. "Your family is very distinguished in its own way of course. Your father has a successful career in..." and here he paused as if searching for the right word and then finding it, "commerce, yes, very successful." Reeves remained silent and the tutor felt obliged to offer up something.

"But," he went on, "have you thought of the Consular Service? Very close cousin of the Diplomatic Service – they work hand in glove together. Indeed the Diplomatic Service would be unable to get the job of diplomacy done without the Consular Service taking so many of those small tasks off their hands – looking after British citizens overseas, issuing passports, helping our merchants in foreign markets, reporting back information to the Board of Trade that I am sure they are very appreciative of. And with your father being in..." and here the tutor paused again before saying "commerce." He continued. "Thanks to your father, you have commerce in your family and I am sure you would take to this part of the mission like a duck to water. It would also be in the fine tradition of your school. After all, you went to Haileybury and its predecessor institution prepared the sons of the officers of the East India Company for service in commerce. Cambridge takes a few Haileybury boys each year." This last fact was added abstractly as though Reeves needed reassurance that Haileybury was an acceptable school.

The tutor paused and listened for any sign that he had given offense. He heard no response and so continued regardless. "The Consular Service is always looking for bright young men with a gift for languages. Not like the Diplomatic Service, where they have to rely on their confidential secretaries to do the translation for them. No indeed, consular officers are expected to know the language of the countries they serve in. And you have shown such a facility," and here again the tutor put a faint emphasis on the word "facility" as though it was something slightly illegitimate, "with languages. I am sure the Board of Examiners would view that very favorably. I have friends at Whitehall who superintend the Consular Service. I can always put in a good word if this is a route you would like to pursue."

"Thank you, Sir, you are very kind." Reeves did not say anything further. The tutor waited a little and then stood up and went to his desk. He opened a drawer, and pulled out some papers.

"Here is an application. Bear in mind that Sir Horace at the Foreign Office is a particular" – the emphasis on "particular" – "friend of mine and I am sure when he knows that we are acquainted, he will give your application every" – the emphasis on "every" – "consideration. Let me know when your application has been mailed and I will write to him." The tutor stood up and Reeves understood that the meeting was over and that the tutor considered that he had done everything that he should for him. Reeves stood up and extended his hand to the tutor, who, instead of shaking it as Reeves expected, placed the application papers in his hand.

Reeves completed his application without any particular enthusiasm. He notified his tutor that he had done so and left the university for the last time. He turned around on the street after passing through the college gate. He had seen it so many times in the rain of a gray autumn or winter day that to see it now in the full sun of early summer was as though he was seeing it for the first time.

He returned to his parents' house for the summer to wait for the outcome of his application. He realized that almost unwittingly he had made a decision on a possible career. When he told his parents, they both expressed a brief enthusiasm. Reeves found himself feeling happy that they seemed pleased and was glad that they had so few questions since he was still unsure what the Consular Service did.

It was August when he got his letter from the Foreign Office inviting him to submit to an interview both by a panel from the Foreign Office and by a panel of the Commissioners of the Civil Service. He was not to appear before the panels until October 3rd.

It was still dark the morning of October 3rd when Reeves left for London for his interviews, taking the same early train that father always took. He, his father, and mother ate breakfast together, talking clumsily and intermittently, his parents seemingly unsure of what was the best thing to say to their son before he appeared before the selection boards. They commented, mainly to each other, on the weather, the headlines in *The Times,* and his father recommended a taxi, rather than the Tube, from Waterloo Station to the Foreign Office in Whitehall. When he left with his father for the train, his mother must have thought he was too big to hug but a handshake was inappropriate, so she did nothing. Reeves thought of how much she always wanted to do the right thing.

On the train, his father and he had a first-class compartment to themselves. His father sat in a seat by the window and Reeves sat on the other side in the far corner, so as not to risk their knees touching. His father had removed the newspaper from his briefcase and kept it folded on his knees for several minutes staring out the window before picking up the newspaper and reading it, pausing to read out loud every now and then an item of foreign news that might interest his son, tying it to a comment that Reeves might serve in the city mentioned in the article. Reeves would respond eagerly each time how interesting he found the piece of news. Once he had an image flash into his mind of his entertaining his parents in some grand consular residence. He thought of how impressed his parents would be. He would love to please them in some way. Reeves wanted to start a conversation with his father during the train journey, but he could not think of how to begin although he tried.

The two parted at Waterloo Station, his father wishing him good luck and giving another unexpected piece of advice to just "answer the questions directly; don't try to be clever," and Reeves walked away to where there was a taxi rank, his father heading in the opposite direction. The rain was coming down hard, the sky was low and black and it could have been night. He turned up his collar and got in a taxi, directing the driver to take him to the Foreign Office in Whitehall. The streets were wet and took on a dull oily shine from the street lights. Men in black coats, their heads bowed under black umbrellas, walked in the wind and rain.

Later in his career, looking back, Reeves was surprised how little he could remember of his interviews by the Boards of Examiners of the Foreign Office. He remembered arriving at the dark gothic pile of the Foreign Office in Whitehall. He remembered a disdainful official who led him down a corridor, up stairs and down more corridors before stopping and opening a door into an anteroom. He remembered that there was a single window in that room that gave out onto the street but little light came in. The wind had rattled the window and the rain had crackled on its glass. There was a fireplace set with tinder and coal, but it was not lit and the room was cold. He remembered sitting there alone for a considerable time. Eventually, he had been taken into an adjacent room, equally dark and cold, and sat in an uncomfortable chair in front of a long table covered with black cloth with four chairs behind it.

One group of four gloomy men and then another set of four gloomy men came into the room, sat down behind the long table like inquisitors and asked him questions in a perfunctory manner over the next two hours. Few of the questions seemed to Reeves to be relevant to his suitability to perform the duties of a British consular officer, however dimly he might understand these duties. There were sometimes conversations among the men as though Reeves was not in the room.

Reeves did remember that towards the end of the interrogation by the second panel, one of the panel members – he had been introduced as Mr. Calthorpe-Browne – turned to the three other board members. "If I may have a word," he said, and then without waiting for the permission he had ostensibly sought, turned to Reeves. "You come with a recommendation from Sir Horace in the Foreign Office. He has heard from one of your tutors at your college, whose opinion he values highly." He looked down at his papers and began: "You have a distinguished uncle." Reeves was unsure of to whom he was referring but before he could inquire as to which uncle he meant, the man continued. "Admiral Edward Seymour is, I believe, a relative of yours on your mother's side." He did not wait for a confirmation but went on. "He led the British Naval detachment that marched to the relief of our besieged Legation in Peking during the Boxer Rebellion of 1900. Have you ever thought of serving in China? It would be good to have one of our representatives there with a connection to the Allied victory over the Boxers. It would be a salutary reminder to the Chinese."

Reeves did not remember how he had replied. He recollected essaying what he thought was an inoffensive comment that he would be honored to serve where the Foreign Office had the greatest need and where he could be most useful. He did add that his studies were in European languages and not Asiatic languages, but did not pursue this point after Mr. Calthorpe-Browne had dismissed it with a comment that once you have learned one language, learning another should present only minor difficulties for a clever man. It was unclear whether he was including Reeves as one of the clever men who would experience only minor difficulties. There was the implication that he disapproved of cleverness. His father's advice may have been right.

Then, abruptly, the interview was over. Reeves did not remember how it was concluded but there must have been a private signal amongst the four of them. They all left the room and an official, perhaps hearing the same private signal, came in by the side door and led Reeves down the many corridors and staircases to the front door, where he said goodbye sternly to Reeves but did not shake hands.

* * *

One morning, perhaps three weeks after he had been before the selection boards, he was at breakfast with his father and mother. The housemaid brought in the morning mail and placed the letters next to his father. His father looked at the envelopes, looked at his mother, and then at his son.

"You have two letters from the Foreign Office." His father's attempt to keep a light tone, knowing the letter would have one of two messages, was forced. He handed the letters to his son, together with a paper knife. Reeves could see that he was anxious and he slit the first envelope from the Foreign Office. It had been addressed to him in flowing copperplate in blue-black ink. He read it and looked up at his parents. There was a pause.

"Well, I was not expecting this," he said, looking at the nervous faces of first his mother and then his father. "I suppose we have Uncle Seymour to blame." He paused, but his parents' expressions did not change. "The Foreign Office wants me in China. I am to go to Peking for two years as a student-interpreter to learn Chinese before being appointed to the Chinese Consular Service."

"Peking," exclaimed his mother, "but that is so far away. I was so hoping that you would be on the Continent where perhaps we could have come and visited. I do not see your father and I getting to China at our age." Reeves seemed surprised that his parents were thinking that they might ever visit him but it pleased him that they thought they might. His father said nothing.

Reeves thought that his parents knew that once he left England it would be several years before they would have the chance to see him again and that must weigh on their minds. He thought about how their age showed that morning. His father was nearly 70 and his mother was over 60 and often, as she put it, 'poorly'. When they visited him at school on the prescribed days, they were always the oldest of the parents who came and this had embarrassed him then. Now he just felt a sadness. Then he began to think about working in a country whose language or ways he did not know or appreciate. Somehow he had ended up in the China Consular Service without intending to do so.

"Do you know what is in the second letter?" asked his mother, unable to keep the anxiety out of her voice. Reeves opened it to find a ticket on the *Orama* from Southampton to Shanghai issued by the Orient Steam Navigation Company, instructions to call on the British Consulate in

Shanghai for a train ticket to Peking and a draft on His Majesty's Treasury for a small sum to cover his "necessary and incidental expenses." He showed these to his parents, not knowing whether to keep a light tone.

His father took a day off work, which rarely happened, to drive Reeves down to the docks in Southampton the day the *Orama* was to sail. He had silently and with great care tied Reeves's trunk and suitcases to the roof of the car with a length of rope he had found in the garden shed. Reeves noticed that his father had had his full name, John Pownall Reeves, painted in neat white letters on each piece of his luggage.

He sat in the back seat, by himself, the new briefcase his parents had given him that morning beside him. "You will have a lot of papers in your new job," his mother had said when proudly presenting it to him. "I am sure this will come in useful." They talked a little on the way down; his mother wondered how long a letter would take to reach China; she hoped the Foreign Office would make sure he got a nice British meal every now and then; they talked about how nice it would be to see him when he got his home leave in seven years; his mother hoped that the local tailors could make warm clothes for the winters; his father encouraged him to get to know the British community in whatever city he was posted. His father had said at one point during the journey that he had often wondered, when Reeves was a lad, what he might do when he was older, but had never thought that his son would end up working in China. His father then laughed but did not turn his head to look at Reeves. It seemed to be some sort of private joke. During the more than occasional silences as all three struggled with how they felt, his mother would sometimes read out the words on the road signs and hoardings.

When they got to Southampton, they said they would not come aboard – "we don't want to be any trouble" – but would stand on the docks, towards the stern of the ship, and wave goodbye. His mother reached in her bag and gave him a small gift wrapped in festive paper and told him to open it on Christmas Day on the ship and they would think of him doing so while the two of them celebrated their Christmas by themselves at the family home. She also gave him two rolls of brightly colored paper streamers and told him to hold one end of each roll and throw them down to them on the docks. They would catch the coils and unravel them as the ship moved out until the distance was too great and the streamers broke in two. They told him he must be getting aboard and they must find a place on the docks to see him depart. His father shook his hand and this time his mother hugged him, far more tightly than she had ever done before. Reeves thought he noticed tears in both his father's and mother's eyes but it might have been from the cold.

Reeves reached his small cabin and suddenly thought of all the things his parents had done for him – the train set one Christmas, the annual trip to London to see the lights on the stores on Oxford Street, their never missing a school visiting day, his father sitting beside his bed for hours when he got a fever one winter, his name freshly painted on his suitcases for the long trip to China. He realized that these were small acts of minor devotions, expressions in their own way of affection and concern, and he wished he could have thanked them, told them that he cared for them. The word 'love' was somewhere in the back of his mind.

He rushed to the stern of the passenger deck of the *Orama*, where there was already a crowd of passengers waving and shouting to the people below. Reeves wedged himself between two couples close to the ship's stern, disregarding their angry looks, and searched the crowd below. He could not see his parents, though he was wearing his glasses. He looked up and down the crowd and several times despairingly waved his arms in the air. He could see no answering response. There was a muffled rumble of the propellers under the water and dock workers cast off the enormous hawsers tying the ship to the wharf. He still could not see his parents and he hopelessly tossed the streamers into the air towards the crowd below. They flew through the air in two long red lines and were caught by two young girls who grinned up at him happily. There were scores of streamers of all colors snaking from the stern of the ship, held on one end by the passengers and on the other end by the people on the dock who had come to farewell their friends. The rumble below the water became louder and the sea at the stern of the ship boiled furiously at the surface.

The ship, nudged by a tug on one side of the bow, began to move away from the dock, Reeves held the ends of the paper streamers until they snapped and fell into the sea, the connection broken. Although he looked for his parents and supposed they must be there somewhere, Reeves never saw them waiting on the wharf to farewell him on the departing ship. They must have been held back by the crowd. He would write to them often.

Chapter 2

Over the two years that Reeves spent in Peking, he learned perhaps two hundred words of an ancient formal Mandarin, spoken within the walls of the Imperial Court for centuries but in few other places in the past three decades. He did learn some of the vernacular Chinese spoken on the streets, but that he had picked up from the servants in the residence for the student interpreters. At the end of his second year, on the day of his last class, Reeves bowed to his teacher and gravely handed him a red envelope containing a number of banknotes. The teacher, with the look of the sadness of generations, took it silently, bowed in return, but not as deeply, and gave him his diploma attesting to his proficiency in the Chinese language. Shortly after, Reeves received his appointment as His Majesty's Vice Consul in Hankow, China. He was to start his duties the first week of January, 1936.

Reeves wondered why he had been sent to Hankow. There had not been a British consul here for three years. Reeves was looking forward to a settlement in one of the so-called treaty ports to administer. The treaty ports were imposed by the victorious British after the Chinese defeat in the Opium Wars of the previous century. Chinese law had no effect in a settlement, British law applied and Reeves imagined himself presiding over the British settlement of Hankow like a minor provincial autocrat – collecting taxes, presiding in courts, commanding a police force, imposing fines and prison sentences. But the British settlement in Hankow existed only on paper. The Nationalist Chinese had seized it a few years earlier after a battle in the interminable civil war that had afflicted China for decades and made it clear that they, not the British, would now rule there.

Reeves would sit in his office in the Hankow consulate for weeks without a visitor, and just the occasional routine notice or bulletin from the Legation in Peking. Mr. Soares, the consular clerk, had shown him how to open the safe, which contained nothing except a few blanks to create new British passports, should a British subject ever come by to renew or replace one. There was not even a code book, which he had been told to expect, although he could not imagine sending a message of such importance that it would require encoding. Mr. Soares also spoke the local dialect of Chinese, a language that to Reeves's mind bore no resemblance to the language that he had been taught by his teacher, or that was spoken by the servants in the student interpreters' house in Peking. In any event, whatever Chinese he had learned there was already beginning to fade.

One afternoon around four, having nothing to do, Reeves told Soares that he was going to the British Club. The Club was still open, although now there were far fewer members than there had been even a few years ago as the British merchants had left Hankow. When Reeves entered its vast gloomy bar, only one table was occupied. A man in late middle age, with a florid face, large mustache, hair combed from one side of his head to the other to disguise his baldness, bounded over and shook his hand.

"You must be Reeves, the new consul," he said, shaking his hand with both of his with rapid vigor. "So great that you are here. I don't know what those Johnnies in Whitehall were thinking, leaving this post vacant all those years. And now you can keep the flag flying. Some of the lads just the other day were saying right here at the Club, that they would not be surprised if the Chinese let us have our settlement back and we become a real treaty port that you could run for us. Nuisance for them to have to run it and they are probably looking for the first chance they have to get rid of it. Come meet my family." This all came out in a hurried jumble as though he had not talked to anyone, at least a white person, in a while. They walked over to the table.

There was a young man very much the image of what his father might have been 30 years ago. There was a thin young woman, perhaps the age of Reeves, in a plain frock of blue cotton without a pattern. It was buttoned to her neck. She was attractive, thought Reeves, although she also gave him the impression of being somewhat nervous. There was a middle-aged woman in a shining silk frock in some sort of green color. She had a very eager smile.

"My wife Mary," said Mr. Murray-Kidd after having introduced himself. "My son Andrew, and my daughter Rhoda." The two sat down. Drinks appeared and Mr. Murray-Kidd talked a lot about his business. He was the director of a large Shanghai trading house that his grandfather had founded. "What the Chinese want, we sell them and what they don't want, we buy." He laughed at his joke, but his family simply smiled slightly. He had evidently used the remark many times. Finally Mr. Murray-Kidd's wife interrupted.

"Mr. Reeves," she said in a voice as eager as her smile, "So nice to meet you. We are so glad to have a British consul back in Hankow. Really, it has been hard to look the French and the Americans in the eye since they have consuls for their settlement. And you so recently arrived from England. You must tell us everything that is happening at home. My daughter has been so looking forward to meeting you to talk about England. There are so few suitable young men in Hankow for her to talk to."

Rhoda looked at Reeves and gave him a small tentative smile before looking away. Reeves thought again she must be very shy. There was a small, simple necklace of pearls around her neck.

At first, Reeves simply was glad of her company, given how few visitors he had and how little he had to do. They would take long drives around Hankow together, which Reeves would justify to himself as 'learning the territory.' They would park by the river, away from the godowns, and talk. Rhoda talked about her life in Shanghai, her schooling in the British school – she was really quite funny about it, and could imitate the accents of some of her teachers quite wickedly – and her desire to visit England, a country she had never seen.

Reeves told her about England, about his family home in the New Forest, and his student days at Cambridge. He told her that she would have to be quite careful in London. It was a tricky city to get around for the first time and there were plenty of traps for the unwary girl. He would love to show her London. He really knew nothing about London; he never had the money that some of his fellow students had to frequent the clubs and restaurants. He certainly knew nothing of the places that might be traps for the unwary girl. But he at least had been to London, even if that was mostly with his parents at Christmas, and he was sure he could find his way around.

Then he saw her looking up at him, her eyes round, her face full of wonder and not at all shy or nervous. "Are there wicked women in London?" she asked, her eyes shining.

"Yes," he said, "Heaps of them. But none as wicked as you, sitting alone unchaperoned in a car with an unmarried man." She laughed softly and reached across and squeezed his hand.

Then, for the first time, he realized that he could live with someone like her. He could take care of her. He could be her guide when she went to England. There was so much that he could teach her. She seemed so willing to listen. He leaned down and kissed her lightly, but on her lips. She froze for a moment but then tentatively returned the kiss. They did this every time they met from then on, she a little more easily as time went on.

They were married in the Anglican church in Shanghai. The wedding breakfast was held in one of the larger hotels. The guests were all friends of the Murray-Kidds and some of the girls that Rhoda had been at school with. There was no one from his side of the family, for obvious reasons. Reeves had the sudden thought that perhaps it was for the best that the wedding was in China. Whom would he have invited himself? There were the members of his boat crew, but he had not really made friends with them. He was the only member who wore glasses and he always felt they lived a more glamorous and easy life that he was not part of, certainly not as though to invite them to his wedding. He had not been invited to theirs.

He had told his parents in a telegram that he was getting married and they had replied by telegram with their best wishes and that they hoped that it would not be too long before they could meet Rhoda. The telegram was read out at the breakfast, people applauded and Reeves wished his parents could have been there. He sent them a tiny slice of the wedding cake in a small silver-plated box. Very many months later, there was a letter from his mother saying the piece of cake had arrived, the fruit cake still moist and the royal icing intact. His father had dribbled a little port on the cake and they had shared the tiny morsel after dinner, thinking of him. Reeves often thought of this distant acknowledgment of his wedding, so far away, his two parents alone in that large dark house on the edge of the New Forest.

Reeves and Rhoda danced together for the first time and Reeves held her tight against him. Because of the troubles in China with the civil war and the Japanese military aggression in the north, they were unable to get away for a honeymoon, but stayed in the hotel for three days before returning to Hankow. Rhoda moved her clothes and a few other items into the consulate.

Within a year after they had returned to Hankow, Rhoda had, after a long period of silence at the breakfast table, announced while looking away at the wall that she had been to the doctor and he had told her that she was going to have a baby. She also added almost as an aside that she was feeling poorly, that she did not wish to disturb him and perhaps it would be better for both of them if she moved into another bedroom, "just until the baby is born and I am better again." Reeves thought that he should express his pleasure and joy and went over to her and kissed her on the cheek. She looked very frightened and held his hand tightly, just as she had done in his car before they were married.

The baby was a girl, delivered by a German doctor in the small European hospital in Hankow, and Rhoda had named her Letitia, a name that had no meaning for her, except that she liked it. Reeves was not consulted. Rhoda's mother sent an ancient Chinese woman to take charge of the baby. She had been Rhoda's nurse when she was a baby and had evidently been kept on as part of the household staff in the event of Rhoda's giving birth. The two of them stayed in their part of the consulate almost the entire day. Rhoda often ate her dinner with the nurse and Letitia, afraid to leave her in case something happened. Reeves became used to eating alone on those occasions, although there were times he missed Rhoda. He enjoyed talking to her, telling her things.

Sometimes before dinner, the amah would bring the baby into the residence's main reception room, so that Reeves could see his new daughter. If she was not asleep, she often was lying awake with a small cough. Reeves would lean over the baby and make what he thought were the right noises – he was an only child and had never been around babies. Letitia would often seem to be looking off into the middle distance and unaware of her father. After a while, he gave up on trying to talk to his daughter. There would be plenty of time when she was older. He wondered how he could be a good father to a daughter. He had no experience or knowledge of babies and small children. He decided that once she began to talk she might enjoy his company. As with Rhoda, he thought there was much he could tell her but could not then think of what he might initially say to a young girl.

It was on Letitia's second birthday, and a few months after the third anniversary of his arrival in Hankow, that Reeves received the news about Mukden. He was to be acting consul there. Reeves found it on the map and saw that it was in Manchuria, in the far north of China. Once again, Reeves remarked to himself, there was no British settlement to administer. The Japanese had taken it over when they had occupied this part of Manchuria. He wondered why he was being sent and what he would do there.

They arrived at the consulate in Mukden on a freezing November day with a biting Siberian wind whipping around them, to see a long low two-story building, set off by itself away from other buildings, as though it abhorred company and preferred to be alone. Dust from the plains and the empty fields around the consulate swirled angrily around the building. The windows were tightly shut, the thick curtains drawn so no light or heat could escape and you could not tell whether the consulate was occupied or abandoned. Only the black smoke of coal fires from each of the several chimneys gave a hint that there might be people inside.

In the few months when the weather warmed, the rains came almost every day. The steel-blue sky would suddenly blacken, a wind would pick up and a driving thunderstorm would force people off the streets and indoors. The servants kept the windows in the consulate open whenever it was not raining, but the wet humid air that came indoors brought mold that spread out on the plaster walls and even to the clothes in the wardrobes and dressers. Rhoda and Letitia almost never went out. Both the winter and the rainy season only seemed to deepen and prolong Letitia's coughing, and, on the few fine days, she never wanted to go outside.

Reeves had few visitors. The King's Messenger came from the British Consulate-General in Shanghai with the official mail, never anyone from the Legation in Peking; a traveler from some British company seeing if there was any business to be had in the region or if the Japanese really had a monopoly; the occasional Japanese Foreign Ministry official seeking to make the case that Great Britain should recognize the government of the new province the Japanese had created in Manchuria, a decision that Reeves had no influence over whatsoever.

Towards the end of his second year, Reeves found Mukden increasingly intolerable. It was early in 1941 and he had been in China for seven years, two years of learning a Chinese as useful in his job as a knowledge of Egyptian hieroglyphics, and five years as a vice consul without a purpose or a mission that he could discern. Following the instructions in the Foreign Office manuals, he applied for the home leave to which he was entitled. He told Rhoda when he next saw her that he had done so. It was the first time he had talked to her in a while. She had been nursing Letitia through one of her illnesses and was staying in a room adjoining the nursery, sleeping only when her daughter was able to sleep. She really was a devoted mother, Reeves thought, and he should not blame her for spending so little time with him. Rhoda had insisted on reading the third carbon of the application for leave retained for the consulate files. After she had done that, her habitual gloom and worry seemed to lift a little and she actually joined him several times for breakfast and dinner.

As Rhoda thought more about the application for home leave, she became more animated. She even seemed to be able to take their daughter's illness in stride. The two of them discussed staying at his parents' house initially, perhaps taking a holiday cottage in Cornwall for a while, looking at schools for when Letitia got older, getting her some proper clothes from Liberty's, seeing a real Harley Street specialist who could tell them why their daughter was so sickly all the time and even going one evening to the West End for the theater. She could wear a long gown and he could wear his dinner jacket. "Think how wonderful it could be to have dinner at the Savoy Grill. I have always wanted to go there." She looked up while he nodded his affirmation of the excellence of the Savoy Grill – a place he had barely heard of – and she smiled shyly. "Perhaps we could even stay a night in the Savoy Hotel." She looked away quickly but she was still smiling.

She now came to dinner almost every night and they continued to talk about places she wanted to go. Reeves had his own suggestions – fun little clubs in London and obscure foreign restaurants in out-of-the-way parts of the City he had heard of as an undergraduate. Rhoda looked up at him with that wide-eyed expression he had come to love in the months before they were married, not knowing that he had never been to the places he mentioned.

* * *

Reeves was never to know why his application for home leave was denied and he was, instead, appointed as the British Consul in Macao. The decision was made in the Ambassador's office in the British Legation in Chungking, the temporary capital of China as the Chinese armies retreated slowly west in the face of the grinding onslaught of the Japanese invasion. It was the end of a very long winter and the Ambassador's office was very cold despite the coal fire in the stove against the wall. Most of the windows in the office were intact, but some had been shattered and covered with oiled white paper. Through the panes of grimy glass that had not broken, you could see perhaps one hundred feet and then there was just a dull gray admixture of damp fog and mist, like a curtain dropped to conceal the horrors of the war that lay beyond. What could be seen, about 50 feet away, were the ruins of the former British Consulate, a building that had stood there for over 50 years, until a Japanese bomb had destroyed it last month. All that remained were some broken walls, and stoved-in beams that were already almost entirely covered with a damp green mold. Last night's bombing of Chungking by Japanese aircraft was on the mind of the Ambassador and the First and Third Secretaries who had been summoned to his office. They had huddled all night in shelters and gotten very little sleep.

The Ambassador spoke first. "Why are you here again?" he asked. He did not mean to be rude. He was simply very tired.

The First Secretary started without looking at the Third Secretary. "It is concerning Reeves, our Acting Consul in Mukden. I do not believe we have had occasion to mention him before."

The Ambassador looked at the First Secretary, who noticed the dark rings under the Ambassador's eyes. "I do not like our consuls in China, at least the few that I have met. I do not think that the China Consular Service attracts first-rate men. Many drink too much and some have taken native women as concubines. In the last century, some were actually insane and we still kept them in their posts."

The First Secretary chose not to respond to this directly. "The issue, sir, is that Reeves has applied for home leave. It creates a problem. There are many consular officers within China of considerably more years of service who have not applied for their statutory home leave. If we grant home leave to Reeves, it could cause a number of our consular officers to make the same request. If we permit Reeves his home leave, we then would have few grounds to deny the others. And we can ill afford an exodus of consular officers from China at this time." The First Secretary stopped;

he was coming to the crux of the matter. "I scarcely need to remind you that the Japanese now occupy half of China and are a direct threat to our preeminence in trade with this nation. And, of course, the Kuomintang has made no secret of its desire to abolish the treaty ports, and take back our colony in Hong Kong. A sudden exodus of our consular officers at this time with a score of consular posts appearing abandoned would send a very bad signal to both the Japanese and the Chinese. I am sure you see my concern."

"Of course I see your concern, I am not a bloody idiot," said the Ambassador. He was not angry, just tired. "What grounds do we have to deny him?"

"On the face of it, none. The regulations around home leave are stark in their simplicity. Home leave shall be granted after seven years of service."

"He has his seven years?"

"Oh yes, sir, two years as a student-interpreter and five years as a consular officer. His application is iron-clad."

"Well," said the Ambassador, his elbows on the table and his hands concealing his face before he sat up and spoke in that same weary tone. "Here is our solution. I have a cable from the Foreign Office here." He indicated the sheet of paper on his desk. "It concerns Macao. Macao is one of the many places in this God-forsaken country I have been obliged to find on a map." The Ambassador rose and walked over to a wall of his office, to which a large map of China was pinned. He stabbed his finger at a point near its base. "Macao is here, on the western shores of where the Pearl River lets into the South China Sea, about as far from this hell-hole of a city as you can get in China. Macao is a colony of our ancient ally, the Republic of Portugal. Apart from that, Macao is of little significance and should be of no conceivable interest to our lords and masters in Whitehall." The Ambassador paused and then began again.

"However, the Foreign Office has awakened to the fact that Macao is a mere thirty-five miles west of the British crown colony of Hong Kong, the bright shining jewel of the British presence in China. And our oriental friends, the Japanese, have taken an interest in Macao. They have sent their ships to visit Macao; they have invested in what little commerce there is there. Their aircraft fly over Macao with impunity. There are rumors that they would like to build an aerodrome in Macao, purely of course for peaceful purposes but which the cynical among you might suspect could be easily adapted to military purposes. We are not at war with Japan – given their war in China, they will never have the strength or resources to take on Great Britain and the West, but we cannot allow them to overly influence a territory, no matter how insignificant, that close to Hong Kong."

The Ambassador again paused; his tiredness making it difficult for him to remember what he wanted to say for a moment. Then he continued. "Here is my point: the Japanese for the last year have had a consul in Macao. He is a Mr. Fukui. A man of both erudition and charm, I am told, who has done much to create a favorable view of the Japanese nation amongst the people of Macao. Whitehall has decided we need our own consul in Macao. There has not been a British consul in Macao since 1865 because there has been no need of one until now. I am proposing Reeves be our consul in Macao. He speaks some European languages; Portuguese, or something like it, may well be among them. He will be appointed as vice consul and his job will be to charm the locals and occasionally remind the Portuguese of their obligations of perpetual friendship under the ancient treaty between our two nations. He does not have to do much or indeed anything. He will just be a presence. His chief task will be to keep the Union Jack flying in front of the consulate. Even one of our consuls should be capable of managing that."

The First Secretary paused awkwardly and then continued, "If I may be so bold as to ask, I very much appreciate our need to balance the Japanese in Macao, but how does that solve the issue of Reeves's application for home leave?"

The Ambassador, closing his eyes, reverted to an annoyed tone. "I don't know. Think of some reason to deny him his leave." He was very tired. "Cite the war with Germany and their submarines in the Mediterranean, the demand for men of his caliber in the Far East, the high regard in which he is held by one and all, his brilliant career to date. Tell him Macao is a little bit of the Mediterranean on the coast of China. It will almost be like home leave." The Ambassador closed his eyes. "If he doesn't like it, he can resign. I am sure it will not be a great loss."

The Ambassador wanted this meeting to end. He stood up. "Well, if there are no objections, then put something on paper so it happens. Wofford, you can sign the order to Reeves; prepare something for my signature so I can cable Whitehall that we have this under control. We all have more important things to do." The two other men rose and all three left the room together, the Ambassador first and the others following.

The letter to Reeves arrived in Mukden five weeks later. The letter was extensive but Reeves only saw that he was to be denied home leave "for the time being" and that he was appointed His Majesty's Vice Consul in Macao. He found Macao, not without difficulty, on the map of China on his wall. He pulled a volume from an encyclopedia that had been left by the last consul in Mukden and read about Macao and its connection to Portugal.

He thought that he should draft an acceptance. But when he returned to his chair, the full import of the position to which he had been appointed, as he conceived of it, struck him: he was being prepared for an eventual posting to Europe. He had been noticed. He had been singled out. There was no other explanation for his being pulled off the Consular Service's China track and seconded to what was really part of Europe. This was the first step in an upward movement in his career. He could not help smiling.

Rhoda entered the office with an anticipatory smile on her face. He had forgotten that he would have to break the news to her that there would be no home leave.

"We have news from Chungking?" Her face was now glowing with expectation. Reeves thought that his clerk might have said something or conveyed something by his expression.

"Yes, my dear, it is good news but not the good news we were expecting," he said, hoping his voice was even, or even uplifting. The eagerness began to slowly fade from Rhoda's face.

"Please tell me what has happened." Now she looked as though she was about to cry.

"Because of the war in Europe and the demands of the consular service in China, they cannot grant me our home leave right now." He looked at Rhoda. Tears were forming in her eyes and one was trickling down her cheek. She did not say anything, forcing Reeves to continue speaking. "But the good news is that I am to be the Vice Consul in Macao. It is a Portuguese town on the coast of China; it will be the next best thing to being in Europe, I think," and here, despite his best efforts to control it, his voice took on a slight tremor. "I believe I have been selected to move out of China to Europe or America. I have to believe this is how it will start." He was breathing hard and his face had a glow to it.

Rhoda looked at her husband, the tears now coming down her face. "I had so wanted to see England. And we could finally find out why Letitia has been so sick. A doctor in wherever this place is will not be able to tell us that. I just wanted the best for her. You were going to show me England and now that will not happen. I had so depended on you."

Reeves stood up behind his desk and started to move towards her. She took a step back towards the door. "Can't you see?" he said, almost imploringly, "We could not possibly go to England now in the middle of the war in Europe. But Macao is the first step in getting the three of us back to Europe, closer to England, and out of China."

Rhoda was crying. "I was depending on you," she stammered between sobs, "I really was. I know this is not your fault, but I was depending on you. I had so loved talking to you about England." She looked up at him. "We need a doctor for Letitia. I know that you love her. I really do. I had so depended on you. I wanted to stay with you at the Savoy." She turned, a hand over her face, and left his office, stumbling a little as she did so.

Chapter 3

The next morning, Rhoda came downstairs to the breakfast room. Outside, the sun was already intense, but the windows were tightly closed against the dust and dirt the wind was carrying from the plains. The air inside was hot and thick. Reeves noticed that her dress of simple blue cotton already had damp stains. She came over and gave him a hug, but it was different somehow, a little perfunctory perhaps. He could not put his finger on what it was exactly. Rhoda sat down at her place at the table, her hands folded in her lap. She evidently did not intend to eat. She was looking away at first when she began to speak and then turned to look at him.

"John," she said, and Reeves had the impression she had thought for a long time about what she was going to say. "I am sorry I was so upset last night. I know none of this is your fault. You have your career and your duties and when they call, you have to answer them." Her tone was even and it was hard to detect an emotion in it.

"The demands of the Consular Service," said Reeves, intending to speak lightly, but his voice trailed off and he added nothing. Rhoda appeared not to hear.

"It was very selfish of me to put my needs ahead of yours and I hope you will forgive me." She was looking down again when she said that, in the same even, flat tone.

"There is nothing to forgive," said Reeves and stretched his hand across the table, hoping she would take it in her hand. She instead placed a hand on top of it and pushed down, a little too hard. She leaned forward and looked at him and suddenly began to speak quickly.

"That is very kind of you." Here she paused briefly. "You always were a kind man; it is one of the principal reasons I was attracted to you." Reeves knew what had attracted him to Rhoda, or at least he thought he did, but he had never before thought of what in him she might have found attractive. It was his kindness. Was he kind, he thought? Rhoda was still talking.

"I know you love your daughter and now that we cannot get care for her in England, I thought I might try the hospitals in Shanghai. There is a very big hospital there now in the American settlement, a French one with the best Swiss doctors from a clinic in Lausanne and Daddy says there are a couple of new doctors at the British hospital. I thought I might take her down to Shanghai and have her examined before coming to Macao."

She paused to see what effect her words were having on Reeves but he was still thinking that Rhoda had found him kind. Not dashing, not handsome, but kind. Was there some element of pity there? Certainly there was no feeling of desire on her part that he could discern. But then he wondered whether he still desired his wife, whether there was any pleasure in her for him. There were the three nights he had spent with her in the hotel in Shanghai after the wedding, but his principal memories of that were not desire, ardor or passion, but his fumbling awkwardness and her trepidation. If he was honest with himself, he found it a bit of a relief when she had moved into the other bedroom when she found herself pregnant. He did not really miss her company. And now all he was to her was someone who was kind. He assumed he would continue to try to please her without really understanding why.

He knew he had to say something and could think of no reason to object to his wife's seeking the best treatment for his daughter.

"I think that is very sensible, my dear. Before starting a new post, it makes sense to make sure we have done all we could for Letitia."

Rhoda brightened a little on hearing no objection.

"I can leave on the train tomorrow and catch the steamer. Your clerk can make the booking. I think it makes so much sense to get a diagnosis and start on a course of treatment if one is recommended as soon as possible." She squeezed his hand with apparent warmth and meaning.

Reeves realized that she had been thinking of this ever since she had heard of the denial of his home leave and his posting to Macao.

"I am so glad that we are in agreement." She stood up. "Please forgive me for rushing off but there is so much to be done if we are to leave tomorrow." She squeezed his hand again and left the room. At the entrance, she stopped and turned with a very slight smile that Reeves thought could convey almost any meaning. "I have thought about Macao; I am sure it will be good for your career."

The next day, she and Letitia were driven in the small consular car with the scratch on the side and the broken headlight to the train station and Reeves was alone. She really is a devoted mother, he thought. My mother certainly was devoted to me. Although she also paid attention to my father and was affectionate to him. But when he was young, he was not ill like Letitia. His mother had time for his father. She probably held him in esteem too and he was not sure Rhoda really held him in esteem. But, of course, with Letitia, she had little time otherwise.

His instructions were to complete his duties as acting consul in Mukden "with every dispatch" and then report "at his earliest convenience" to Hong Kong where he would be briefed by the staff of the Colonial Secretary and the Commander of British Forces as to the situation in Macao and the surrounding region. He was then to proceed to Macao to assume his duties. Reeves did not really know what 'complete his duties' meant, but he wrote one final report of his observation of the movement of goods trains south and west. It was his fifth report on the movement of goods trains in the same number of months, but no one had complained, or given any indication that they had read them.

He superintended the packing and shipping of his now large collection of Chinese furniture and artifacts, picking up many of them to look at them with affection and wonder before giving them to the Chinese workers packing them in straw in the wooden crates. It gave him a particular pleasure when he saw the packing cases, stacked on handcarts ready to go to the train station, addressed in black letters to "His Britannic Majesty's Consulate, Macao, Republic of Portugal, Republic of China." On the

King's Messenger's last visit, there was a letter from the consul-general in Canton congratulating him on his appointment and adding, Reeves thought, an unnecessary reminder that Reeves now reported to him.

After a train and two steamers, both overnight, Reeves arrived in Hong Kong in the early morning and went to his hotel, one that had been selected for him as appropriate for his position, grade and seniority. He found nothing in either his accommodations or the service he received either to offend or to commend.

The next morning, he received a desultory briefing on the military situation from a very young army captain, who made no effort to conceal his suspicion of why someone from the Foreign Office needed to know anything about the strengths and dispositions of the Japanese and British armed forces and confined his comments to a high level of generality. Reeves did learn that the Japanese military, with 60,000 troops, occupied all of Canton Province, which bordered Hong Kong and Macao on the north, and Reeves received the same assurance that the Japanese were too weak to risk war with the West by menacing either place. A member of the Colonial Secretary's staff talked to him only about Hong Kong and its commercial supremacy in China and Asia. He asked Reeves "to keep an eye on Macao and the Portuguese" to make sure they and the Japanese did nothing to upset this supremacy, without explaining how this was to be done.

He had no further appointments and spent the remainder of the day wandering the streets of Hong Kong. He passed the Lane Crawford department store with its British goods in the windows and resolved to write Rhoda suggesting that she stop in Hong Kong on her way to Macao and purchase what they needed for a proper English Christmas. He might even join her and show her around, although he was seeing the city for the first time today. Her daughter might find the warmer air agreeable. He thought he might hold her hand while she walked. She had never done this to date. He wanted to be a father to her, to have her finally talk to him, and have her even look up to him. She seemed to live in her own world, one that she seemed to share occasionally with her mother but from which he was excluded. He wanted her once the war was over to meet his parents when he finally got his home leave. He hoped his parents lived long enough to meet both her and Rhoda. Perhaps some of his classmates from Cambridge would want to get together and Rhoda could meet them too. He wondered how he could write to them if this all should eventuate.

The next morning, very early, because the ship left at eight in the morning, a taxi took him down to a dock where the steamers went back and forth on the four-hour trip across the Pearl River Delta between Macao and Hong Kong. A sign on the little wooden ticket office with a green tin roof announced the Hong Kong, Canton and Macao Steamship Company.

And then he saw it. Tied tight against a wooden pier, by itself and at a distance from the other vessels in the coastal trade, was a two-decked steamer, its brilliant white paint gleaming in the early morning sun and contrasting with the dark forest-green of the lower half of the hull. The ship was not large, perhaps just over two hundred feet in length, but seemingly perfectly proportioned for its task. Reeves thought it would be wonderful to take this ship along the China coast, or, even more wonderfully, to sail without purpose amongst the archipelagos and islands of the South China Sea. There was a single smokestack out of which came a lazy drift of black smoke, as though somewhere inside there was a welcoming hearth with a kettle on the hob. But what Reeves would remember long after he had left Macao was the large Union Jack painted on the side. It had been a long time since he had seen so prominent a sign of his native land and he felt a surge of pride and affection; from where that came he did not know. The ship's name, painted in black on the little sharp upright bow, was the *Sai An.*

Exactly at eight, the steam whistle of the steamer blew in a high-pitched squeal, sounding, to Reeves's ears, more like the calliope of the county fairs he remembered his parents taking him to when he was a boy, than something belonging to an actual steamship. Far below, there was a soft shudder from the engines, the waters at the stern of the boat began to bubble, dockworkers unloosed the hawsers binding the ship to the dock and the *Sai An* began to move.

Reeves stayed on the deck outside his cabin as the ship left Hong Kong, looking at the small islands they passed and the low rolling hills, still covered in part in mist, of the coast of Southern China. There was a lush, warm, fertile feel to this part of China. Somehow he had left the low gray skies and the cold damp twilight of northern China for somewhere he found hard to credit was part of the same country. The *Sai An* gently rocked from side to side as it moved west towards Macao. There was the caw of sea birds circling around the ship, and the faint creak of the iron plates of its hull. Reeves was on the side of the ship in the shade, the breeze was warm and he had not smelt sea air in a while. He was thinking that he might spend the remaining hours of the voyage outside on the deck and not go to his cabin. The sun rose higher in the sky and the sea ahead turned from a gray-blue to a silver, rippling like foil.

Reeves did not know how much time had passed, but it must have been a few hours, when he realized that they had come closer to the coast. The green hills that he had seen from afar were now almost emerald and no more than a few hundred yards off the starboard side of the *Sai An*. It was nearly noon; the sun was almost overhead and the sea was a brilliant gold.

Then Reeves noticed what was ahead of him. His first thought was that he was looking at a small Italian hill town on the Mediterranean coast magically placed on the edge of the South China Sea. Was this Naples? Capri? Everything about Macao spoke to him of the pictures he had seen of small towns in the south of Europe – the low sea-wall that curved elegantly around a harbor, the single row of tall trees, their branches shading the road and promenade from the noon sun, the large houses with balconies and tiled roofs, the spires of the many churches rising above those buildings, the castles or fortresses at the tops of the hills and jagged walls with crenelations following the rolling ridgelines.

But then Reeves saw the colors. Each house, each building and each church was a different pastel. There was lemon yellow, apricot, the blue of birds' eggs, a salmon, another pink, a scarlet, a white, a pistachio green, a lime green, the teal green of a calm sea. This was not Europe so much as a fairytale.

As the ship came closer to the coast, Reeves saw that they were approaching a harbor crowded with junks and sampans, most lashed together side by side, others slowly moving, rowed by long sweep-oars at the stern. Looking down on the nearest junk, he saw a naked child dive off the bow. The child had the end of a fishing net in his mouth, and he swam out into the harbor in a strong swift breaststroke, towing the net behind him. He changed directions a few times to spread the net out. When he released the net and rolled over, Reeves saw that the smooth-skinned swimmer was in fact a girl. She could have been no more than ten years old and she caught his eye, looking at him with an innocence that belonged in Eden before the Fall. The men waiting on the deck of the junk hauled the net in and a single small silvery fish flopped onto the deck.

There was a shudder of the engine that shook the entire ship and the *Sai An* came to a stop alongside the wharf. A steward was waiting with his luggage further down the deck.

There was a separate gangplank for the first class passengers and Reeves went down, the steward with the luggage following. A Portuguese customs official in a white uniform asked in quite good English to see his passport. When Reeves produced his maroon diplomatic passport, the official handed it back quickly, stepped back and saluted and gestured away from the harbor and towards the city of Macao, as if he was saying that all this is now yours.

He had been expecting someone from the new consulate to meet him. He had been told that a clerk, Mr. Gonsalves, had been engaged and a building rented that would be both his residence and the consular office. He stood on the street at the end of the pier and looked in both directions. On the left, up the street, a man leaned against a taxi. He made no effort to see if Reeves was a potential customer but stayed by his taxi, looking at the passengers coming off the ferry. There was a row of about seven rickshaws, each with the ends of their two long shafts lying on the ground and the seat for the passenger high in the air. The Chinese who would pull the rickshaws were all women, some young, but two very old, with brown wrinkled faces like dried fruit. They squatted on the ground between the shafts, staring at Reeves, but not expecting him to ask them to take him anywhere. None of the passengers from the *Sai An* still in the street seemed to need a rickshaw.

At that moment, a man came down the street at a quick trot. He looked Portuguese, with his olive skin and thin mustache. He had a round red face with a big smile. He was wearing a khaki suit and a broad-brimmed straw hat. It had a scarlet hat-band around the crown. His jacket was unbuttoned and was flapping behind him. Reeves could see the man's large stomach pushing hard against the fabric of his shirt. "Consul Reeves," he shouted breathlessly, "Please sir, Consul Reeves, please forgive me but I could not get the car down closer. I am late, I know." The man stopped and took off the broad-brimmed hat and mopped his brow with a handkerchief he pulled from his trouser pocket. He was a little out of breath and said nothing for several seconds, just breathing hard in quick little pants. There were drops of sweat on the tips of his mustache. "I am Mr. Gonsalves, your consular clerk. I was the deputy to the head clerk in the Canton consulate before coming here. I speak English, Macanese, Portuguese and Cantonese. I can do the typing and some shorthand. I will give you great satisfaction." He smiled and extended his hand, which Reeves shook. His accent had the English and Chinese tones, plus something from one of the European Romance languages. Reeves assumed it was Portuguese, although that was not a language he had studied.

"Mr. Gonsalves, it is a pleasure to meet you. I was beginning to worry about what was going to happen to me." Reeves extended a hand and Mr. Gonsalves took it in both hands, pumping it up and down.

"You will love Macao. So many of my relatives live here. It is a very nice life." Mr. Gonsalves gestured to the steward from the steamer to follow him and turned away from the wharf. Reeves looked back on the *Sai An*, just to see the Union Jack against the white of the upper deck.

When the three rounded the corner, Reeves saw the car waiting. It was American, thought Reeves; only the Americans would make something of that size. It was black, sleek, with headlights that were set like a wicked pair of eyes into the curved wheel covers. Two other lights were set lower behind the front fenders. Wide strips of chrome ran the length of the car and caught the light of the sun with sharp flashes. The windshield was divided in two and was raked back slightly on either side, as though it was looking for every advantage to achieve a hitherto impossible velocity. From where they stood, the curved bonnet that concealed the engine seemed longer than the cab of the car and Reeves tried to imagine the power of the engine it concealed. The car was highly polished to an almost ebony and it sparkled in the sun.

Reeves thought he had never seen anything so beautiful. He could not wait to drive the car himself. He imagined how happy he would be doing that. Reeves and Mr. Gonsalves got into the car, Mr. Gonsalves in the front next to the driver. Mr. Gonsalves turned around and smiled expansively. "This is a new car. It is a Studebaker. It is for you." Reeves thought of the battered black Austins that had been assigned to him at his last two postings and thought that the Studebaker must be some sort of sign of his increased importance.

The driver put the car in gear and eased forward. The engine made a sound between a growl and a purr. Reeves closed his eyes and listened.

The car left the port and in a few minutes was climbing a hill. Perhaps two minutes later, the car glided to a gentle halt. Mr. Gonsalves turned around in his seat again. "Here we are, sir, your new home and office."

Reeves saw a perfect two-story townhouse in the Italian Renaissance style. The afternoon sun washed the white dressed stone blocks out of which it was built with a glowing yellow. There were balconies and balustrades and tall windows that hinted of elegant reception rooms behind them. There was a small front lawn, rimmed with a bed filled with pink flowering plants. A small lemon tree, no more than four feet high, was in full fruit and the yellow lemons also caught the afternoon sun. The Union Jack flew in the afternoon breeze that came off the South China Sea from a flagpole in the middle of the roof above a balustrade that ran the length of the building. A highly polished brass plaque at the side of the big main entrance read in large black letters "Consulate of Great Britain, Macao" and underneath in equally large letters "*Consulado da Grã Bretanha, Macau.*" The royal coat of arms in bright enamel colors was in the middle. Reeves felt absurdly happy to be here.

A Chinese man in a white jacket opened the front door and a second man came out to get the luggage. Mr. Gonsalves, coming up behind Reeves, pointed to the man at the front door. "I have hired him for you. This is your Number One Boy. He will take charge of your house. Find other maids and servants. Your wife will like him when she comes." Reeves thought how pleased Rhoda would be to come to Macao and find a fully staffed house. He would take pleasure in introducing her to the servants. Perhaps they could choose an amah for Letitia together. Perhaps she would think she was in Europe.

The Number One Boy led him into the house and went and opened all the doors on the ground floor. The windows in each room had been opened at the bottom and a slight cool breeze was coming in. The shutters had also been opened and in the front rooms the sunlight flooded in and gave the fresh wax on the dark wood floors a silver sheen. At the back of the house, facing a small walled garden with an orange tree in fruit and benches you could sit on under the shade of royal palms, was an office and an outer anteroom. This was where Reeves and Mr. Gonsalves would work.

They went upstairs. Reeves decided which bedroom would be his, which his wife's, and which the nursery. He then suddenly thought that perhaps in this more benign climate, Rhoda would feel better and want to share a bedroom with him. He turned that thought over in his head for a while. Mr. Gonsalves told him his packing cases with all his household effects would arrive at the consulate tomorrow or the next day. They were already in a warehouse down by the *Porto Interior*.

Without furniture, Reeves spent the night at the Hotel Riviera. He went up to the Delicias Bar on its roof and found a table from which he could look down on the *Praya Grande*, the name he had learned for the tree-lined boulevard that curved around the *Porto Interior*. He saw the top of his long black car at the hotel entrance waiting for him. He saw the banyan trees and their leafy branches shading the road and the paved path on the water's edge. He watched the sun, huge against the horizon, turn the South China Sea gold and the innumerable junks still sailing become black silhouettes as if they were embroidered on a robe. He drank gin with ice over a few hours while an orchestra played soft lilting music he did not recognize. Several couples were dancing, close in each other's arms. Reeves watched them and did not eat dinner before going to bed, the music of the orchestra still swaying in his head.

Late the next morning, Reeves himself drove back to the consulate. Entering the house, Reeves found all his Chinese furniture and artifacts neatly placed in lines and groups in the front hall. Reeves took his time to direct their placement in the rooms. There were scrolls of calligraphy, landscapes and portraits of extended Chinese families to hang on the walls. There were Ming tables with delicate twisting rails, Chinese scholar chairs with a single Chinese character cut into a flat vertical back, blackwood cabinets and narrow altar tables to be arranged in the several rooms. On their surfaces, he placed his treasures – small temple bells, a bronze Buddha from the Song dynasty, ceramic and porcelain bowls and plates in sea blue and celadon, a pair of embroidered slippers from the Manchu court, a statue of Guanyin, the Goddess of Mercy, in wood with traces of the original polychrome still remaining. For the first time, he had all his possessions, collected over seven years, out to be seen. The lights of the electric chandelier reflected off the polished woods, bronze and ceramics like glinting stars. The scrolls hung down with their misty enigmatic landscapes into which Reeves would sometimes think, when he was having a drink by himself, he could disappear.

He went back into the front hallway where a framed photograph of George VI in his coronation robes had been hung. A Union Jack hung down on a stanchion next to it. Mr. Gonsalves and the Number One Boy were watching him but he paid them no attention. He was thinking about how pleasant all this was; he wondered how he could make himself useful here in Macao and, he hoped, attract the favorable attention of the Foreign Office. He smiled to himself.

Chapter 4

The next day, Reeves went to his office that faced the back garden with its inviting benches in the shade and orange tree and wrote to Rhoda. He said that there was an English department store in Hong Kong that would have everything they needed for Christmas. It was only June but the Christmas goods were already on sale. He could meet them in Hong Kong and show them around. He said she would love Macao and that he was sure the warm weather would do wonders for Letitia's health. The almanac for 1941 indicated that the warm weather he had found when he arrived in June would continue almost the whole year, he told Rhoda. Letitia would thrive here. He said that he was due to present his credentials to the Governor of Macao in a few days and she would no doubt be meeting him herself soon after her arrival. He said the Legation in Peking had already entrusted him with an assignment for his meeting with the Governor, which he was sure she would understand he could not go into in this letter. He told her of the lovely house on a hill that awaited her. He mentioned the little lemon tree in the front garden.

Rhoda replied within the week. She was sorry she had left so precipitously but she was not herself with the worry about their daughter. She had made appointments with the leading doctors in the European hospitals in Shanghai and had already seen two of them. Those two were really worse than useless. Just wait until Letitia grew up some more and they were sure she would grow out of it. Of all the things to say. But thankfully there were still some specialists elsewhere to see and tests to conduct. Perhaps he was right that a warm climate might prove a cure. She would come down to see him as soon as Letitia was done with the doctors and she judged that Letitia could travel. It might be some time. She would very much appreciate his meeting them in Hong Kong.

Having a proper Christmas would be a tonic, as she put it. The new house sounded lovely. Rhoda put three Xs on the bottom of the letter and Reeves realized, with regret, that in his letter he had not done the same. He thought of his daughter with her strange distant stare. He hoped the doctors could help her. That would be nice.

When he had walked into his office on his first morning, Mr. Gonsalves had brought in two pieces of correspondence on a silver-plate salver. The first was the set of instructions from the Legation in Peking that Reeves had alluded to in the letter to his wife. Mr. Gonsalves had decoded them for him, using a version of the consular code. They listed the issues he was to raise with the Governor and policies which the Legation wanted the Governor to embrace. Reeves was to report back "forthwith" with a detailed account of the Governor's responses.

This was the first time Reeves had been given anything like a diplomatic assignment. Consuls did not try to bend the wills of sovereign nations to that of His Majesty's Government. That was a job for a diplomat. And he was not a diplomat. He had studied languages at Cambridge and never even so much as read a book on diplomatic history. He reflected that all he knew about diplomacy came from reading newspapers. Nevertheless he had been asked. Like the posting here, that must mean something. He was given tasks not normally given to a consul. He was being both tested and groomed for higher office. He felt pleased.

The second piece of correspondence was an invitation to a garden party at the Governor's residence and an attached letter inviting him to present his credentials to the Governor in a private ceremony immediately before. Reeves wondered whether it was proper to raise the issues the Legation wanted him to raise on that occasion and then he decided he would do so. It seemed silly to make a separate appointment and have another meeting. Perhaps actual diplomats thought otherwise.

The afternoon of the garden party, Reeves put on his consular uniform for the first time. He had had it made by a tailor in Peking at the end of his time there as a student interpreter. This was his first time wearing it; in his last two postings, he had not had an occasion to. The Chinese and the Japanese authorities in Hankow and Mukden preferred that the European consuls in the settlements they now occupied be as invisible and as inconsequential as possible.

There was a tall mirror in the hallway of the consulate and now, twenty minutes before he was due at the Governor's reception, he looked at himself in his uniform. It was the tropical uniform in white drill, with nine gilded buttons with the royal coat of arms in the center of his jacket coming up to a high upright Prussian collar around his neck. Reeves looked at the silver embroidery on his cuffs, on either side of the single row of gold buttons on his jacket and running up the sides of his trousers. He hitched the small harmless sword onto the strap on his white belt and put on his tropical helmet with the single strand of silver bullion loop around the base. Here he was, he thought, going to a party dressed like something out of a comic opera from the last century, and he had members of his boat crew and classmates in the drab khaki of the Army or the blue of the Navy fighting a real war on the other side of the world. He started towards the door and the waiting car on the street outside.

At precisely the hour appointed, the newly polished Studebaker passed through two black wrought-iron gates and into a forecourt of the *Residencia do Governador.*

It was a fantastical building. As the car pulled out of the dazzling brightness of the morning sun and into the shade under the portico with its four solid white pillars, Reeves took in a small compact palace in a miscellaneous mixture of the classical, baroque and several other styles and painted, like no palace in Europe he had ever heard of, in a cheerful bright pink, with its corners, roof lines, cornices, pillars, windows, and shutters outlined in what he thought looked like the shiny white royal icing he remembered from the Christmas cakes of his childhood. There were gardens, lawns, tall trees whose branches touched to form canopies, and fountains surrounding both sides of the palace and ascending the hill. All of this, he thought, on the coast of southern China.

The car stopped in the deep shadow under the portico, and for a moment Reeves's eyes, habituated to the bright sunshine, were unable to see anything. Then he saw two tall doors, in a dark varnish and highly polished, open and a man about his height in a white uniform come down the three steps to the driveway. Reeves first thought he was the butler, but then he noticed that he had a row of ribbons on his chest and the stripes of a naval captain on his shoulder boards. He must be the Governor, thought Reeves. Before his driver could get out of the car, the Governor had strode over to the car and opened the door for Reeves to exit. Reeves got out of the car, stood up, but then turned around without greeting the Governor, to retrieve his sword that had been lying on the seat next to him and attached it back onto his belt. He was looking down to do so, fumbling with a clasp and conscious of not having yet caught the eye of the Governor. But then what was worse, Reeves had to turn back again to pick up the peaked pith helmet with the single strand of silver piping, and the envelope with his credentials, his sword nearly entangling itself between his legs. Reeves finally stood erect, his helmet under his arm like a package, and with an embarrassed smile faced the handsome man in the naval uniform. His driver had turned the motor of the Studebaker off and all that could be heard for a moment was the sea breeze rustling the leaves of the many trees of the palace gardens.

"You must be Vice-Consul John Reeves," the Governor said warmly and extended his hand. "I am Governor Gabriel Maurício Teixeira, the Governor of Macao. We welcome you here. Given the centuries of friendship between our two countries, you are long overdue."

Before Reeves could shake the Governor's hand, he had to transfer his helmet under his arm and the envelope in his hand. He did this awkwardly and then shook the Governor's hand.

"I am indeed John Reeves, the new British consul." Reeves was conscious of a slight stammer in his voice. This was more than a social call; here he was to meet the senior representative of his host country and to be formally acknowledged as His Britannic Majesty's representative in that country. This was the first time during his brief consular service that it had actually happened. In Hankow and Mukden, there was the fiction – a fiction because the Japanese and Chinese had removed the

British from any authority – that he was not going to a foreign country but to a little part of Great Britain demarcated in a city in China, ceded, unwillingly but nevertheless ceded, to the British crown. Here in Macao, he was at least in a real country and with a real consular role, even if one, at least now, of small importance. Macao seemed a very long way from the center of the world stage.

"My pleasure to meet you. I wanted to greet you personally away from the other guests. It is often hard to talk with other people around. Let us go inside." The Governor turned and took off briskly for the open doors at the head of the steps.

Reeves followed as closely as he could, the fingers of his left hand grasping the looped guard of his sword to prevent it from swinging back and forth as he ran behind to follow the Governor, his other arm grasping the helmet. He thought that the Governor was very like his two uncles, the Admirals: the same brusque manner, the clipped, almost staccato way of speaking as though every other sentence was an order given on deck, and a disdain for the niceties of civilian life. Reeves found himself in the large entry hall of the Governor's residence. A servant took his helmet, to Reeves's relief.

"Come, let's go upstairs to the library where we can sit. We can join the party later." They went up the stairs and entered the library which was almost entirely dark, save for shafts of sunlight coming through cracks in the shutters.

"Open those shutters and windows," said the Governor brusquely to a servant. "This is like being in the hold of a ship. I do not know why they think the only way to stay cool is to shut us up as though we are in a packing case. There is a perfectly good breeze coming off the sea." The servant opened each of three double sets of windows in the room, pushing them like French doors against the wall of the library and then opening the shutters against the outer walls of the residence. Light flooded into the room and Reeves saw that the wallpaper was the color of limes. Books filled the shelves and several model ships were displayed on tables. A cool breeze off the sea wafted in and Reeves could hear an occasional motor car on the *Avenida da Republica* below. The servants left.

The Governor pointed at one of two easy chairs close to a window. Reeves sat down, this time pushing his sword to the side in time, and the Governor took the other chair. A table lay between them with a decanter of a golden orange liquid and two glasses. There was also a coffee pot, two cups, silver jugs, forks and knives, a pair of tongs, folded napkins and plates of small cakes and tarts.

Reeves began by somewhat abruptly thrusting out the envelope containing his credentials. "My credentials," he said clumsily and then immediately worried that he had done the wrong thing. The invitation had talked of a ceremony. The Governor smiled in an amused way, took the envelope and laid it on the table, paying it no further mind. Reeves decided he needed to start again with what he thought would be diplomatic niceties.

"Your Excellency, let me compliment you on your English. It is really quite excellent and I am ashamed to say that I have no Portuguese. I studied French, Italian, German and Spanish and it is my hope to master the language while I am here."

The Governor waved a hand in dismissal. "Everyone took English lessons at the *Escola Naval* when I was there, and once Portugal declared war on Germany in the last war, I was sent as an exchange officer with the British Navy. I served for a year as a young lieutenant on the *HMS Ambuscade*. Just missed the Battle of Jutland. That's the ship there." The Governor turned in his seat and pointed out the model of the gray warship with the white ensign that Reeves had first seen trapped in a beam of light that had come through the gap in the then closed shutters.

The Governor stood up and poured coffee into a small demi-tasse cup. He also poured a glass of the orange-colored liquor into a glass. "Take this – Madeira. Braces you for the rest of the day. I got used to the noon tot of rum when I was on one of your ships." Reeves took the coffee and did not object to the proffered glass of wine.

The Governor raised his glass and Reeves did the same. They touched glasses, and both drained theirs. Reeves soon felt that warmth inside him and calmness of mind that always came from his first drink. The Governor put down his glass and continued: "Welcome to Macao. I am told the last British consul in Macao departed eighty years ago. Your arrival is long overdue, given the long history between our two countries. The Anglo-Portuguese treaty is the oldest treaty of its kind in the world, and despite some ups and downs and setbacks, some recent, it still stands."

Reeves thought at this stage he should begin with his assignment from the Legation. He had never done this before and wondered if there was special training for those accepted into the diplomatic service. "Governor, I can assure you that His Majesty's Government has the utmost respect for the treaty and for the friendship between our two countries that it embodies and it has made every effort to abide by both its letter and its spirit." The words sounded hollow and slightly ridiculous in this enormous room. The Governor was looking at him directly. He had raised one eyebrow and he had a slight smile on his lips.

"Come, Mr. Reeves," he said, "We are both men of this world and we can talk directly and frankly. We will both be dealing with each other for a while. Let us get off to a good start and be candid, you and me, and that will make this meeting and all the rest of them to come so much easier. We both know that the British have abided by the treaty when convenient and ignored it when not." The Governor paused for a moment and then continued while still looking directly at Reeves. "Can I offer you another?" he said after a pause. The Governor took the decanter of Madeira and offered it to Reeves.

Reeves poured himself his second glass, his coffee untouched. He really did not know what to say; this all was quite difficult. He did not know when Britain had abided by the treaty with Portugal and when it had not. He bought time by taking a sip of his Madeira and looked back at the Governor. The Governor had picked up one of the cakes on the plate with his fingers, ignoring the silver tongs lying nearby and was eating it, looking at it in his fingers between bites. Reeves decided with a slight feeling of desperation to plunge ahead with the points that the Foreign Office had instructed him to make and to make no further mention of the ancient treaty of friendship between the two countries.

"In view of the state of war that now exists between Great Britain and Germany…" Reeves stopped. This sounded impossibly pretentious. Of course the Governor would have known that Germany, France and Great Britain were at war. They had been at war since 1939 and it was now early summer in 1941. The newspapers had talked of nothing else. Everyone knew it. Although perhaps it would be easy to forget that there was a war in Europe when you were living in this tranquil coastal town 6,000 miles from the fighting.

Reeves went on without any real conviction that he was doing the right thing. "... and the long friendship between our two countries..." Reeves stopped again. He had invoked the treaty without intending to and the Governor had already told him that its obligations had been disregarded by England when it suited its purposes. But he was in too deep and felt he had no choice but to continue. "... His Majesty's Government would urge and hope that the Government of Macao would take strict measures to prevent the transhipment of wolfram – tungsten – from French Indochina and the Republic of China through Macao when its ultimate destination is Germany." He stopped talking, a little flustered.

The Governor had taken another cake and was eating it while twisted around in his chair to look at something on the harbor below. He turned back and faced Reeves, wiping his fingers on one of the napkins.

"Consul Reeves," he said, as though 'consul' was a rank in the military. His voice had now a slight weariness as though he found it painful to speak. "I am sure you are aware that Portugal has declared its neutrality in the current war between Germany and Great Britain, a fact acknowledged and recognized by the British government within a day of the outbreak of hostilities. As a neutral party, we cannot show favor or disfavor to any of the belligerents. We sell wolfram to Germany and we sell wolfram to Britain, and we will sell it to anyone else on the identical commercial terms. That is the action of a neutral party. Mr. Reeves, even if I were to agree with you wholeheartedly, I have no power to stop any trade my government has authorized. This is a subject that your Ambassador in Lisbon should take up at the highest level; two unimportant people like us far from the capital have no influence over that decision."

Reeves had no argument in response. He thought to himself that perhaps the Foreign Office had been justified in not considering him for the Diplomatic Service. He had no idea how to deftly fashion an argument for persuading a nation to renounce its neutrality and to join an alliance against another country with which they had no quarrel. That was quite beyond him. It was thus with a feeling of hopelessness that he began the final point that his superiors in the Foreign Office had instructed him to urge upon the Governor of Macao.

"Your Excellency," he began and immediately thought that this formality was unnecessary with just the two of them in the room and the Governor smiling in such a friendly manner, "My government has instructed me to urge that Macao continue to permit the free passage of arms and weapons intended for the Republic of China through the ports of Macao." He put that word in the plural and then remembered that Macao had only one port. "His Majesty's Government, although not at war with Japan, is supporting the Republic of China in its resistance to the Japanese invasion and in view of the longstanding friendship, and the history of supportive alliances for the interests of our two nations, we are making this request." Reeves let his voice trail off.

"My dear John," the Governor said, addressing him for the first time familiarly by his name, "Please tell your government that I am entirely sympathetic to this request. As well as my great affection for Britain and its people, I hold no brief for the Japanese. They have committed atrocities against the Chinese people. But they have conveyed to us that it is a violation of Portugal's neutrality for Macao to appear to be aiding the enemies of Japan. We have no choice but to agree."

The Governor raised both hands as though asking for understanding. "I have 1,500 troops, a gunboat and, for the moment, a small warship to defend Macao. We estimate that there are perhaps 70,000 Japanese troops in the province immediately to our north. If provoked, I doubt that they would respect our neutrality. It would take them an hour to seize Macao. I do not think the British would come to our aid if the Japanese were to violate our neutrality."

Reeves slid to the edge of his chair, aware once more of his sword. "His Majesty's Government is keenly cognisant of its obligations under the various treaties between our two nations and would regard any aggression by Japan towards Macao with the utmost seriousness." He could not believe how silly his words sounded. 'Utmost seriousness' – what on earth did that mean? "And," he added as a hasty afterthought, "I am assured that they would take the appropriate action."

The Governor did not say anything for what seemed a long time to Reeves but was probably only a few seconds. He raised one eyebrow and looked at the consul. "Mr. Reeves, you know all too well that if the Japanese were to occupy Macao, the British would be powerless to help. You need your army and navy in Europe to fight the Germans. You are not going to move them east to protect Macao and leave Britain naked and undefended. In any event, their first task would be to protect Hong Kong, not Macao."

The Governor stood up and turned away from Reeves to look out towards the harbor where a tiny warship, the *Goncalo Velho,* floated gently at anchor, rocking slightly in the small waves. Its three small gun turrets stood like ornaments on its deck. The Governor's eyes were fixed on it.

"Please tell your government not to worry about Macao. Macao is of little importance in the affairs of this world; the great events that concern our statesmen and generals take place elsewhere, but not here." The Governor turned back from his contemplation of the small toy-like Portuguese warship, and smiled at Reeves.

"Come, Mr. Reeves, do not despair, there will always be a place for us somewhere. We will find it. It is undoubtedly not Macao. In the meantime there is a party on the lawn outside. People are happy. Let us go downstairs and join them." He stood up, put an arm around Reeves who had also risen and steered him out of the library, down the staircase and to the lawn where the garden party was in progress. Reeves could hear laughter and talk before he saw any guests. His credentials lay forgotten on the small table with the debris of their tea.

In the car returning home, Reeves realized that his first diplomatic assignment had ended if not in failure, then in a reaffirmation of the status quo. He had changed nothing. He replayed in his mind the various phrases that he would include in his cable recounting his meeting to the Embassy in Chungking that he hoped would disguise what he saw as his failure: *"impressed upon him the importance..."* *"He appeared to take on board..."* *"Sympathetic to the concerns of His Majesty's Government, but mindful of local military and geographical constraints"...* *"acknowledgement of the long tradition of amity between our two countries"... "will raise at the highest level in Lisbon."* Reeves knew that such phrases in his cable would lie like sludge on the bottom of a well, tainting whatever else he said. He thought that whatever faith that had been placed in him in sending him to Macao would now seem unjustified. His prior thoughts of early promotion he now thought were delusions. He was conscious of disappointing Rhoda.

Chapter 5

When Reeves sat down the next day to write to Rhoda, he hesitated at first. He was going to describe how nice the garden party was and then remembered how uncomfortable Rhoda was at social events. He decided to just give it a sentence or two with the implication that he too had not enjoyed it and only stayed as long as politeness required. He described the presentation of his credentials as a "private ceremony in the Governor's library," adding as an afterthought, "I so wished you had been standing there next to me in one of your nice frocks." He said he had been "quite forceful" in advancing the points the Legation had wanted him to and then added "You would have been proud of me." He said he wanted to show her and Letitia the Governor's palace – "like something out of a fairy tale" and then remembered how he had tried to read his daughter fairy tales from an old illustrated book, but she would claw at the pages and, before long, wiggle out of his lap without saying anything and run out of the room. He hoped Rhoda was having better luck with the rest of the doctors. He wanted to know his daughter.

Reeves had drunk sparkling wine at the garden party and then moved to gin and lime juice. He had his first Portuguese egg tart. He had met a very fat man in a white jacket and pants. The man's neck was especially fat and looked as though at any moment it might burst through the collar of his shirt and cause his small red bow-tie to fly off, as though an exotic insect had been startled. Despite his weight, the man had come across the lawn in a series of little springing hops and introduced himself with his impossibly long Portuguese name and his title of the Harbormaster of Macao. He started talking immediately and was not to be interrupted.

As sweat trickled down his round cheeks, the Harbormaster enthusiastically explained the principal exports of Macao: fireworks, incense, fish sauce, walnut oil, matches and heavy hemp mats. Reeves thought at the time that they were an odd miscellany of goods; who on earth bought them? The Harbormaster became louder on his plans to turn Macao into a rival to Hong Kong – deepening the harbor, something about finishing a railway connection, something about the importance of the telegraph company.

Reeves was skeptical. He had seen a small barge-like boat lying at anchor in the *Porto Interior*. It had a tall crane at the back with some sort of bucket or scoop hanging above the boat's deck on a thin wire cable. The barge lay away from the other boats, rocking peacefully in the small swell from the flow of the Pearl River. The scoop at the end of the crane would occasionally drop into the water to pull up a small piece of the seabed to deepen the harbor. Reeves had thought of that insignificant scoop dipping into that immensity of sea and pulling up, piece by piece, small bites of the seabed, while the mighty Pearl River flooded down its sheets of silt to almost instantly fill the hole. There was rust on the scoop and on the hull of the boat. Two deck hands had been sleeping in a shaded part of the stern.

The Harbormaster had said a lot; Reeves summarized what he remembered in a cable to Chungking, making the case, somewhat deftly he thought, that Macao was not an economic threat to the commerce of Hong Kong. He was sure that people must know already that Macao would never be a serious rival to Hong Kong, but he was determined to do the job he was asked to as well as he could. Perhaps if the right people saw the cable they would find it interesting and perhaps remark on its author. It seemed to be an important issue to some of them.

Reeves was wondering if he should talk to someone else when a tall young man came up to him and pulled the Harbormaster aside. The young man was broad-chested, and had a grin that seemed to come from a bubbling well-spring of vitality within him. He was not wearing a jacket or tie, but a khaki shirt and pants. The shirt was open to the second button and he had a red bandanna knotted around his neck. Reeves had never seen anyone with a knotted bandanna except a cowboy in a Western film. He found himself staring until the stranger caught his eye and Reeves glanced away, but, he thought, not quickly enough. The Harbormaster and the man finished talking and then the Harbormaster turned towards him with the extraordinary young man.

"Allow me to present to you the new British Consul, Mr. John Reeves. I have been telling Mr. Reeves about my plans for Macao and the industries we are building here."

Redden took one long stride over to Reeves and grasped his hand from his side before the startled consul had a chance to raise it. "Ed Redden and a pleasure to meet you, John. I manage the Macao station for Pan American Airways." Reeves was taken aback by the man's American accent and the easy way the man had used his first name, and was going to reciprocate, but found he couldn't. He had not met many Americans before.

"A pleasure to meet you also, Mr. Redden." He freed his hand from the tightly enveloping handshake. Redden slapped him on the back and strode off. Reeves thought it was time he went home.

Over the next few weeks, there were visits from most of the British community in Macao, the heads and senior officials of the electric and water company, invitations for lunch and dinner from prominent Macanese businessmen, especially those with interests in Hong Kong who thought Reeves might be useful, and some government officials. The Governor even called to see how he was "settling into his new berth." Reeves recognized it as a naval expression; one of his uncles had used it asking about how Reeves was getting on at school. He filed further reports on the economy of Macao with further evidence that it would not present an economic challenge to Hong Kong. Again, he thought that this should hardly come as a surprise to anyone, but it might be useful and even important to have it further documented. Everyone in Macao seemed to treat him with respect, which was a new sensation for Reeves.

Perhaps a week after the garden party, Mr. Gonsalves came into his office. He had a small sheet of paper in his hand. "I have just received a message from Mr. Redden at the Pan American hangar. He is inviting you to watch the big American airplane land." Mr. Gonsalves then looked down and read from the paper as though he was dealing with a language he was not very familiar with. "He said the plane took off 30 minutes late from Manila, so come down about noon. He also said do not dress up; you are going out on the launch to the plane and you can..." here Mr. Gonsalves paused – "... shoot the breeze with the pilots and the passengers staying aboard." Mr. Gonsalves looked across at Reeves and raised an eyebrow as if to inquire whether he had understood the message.

Reeves marveled at the informality of the language, the American argot. He could not imagine leaving a message in such *casual* language. And what did 'do not dress up' mean? What on earth was he to wear to greet an American aircraft as the senior British consular official if Mr. Redden were to dress like a cowboy? What did 'shoot the breeze' mean? In the end, he decided to wear gray trousers, his blue Cambridge blazer and a white shirt, open at the collar, with the collar of the shirt laid over the collar of the blazer. It is what he would have worn if he was going on a picnic in England and this seemed to him the closest parallel to this present invitation.

Reeves, dressed as if for his picnic, drove himself down to the *Porto Exterior* – he hoped Redden would be there to see him arrive in the black Studebaker – and pulled up in front of a small wooden building, painted pink like so much in Macao, and trimmed in white. It looked like it belonged on a lido on the Amalfi coast. Above the door was a white sign with blue letters reading 'Pan American Airways System' and below on the left hand side was a small brass plaque, polished so that it dazzled in the bright sun, with the words '*Sociedade Aeroportos Pan Americana de Macau.*'

On the harbor seawall just beyond the building, he saw a short wharf going into the harbor. A large white motor boat was tied alongside it and someone, his head away from Reeves, was bent over an open hatchway. The man straightened, jumped up onto the stern and then leaped onto the wharf. Reeves recognized him as Redden. Redden saw Reeves, broke out into a broad grin and waved an arm back and forth vigorously. He ran down the wharf towards Reeves. Reeves reached back unconsciously and put his hand on the car.

"John," he shouted, although by now he was only a dozen yards away, "You made it." Reeves tensed at the use of his first name, although he had steeled himself that it was going to happen, just as in the movies. Redden was up to him by now and extended his hand. He tightly grasped Reeves's, but not so tight that it hurt. Redden was sweating and his shirt was damp.

"Ed," said Reeves and awkwardly paused before continuing. "Thank you for inviting me. I am looking forward to seeing this plane. I have read so much about it."

"It is a doozy, eight days ago it was 7,000 miles away on the other side of the Pacific in San Francisco," said Redden, who put his hand on Reeves's shoulder and pushed him towards the building. "Let's go inside out of the sun for a minute. I talked to the radio boys and they reckon that we have about 30 minutes to touchdown. I finally got the launch humming."

Inside the building above the couches and chairs for the passengers, there were several framed airline posters for the cities and countries you could fly to on Pan American. They were all far from Macao.

Reeves stopped at one poster and looked at it closely. It showed a native woman in the near foreground stretched out languidly on a hilltop, a garland of flowers around her head and her long black hair falling on her bare shoulders. Her skin was a lustrous golden brown; it almost shone. She wore a simple white cotton dress, very tight around her, patterned with red hibiscus flowers. Palm trees extended over her to provide shade, and exotic flowers and plants grew nearby. She had propped herself up on one elbow, while her other arm was stretched out on a thigh, to watch in the middle distance an enormous aircraft, with four engines and two rows of windows in the hull, motionless alongside two craggy mountains streaked with red from a dawn or sunset, the same light that had turned the native woman's bare shoulders and back such a golden brown. The plane was about to land on its floats in the impossibly blue lagoon below.

"Fly to the South Sea Isles" read the words on the top of the poster, and "Via Pan American" along the bottom. The languid woman with her promise of untold delights was waiting for the plane and perhaps a particular passenger.

Reeves tried to imagine gliding down from the sky in some sort of flying ocean liner to an uncharted tropical paradise in the South Seas, where a beautiful woman would be waiting for him. He remembered his clumsy fumbling with girls at university and then here he was, a British mid-level civil servant in an obscure posting. Languid women in tropical gardens did not wait for people like him. He had his life with Rhoda and his daughter. They would be here soon, he was sure. His daughter would surely get better and Rhoda and he would finally grow close. He would make a success of his time in Macao.

He heard the voice of Redden. He was standing at the doorway in the sun, the *Porto Exterior* behind him. Redden with his blond hair and broad shoulders looked like he had stepped out of a film. Reeves was conscious for the first time in a long time, since he rowed, of wearing glasses.

"I got the word from the radio boys up on the hill. Twenty minutes to landing. Let's go."

Redden ran down to the end of the wharf, expecting Reeves to follow, and sprang into the launch, very gracefully Reeves thought. Redden held his hand out to assist Reeves in getting into the boat and he grasped Redden's hand, feeling the damp sweat on it.

The launch shone white in the sun, except for a mahogany deck behind the bow. But it was varnished and polished to a high finish. The rear half of the launch was open, with cushioned seats and banquettes to recline on. The forward half of the launch behind the mahogany deck with the console and controls was enclosed by a cabin. There was a large searchlight on the top of the cabin. The launch looked like it was capable of a long journey taking it far from Macao. There was an eager vibrating ticking from the engine hidden from view somewhere. A small American flag hung from a staff, angled back at the center of the stern. A slight breeze ruffled it a little.

"This is a real beauty," said Redden, turning the wheel and opening the throttle. The engine noise increased and the launch eased out into the *Porto Exterior*. "Chris-Craft, nothing finer. Thirty foot long, 160 horsepower Kohler engine." Reeves felt flattered that Redden assumed he would know the virtues of a Chris-Craft and a Kohler engine and need only to mention their names. He had never heard of them before, but, regardless, he had been accepted into a fraternity of which Redden was a senior member. He was pleased but kept his pleasure to himself.

The launch motored slowly through the *Porto Exterior* towards the break in the sea wall that would lead to the South China Sea. Soon they were in open water.

"Brace yourself," said Redden, turning the launch west and away from Macao, pulling back on the throttle. The hidden engine howled; the bow of the launch lifted suddenly and the boat shot forward, skimming over the tops of the waves, Reeves gripping a handrail tightly so he did not tumble. The launch raced along for several minutes before Redden abruptly slowed it and turned it back in a tight arc towards where it had come from. In a few seconds, the motor was at a low throb and the launch halted in the sea. Macao and the coast of China were much smaller against the horizon

"This should do it," he said, "Not much wind today. Plane will land from the east, should stop about here, and we can lead it into the *Porto Exterior*." He reached under the console and pulled out an enormous pair of rubber-covered marine binoculars, put them to his eyes and stared into the eastern sky.

After several minutes, Redden lowered the binoculars and pointed without saying anything. Reeves looked in the direction Redden had indicated, his eyes squinting against the bright sun and brilliant blue sky. Then he saw, not a speck, but a small black mass low on the horizon. It was no longer black but silver. For moments it seemed to be motionless, not moving or growing in size, but just suspended in the sky. Then Reeves realized that he could perhaps make out a wing and some sort of hull suspended beneath it. Sunlight glinted off the silver hull. Then he saw, just before he heard them, the four engines on the wings, and the bow of the aircraft – was it called a bow? – sloped up like the head of a leviathan just raised above the water. The aircraft grew in size until it seemed immense, menacing, brutal, in the air above the sea.

The engines of the aircraft were much louder now as it approached, perhaps twenty feet above the water. Reeves was astounded that something that large, that heavy and that substantial could be so suspended in the air. It was as though a small ocean liner was flying by them. Then the aircraft delicately descended that last fifty feet and gently touched onto the South China Sea. The engines roared and the sea on either side of the enormous plane came up in a single sheet of water, catching the sunlight in a myriad of rainbows. The aircraft glided across the sea and came to a stop, resting in the water, right near the launch as Redden had predicted. The four engines were now a little quieter, but just a little. The noise still deafened Reeves.

He looked at the huge aircraft now lurching from side to side in a slight swell; he had never seen anything remotely like it. He saw far above him the tail wing with its three upright fins as the launch passed alongside the hull. There were portholes set into the hull but he was far below them and could not see inside. The wing on the top of the hull was high in the air; Reeves could not estimate the height but he thought it was as high as a four- or five-story house. It cast a broad shadow over the launch as it passed close. He saw the Pan American logo and the large American flag on the fuselage, painted to look as though it was fluttering in the wind, but this aircraft was not from another country; to Reeves it was from another world altogether. He knew that Great Britain, the country he represented, had nothing like it.

The launch took up a position about one hundred yards directly in front of the aircraft and halted. Redden stepped back into the open stern of the launch and waved at the plane. High above, at the front of the plane and on the top of the fuselage, a windshield swung open and upwards and an arm, in the sleeve of a blue uniform jacket with gold stripes around the wrist, came out and made a circular motion. The four engines below the wings slowed and the noise dropped so that Redden and Reeves could converse without shouting.

"It's taking off again," said Redden. "Does this sometimes. Passengers want to get to Hong Kong. No real interest in seeing Macao. Have to touch down here to preserve our landing rights. Hong Kong is the big important city but Pan American wants you Brits to know that we don't need Hong Kong to have a base on the edge of China. If you know we have Macao, then you can't threaten us with taking away our right to land in Hong Kong. You Brits want to keep Hong Kong and its connections to China to yourselves. But we'll always have Macao as our gateway to China." He laughed and patted Reeves on the back.

Reeves thought of that war-torn country, engaged in a bitter and bloody war with Japan, swept by frequent floods and famines, oppressed by war-lords and the battles between the Nationalists and the Communists. He had been a vice consul in two obscure cities in China before Macao, trying to defend the interests of Great Britain. Right now, he could not really even define those interests. He wondered why anyone would want to pass through a gateway to China.

"We'll watch it take off and then head back. Pity you won't see inside. Like a de luxe hotel. Couches and coffee tables, dining rooms, sleeping compartments, bathrooms with running water, lounges, a kitchen with a steward who will cook you anything you want and a barman who will make you a drink anytime day or night. A palace in the sky."

A series of deafening cracks like sliced thunder shattered the early afternoon tranquility of the South China Sea as the aircraft's engines began to increase power. Then Redden was giving a thumbs up from the launch; the sea plane turned slowly into a mild wind coming from the west and waited. The aircraft was shuddering with a suppressed energy, like a caged beast which knew it would be released soon, but the plane did not move.

Then, in a flash, the plane glided forward with a grace and an ease that belied its immensity. It slid forward in a mist of spray and seconds later had lifted above the surface of the sea and was floating away above the water, the sun sparkling on the silver sides of the hull. It lifted higher and higher into the air heading west.

Then it began a gentle broad bank around in the air, still sparkling in the sun, and perhaps only two hundred feet in the air turned back east towards the launch and then Hong Kong. In a few seconds the plane passed over the launch to its port and Reeves saw the four engines, the spread of the wing that would have stretched the length of some of the streets in Macao, the huge hull hanging beneath. He saw the windows in the hull and wondered if anyone was looking out at him. He wondered who was sitting in the drawing rooms, reception rooms, and dining room. Would they take up the carpet and start dancing on sprung hardwood floors below? Had anyone retired behind a thick blue curtain in a sleeping compartment? The plane suddenly climbed higher, the reflected sunlight turning all of it golden, like a small sun rising heavenwards. You could not tell it was an aircraft any more. Then, in a literal flash, it disappeared, somewhere up in the air, on its way east, through the summer sky.

Redden was at the stern of the launch following the aircraft in the sky through the pair of binoculars. Reeves was by himself in the forward half-cabin. He had so many thoughts. He wondered when Rhoda would join him; he thought of the girl in the travel poster who would never be waiting for him; he thought of that immense flying palace that had just vanished into the sky. Only the Americans had such a thing and suddenly England, of which he was the only representative in Macao, began to look insignificant. And what did that mean to him? Did that make him insignificant? He wanted very much to make a difference, even if in a small way, but a difference nevertheless. But he felt small and helpless in the shadow of the immensity of the Pan American Clipper. Redden put down the binoculars and smiled. "We'll head back in. I'll buy you a drink when we get back to the hangar. Then we can go for lunch." Reeves thought at least he and Redden could be friends. He would like to have friends. He would make a difference in Macao even though it was small. He would have a career with meaning. He would be promoted. His next post would be in Europe where the battle for the future of civilization was just beginning. He would have a part in that. He had been sent to Macao to prepare him for Europe. Britain would have aircraft like the one he had just seen. The coast of China was a line of smudged shadow on the horizon.

Chapter 6

For Reeves, that first summer of 1941 in Macao was peaceful, even blissful. The war in Europe was very far away. Japan was consumed with fighting the Chinese and, he was assured repeatedly, despite its belligerent posturing, too weak to make war on the West. Reeves spent many of the weekends, and even some of the weekdays, with Redden. They would sit with friends in the Pan American hangar or Redden would take them out in the launch far out into the South China Sea – the cost of petrol never seemed to be an issue – and then, after a few hours of idle talk in the sun, they would return. Sometimes if the Clipper had landed and would be laying over in Macao for longer than an hour, the pilots, engineer and navigator would come ashore and join them in the hangar. The crew would talk of the weather they had encountered on the long days over the Pacific, the sweethearts and wives who would be waiting for them back in San Francisco, where to get dinner that night in Hong Kong, a bar near their hotel with naked Chinese girls dancing. It was a tight, intimate sodality of men. Redden was a member and Reeves hoped he could be too. He had never really had friends.

He wondered how Rhoda would find Redden. He hoped that she would like him. In any event he would find out soon. That hot summer had become a cooler autumn and Rhoda had written in late November that she thought it was time for Letitia to come to Hong Kong. The doctors had done nothing for her and one doctor at the American Hospital had suggested Letitia see a psychiatrist. Imagine the nerve, asking our daughter to see a looney doctor as though she wasn't really ill. She was done with doctors. We would have to take care of her ourselves. Rhoda planned on leaving soon to arrive in Hong Kong in early December. It would be lovely if he could take leave for a day or two, join them to do the Christmas shopping and help select a present for Letitia. Reeves had written he would come just a few days after her arrival. By then, the Macanese would be getting ready for Christmas, and slipping out of the office should not be an issue. They would take their time in Hong Kong – perhaps just the two of them could arrange to have dinner in the Hong Kong Club. Rhoda wrote back – Reeves thought her tone was almost affectionate – and said that sounded lovely, she was looking forward to seeing her new home. She gave details of her arrival by steamer and the hotel at which she and Letitia would be staying.

* * *

Reeves woke the morning of December 8th, six months after he had arrived in Macao almost to the day. It was just before seven. The window in his bedroom was open and faced the street. A breeze with a slight chill came in with the morning light but there were no sounds beyond a few bird calls. There were certainly no people or vehicles on the streets. Nothing, thought Reeves, remembering what the Governor had once told him, happens in Macao before eleven in the morning. Then a faint whine of a single plane heading east could be heard for some seconds but the silence resumed shortly.

Reeves got up and knotted his robe around him. He went downstairs to his sitting room and sat down in an easy chair. The Number One Boy knocked and, without waiting for a reply, opened the door carrying a large shiny lacquered tray. On it was Reeves's breakfast – tea in the British style with a teapot, strainer, cup and saucer and milk, and toast in a nickel-plated rack, which held the four thin slices vertically, like letters in a letter-rack. But there was also a bowl of congee – Chinese rice soup – and a small plate of sliced pineapple. He set it on a low table before the consul. Reeves ate the pineapple with toothpicks, rather than a fork. The Number One Boy would wonder why this white man had such odd habits.

Before beginning his breakfast, Reeves walked over to a large radio console of a polished mahogany veneer. It stood over four feet high. Reeves loved the words 'Radio Corporation of America' in gold letters across its top. There was a dial in the center of the console with the names of about thirty cities around its circumference like markings on a clock. The dial held out the promise that, with a twist of a knob, a pointer would alight on one of these cities – Quito or Stockholm or Sydney or Kansas City – and, thanks to the the Radio Corporation of America, Reeves could hear the same news and music as the citizens there were listening to, thousands of miles away on the other side of the world. But apart from an occasional ghostly burst of strange voices or music late at night, all Reeves could really receive on the radio was the BBC.

He sat down in the easy chair before there was any sound from the radio. It took some time to warm up and the first sounds would just be the crackle of static, then a random word or note of music, before the newsreader of the BBC Overseas Service could be heard. It was as though the announcer had to approach from a great distance through dry undergrowth before he could make himself understood. It was 7:30 in the morning and Reeves was expecting the news from England and the latest football results. He wondered, while the radio warmed, if his parents in England would be listening to the same program. He remembered fondly, as a small boy, playing by himself with his toys in the living room while his parents sat in solemn silence on either side of the fireplace to listen to the evening news on the BBC.

Then came complete sentences, with each word precisely and calmly enunciated, and for a moment Reeves heard only the sound of the words and not their meaning. Then he understood what he was listening to. The newsreader was explaining in his measured diction, that aircraft of the Japanese Navy had attacked the American naval base at Pearl Harbor in the American territory of Hawaii in the Pacific Ocean; that details were scant at the moment, but several American naval vessels, including battleships, were believed to have been sunk. Japanese losses were unknown. The American president was expected to address the United States Congress that evening. Reeves heard the date December 7th, which was yesterday, and thought that this must have already occurred. Then he remembered the international date line and that Macao was a day ahead of London. This had just happened and perhaps was still happening.

There was a rustle from the trees in the garden at the back of the house from a sea breeze and the smell of leaves and sea salt swept through the open windows into the room. The BBC was continuing with an account of the 'grave concern' with which His Majesty's Government was viewing the events in Hawaii and how they were 'closely observing the situation.' Then came a screaming roar from outside and Reeves, turning to the large window facing the street, caught sight of some dozen aircraft racing east, low in the sky.

Forgetting he was in his dressing gown and pajamas, Reeves ran to the front door, pushed it open hastily and stood on the front step of the consulate facing the street. He looked up and there were perhaps an additional 30 aircraft, engines howling at a deafening pitch, flying in close formation very low over Macao. He could not make out their markings and in seconds they were gone, the sounds of their engines trailing off and becoming very faint. A shudder of pigeons took to the air in a frantic nervous beating of wings before settling somewhere out of sight. The outside was still in shadow as the sun had not yet risen over Guia Hill. The curtains on each of the windows of the Japanese consulate next door were tightly closed. He returned inside to the sitting room to finish his breakfast. The announcer on the BBC sounded a long way away, thought Reeves, before remembering that the newsreader was in London, seven thousand miles from Macao.

He was sitting there, half paying attention to the voice on the radio, when there was a bang on the door and Mr. Gonsalves fell into the room. He was unshaven, without a tie, his jacket open, and not all the buttons on his shirt were fastened. His face was shiny with sweat. For a moment, he could not speak as he gasped in short frantic bursts and tried to catch his breath. Finally, his words rushed, tumbled and fell out of his mouth.

"They are bombing Hong Kong, they are bombing Hong Kong. My uncle in the rope factory there was able to call an uncle here with a phone in his home. The Japanese are bombing Hong Kong. He has seen the planes." Mr. Gonsalves sat down, or really collapsed, in one of the other easy chairs in the sitting room. Reeves was conscious that he had never invited Mr. Gonsalves into this room before and that he himself was in a dressing gown and pajamas. "The docks are on fire and there are burning buildings. There are no British planes in the air to fight them. Those must have been Japanese planes a few minutes ago over Macao. Perhaps they turn around and bomb Macao next. We are so close to Hong Kong." Mr. Gonsalves slumped back and fanned his face theatrically with his hand and said no more.

From somewhere outside, now quiet again, came two quick shrill sounds of a steam whistle, not very loud and not very close. Reeves thought he had heard it before but could not remember where.

"What was that?" asked Reeves. "Are they trying to sound some sort of air raid alarm?" He was sure the Portuguese did not have proper sirens and would have to improvise with something like factory whistles.

Mr. Gonsalves stopped fanning himself with his hand and with a surprisingly graceful gesture brought his wrist around so he could examine his watch. It was an American brand, bought off a US Navy sailor in Shanghai, and he was very proud of it. "No," he said in an airy voice of authority, seeming to forget the Japanese bombing of Hong Kong, "It is the first whistle of the Hong Kong steamer. It will depart soon." He resumed his fanning.

"The *Sai An?*" said Reeves, standing up suddenly, and his dressing gown opened to expose his pajamas. "The *Sai An?* It cannot sail to Hong Kong now. It will be sunk by Japanese bombers. It has to stay here until this situation is resolved. We have to stop it."

Mr. Gonsalves looked at Reeves and his blue striped pajamas. "I could call the Harbormaster but his office does not open for two hours. It is too early to call the Governor. They are the only two people who can stop a ship from sailing from the harbor. Perhaps the police chief."

Reeves stood looking off, his eyes unfocused. He loved the *Sai An,* even more so since he had seen the Pan American *China Clipper.* That may be the future, but this gentle ship, all in white with the Union Jack on each side, its rounded bridge, the graceful sweep upwards of the bow and stern, represented a love of England that he was now just discovering in himself. The thought of the *Sai An* destroyed by bombs dropped from the air horrified him.

"Wait there while I get dressed. We are going down to the harbor and we will stop it from sailing." Mr. Gonsalves wondered how he would do such a thing. Reeves was not in a China treaty port with authority over British shipping. He was simply a British consul in a distant province of Portugal, where Portuguese laws applied and the Portuguese ruled. Reeves abruptly left the room.

In a few minutes he returned, holding the door of the sitting room open. "Come, come," he said impatiently to Mr. Gonsalves, "We need to get down to the harbor. I will drive us." Mr. Gonsalves did not move at first but stared at Reeves. He had pulled a pair of navy trousers over his pajama pants, which stuck out under the cuffs of the trousers and over the top of his trouser belt. He wore a jacket of a similar, but still different, color that evidently belonged to another suit than the one the trousers came from. He still wore his pajama top, but had buttoned his jacket across it as though that was sufficient for him to consider himself dressed. He had not changed out of his bedroom slippers. They were of some scarlet material and there was a stork caught in flight embroidered on each in silver thread. Mr. Gonsalves's face was without expression as he followed Reeves out of the room.

Reeves and Mr. Gonsalves ran out of the front door of the consulate. There was no servant there to open it for them. The Studebaker was parked outside, shiny with the morning dew. Reeves ran around to the driver's side of the car and got behind the wheel, with Mr. Gonsalves next to him in the front passenger seat. The car started, Reeves pushed down on the accelerator and swung the steering wheel to the left hard. The car made a sharp turn with a harsh loud scrape of the tires and headed rapidly down the *Calcada do Gaio* towards the *Porto Interior*. Reeves pushed frequently on the button for the car horn, which made a mournful klaxon sound, even though there were no people or vehicles about to impede their progress.

Once on the *Praya Grande* and closer to the docks, there were a few pedicabs and handcarts on the road and people were slowly crossing from one side to the other. Reeves pushed repeatedly on the car horn button and the klaxon went from a slow mournfulness to a frantic urgency. The pullers of handcarts, the drivers of pedicabs and those engaged in slow walking across the street were surprised by this noise disturbing their peaceful morning and, rather than moving out of the way, stopped where they were and stared at the consular car with its insistent horn. Reeves wound down his window, leaned out, waving his arm and yelling. The people on the street gradually began to comprehend what was expected of them and slowly, one by one, moved aside. The Studebaker leaped into the space they had just vacated and then abruptly halted until the next group cleared a space in the road. The car jerked down the road in this fashion until it reached the ferry pier. Reeves turned on to it and then brought the car to a sudden halt. He stopped before the rows of fish laid out on the road by fishermen to dry in the sun.

The *Sai An* had a full head of steam on her, judging from the smoke coming out of her one stack and the low thudding of its engine. But it was still tied to bollards on the pier by stout hawsers and the passenger gangway was still in place between the ship and the pier. People, all Chinese, were standing on the pier in groups looking to say farewell to friends and family on the ship. They pointed up and yelled when they recognized someone standing on the open part of the deck. Reeves thought that they could have no idea of the bombing of Hong Kong.

He had climbed out of the car, remembering to take the keys with him, and began to walk quickly towards the gangway. He would have run if he had not been wearing slippers. The people on the pier, seeing a strange white man in the pants and jacket of a suit over a pair of pajamas, stepped back on either side, pushing on the people behind them and staring. Mr. Gonsalves, conscious that his *patrao* must look ridiculous, hurried behind him shouting between gasps for air *joeng hoi, joeng hoi* – make way, make way in Cantonese. He wanted the consul off the wharf where someone important from Macao might see him. Mr. Gonsalves knew his shirt was stained with sweat, that it was partially unbuttoned, his jacket was flapping, and that he had not shaved or put on a tie. But he thought he must look more respectable than the consul.

Reeves thought that the *Sai An* looked beautiful. The Union Jack on its side had also been repainted in bright red, blue and white enamel. He had not seen England in nearly seven years and he did not expect to see it for several more. This was as close as he would come to England for quite some time.

He walked up the gangway, worried that if he went too fast, he would lose a slipper. A Chinese officer in whites stood on the deck at the top of the gangway, holding a clipboard. He moved forward with his hand outstretched as though he meant to bar this crazily dressed white man from coming aboard the vessel. But Mr. Gonsalves, coming behind him shouted in Cantonese, between puffs and wheezes, that this man was the British consul in Macao, he had an urgent message for the captain and that it was so urgent that he had not had time to dress properly. He himself was the secretary to the consul and he had come across town to deliver the urgent message to the consul and he too had not had time to dress. The officer, thinking that this could be the only explanation for these two people, stepped aside and pointed to the door to the bridge.

Inside the bridge, there were two Chinese officers standing forward but Reeves could not immediately see the captain in the dimness of the cabin. A loud angry voice with a Scottish accent came from somewhere at the rear of the bridge.

"Who the hell are you and what are you doing on the bridge of my ship? How dare you come on to it, dressed like that? What the hell do you want?" Reeves could see a figure in a white uniform rising from some sort of a desk and coming towards him. He was conscious of a slight quaver or nervousness in his voice when he began to speak. He wished he could come across as more authoritative.

"I am John Pownall Reeves, His Majesty's Consul in Macao," he began and wondered why he had used all three of his names. "Forgive me my costume, but I dressed hastily and came down here immediately as soon as I heard the news." The captain had advanced and now was in the light coming through the bow windows of the bridge. He looked up and down at Reeves and grinned. Reeves recognized Captain McDougal whom he had met somewhere, at one reception or another.

"No wonder I did not recognize you, Reeves. You don't often see the senior British civil servants in their pajamas in broad daylight. No wonder I have a hard time," and here he waved generally in the direction of the two Chinese officers who were now staring quite openly at the consul, "convincing my Chinese officers that all white men are not fundamentally insane. You are not making my task any easier." He laughed again and put his hand on Reeves's shoulder as though comforting a relative who he thought was a little simple. He continued in the same amused tone. "Now what is the news that you raced out of your bedroom to tell me?"

Reeves raised himself to his full height, hoping both that it would give him a little more authority and that doing so might cause Captain McDougal's hand to fall from his shoulder. "You may not have heard the news but the Japanese Navy has attacked the American naval base at Pearl Harbor – in Hawaii."

"I know where Pearl Harbor is," said McDougal a little testily. He had dropped his hand from Reeves's shoulder and stepped back one pace. "It is two thousand miles away and I assure you that I have no intention of sailing there. Just the forty miles east to Hong Kong and back."

Reeves swallowed and continued. "I have it on good authority that aircraft of the Japanese Armed Forces within the past hour have attacked and bombed Hong Kong and its harbor. I can only assume that a state of war exists now between His Majesty's Government and Japan."

"On good authority? Only assume? You don't actually know? Surely someone would have told you if that was true. You are the British consul, aren't you?" McDougal's tone was both sarcastic and amused.

Reeves hesitated and then continued. "I received this information through informal channels." He hoped that McDougal would not press him as to what those channels might be. He did not want to tell him that they consisted of a single phone call from a relative of his secretary, who happened to be in Hong Kong. He was glad that Mr. Gonsalves was waiting outside the bridge and would not be tempted to interject to clarify the situation. "I am sure that by the time I return to the consulate there will be an official notification awaiting me. One cannot expect that in a time of war that everything will continue to operate in a timely and orderly manner."

"Mr. Reeves, you are very kind to come down to the harbor and give me this news, even before you had it from an official source. But I do not see what it has to do with me. I am the captain of the *Sai An* and in a few minutes, I will sail to Hong Kong, discharge my passengers and cargo, load more passengers and cargo, and return to Macao."

"Don't you see?" said Reeves, his voice rising and he worried that he was sounding more hysterical than urgent. "You cannot sail. You risk this vessel and all its passengers being attacked and possibly destroyed by the Japanese before or once you reach Hong Kong. As the British consul, I cannot permit you to sail and I am hereby ordering you to remain in the harbor of Macao awaiting further instructions." He stopped speaking, unsure of what to say next.

"Mr. Reeves," said Captain McDougal. He had a patronizing smile. "I am sure that you have all of our best interests at heart. The *Sai An* may have a large Union Jack on its side, but it is owned by a Chinese company with Chinese owners and is flagged in China. I am sure the owners thought it was great advertising to paint the British flag on its side, but they did not intend, I am sure, to have its timetable determined by the British consul in Macao. I have received no instructions from the owners and in the absence of those or an explicit direction from the

Harbormaster in Macao, who actually has some authority over my vessel, I intend to keep to my schedule. Now, if you would not mind, I must ask you to vacate my bridge and go ashore. We sail," and here McDougal pointedly looked at his wristwatch, "in a few minutes."

"Captain McDougal, with all due respect, you cannot sail." Reeves paused for a moment, then he plunged on. "Should you defy my instructions to stay in the harbor at Macao, I shall report to your owners that you deliberately placed your vessel in harm's way and risked both its and the passengers wellbeing despite being in possession of credible evidence of the danger that you were putting them in." Of course that would sound ridiculous if the *Sai An* simply left Macao in a few minutes and returned that afternoon unharmed. But then, as if emphasizing the points he had just made, a squadron of planes flew in a deafening scream so low over the *Sai An* that the windows on the bridge rattled. The red Rising Sun of the Japanese armed forces could now be seen clearly on the wings and fuselages of the planes in the few seconds before they disappeared on their way east. Captain McDougal turned from the windows of the bridge where he had been following the planes and seemed to have made his mind up about something. He said something harshly in guttural Cantonese to the two Chinese officers. One of them left the bridge immediately and could be heard shouting something down to the dock. The other spoke loudly into a speaking tube. What was the distinct rumble of the ship's engine below became a low, almost inaudible, throb.

"Very well Mr. Reeves, I will hold the ship in port, pending clarification from the ship's owners as to my instructions. I will cite our conversation here as my grounds for not sailing. I am sure you are prepared to live with the consequences if they choose to protest your interference to your superiors in the Foreign Office. And now I suggest that you leave the vessel to return to the consulate before you are trapped by a mob of angry passengers who will be rapidly coming to the realization that they will not be traveling to Hong Kong for the foreseeable future." McDougal stared at Reeves, his face now angry, not liking the situation in which Reeves had placed him.

Reeves shook the captain's hand and said something about thanking him for his cooperation and hoping that they met again soon. He turned and stepped out of the bridge onto the narrow side-deck. Mr. Gonsalves was waiting for him, a look of anxiety on his face. In the breeze coming off the harbor, his face no longer was covered with drops of sweat, although there were still large damp patches on his white cotton shirt, tight over his chest and stomach.

"What did he say, Mr. Reeves? Is the ship staying in Macao?" He looked at Reeves in a worried manner.

"The *Sai An* will not sail," said Reeves, not quite believing it himself. He had never done anything like this before. "Let us return to the consulate. We need to prepare. I intend to hold a reception at lunchtime today so that I can speak to the British community and there is much to be done, not the least of which is for you to telephone around and issue the invitations. There is not a moment to be lost." He realized that he was intending to speak to the British community to inform and reassure them without actually knowing what was happening. Perhaps there would be further information back at the consulate. He would think of something; this is what he had to do.

In the car returning to the consulate, Reeves suddenly thought of Rhoda in Hong Kong. She would be having breakfast at the Gloucester Hotel. He wondered how she was. He imagined she was very frightened – she was by disposition nervous and even if the bombing was confined to the dockyards, she would be very scared. Would she be a source of comfort to Letitia? Would he have been under the circumstances? Perhaps Letitia's indifference to the world would serve her well and she would not notice the chaos of a city under attack. He felt he should be in Hong Kong with her. A husband should somehow take care of his wife.

Then he remembered that he was meant to travel to Hong Kong in a few days and the three of them return to Macao. He was not sure that the Foreign Office would let him travel into a war zone, when he had no official business there. And how was he to get there, and he and Rhoda return, when he had stopped the ferry from the sailing that connected these cities? Perhaps some sort of normality would return soon and the *Sai An* could resume its short little voyages back and forth. In any event, she was the wife of a British consul and someone official would surely take care of her. She would be fine. He would put in a call to her as soon as he got home.

Once back at the consulate, Mr. Gonsalves first tried to telephone the Gloucester Hotel so that the consul could talk to his wife, but the exchange was unable to reach Hong Kong. Reeves asked him to keep trying. Mr. Gonsalves in the meantime made many telephone calls and managed to gather a small group of people. The Governor had declined, but someone from his staff did come. There was the Harbormaster by himself; Mrs. Fletcher, the wife of the head of the Electric Company (her husband was in England but would soon return to Macao); Mrs. Joy Wilson from the consulate staff; Pat Heenan of the Royal Insurance Company; Ed Redden from Pan American; Mr. Cassim Moosa, an Indian who had a claim as a British subject and whose family had owned a general store on the *Rua Central* for generations, with his wife, a shy lady in a scarlet and yellow sari and a small gold ring through one nostril (other Indian merchants Mr. Gonsalves suspected were supporters of the Indian Independence League and could not be invited); the three cadets from the Malayan Civil Service who were in Macao to learn Cantonese and were delighted to find their studies interrupted for a noon-time drink; Mr. Enrique Nolasco, a local lawyer who was also the honorary Dutch consul (Reeves was to learn that his mother was the daughter of Prince Teles de Menezes back in Portugal); Mr. Borras of the China Maritime Customs; Mr. Braga and his wife – he was the preeminent historian of Macao; the Lammerts and the Galloways; and other Portuguese who Mr. Gonsalves assured Reeves were British subjects and were already registered at the consulate as such. Reeves had changed into a dark blue suit, a white silk shirt with a thin blue stripe running vertically through it and a tie in the colors of his university. He had put on black socks, but was still wearing his scarlet slippers with the storks embroidered in silk thread.

All in all, perhaps twenty-five people gathered in the largest of the reception rooms at the consulate. There were bottles of wine and sherry, a single bottle each of scotch and gin, a pot of coffee and one of tea, glasses, cups and trays of small sandwiches and Portuguese sugar cookies. The conversation amongst the guests, as might be expected for those who had their first drink at noon before having lunch, was loud and, despite the solemnity of the occasion, there was occasional laughter. Reeves had had his first glass of wine at around 11:30am, before the first guest had arrived, and now, at around 12:30pm when he tapped a glass to get the gathering's attention, he had already had a second. The crowd slowly hushed and the last person loudly talking realized that everyone else was silent and stopped his conversation in mid-sentence, his words hanging very loud in the silent room.

Everyone was looking at Reeves and he began, a little too quickly. "Thank you all for coming on such brief notice. I thought it was important for all of us in the British community to gather together here today." He remembered Redden and some Portuguese were there, and added "and the Western community as well."

He stopped for a moment, then remembered the sheet of paper in his hand. He brought it in front of him and held it with two hands. He looked at the expectant faces of his silent guests and began. "You will have heard the news reports on the radio and I am sure that there are rumors even now as we speak. But I have just received the following dispatch from the Foreign Office in London and let me share with you its salient points." Reeves knew that he made it sound like the cable had been addressed to him exclusively, rather than having been sent to every British mission in the world in clear text without even having been coded. He pushed back his glasses, looked down and began to read:

"On the evening of December 7th, His Majesty's Government in the United Kingdom learned that Japanese forces, without previous warning, either in the form of a declaration of war or of an ultimatum with a conditional declaration of war, had attempted a landing on the coast of Malaya and bombed Singapore and Hong Kong."

"In view of these wanton acts of unprovoked aggression, committed in flagrant violation of international law, and particularly of Article 1 of the Third Hague Convention, relative to the opening of hostilities, to which both Japan and the United Kingdom are parties, His Majesty's Ambassador at Tokyo has been instructed to inform the Imperial Japanese Government, in the name of His Majesty's Government in the United Kingdom, that a state of war exists between the two countries." He paused to let the awful solemnity of the declaration of war sink in. No one said anything. Their faces were serious, even grim. Everyone was looking at him.

Reeves went on, quoting from the cable, about how the United States and the Royal Netherlands Government had also declared war on Japan, that the three powers had strong land, air and sea forces in the region, that they were prepared to strongly resist and repel any invasion or incursion. He did not know how to finish but finally said that we were gathered in a territory of Portugal, that he had been assured by Governor Teixeira that Portugal would maintain neutrality (it was in a totally different context, but these people did not need to know that), he had had no indication that Japan would not respect Portuguese neutrality and that we all would be safe here. Now was the time for all of us to come together in solidarity and he could assure each and every one of them that the full resources of the British consulate were at their disposal. He was not sure what those resources were or what he could do to help in a situation like this, but the remark was greeted with enthusiastic applause, sounding very loud in that closed room. He decided to end his remarks, put down the paper and picked up a glass of wine that was lying on a side table. He raised it, a little too high, and said, "To King and Country." The gathering raised their glasses, even the Portuguese and Mr. Redden the American, and repeated "To King and Country."

Reeves stepped away from the wall and joined his guests in conversation. He wondered what Rhoda would think if she was here. He was sure she would admire him. His thoughts turned back to this morning. He had raced down to the harbor and saved a ship from destruction by Japanese bombers by dint of nothing but the force of his own words. Then he had rallied the British community, who seemed now to be looking up to him for support and guidance. And he had done this in scarlet slippers with embroidered silver storks. He was very happy and picked up another glass of wine. He would ask Mr. Gonsalves to try the Gloucester Hotel again to reach Rhoda once the reception was over.

Chapter 7

Rhoda lay on her side on a thin stained mattress on a metal cot. There was only a single worn gray sheet on the bed – no blanket or pillow – and she was lying under it, pulling it up as far as she could, trying to cover her face. When she pushed her knees up to her chest and bowed her head, she succeeded. She was trying to be brave, she really was, but she was crying, not loudly, but in small sobs she hoped could not be heard. The room was a long dormitory containing around thirty small beds pushed close together. The beds occupied almost all of the floor. The electric lights did not work; a dim light came from the small windows, but not much as it was a gray winter morning. A few of the beds had mosquito nets hanging down, but all of these had large tears in them and would not have saved a sleeper on the bed from being bitten. The nets swung slowly back and forth in the chilly draft like melancholy ghosts.

There were thirty women and perhaps fifteen children pushed into that room, most lying on the beds as there was not enough room for all to stand. Most of the women were in light frocks as though it was a summer's day and they were going on an outing. It was December 27th and it was cold in the Hong Kong winter. The women folded their arms as some protection against the cold; a few wore cardigans that they pulled tight around them, clutching the edges with clenched fingers. Some of the glass in the windows was smashed, but even those windows that were intact were open despite the chill wind. The women and children had not changed clothes or washed in several days and the air in that close-packed room would have been unbearable had the few functioning windows been closed.

Rhoda sat up, her eyes red and wet. She hoped no one would notice. She had to pull herself together. Her daughter depended on her. Letitia was sitting at the foot of the bed, looking down at the floor and holding the handle of a small rattan case, pulling it tightly against her as though she was afraid of it being taken away, although it was very small and could hardly have held very much. Letitia was such a strange girl, thought Rhoda, not for the first time. She rarely displayed affection towards her mother and seemed to be lost in her own thoughts much of the time. She coughed constantly. Rhoda supposed that what she felt towards Letitia was love, but she could not be sure. Soon it would be time to line up in the kitchen for whatever food there was. She needed to make sure that Letitia was fed. Yesterday there was a bowl of some sort of soup and a single boiled potato. Rhoda had tried to give part of her potato to her daughter, but she had refused it. If her husband was here, he would have made things better. She felt sure of it.

* * *

Rhoda and her daughter had arrived in Hong Kong on December 3rd. She had booked a room at the Gloucester Hotel where her father always stayed, and when she got there she was pleased to see that the other guests were almost all English, with a scattering of Europeans and Americans and just a few Chinese. Rhoda would talk happily to her daughter about the nice shops they were going to visit that day to buy what they would need for Christmas in Macao, and how Letitia would finally see her father again after all these months. He was going to come to Hong Kong, especially to see her and to help them onto the ferry that would take them to their new home in Macao. He would make sure that their cabin was on the sunny side of the boat so they would be warm. Because she was the wife of a vice consul, she would have a cabin, even though the voyage was just a few hours long. The warmth would be good for Letitia's cough.

On the morning of December 8th, there were just a few other people in the dining room when Rhoda and her daughter went down for an early breakfast. Rhoda nodded at the other guests without saying anything, just as she had seen her father do in the dining rooms of the Shanghai Club. They were shown to a table by the window with a nice view of the harbor.

The quiet of the dining room of the Gloucester Hotel was suddenly shattered by an enormous noise outside. Rhoda looked out the window and saw dozens of aircraft flying overhead just above the roofs of the buildings. Their engines made a deafening angry roar that shook the windows of the dining room. In seconds the aircraft had risen steeply in the air and were flying in a circle over the docks on the Kowloon side of the harbor. Planes peeled off from the circle one by one, very quickly, and dove down on the docks like furious metal sea-birds attacking creatures on the beach. Rhoda heard the explosions first, dull thumps that nevertheless were loud enough to startle her and she gave a little scream as the first shockwaves from the bombs furiously rattled the windows. Her daughter, staring down at the table, started to cry. Rhoda, very scared, reached across to comfort her but grasped her daughter's arm too tightly and Letitia cried a little louder. Rhoda loosened her grip and stroked her daughter's arm.

"For God's sake, get away from the windows," yelled an Englishman. "Come back here against the wall." She stood up clumsily, almost falling but righting herself and grabbing her daughter, pulling her across the dining room and against the wall furthest from the windows, where the other guests were already crouching. For the next 45 minutes, the planes continued to roar over the hotel like hornets to dive onto the Kowloon docks. The bombs exploded every few seconds and Rhoda gave a start each time, though she was determined not to cry out. Letitia sat on the floor with her legs outstretched, tears running down her cheeks but otherwise silent. Rhoda, crouching down, put one tight arm around Letitia. Her daughter was a comfort to her right now.

Then the planes stopped coming and the bombing ceased and there was silence. Black smoke was rising from the harbor side on Kowloon and blotting the blue winter sky. Then, very faint, distant sirens could be heard.

The Englishman looked as though he was about to say something when the door to the dining room opened and the manager of the hotel almost fell in. "The Japanese," he gasped, having evidently run up the three flights of stairs from the lobby where his office was. "They have attacked Hong Kong. And Malaya. And America. We have declared war. We are at war with Japan." He looked in a horrified manner at the guests and stopped speaking.

The manager caught his breath and continued. "I have been in telephonic communication with the senior police officials just now. The situation is very fluid" – he said 'fluid' with a great deal of emphasis as though the word would have a significance for everyone – "and they are still gathering information. In the meantime, they suggest that we all remain in the hotel and not venture out. It might be dangerous and they will need to keep the streets and roads clear so that the authorities can move around unimpeded."

Rhoda walked over to the manager. She explained, straining not to cry, that she was the wife of His Majesty's Consul in Macao and she needed to book passage on the first ferry there. It was imperative that she rejoin her husband in view of what had just happened to assist him in his vital duties. Her place was by his side, she explained. After living apart for so long, she so wanted to be with him. She was convinced of it now when perhaps she had had doubts before.

The manager was apologetic, but all shipping out of and into Hong Kong had been suspended. The *Sai An*, the regular ferry between Macao and Hong Kong, was still in Macao, he had been told. Rhoda, still struggling to stay calm, said, "Then I will need to speak to my husband by telephone. Can you have your operator place the call to the British consulate in Macao and you may bill it to my room?" The manager wrung his hands and contorted his face into a parody of sorrow and apology. "I am so sorry, madam," he said, "but all the phone lines are now reserved for official and military purposes. It is impossible to telephone Macao, or anywhere outside Hong Kong."

"There is a war on," he added in an unnecessary explanation.

Rhoda went back to her room and realized that there was no way of reaching either her father in Shanghai or her husband in Macao. She was all alone with her daughter. She did not cry, but lay on the bed silently. Her husband was an important official with the British Foreign Office. He would have influence and would know what to do. In the meantime, she must try to be strong. Her daughter depended on her.

The bombings continued over the next several days, sometimes at night, when they were roused out of their rooms by the hotel staff banging on their doors and they stumbled down stairs in the dark to the hotel cellar, where they crouched down, packed against the other guests while the bombs fell, some very close and loud, shaking the walls and floor. There was very little food to be had. The water was also on for just a few hours a day and Rhoda was very proud of herself for remembering to fill her bathtub as much as she could before the water was turned off. She would scoop it into the sink with the lid from a jar of face cream and wash Letitia's face, and then her own. She wanted so much to tell her husband how she had coped. He would be proud of her.

Then very early one morning when the explosions seemed to increase in both volume and number, Rhoda heard the manager running down the corridor of the hotel, banging on the walls and doors, ordering everyone down to the hotel lobby for an important announcement. When she came down to the lobby, it was crowded with the other guests. There was a very young British army lieutenant standing by the unmanned reception desk. He stood with a swagger stick under one arm, the other arm behind his back and his legs apart. He was smiling wanly. He was trying to look confident and in charge, Rhoda thought, but he had the face of a schoolboy and looked scared, tired and haggard. His uniform was rumpled as though he had slept in it and it was stained down the front. When he thought that all the guests were in the lobby, he rapped the reception desk for attention. It was an unnecessary gesture as the room was silent and everyone was looking at him.

"We will be moving our forces to establish a line of better advantage." His young voice sounded very weary and he made no effort to say this in a positive way. "Some of this line will be very close to this hotel. HQ has determined that the British subjects staying at this hotel" – when he said 'British subjects' the Chinese people looked at one another and realized that whatever this officer had to offer would not include them – "would be more conveniently accommodated at the Repulse Bay Hotel on the south side of the island. We have arranged transport. Two lorries will be here in about a half hour. I regret that because of space, you may only have one suitcase per person. Please be down promptly in a half hour; the lorries are needed elsewhere for urgent war work and they will not wait. Are there any questions?" His tired black-hooded eyes looked up around the room but Rhoda had the impression he was looking into the distance. Not waiting for questions, he turned and walked out of the hotel.

Rhoda and Letitia were among the first down. The manager was down in the lobby. Rhoda told him about the Christmas parcels that she was obliged to leave in her room and asked him if he could have the staff put them in a safe place until her return once this situation was resolved. The manager seemed astounded at this request and made no reply. Then an army sergeant in a red beret with some sort of brush on its crown was saying something like anyone who wanted the scenic tour of Hong Kong should get in the lorries right now, otherwise they would miss tea-time at the Repulse Bay. No one even smiled as they filed out and took their places. The women sat on benches on the open beds of the trucks, the men on the floor in the narrow space between, the suitcases jammed amongst them. The explosions were much louder and seemed closer. Rhoda could see flashes like lightning with each explosion but she could not tell what was happening. A cold damp mist came down with a cutting breeze as they pulled away and she shivered in her cotton frock. Letitia was sitting on the floor of the lorry bed at Rhoda's feet. She too was in a cotton frock without a cardigan.

The Repulse Bay Hotel still looked magnificent. The mist had cleared and the hotel was caught in the gold of the morning light an hour or so after sunrise. Nestled low in the hills, a few hundred yards from the beach, the hotel seemed just a few stories high. Two broad stone staircases ran up to a deep veranda shaded by red-striped awnings that ran the entire length of the hotel. How pleasant, thought Rhoda, it must have been to sit and drink tea in the shade and look out over the gardens down to the beach and the South China Sea. But no one was on the beach and there were coils of barbed wire strung in several rows on it. This must have been very recent as no one was talking about war when she arrived in Hong Kong just two weeks ago. Someone had started to dig a trench in the lawn but had stopped and left a deep gash and some dirt piled close to the stairs. The hotel looked abandoned; there were sandbags stacked against some of the windows facing the porch and around the base of the two staircases. There was no one sitting on the porch, perhaps because there were no chairs or recliners. No one from the hotel was there to meet the two lorries; indeed Rhoda could see no people at all.

Rhoda and the other guests from the Gloucester Hotel climbed out of the lorry with their suitcases. Someone kindly handed Letitia down to her. They crowded into the lobby where a major shouted at them to stay away from the windows, as there were reports of Jap snipers. Rhoda and Letitia were put in a room with five other women. They slept on the floor when they slept at all. There was one meal a day and that was often just a thin soup and a few vegetables.

Several days later, Rhoda, her daughter and the five women were woken by a soldier banging on their door and ordering them down to the lobby. There, an officer, his uniform stained with mud and torn in patches, told them that the Japanese were close and that British forces were going to make a stand around the hotel. For their own safety, everyone was to take shelter in a drainage tunnel under the hotel that led from the hotel to the beach. "You will be quite safe there," he said but he did not sound convinced.

A soldier led the guests into the hotel's conservatory where a manhole in the floor was open and the guests climbed down metal rungs into a drainage tunnel, large enough for an adult to stand if he bent over a little. There was mold and slime on every surface. Every now and then, a few inches of waste water washed through the tunnel. If they did not stand up in time, they became wetter and dirtier. There was a faint light at the end of the tunnel where it opened onto the beach. They had nothing to eat or drink for the nearly 12 hours they were down there, and towards evening, the smell of urine was very strong. Even underground, they could hear gunfire and a few times during the day, artillery or mortar shells exploded on the beach close to the open end of the tunnel. The noise echoed horrifyingly up the drainage tunnel, deafening the occupants, and the acrid smell of explosives blowing into the tunnel caused many to choke or cough.

Rhoda held Letitia tightly to her. Letitia seemed to have no reaction to having been thrust underground into a sewer. That is the advantage of not paying attention to the world around you, thought Rhoda. It must be a marvelous gift sometimes. The only way she thought she could cope was to tightly close her eyes, not talk to anyone, and shut the world off. If she did this, she thought, she could hold herself together until her husband rescued her and Letitia.

One day in the tunnel, a man insisted on talking to her. He was an American businessman and he talked despite Rhoda having turned her head away. His voice was loud in the tunnel. He told of arriving in Hong Kong on the Pan American plane from Manila, that he was due to fly back to Manila the day the Japs attacked, that they had all assembled early but the plane had been bombed. He talked on and Rhoda was able to keep most of his words out of her head, until he started talking about the Japanese soldiers invading Hong Kong. He had heard from a man high up in the government that the Jap soldiers had been able to advance so far because they had special training. Stuck twigs and branches into their uniforms and helmets and crawled along the ground like snakes. Could not be seen. But that was not all. They had German shepherd dogs with them and they were also trained to crawl on their bellies through the undergrowth. He was growing more excited and louder as he was telling this story. They creep up on a British soldier in the line. He cannot see them because they have blended into the landscape. The first thing he knows is that a dog has leapt on him and is trying to tear his throat out with its teeth. Then, while he is trying to fight off the dog, a Jap soldier leaps up and charges him with a bayonet. He can't even fire his weapon before he has been stuck like a pig and is dead. From then on, when she had her eyes closed, all Rhoda could see were savage dogs suddenly leaping out in front of her, jaws open, and trying to sink their teeth into her throat. She held back her tears.

On the morning of the fourth day, they were told not to go down from their rooms to the drainage tunnel, but to assemble in the lobby of the hotel. There the guests found two weary ragged British officers and a dozen Japanese soldiers and one Japanese officer. He had a curved sword at his side.

One of the British officers, trying to talk loudly but his voice coming out in a weak, gravelly dry sound, not much louder than a whisper, asked everyone to gather around him. He told them that he had come from British HQ, had spoken to the Governor and that the Governor had determined that further fighting would be futile. Here his voice quavered and some of the hotel guests wondered if he was going to cry. But he recovered and went on to say that the British Army and their Indian and Canadian allies would surrender. All Allied civilians were to be interned for an unknown duration. The people in this hotel would proceed to St. Stephen's College, a boys' school several miles from here, where – and here he paused again as his voice caught – accommodations would be provided. "Merry Christmas," someone said quietly and then everyone remembered it was Christmas Day. The two British officers took a step backwards and the Japanese soldiers moved forward.

The soldiers came and inspected each guest, removing their watches, jewelry and rings. An aide to the officer stepped forward and said in creditable English that everyone should remove their hats and bow towards the colonel, pointing at the officer. He spoke very softly, but since there were Japanese troops standing around with rifles and bayonets, everyone obeyed.

The crowd of guests that walked out of the hotel that morning were largely women, but there were some men and children. Each adult held a suitcase, some large and some small. They shuffled and stumbled down the hotel lawn towards the road in a ragged straggling line. Japanese soldiers with bayonets fixed in their rifles urged them forward in short guttural shouts. Rhoda was holding her daughter's hand with her free one, afraid she might get left behind or lost. They began the long march towards St Stephen's College. Rhoda could not help thinking of German shepherd dogs, crouched in the underbrush along the road, ready to sink their teeth into her and Letitia's throats.

* * *

Reeves was never able to complete a telephone call to the Gloucester Hotel to his wife on the day the bombing began or in the subsequent days. The ferry service remained suspended between the two cities with the *Sai An* at anchor in the *Porto Interior*. He called on the Governor and asked for his help. The Governor cabled the Portuguese consul in Hong Kong – the Japanese had left him alone – but the consul was unable to discover any information. Reeves cabled the Embassy in Chungking; they replied saying that they had opened a file on the subject, but conditions in Hong Kong at the moment were reportedly chaotic and they had little direct information. They were dealing with thousands of inquiries on missing British subjects.

Reeves wondered if his wife and daughter had become unexpected casualties of war and that he would be a widower with nothing but a memory of his married life. He had such hopes for their lives together in Macao. The tone of Rhoda's letters indicated a new affection towards him. She would see him in a different role, dealing with problems and having the respect of the British and Portuguese community. They could share a bedroom. Letitia would grow out of her illness and he would be able to talk to her. He anxiously continued to make inquiries of the Governor's staff. He thought it futile to cable the embassy in Chungking again; his inquiry would not be a priority.

A week after the Christmas Day surrender of Hong Kong by the British to the invading Japanese army, Mr. Gonsalves came into the consul's office and said that the secretary to the Japanese consul was in the waiting room and would there be a good time for the Japanese consul to call on Consul Reeves. Reeves at first did not know what to say. The two countries were at war and diplomatic relations between the two had been sundered. The Foreign Office had sent instructions to its posts in neutral countries with Japanese diplomatic and consular representation that, should a British official encounter a Japanese official, they were to be greeted with 'cold civility.' But this seemed to cover the case of random encounters; there were no instructions on how to deal with an actual request for a meeting. Should it be declined or should it be conducted with 'cold civility'? In the end, Reeves decided that Mr. Fukui had always been gracious to him and that his curiosity as to what Mr. Fukui could want was greater than any need to placate a distant Embassy in Chungking, a thousand miles from Macao. He told Mr. Gonsalves to set the meeting for 3:00pm that afternoon.

Exactly at three, Mr. Gonsalves came into the consul's office and said that Mr. Fukui was waiting in the reception room. Reeves entered the room and Mr. Fukui immediately rose from the sofa and bowed gravely. He was beautifully dressed in a dark-blue suit with a thin white stripe running vertically through it. Reeves was aware suddenly that he had not put on his jacket and he was dressed in a pair of white tennis slacks. He was wearing a red tie with a bright pattern, which he realized looked frivolous when contrasted with Mr. Fukui's formality. Reeves felt a slight awkwardness come over him and he was glad of the interruption when the Number One Boy came in with the tea.

They both sat there in silence for a minute, on two opposing sofas, both holding the saucer with a cup of tea with two hands just above their laps. Then Mr. Fukui began to speak. He talked of the autumn weather, how pleasant it was for it to be a little cooler, the blue skies and warm sun that came at noon, that the hibiscus on a neighboring house was still in flower, that it was delightful to hear church bells. Reeves did not reply but wondered to himself where Mr. Fukui had learned the word 'hibiscus.'

Mr. Fukui then paused, put down the cup and saucer, and looked down and then up. In a slightly softer voice, he went on to say he deeply regretted the current unpleasant state of relations between Japan and Great Britain, that he and his colleagues in the Foreign Ministry had worked tirelessly to avoid war and would work tirelessly to see that the interests of Japan, Great Britain and its allies could be united once again and that peace could be restored. He would hope that reasonable men would be able to reach a reasonable solution to our differences, although he was sure that all parties understood, given the complexities of the situation, that this would take time. Reeves thought that 'unpleasant' was a pretty funny word for bombing Hong Kong and sending thousands of troops over its border to occupy it, but Mr. Fukui was obviously so pained by what he was saying and seemed to be such a nice man, that he let it pass.

Then Mr. Fukui brought up Reeves's wife and daughter. Mr. Fukui had said he understood his wife and daughter had been in Hong Kong when, and here he stopped, thought for a second or two, and then continued, on December 8th and that so far had been unable to travel to Macao to join him. He knew how much this must distress him. He had been in touch with the Foreign Ministry and had been told that they were both well and staying with other British subjects in Stanley on the south coast of Hong Kong Island. The Foreign Ministry representative in Hong Kong was doing all he could to arrange their release.

Here Mr. Fukui took off his glasses and removed a handkerchief from a pocket in his jacket to polish the lenses. He smiled vaguely at Reeves, who wondered if Mr. Fukui could actually see him without his glasses, and began talking as though he was sharing a private joke. I am sure, he said, an experienced diplomat like yourself, you appreciate the issues the Foreign Ministry has in Hong Kong. Hong Kong is now under a military administration, when we in the Ministry had urged it be placed under a civil administration. Sometimes the Army and the Foreign Ministry do not see everything the same way. He looked in the direction of Reeves without giving the appearance of actually seeing him. I am sure that you have had problems dealing with your army, he said. They never seem to understand what we diplomats are trying to do. He smiled as though he was attempting to establish a common bond, one civil servant to another commiserating over shared problems. Reeves had never had to deal with any army or had faced any problem remotely like Mr. Fukui was describing and said nothing. A consul in Japan seemed much more important than a British consul. Mr. Fukui continued. We are urging that Mrs. Reeves and your daughter be released from their accommodations in Hong Kong and be allowed to come to Macao. Please forgive me, he said, but this may take a little time. People need to be persuaded. In the meantime, my colleague from the Foreign Ministry will deliver food parcels to Mrs. Reeves and try to see she is as comfortable as possible. He finished polishing his spectacles and put them back on. He then stood up and bowed. When he rose again, Reeves saw his eyes were full of tears. We are doing all we can, he said. Now I have taken too much of your time already and I will leave you to your duties.

He bowed again and turned to leave the room. Reeves was barely able to thank him before he had left the sitting room.

* * *

One afternoon, at the end of the third week of January, a Japanese officer came into the dormitory where Rhoda and Letitia were staying with the other women and their children. They had been there for nearly four weeks. The Japanese officer was accompanied by two soldiers; all three wore swords. They came over to Rhoda's bed where she was lying, as were most of the women. Everyone had just had a meal of a cold brown soup mixed with porridge and they did not want to go out into the winter chill. Letitia was sitting on the end of the bed, holding onto her tiny wicker suitcase.

The Japanese officer swung his sword around, still in its scabbard and attached to his belt, and slapped it against Rhoda. "Wake, wake," he said, "You leave the school." His accent was clipped and the words pronounced in a harsh and guttural way, although they were distinct enough to be understood. The women in the dormitory stared, saying nothing, wondering if she was to be taken off to an actual prison or for some form of brutal punishment, or – they all thought this, though none was willing to say it – execution. They also wondered if it was just Rhoda who was to be taken away, and whether they would have to look after that odd little child who kept so much to herself.

Rhoda picked up her suitcase; tears came down her face and then she appeared to keep herself under control. One of the soldiers took her by the arm and pushed her after the officer who was already walking towards the door. The other soldier, who looked very young, took Letitia's suitcase from her and then took her by the hand gently, as though he was her elder brother taking her outside to play together.

The women remaining in the dormitory looked at the departing woman and child. They all had lived through the Japanese invasion of Hong Kong. Not long ago, they had seen bodies of men and women, white and Chinese, that had been shot by the Japanese and left on lawns, streets and in the corridors of houses and office buildings. And they all knew of men who had been separated from the internees, taken away and never seen again.

Rhoda followed the Japanese officer towards the gate in the wire fence that had been thrown around the school in the second week of the internment. A guard opened the gate and on the other side of the road running alongside the fence was a black sedan with the Argentinian flag flying from a short metal staff on a mudguard. The driver remained in the car; a Chinese man was leaning up against the car with his arms folded. He had close-cropped hair, a small scar down one cheek and was chewing a toothpick. The Japanese officer had turned back and Rhoda was in the middle of the road by herself; the soldier with Letitia was still holding her hand and was walking her towards the car. The Chinese man with the toothpick stepped towards Rhoda, took her suitcase with one hand and her arm with the other.

"I am Rudy Choy. I am here to get you back to Macao. Get in the car. We are leaving," he said in unaccented English. She opened the car door and randomly thought of the time – before she had nightmares about dogs attacking her throat – when she had had a different life and someone else always opened car doors for her. The Japanese soldier holding Letitia's hand took her around to the other side of the car, opened the door for her, let her climb in and placed the tiny suitcase at her feet. Rudy Choy placed Rhoda's suitcase in the boot of the car, got in the front seat next to the driver, said a single word to him, and the car pulled away.

The car looked as though it was capable of great speeds, but it was forced to drive slowly on the rutted gravel road that ran from St Stephen's College back to the north side of Hong Kong. Sometimes the car was stopped by Japanese soldiers blocking part of the road. Rudy would show the soldier in charge of the roadblock a piece of paper that must have been some sort of a pass and they were allowed to continue. Most of the time the soldiers saw the flag on the mudguard and waved the car on.

After about 30 minutes they came to the harbor at Aberdeen. Within the breakwater, the harbor was packed with sampans and junks, row after row. "We get out here," said Rudy, turning to the woman and the girl in the backseat. "Over there," he said, indicating the far side of an open-sided building, "we have a boat." The car pulled away and turned in the road to head back the way it had come.

The three crossed through the building to a wooden wharf with a junk waiting alongside. It faced forward out into the harbor. The junk had a single mast, but the sail was furled. Rudy helped the two onto the boat. "Get inside," he said, pointing to the high cabin at the stern. They went inside; the door was shut behind them. There was no window or, if there was, it was tightly shuttered and it was very dark, with just a few murky shards of light coming through some chinks in the wooden walls. Rudy shouted through the closed doors: "You have to stay here until night time. Not long now. Then we take you to Macao."

They stayed in the cabin. Chinese men brought rice and some dried fish, and water for them to drink. The cabin smelled of decayed fish, motor oil and human sweat and urine. Rhoda and Letitia sat on the floor and leaned against the far wall of the cabin. Rhoda sustained herself with the thought that she would soon see her husband and her new home; Letitia said very little but did not loosen her grip on her little wicker case. Rhoda tried to hush her every time she coughed.

Then they could tell it was night because no light came through the cracks in the wall into the cabin and they were sitting in total darkness. Suddenly there was a loud thudding of an ancient diesel engine starting, the timbers of the junk shuddered and the boat unexpectedly jerked forward. Sickly warm fumes from the engine came into the cabin.

They could not tell how long it had been when Rudy finally opened the door and motioned for them to come out. They were clear of the harbor and motoring in the darkness. There was a full moon and some stars; the junk had no running lights. A wind had sprung up and Rhoda and Letitia were shivering. Rudy went into the cabin and came back with two gray blankets, crusted with dirt and filth. He placed them one by one around the shoulders of the two. They did not take them off and stood on the side of the boat looking at the moon-streaked sea and the blackness beyond.

The journey to Macao took almost the whole night. Rudy had talked at the beginning about the risk of being stopped and arrested by Japanese patrol vessels. In the end they only saw one, slowly coming towards them in the distance, a beam of bright light from its big bow-mounted spotlight moving in jerks back and forth over the water in front of it and occasionally stabbing out to either side. But the junk slipped into a bay on a nearby island and cut the engine. The patrol boat went by without seeing them, the beam from its spotlight flickering from side to side.

As they approached the *Porto Interior*, Rudy came forward and pointed into the darkness. "Macao," he said and then disappeared. Rhoda could see the light of dawn in the east forming a pale golden corona over the hills of Macao, but the western part of the city facing them was still dark.

She stared into the blackness trying to make out her new home but could only see the crown of light on the hills. She held her daughter around her shoulder, pulling her as close as she could to herself. This is where we will live, she whispered to her daughter as they looked into the darkness. They came into the harbor, but did not stop at the wharves where the ferries docked. Instead, they motored north, away from rows of anchored sampans, to where there was a shipyard with several half-finished junks lying on their sides. The boat pulled alongside a short stubby wharf. There was no one on it and no one around. Rhoda wondered where people lived. Rudy gently lifted the blankets off the shoulders of Rhoda and Letitia and helped them on to the wharf. He followed with the two suitcases.

On the road at the end of the wharf was a Macao taxi, its engine running, its lights off but the sign on the top of its roof illuminated. Rudy guided them into the backseat. Letitia climbed on her mother's lap and pushed her face into Rhoda's chest. Rudy had turned and gone back to the junk before the taxi had even pulled away. He did not wave or say anything.

The taxi headed uphill and, with no other traffic on the streets, was in front of the consulate very quickly. Reeves and the Number One Boy were standing outside on the steps. The Number One Boy had received some sort of message somehow – it had not come by telephone – and had woken Reeves, telling him that he needed to get dressed and wait by the front door. He spoke with such urgency that Reeves had not thought to question him further. Next door, Mr. Fukui and his secretary, already dressed in suits and ties, were standing on the pavement in front of the Japanese consulate. It was that time when they took their morning walk, although they made no effort to set off but stood waiting and watching. The driver came around and lifted Letitia down, then helped Rhoda out. He put the suitcases down on the ground.

Rhoda stood and looked at the trim neat building, now gold in the dawn light. She saw the Union Jack on the flagpole on the roof, the stone steps shiny wet from a recent scrubbing, the polished brass plaque announcing that this was the British consulate, the warm lights in the windows and the immaculate little lawn, the tree with its yellow lemons, and the flowerbeds, before she saw her husband. She stared at him for what seemed minutes. Neither one moved and then Rhoda took her daughter's hand and ran down the short path to the front steps and threw herself at her husband, flinging her arms around his neck and pushing her weeping face into his shoulder.

"Oh John, oh John, I dreamed of dogs with their teeth ripping my throat; there were soldiers with guns and planes dropping bombs. I needed you so much." She was saying something else but Reeves could not hear it between the sobs and her face pressed into him. Reeves put his arm around her shoulder and pulled her closer to him and took his daughter's hand in his other. She was looking at the lemon tree. Reeves told Rhoda she was in Macao now, the war was far away, she would be all right.

Chapter 8

That first morning in Macao, Rhoda had sat in the dining room with Letitia on her lap with Reeves on the other side of the table. The Number One Boy had brought in eggs, tea, toast and jam and Rhoda had said that it all looked lovely, but after the sea voyage, she could not possibly eat anything. She still gave an occasional sob. Letitia took a piece of buttered toast and stared at it a lot before eating it, as though she was trying to remember what it was. Reeves leaned forward anxiously and tried to draw her out about her experiences in Hong Kong, but all Rhoda had said was that it was horrible and she simply could not talk about it right now, perhaps later. She reached across and tentatively touched her husband's arm. Reeves told her all about Macao and how much she would love it.

After breakfast, Reeves showed her around her new home in the consulate. When they reached the second floor landing, Rhoda looked at one of the rooms and asked to take it to sleep in. I have been sleeping so badly, she explained, I do not want to disturb you. I am sure it will not be long before I am better. She quickly touched her husband's arm again, without catching his eye.

Rhoda threw herself into the care of Letitia. She would bring her down to the sunny back garden of the consulate and they would sit together by themselves on a bench under an umbrella near the orange tree. Reeves could see them from his office window. Rhoda tried to engage Letitia in conversation or read to her from children's books but she had little reaction. Sometimes the only words that Letitia spoke in the day were in a Cantonese she must have learned from the Chinese woman whom the Number One Boy had hired as her amah. Rhoda ate many of her meals with Letitia as though she could alleviate her daughter's illnesses by her presence. When she dined with Reeves, she found it hard to talk. Oh John, she would say, it was so horrible, and look away. Reeves said he understood, although he really did not know what she had been through. When he tried to tell her about his day, she looked at him blankly, not taking it in.

Through the Governor's office, Reeves arranged for Dr. Gomez Santos, who headed the Medical Services Department for all of Macao but who also had a specialty in gynecology, to examine Rhoda. He decided that her problems were all psychological – the trauma of her time in Hong Kong, and she should rest and avoid excitement. "Then she will be a proper companion to you," he had added, looking at Reeves curiously as he came out of what was clearly her room and not the marital one. He had also concluded that Letitia's health would improve and she would talk more once she was older and there was nothing to be done in the meantime. She should be left alone to develop in her own way. Dr. Santos was driven from the consulate in his official car and did not see either of them again.

Reeves thought that Rhoda might assist in some way with the British refugees now arriving in Macao. This would give her a purpose after all and, as the wife of the most senior British official in Macao, the women among the refugees would look up to her, as the Portuguese and Macanese women looked up to the Governor's wife. Surely this would make her feel better. Rhoda told him one afternoon when Letitia was asleep and she was resting in her dark room with the curtains pulled that she would really try to help when she felt better. Reeves could see her, small and frail, staring at him in the dim light, trying to see if he understood.

* * *

Every day British refugees arrived in twos and threes and sometimes more in Macao, which still clung to its precarious status as part of neutral Portugal and a haven from the war and terror surrounding it. The refugees were escaping from Hong Kong by junk or sampan, and they were escaping from China to the north, fleeing the British settlements in Canton, Shanghai and the other treaty ports now occupied by the Japanese Army. Those refugees from the north finished their long journey to Macao by walking down a road lined with scarlet-flowered flame trees, the branches of which were said to resemble a soaring phoenix. The road ended at the *Portas do Cerco,* a high arched gateway, set in a thick wall painted a canary yellow, and which marked Macao's northern border with China. The wall, set in a large empty field, extended only twenty feet on either side of the gate and a person not wishing to pass through the gate simply walked around it before resuming his journey down the road. The few Portuguese soldiers and customs officials who lounged on the wall's shady side would have done nothing to stop them entering Macao. Everyone was welcome in Macao.

Many of the refugees came to the British consulate on the *Calcada do Gaio* seeking help. Reeves had no issue with accepting some as British. They were white, had British passports, spoke with accents that Reeves could trace both to a region of England and to a place within its class structure, wore clothes he thought of as English, and talked of English schools, food, friends and relatives. He conversed with them in a reception room, gave them tea, took their names and promised to be back in touch.

Others caused Reeves to pause. They claimed to be British subjects but often only had local identity cards which made no mention of nationality. The refugees looked Chinese and had Portuguese last names, or they looked Portuguese (or partially Portuguese) and had Chinese last names, or they looked Portuguese and had Portuguese last names, but had lived in Hong Kong or the British settlements in the treaty ports for generations and said they were British subjects. Some were dark-skinned with almost incomprehensible accents, and claimed to be British subjects because of a parent from India or Ceylon. One said he was born in Peru but his parents were British subjects from India – Tamils from Madras, where they had once worshiped in the Anglican cathedral there. What Reeves remembered in the end was their weariness, their thin children, the blank despair in their eyes, the way they all looked up to him as their last hope. He decided that somehow he would take care of them. He had never done anything like this. He did not know where to even begin.

Reeves cabled the Legation in Chungking and asked for instructions. For the sake of simplicity, he had written simply of British refugees from Hong Kong without referring to the racial and ethnic *melange* of the others claiming to be British subjects. There was no need to complicate things. The Third Secretary had replied with the alacrity of one relieved to find he bore no responsibility for solving a problem, that the refugees in question came from a British colony, not a foreign country, and thus responsibility for them was properly the province of the Colonial Office and not the Foreign Office. He had forwarded Reeves's cable to the appropriate officials in the Colonial Office and told him that he should hear back in due course. The implication of the Third Secretary's message, at least to Reeves, was that he should not mention this matter to him again.

To Reeves's surprise, a cable came within a week from the Colonial Office. It read that he should make appropriate arrangements for the relief and support of all British subjects displaced by the occupation of our colonies and settlements by the Japanese and that funds to underwrite his endeavors would be wired, via the British Embassy in Lisbon, to the consular account in the *Banco Nacional Ultramarino,* Macao. Reeves thought of that august building on the *Avenida de Almeida Ribeiro*, with its tall arches shading a colonnade and its cool dim interior with high ceilings and clerks in jackets and ties behind polished brass grills. He thought of the money traveling thousands of miles by telegraph wire across a violent and war-torn world. The cable talked about keeping accurate accounts, making prudent expenditures, the avoidance of extravagance and waste.

Reeves took from the message from the Colonial Office that they recognized the immense responsibility he had taken on, that the Foreign Office must have commended him to the Colonial Office and that this must augur well for his prospects within the Consular Service. He would need to show initiative and he should seize the moment if the Colonial Office was, in its turn, to give a good account of him to the Foreign Office. This was very different from drafting reports on the economy of Macao. There was the immediate issue of what to do about the British refugees until the funds from the Colonial Office came. That might be weeks and he had to find food and shelter for them right now. He again thought of their faces when they had waited in the consulate. He thought of the horrors of war they had been subject to. He needed to solve this problem if he was to give a good account of himself. He called out to Mr. Gonsalves in the outer office.

Mr. Gonsalves entered, wiping his face with his handkerchief, although it was not hot today in the consulate. Reeves paused as though for some dramatic effect and then went on. "The Colonial Office will put us in funds to support all British subjects fleeing the Japanese onslaught. The issue, Mr. Gonsalves, is that I do not know when the money will arrive – it could take weeks or even months – and the problem we have is immediate. We must house and feed these people. There are now a few hundred. Their numbers increase every day." Reeves sat in his chair behind his desk and waited to see what Mr. Gonsalves would say.

"We borrow the money so we can start straight away," said Mr. Gonsalves simply, as though it were the easiest thing in the world. "You see my friend Y.C. Liang." Reeves stared at Mr. Gonsalves and thought, not for the first time, that every British consul in China could disappear and their consular clerks would take over and do a far superior job. The clerks were almost all of Portuguese, or partial Portuguese, descent. Their families had lived in the cities for generations. The clerks spoke not only excellent English but also the local Chinese dialects. They had friends everywhere. They were wise in the ways of the East that Reeves and his fellow consuls were not.

The next morning, Reeves found himself in the Wong Tai Company on the *Rua de S. Domingos*. He would have ordinarily paid the Wong Tai Company no mind, even in the unlikely circumstances he had an occasion to walk down this nondescript street. It was a small shop, selling a miscellaneous selection of ironmongery, household goods, a few electrical appliances, and children's toys. The contents of the store were all jumbled together on the floor or on shelves, piled on top of one another in no particular order and often covered with dirt and dust as though they had lain there untouched a long time and the shopkeeper did not care whether you bought anything at all or even looked at what was ostensibly on offer. There was a single lightbulb hanging from a wire in the ceiling, making it difficult to see in any event. An elderly Chinese clerk in shorts and a singlet sitting on a stool in a corner looked up from his newspaper at Mr. Gonsalves and opened a door on the back wall of the store. He gestured and Reeves and Mr. Gonsalves walked through it.

Standing behind a desk in the room behind the door was a tall handsome Chinese man somewhere in his thirties. He had long hair swept back and was wearing a silk dress shirt with French cuffs, fastened with jade and gold cufflinks. He wore no tie and the shirt had the top two buttons open. Reeves noticed how good-looking the Chinese man was and thought that he looked like he could star in a movie. The man gave what Reeves thought people might mean by a brilliant smile and came round the desk. He put both of his powerful arms around Mr. Gonsalves and hugged him tightly. Mr. Gonsalves pushed him back in an embarrassed manner and introduced Reeves to Mr. Y.C. Liang. Mr. Liang gave another smile and motioned for the two of them to sit. He returned to his side of the desk and sat down, still smiling, resting his elbows on his black polished desk with his fingers forming a pyramid, and waited.

Mr. Gonsalves started to explain how the consul had suddenly been given responsibility for a large number of British refugees and that he had been assured by the Government in London that money would be forthcoming. But explained Mr. Gonsalves, the consul did not know when the money would arrive and he needed to provide help now. Mr. Liang's broad smile was now a slight grin. He held up his hand.

"I quite understand," he said in excellent English. "You have to feed them, house them, clothe them and find schools for their children and doctors for when they are sick. It is like having a very large family. Of several hundred people I understand." He flashed a smile, then reached into a desk drawer, pulling out two forms in Chinese characters. He completed them both, again in Chinese and gave one to Mr. Gonsalves. "Take this to my friend Mr. Lee at the Po-Hing Bank on the *Rua dos Mercadores*. The money will be in your account at the *Banco Nacional Ultramarino* by this afternoon if you get there soon." And then he turned to Reeves with that winning smile and handed over the other copy. "Here is your note of the amount I have lent the British Government for your records. I am charging no interest and you can repay me when London sends you money – or when you have won the war." His smile could not have been broader. The war had just begun and Reeves thought of what was happening in early 1942. Far from Macao, the Japanese army and navy was thrusting west and south. Soon they would have conquered China and Burma and be at the border with India. They had taken Singapore and were seizing the Dutch East Indies. An Allied victory was far from assured. And he had no idea when the Colonial Office would remit the promised funds.

Here was a Chinese man of apparently immense wealth who was placing a lot of faith in him and the British Government. Where did he come from and where did he get his money? Why was he doing this? What was the Po-Hing Bank? He had never heard of it. There was a whole world in the East concealed from him. He would never understand the Orient. And here he was, part of the China Consular Service. He was no wiser now than he had been as a student in England all those years ago.

Reeves and Mr. Gonsalves arrived back at the consulate before lunch. There were already a few people in a line on the pavement. Their eyes followed the two as they entered the building. "What shall we do now, Micao?" asked Reeves and Mr. Gonsalves remarked to himself that this was the first time that Reeves had used his first name.

"We find some places for them to live. It is simple. Now we can pay rent; everyone will want to deal with us. I will make some telephone calls. I know who to call. We can look this afternoon." Mr. Gonsalves went back into his office. Reeves wondered whether if he went to the dining room for luncheon his wife might join him. He wanted to tell her about how he was going to take care of the British refugees. But then he remembered that Letitia had taken a turn that morning and Rhoda would be occupied with her. He did not want to burden his wife. He ate lunch in his office alone and read the *Macau Tribune*. It contained little of interest.

At 2:00pm, Mr. Gonsalves came into the office. "We can look at places to put the British people. There are some vacant buildings." He stood and waited, his jacket on, holding his hat. He was expecting to leave immediately and Reeves thought that he had assumed that Reeves's afternoon was free. He felt annoyed for a moment and was about to delay departing to show Mr. Gonsalves that he should not presume. But then he thought that he had nothing to do this afternoon and until the problem of housing the British refugees was solved, that he could not proceed with anything else. He put on his jacket, leaving his hat behind, and left his office, Mr. Gonsalves following.

Mr. Gonsalves had insisted on using the consulate driver and gave a destination to the driver in that sing-song Cantonese that Reeves could not understand. It bore no resemblance to the Chinese he had learned in Peking and which he had now, from desuetude, largely forgotten. They went along the *Praya Grande* past the pink and white wedding-cake-like building housing the Governor's offices. A Sikh policeman on traffic duty standing on a raised platform watched them as they went by. They were the only car on the road and he did not even wave. So far, thought Reeves, the war does not seem to have changed much in Macao. They stopped in front of a building on the northern end of the *Praya Grande*.

It was some sort of a warehouse. There was a Chinese sign over the door but Reeves could not read the characters. In any event, from the leaves and papers that the wind had blown against the door, no one had gone in or out for some time. There was a black mold staining the plaster of the walls; the windows in the front were tightly shuttered and the windows on the side had been bricked up. Two Chinese men stood in front, their faces without expression.

"The owner's agents are here. You will need to decide quickly. Owner likes to deal only with other Chinese men." Mr. Gonsalves got out of the car and one of the two Chinese men kicked the litter away from the door. He took a large key out of his pocket and after a while, was able to open the door. He pushed it open and motioned in a single curt movement of his arm for Reeves and Mr. Gonsalves to follow him inside.

At first Reeves thought it was totally dark inside, and all he could sense was an overwhelming smell of damp and dirt and dust and mold. Then he saw, far away, a faint light from two windows on the rear wall and he realized that the building was far deeper than he thought any building was on the *Praya Grande*. He could pick out in the faint light from the rear windows a few large wooden crates but otherwise there was just an enormous expanse of empty filthy floor. There was a narrow staircase on the right hand side of the warehouse and the four of them went up. There was a second floor, equally vast and empty with that same smell of dirt and decay, and the same faint light from the two windows at the rear.

"We cannot ask people to live here; this is entirely unsuitable." Reeves spoke in a normal voice to Mr. Gonsalves, assuming without thinking about it that the two grim Chinese men close by them did not speak English.

Mr. Gonsalves put his hand on the consul's shoulder and leaned towards Reeves's head. He spoke in a low tone with a nervous rushed urgency. "These are Wong Kong-kit's men and this is his godown. You cannot make him lose face by not renting the building. I have talked to his people. They will put water and bathrooms in, more windows and walls to divide it. They will build a kitchen in the garden at the back. You can talk to the electricity company about turning the electricity on. They will listen to an Englishman."

Reeves looked around and could not imagine this dank cave-like space made suitable for British refugees fleeing their villas on Hong Kong's Peak or the British settlement in Shanghai. What would the Colonial

Office say, and what might they report to his superiors in the Foreign Office? But all he asked was "Who is Wong Kong-kit?"

"A very important person in Macao. Someone good to have as a friend. One day you will meet him." He turned to the two Chinese men. He talked in Cantonese for a few minutes and their faces seemed to relax, if only slightly. They nodded at Reeves. Mr. Gonsalves turned back to Reeves and continued in that same urgent whisper. "I have told them that their terms are fair and that we will rent the warehouse. I have told them that I will make arrangements to make the first payment to Mr. Wong Kong-kit this afternoon and I have told them we hope he can start on the improvements as soon as possible. Please sir, shake their hands and smile. It is very important." Reeves wondered how he seemed to no longer be in charge, but he did as requested.

They looked at a number of other places and Mr. Gonsalves insisted on renting every one of them, telling Reeves if he did not rent them, he would have nowhere to house his refugees. One of the buildings they rented was called the *Chacara Leitao.* This was some sort of rambling farmhouse or villa on the *Estrada de Cacilhas.* Reeves saw that there were some large gardens around the house but then he noticed that the rain ran down off Guia Hill behind the villa and, having nowhere else to run, formed stagnant pools of dark brackish water in what should have been a lawn. Even in the cooler weather, he could see the mosquitoes in small dark swarms. He thought of malaria and yellow fever.

Another rental was a group of cottages in the *Barrio Tamagnini Barbosa,* and the last rental were several houses in a poor neighborhood near the facade of the ruined cathedral of St Paul's. On each occasion, there were two unsmiling Chinese men to meet them and each time, Mr. Gonsalves told Reeves in that same urgent whisper he had no choice but to rent the houses, invoking the name of Wong Kong-kit. He even told Reeves that he had already rented a building to house the Malay and Indian refugees with a claim to being British subjects. It was in a Chinese *barrio* and there was no need for Reeves to see it. It was entirely suitable. Reeves did not voice an objection to any of this. He never did visit the building where the dark-skinned British subjects from Malaya and India were housed.

By the end of the day, Y.C. Liang's money was almost all spent on rent payments to Wong Kong-kit. Reeves could do nothing but wait for the funds from the Colonial Office. He had no idea when they would arrive and in the days he spent waiting, he had been consumed by the enormousness of the task that now fell to him. Nothing in his professional career had prepared him for this. He had been a solitary consul in remote parts of China. He had written reports and never heard anything again about them once they were submitted. He had given a reception on the King's birthday and a dinner occasionally to members of the British community and local officials and dignitaries. Sometimes in Mukden or Hankow, he had the feeling that if he had absented himself from his office for a month, no one would have noticed. When he had arrived in Macao, he was determined to make himself useful and to get himself noticed. But the scale of this was enormous. Several hundred people, and that number increased daily, now depended upon him and some might actually die – *actually die* – if he did not act. Sometimes he found himself lying awake for hours at night and in the early morning, his mind racing nervously, his chest tightening with fear. He wanted to talk to Rhoda and tell her how he felt. She was a good listener, or at least she had been when they first met. But Rhoda was in her room, its door was shut, and he knew she too had her demons roused by her imprisonment in Hong Kong that he was unable to placate. The Portuguese doctor had said she needed rest and should not be disturbed. He thought she would be better off if he did not go in there. Perhaps there would be an opportunity to talk in the morning. He had always loved telling her things. He thought his parents would be impressed with what he was doing. Surely the Legation in Chungking would not censor a description of his taking care of British refugees. He resolved to write to them the next day. He imagined his mother reading the letter aloud to his father over breakfast. They both would be smiling and thinking of him.

* * *

The first draft of funds from the Colonial Office had arrived at the *Banco Nacional Ultramarino* in just over a week. He had been so surprised when Mr. Gonsalves had told him that he had driven down to the bank to ask the manager himself whether this was true. Talking to Carlos Eugenio de Vasconcelos, the manager of the BNU – Reeves loved to say his full name out loud – he was confronted with the fact that he now had the almost unimaginable sum of fifty thousand pounds sterling to spend as he saw fit and he could not even think of what that might be in Macanese patacas – millions and millions, he imagined. To his surprise a calmness, almost a serenity, settled down on him like a falling of pure white snow. He felt a tug of happiness that he had not known for a while and, even though it was near lunch time, he did not feel the urge to have a drink.

Happiness mingled with resolve – part of him was still surprised at the new person he had become – and he looked on the job that lay before him with a calm detachment. He considered that there were really only two possible outcomes to what he had to do: he would either be sacked or promoted and that there was not one person he could call on to counsel him. He was truly alone and that, again to his surprise, did not concern him in the least.

He rented, with Mr. Gonsalves's help, a building on the *Praya Grande* as a kind of second consulate. He would have an office there, as would Mr. Gonsalves, and that is where they would take care of the British refugees. Mr. Gonsalves spoke to Wong Kong-kit's men, and workmen moved in old, scratched, battered desks, chairs, shelves and cabinets. He wondered where Wong Kong-kit had found the furniture. He suspected that he might have taken it from people who still had a need for it or could have sold it profitably.

Mr. Gonsalves found A.A. Swemmelaar to head all the relief work. He was a Dutchman; Reeves had explained that he wanted someone who was not British and who could appear to be entirely objective. He found Wilfred Aycock to interview the refugees. Mr. Aycock came from the

Cable and Wireless Company in Hong Kong and had a large walrus mustache and an accent from the English Midlands. To most people, he could not have been more English. But Mr. Gonsalves knew that his parents were from Mauritania and that his wife was Portuguese. They went to the church in the same parish as Mr. Gonsalves and his wife and that gave him comfort. He did not expect the consul to understand the mixture of races that made up the people of Macao and their tight bonds of family and church. Mr. Jerry Silva was hired to keep the accounts. Reeves himself had engaged a young man named Micky Sousa to help him. He had no book-keeping experience at all and was hired simply because he was nicely dressed when he came to apply and engaged Reeves in conversation. The three of them devised a system of their own to keep track of the enormous sums they would be spending for destitute British refugees. It bore no resemblance to the accounting methods prescribed in the *Consular Instructions*. This may have been reckless but Reeves concluded that his system was simpler and more efficient and that he would ultimately be judged on results, rather than whether he had followed procedures. There was a war on; he would surely be granted some latitude. He was taking care of things; he had resources; he had an organization. He began drafting an account of what he was doing to the Colonial Office. He would copy it to the Foreign Office and they would put it in his file. It would be noticed when he was next considered for promotion and advancement. He felt the excitement well up within him.

Chapter 9

Reeves after a week started going upstairs and seeing his wife in her room, at first just putting his head in the door and inquiring after her, then entering and spending a little time with her. Then the Number One Boy told him she was now taking two meals a day and was awake for much of the day. When he went up late the next morning, she seemed actually glad to see him. She was sitting up in bed wearing what she called a housecoat buttoned to her neck and a breakfast tray was lying on a side table. She had eaten something from it. When Reeves entered, she raised a finger to her lips and pointed in the direction of Letitia's room.

"She was awake much of the night," she whispered, "but I think she has gone down now. I am going to get dressed and go with her and her amah to the park when she is awake. It seems such a lovely day and a pity to waste it. Perhaps we could all have tea early in the garden this afternoon. Have there been any letters for us?"

Reeves knew why she was asking. She was hoping for news of her parents and brother now that the Japanese had seized Shanghai and the international settlements there and interned the British. There had been no news either from the Legation in Chungking or the International Red Cross. He knew she was thinking that they were living under the same horrendous conditions that she had been subjected to in Hong Kong. Rhoda's account to her husband of the Repulse Bay Hotel, the drainage tunnel, and her imprisonment by the Japanese had come out in small random fragments over days as it forced its way back into her memory. But Reeves had heard other accounts of the fall of Hong Kong and was able to piece together a picture of what Rhoda had been subjected to. No wonder she had been so high-strung. It was as though she suffered from shell-shock, like the soldiers from the Great War he had heard about.

"Nothing so far," he said in what he hoped was a comforting voice and found himself reaching for her hand. "But the mails are very irregular at the moment." He changed the subject when he saw her face fall. "An expedition to the park sounds like a splendid idea and then tea in the garden for the three of us would be a treat. I will arrange for ice-cream for Letitia. I am sure I can join you." He told her about finding housing for the refugees, how useful Mr. Gonsalves had been, how he had borrowed an enormous sum from one of his friends to tide them over until the remittances from London had arrived. Rhoda's eyes had widened and she squeezed his hand.

"Are you allowed to do that?" she had asked anxiously but she was smiling when she said it.

"By the time they tell me I can't do it, it will be months from now and the money will have been repaid. Sometimes in wartime, you have to seize the initiative." He noticed that Rhoda was looking at him as though she was seeing a different man than the one she thought she knew.

The next time he saw her, he had more good news. "I have found a doctor for you and Letitia. I did not think that Dr. Santos was satisfactory." Reeves had brooded over Dr. Santos ever since he had said Rhoda would eventually recover and "be a proper companion" to him. The implication of that off-hand remark about a profoundly personal matter weighed on him.

"I did not like Dr. Santos," Rhoda replied, "I was so hoping to find a doctor with proper training and English I could understand better." She squeezed his hand again and looked up to him.

"You will like Dr. Gosano," he said. "He was trained by the best British doctors at our university in Hong Kong and to listen to him, you would think he was British through and through." Rhoda still held Reeves's hand and squeezed it again.

Reeves had searched for actual British doctors in the previous weeks. He needed to provide medical services for the British refugees whose welfare he was now responsible for. He thought it best to establish a medical clinic and make its staff salaried employees of the consulate, rather than paying fees to Portuguese doctors. There were no British doctors among the refugees, but Mr. Gonsalves found three graduates of the University of Hong Kong School of Medicine (Drs. Ozorio, Gosano and Ribeiro) who were unable to practice in Macao because they did not have the appropriate certificate in tropical medicine from the *Faculdade de Medicina da Universidade de Lisboa*. Reeves spoke to the Governor who was only too willing to waive the requirement. Mr. Gonsalves found a small building for the clinic on the *Praya Grande* close to the consulate and Reeves found himself approving another payment to Wong Kong-kit. Reeves was taking the initiative again.

Dr. Eddie Gosano spoke perfect English and there was little trace of a Chinese mother in his Portuguese face. Reeves invited him to come to the consulate and examine his wife and daughter. Dr. Gosano quietly counseled rest and patience on Reeves's part, just as Dr. Santos had advised. But Rhoda warmed to him; she knew he was the closest to a real British doctor that she would find in Macao. Dr. Gosano would often come round to the consulate after he was done in the clinic and play mahjong or canasta with Rhoda, bouncing Letitia on his knee during the game even though she was nearly six, and talking to her in both English and Cantonese. Reeves noticed that Rhoda looked forward to his visits and he did not object. Both she and Letitia would come down to the living room and wait when they knew he was coming.

On one of these visits, Dr Gosano took him aside and asked to speak to him about the clinic. Reeves took him into his formal reception room and they sat down in adjacent armchairs. Dr. Gosano told him about working without anesthetic or proper disinfectants. He told a harrowing story of having to remove an infected boil from the lip of a young girl who had fallen off her bicycle with just a heated razor blade. "She screamed, oh how she screamed." Reeves thought of Letitia in the same situation. Dr. Gosano told of the prices Mr. Nolasco at the *Farmacia Popular* charged for medicines – "twelve British shillings for one tablet of sulfathiazole" – and that none of the refugees could afford that. He told of malnutrition amongst some of the refugees and the rashes, pustules and boils they suffered from. Dr. Gosano pulled out a piece of paper and handed it to Reeves. It was a list of medicines the clinic needed. Reeves saw aspirin, sulfa drugs, sera for injections, quinine, maltose, and cod liver oil, among others. Dr. Gosano said he would say goodbye to Rhoda and Letitia and then he really must be going.

Reeves stood by himself for a while. Where on earth was he going to get the medicines the clinic needed? And proper food for the refugees? It was easy to forget that not everyone lived like him. He along with the merchants, middle class and government officials had access to special warehouses for food and wine. There was a special clinic for them at the hospital. He knew the poor Chinese were suffering and that the *Santa Casa de Misericordia* was doing yeoman work amongst the hungry and poverty-stricken, but he rarely saw people like that. Young Stanley Ho who worked for Dr. Lobo, the director of the economy in Macao, had come round one day with a gift of a bottle of scotch – Johnnie Walker with the seal over the cork still intact – and a carton of American cigarettes with a picture of a camel. Reeves had started to protest that this was too generous but Stanley had simply waved away his objections with the remark that you can get anything you want in Macao if you know the right people and have the money.

The next morning, Reeves explained the issue to Mr. Gonsalves. "We have to get medicines; we have to get better food and we have to get it all at a better price." He paused and there was a minute's silence. Then Mr. Gonsalves spoke:

"I will arrange a meeting with Wong Kong-kit. He will help us."

Two days later, at around noon, Reeves and Mr. Gonsalves were driving to where Reeves was to have lunch with Wong Kong-kit. Mr. Gonsalves had insisted on coming with him, at least as far as the place for lunch. "It is Wong Kong-kit's own eating club. It is hard to find and it is behind one of the brothels on the *Rua da Felicidade*." He had said this as matter-of-factly as though he had been referring to any common landmark that you might refer to in giving directions to a traveler. Reeves had never seen a brothel before and could think of nothing else on the short drive over.

He had not asked who Wong Kong-kit was and whether he should be dealing with him. There was a war on; Fortune favored the brave.

The car turned into the *Rua da Felicidade*, drove a little way down and stopped. Mr. Gonsalves and Reeves got out of the car. There was the urgent nervous clicking of mahjong tiles from behind the shutters of the gray-brick houses, none of the bright pastels of the other houses in Macao. Mr. Gonsalves took Reeves by the arm and steered him quickly down an alley alongside one of the houses.

They had gone about 20 yards and then turned a corner and went down an even narrower alley. Reeves was sure that the sun had never been able to penetrate even a part of it. His nostrils were struck by a foul odor and then he saw the open wooden tubs of human excrement waiting for collection by the night soil man. The tubs were full almost to the brim and Reeves wondered how they could be picked up without their slopping over. The pavement of the alley was damp and slippery and Reeves concluded that tubs must have spilled a little.

Deep down the dark alley, they came to a building standing by itself. There was no sign of the brothel Mr. Gonsalves had mentioned and Reeves felt a small pang of disappointment. The ground floor of the building had its shutters flung back to expose a filthy kitchen. A man in a singlet stood behind a thick wooden table and hacked at a plucked chicken with a cleaver. He did not wear an apron and he had stains of blood and viscera on his singlet. He tossed the pieces of chicken into a blackened pot on the ground. There was blood on the floor from the hacked chickens and the room smelled of rancid cooking oil, the smoke from a fire, and the fetid odor of night soil from the alley.

Mr. Gonsalves walked through the kitchen, Reeves following him, and up a flight of stairs at the rear. At the top of the stairs was a beaded curtain. "Walk through the curtain," Mr. Gonsalves whispered, "Wong Kong-kit is waiting for you. I will wait in the car." He turned and almost ran down the stairs to the kitchen and the alley as though he did not want to be there at all. Reeves heard the clatter of his shoes on the worn wooden stairs and thought he had no idea what he was doing.

Reeves walked towards the beaded curtain. I suppose it had to be a beaded curtain, he thought to himself. He pushed through it, the strands of beads brushing against his head and forehead. He was nervous and apprehensive as to what he might find.

He was surprised to find an immaculate and well-lit room. There was a small chandelier hanging from a chain in the center of the ceiling and several red paper lanterns hanging elsewhere from the ceiling, and the light in the room was pleasant and warm. The dark brown floor had been scrubbed, waxed and polished to such an extent that you could see blurred reflections of some of the Chinese lanterns in it. There was a round table in the center of the room with platters of fish, small pieces of chicken and pork, vegetables, and several covered porcelain and silver tureens. There was a Chinese girl on a carved black chair in a far corner playing a pear-shaped lute very softly. She did not look up, but concentrated on her hands on the frets and strings. Reeves thought how pretty she was. Two other Chinese girls in silver and gold cheongsams sat on chairs against the wall. They had their hands in their laps and looked up expectantly when Reeves entered. They were pretty too. On the far side of the table from the entrance with the beaded curtain, a man stood up slowly. He did not extend his hand. A floor fan on a stand moved from side to side and Reeves could feel the warm air on his face.

"Consul Reeves," he said, "I am Wong Kong-kit." He sat down. Reeves saw a tall man, much taller than the Chinese from southern China he was used to in Macao. He had prominent cheekbones and Reeves wondered whether he could have come from the north of China, where the Mongol influence could often be seen. He had the beginnings of jowls and a double chin; his shirt was tight around his large stomach. But there was no denying, looking at his chest and shoulders, that he was a strong and powerful man. Reeves had the impression that he could have hit him very hard if he had so chosen. He gestured for Reeves to sit down.

"You have some business to talk about," said Wong Kong-kit. He spoke good English, but his sentences had the clipped staccato rhythms of Cantonese and they came out in little bursts. "I am always happy to help my British friends. I did business in Hong Kong before the Japanese came. I still do business there but not so much with the British. I have a lot of friends in Hong Kong." Reeves thought he meant that now he did business with the Japanese, but chose not to say anything. "But before we do business, first we must eat. Sometimes the English do not want to eat before they do business. Do not be like that." He almost spat the words out and Reeves could not help feeling that he had been reprimanded. Wong Kong-kit put his fingers into a bowl and pulled up a fistful of dried sunflower seeds. He pushed them into his mouth, chewed for several seconds, the noise of the crunching seeming quite loud in the enclosed room, and then leaned over to hawk the shells into what looked like a brass chamber pot on the floor next to him.

Reeves heard a scrape behind him. One of the Chinese girls had pulled her chair forward so that it was slightly behind that of Reeves, but almost next to him, very close. He glanced to his side. The girl was looking down demurely at her clasped hands in her lap. What on earth was she doing? The other seated girl had similarly pulled next to Wong Kong-kit. The girl with the pear-shaped lute continued to play that soft tuneless Chinese music that Reeves thought he would never understand and would certainly never like. The girls, without leaving their seats, leaned forward as one and placed a bowl before each of the two men. Then, removing the lids from two small silver pots, they ladled out a small portion of something white in a brown liquid into the bowls. Reeves smelled the sharp odor of liquor and looked at the bowl. There were tiny white beads of something – sago? tapioca? a Chinese caviar? Wong Kong-kit was grinning at Reeves. The two girls, once they had finished serving, leaned back in their chairs and folded their hands again on their laps, their eyes cast down.

"We will need our strength when we do business later on. So we start with snake blood and snake eggs in my favorite Portuguese brandy. Drink and eat and all your insides will be strong and happy." He ate a spoonful of the liquid from the bowl and then looked across at Reeves without expression. Reeves knew what he had to do. It was really like the bullying rituals he had known at school and some pride in his Englishness and his position as His Britannic Majesty's Consul – the four words actually flashed through his mind – compelled him to smile and take a spoonful of the snake blood and snake eggs in brandy. It did not have much of a taste apart from the brandy; if it wasn't for its rough texture – could a liquid have a texture? – and if he had not known what the liquid actually was, he might have even liked it. Wong Kong-kit watched him the whole time then took up his porcelain spoon and ate another mouthful of the snake eggs and brandy. Reeves, still conscious of his position and what he thought were his obligations, did the same. He wondered if it and the rest of the food had been prepared in that filthy kitchen downstairs. He could taste nothing except the harsh rasp of cheap warm Portuguese brandy. In seconds he felt his mind suffused by the beginnings of that tranquil calmness that the first drink of the day always brought. They both finished their bowls of snake blood and snake eggs.

"Excellent," Reeves said with a smile to Wong Kong-kit. He smiled back.

As soon as he had finished, the girl in the chair just behind him leaned forward and placed a glazed clay cup without handles next to him. She filled it up from a jug on the table with a clear liquid that Reeves recognized, from its smell, as distilled rice wine. When he looked up, Wong Kong-kit was holding up his cup to him.

"*Ganbei*," he said, "We will be friends for a long time." This seemed to Reeves at the time to be more of an order than a hope or wish. He swallowed the entire contents of the cup and put it down on the table with a small bang. Reeves did the same. Immediately the two girls in the chairs behind them filled the cups up again. Wong Kong-kit immediately raised his cup again and proposed a second toast.

"The British people in Hong Kong and the Chinese people in Macao. Friends for a long time." Reeves repeated the two phrases and they drank together at the same time. The meal continued. Reeves did not have to choose dishes; the girl seated just behind him would reach forward and place various items on his plate. There were two small birds, like sparrows, that had been plucked and fried. The feet, claws, skull and beak had been left on. Reeves watched Wong Kong-kit pick up the whole bird, put it in his mouth and begin chewing. After a minute or so he leaned to the side and spat out the bone fragments that he had not swallowed into the brass chamber-pot. Reeves had no compunction in doing the same. There was chicken and pork, rice and various vegetables. The toasts continued, Reeves proposing the health of the Governor, happiness to the people of Macao and a successful harvest for the farms in Canton across the border. Wong Kong-kit said *ganbei* to each of these, but when Reeves proposed a toast for an Allied victory over the Japanese, Wong Kong-kit simply finished his cup of liquor.

Eventually, for no reason that Reeves could discern, the girls stopped serving and the meal came to a halt.

"Now we do our business," said Wong Kong-kit, picking his teeth with the one long fingernail he had; the rest were bitten to the quick. He waved a hand, there was a scraping of chairs while the girls who had served them moved back to the wall. The girl playing the lute ceased, put her instrument on the floor next to her and folded her hands in her lap with her head bowed. She did not look up once. "How can I help you?"

Reeves did not pay attention to the amount he had drunk. He liked to drink and drinking brought him a peace and solace. He could drink and still accomplish much, if not most of what the outside world demanded of him, while staying within his own peaceable kingdom where drink had taken him. He began to speak with a fluency that always pleased him.

He began by thanking Wong Kong-kit for the many excellent properties he had provided for the numerous refugees now under the consul's care and that he further appreciated the repairs and improvements that he had arranged to render the buildings suitable. He then described the task he had been given of taking care of their shelter, sustenance (he was unsure if Wong Kong-kit understood that word), health and well-being. That he was in receipt of (the part of his mind that was detachedly observing him speaking wondered why he didn't simply say 'he was given') funds from the British Government to undertake this and that the funds were now in his account at the *Banco Nacional Ultramarino.* He said that because of the exigencies (again, why that word with this man?) of war, the people under his charge suffered from an inadequate diet and a shortage of essential medicines and thus were plagued by illnesses and other physical debilities that could be remedied if adequate provision could be made. He was led to understand that Wong Kong-kit could possibly be of assistance. He finished by thanking him for the excellent lunch which he thoroughly enjoyed and then thought that perhaps that last piece could have been saved for the end of the meeting. Wong Kong-kit had stared at Reeves, expressionless, throughout his speech but now that it apparently was over, he snapped out four words:

"What do you want?"

Reeves was a little taken aback by this abruptness, but then the detached part of his mind asked why he was expecting him to reply elaborately and at length as an Englishman might have.

"Medicines are a priority," he said, reaching into his pocket and pulling out the list that Dr. Gosano had given him.

"Read to me," said Wong Kong-kit and Reeves thought that perhaps he could only speak English and that he had never been taught to read it. Reeves named each medicine on the list one by one. When he got to cod-liver oil, he stopped and looked up brightly at his lunch host.

"I was thinking," he said, but this actually was the first time that he had had this thought. The brandy and spirits had freed it from whatever part of his brain it had been entrapped in. "I was down in the *Mercado Municipal* – the big one on the *Rua da Praia do Manduco* – the other day and was looking at the fishmongers' stalls and saw the trays of fish livers. It would not be hard to set up a small laboratory or factory to extract the oil. We could put it in the clinic. It could provide enough to meet our needs." His voice became even more enthusiastic. "Any surplus could be sold to defray the expenses of the clinic. I am sure we could get a good price given the demand in Macao."

Wong Kong-kit's expression did not change. Neither did the tone of his voice. He simply rapped a single knuckle softly on the table. "You don't make fish oil. You buy it from me. You don't sell fish oil. My friends sell the fish oil in Macao. OK?"

Reeves agreed and then he wondered why he had assented so quickly. It would be hard to make the case that his luncheon host had threatened him or that there was even menace in his voice. He went on to read the rest of the list. When he had finished, Wong Kong-kit was silent for a minute. Then he said, "You need food – rice, meat, fish, vegetables?"

"Some of the diseases my doctors have identified are the result of a poor diet. We need to improve it. We would be grateful for your assistance."

"Rice is hard to get. Best rice comes from Amoy, but that needs to come by ship. We can get rice in Canton and we can bring it to Macao by snake boat or junk. Short trip, but we have to do it at night. My men bring all the rice from Canton. Japanese do not bother us. Vegetables and meat, the women walk over the border at the wall with it in baskets. We talk to the Japanese soldiers and they do not bother us. Medicines come from Chungking. Americans have boxes and boxes of them. My friends will bring them down for us." Reeves wondered why the Japanese did not bother this smuggling operation and then he decided that there was no need to think about it. Money and bribes no doubt. He certainly was not going to mention it in his reports to Chungking.

Wong Kong-kit leaned forward a little in his chair but his tone or expression did not change. "You and the English do not sell any of this. Just for you, no one else in Macao. No one sells the rice; no one sells the medicines. My men bring the vegetables and the meat right to my houses where the Englishmen live. They pay the men. They eat the food. They do not sell it. You give out the rice to the Englishmen but just enough for them to eat. No Englishman is to sell my rice. You have a shop for the medicine and you give only enough to help the sick person. No one keeps medicine in their pocket to sell. OK?" He rapped a single knuckle on the table, as he had done once before.

Reeves remembered that Dr. Gosano had suggested that a dispensary be established at the clinic to ensure the best distribution of medicines to those most in need. Now Wong Kong-kit was suggesting the same thing, but this time to prevent competition for him in the black market. It was the same with the distribution of rice. But, regardless, it seemed like an excellent suggestion. It would enable Reeves to keep control and that seemed something to be desired.

"Those seem eminently sensible suggestions," said Reeves. "I agree wholeheartedly. No one wants to see profiteering or the pocketing of illicit gains." Wong Kong-kit's expression did not alter. There was a brief silence before Reeves went on. "How do you suggest we proceed?"

"Give me some time. You ask a lot but I can do it. My men will talk to Gonsalves. I will see what I can supply and when I can give it to you. My men will tell Gonsalves the price and he can pay us."

Reeves sat up and said, almost, but not quite, indignantly, "We should know the price in advance to ascertain whether it is acceptable before we accept delivery of any medicine or food."

For the first time, Wong Kong-kit smiled. "You will be happy. Men of business do not argue about such things." At some hidden signal, the chairs scraped, the two pretty women slid forward and poured each man a cup of the rice wine liquor. Wong Kong-kit stood up and held his cup up. "Now we are friends. I help you. One day, you will help me." Both drained their cups and Reeves hoped that he could have another. But Wong Kong-kit had his arm around him and was escorting him out of the room, through the beaded curtain.

* * *

Within weeks, a supply of rice arrived and further supplies periodically after that. Reeves arranged for it to be stored in a shed behind the consulate where he could keep an eye on it. The medicines listed in the paper that Reeves had given to Wong Kong-kit took a little longer to arrive. The medicines went straight to the clinic where the three doctors set up a dispensary in one of its rooms. Wong Kong-kit had sent men to put thick iron bars on the window of the room used as a dispensary and replaced its thin wooden door with one made of stout planks of wood held together with wide iron bands. Mr. Gonsalves wondered why he had done that, as no one in their right mind would steal Wong Kong-kit's medicines. He was glad that Reeves approved the payments Wong Kong-kit demanded without questioning them. They were reasonable considering the war and cheaper than anywhere else on the black market.

Reeves told Rhoda and Letitia all about his lunch when they had tea in the garden that evening, which they now did a few times a week. The Number One Boy brought out ice-cream and Letitia ate it slowly and solemnly, looking at Reeves all the time. He said he had had lunch with a Chinese gangster and Rhoda had gasped, which had pleased him. But now Dr. Gosano would have enough medicine and the British refugees would have enough food. That would be part of his next report to Chungking. He leaned towards Letitia sitting on her mother's lap and imitated in a comic manner the tuneless music the Chinese girl had made with her lute. Letitia actually smiled and so did Rhoda. Reeves could not remember the last time he had seen either of them smile, perhaps in the case of Letitia ever.

Chapter 10

Winter came early in the autumn of 1942. Even in October, cold rain blew in from the South China Sea and a damp chill settled over Macao. It was colder than anyone had remembered for a long time and low leaden clouds hung over the city for weeks, blocking the sun. The weather caught the somber mood of Reeves and the British community. In the year since the fall of Hong Kong, the Japanese were undefeated in their continuing conquest of Asia. An Allied victory looked very distant and not very probable. They felt very much alone on this small peninsula. Reeves's mother wrote about the severe food rationing in England, how his father's importing business was struggling during the war and the German bombing of so many cities in England. It must be nice to be out of all of this in the East, she said. One of the members of Reeves's boat crew at Cambridge was killed when the corvette he commanded was sunk by a submarine in the North Atlantic. He had sat directly in front of Reeves in the shell and the first image that came to Reeves's mind when he read about the death was the back of the dead man's head. Reeves found it hard to recall his face, but eventually did.

Rhoda made the decision when Letitia turned six to send her to a girls' primary school that many of the children of the British refugees attended. She thought Letitia would benefit from being around some girls of her own age; perhaps being alone at the consulate with just her parents and amah was part of the problem. The school was run by Italian Canossian nuns and Rhoda worried about how Letitia would learn to speak in English from Italian nuns, but there seemed no other choice. In the afternoon, when the driver brought her back to the consulate, Rhoda would take her to her room and read to her from such children's books as she was able to find in English. Rhoda was gratified that Letitia would sit quietly and appear to listen. Rhoda thought she was understanding the books even if she could not read them. Letitia still had little to say and Rhoda's heart would silently break each time she asked a question and Letitia would just stare silently.

Rhoda had also joined a group of English women who had started a vegetable garden on the grounds of the former hippodrome. There were Chinese to do the actual work but the British ladies supervised them and Rhoda was happy to be part of them. There were three dairy cows in what were the former stalls for the racehorses and the ladies hoped the milk, treated and refrigerated at the *leitaria* near the ice factory on Green Island, would go, along with the vegetables, to the refugees and needy children. Rhoda would come back, sometimes in coveralls with a scarf tied around her head, and tell her husband about all that the Ladies Committee for Wartime Relief hoped to accomplish. "I feel so useful now," she said to Reeves, collapsing into a chair in his office one afternoon. "I am really pulling my weight for the war effort." Reeves noticed there was not a trace of dirt on her clothes, but then, what was he really doing for the war?

The refugees now arriving in Macao were all poor Chinese, and they flooded in by the hundreds every day, fleeing a China ravaged by warlords, civil war, famine, disease and the brutality of the Japanese occupation. The government collected as many of the refugees as they could in the backs of trucks and took them to camps on what once had been open fields on the outskirts of the city. The police did the same, but there were untold numbers of refugees still living on the streets.

The rice harvest had been poor that winter in Canton, which bordered Macao and where it procured nearly all its foodstuffs. The soaring price of rice put it out of reach for nearly all of the refugees. The Church and the Macao Government did their best to care for them, but there were simply too many refugees and too little food. Reeves saw the newly arrived Chinese scavenging in the rubbish on the streets, setting primitive traps for rats, entering gardens to gather papaya leaves to chew on, picking up crab shells and fish bones on the wharves of the *Porto*

Interior, shuffling along, the few clothes that they had on when they had crossed the border during the summer now pitifully inadequate in the cold wet winter wind; scores died every day on the streets. If they did not starve, they died of exposure to the cold, dysentery, cholera, other fevers or simply despair. When Reeves went to the *Banco Nacional Ultramarino* to collect the latest remittances from London, he sometimes stepped over a corpse under its tall elegant arches, already beginning to rot and its face covered with lice and other vermin. The Mozambique soldiers from the garrison were ordered to clear the streets of the bodies and they patrolled in municipal trucks to collect the corpses. But the refugees were dying in great numbers and many lay dead in the streets for days before they were removed.

Reeves was walking one afternoon near that part of the *Porto Interior* where there were only old tenement houses, some leaning to the side, some whose upper stories had collapsed. Only the very poorest Chinese lived there, dozens to a room. Some tenements had roofs of corrugated iron and they extended out over the footpath to provide shelter from the heat and rain. Lying on the sidewalk under one roof, there were a dozen or so men. At first, he thought he was seeing more corpses – he was surprised how unremarkable he now found dead bodies and he wondered what this said about him. Was he growing in the job, or was this a numbing of his soul? He put the thought out of his mind; he preferred right now not to reach a conclusion.

As he got closer, he could see that some, but only some, were alive, their chests moving up and down almost imperceptibly, their eyes staring up, and then sometimes their heads slowly rolling from one side to the other and their lips silently mouthing words that only they could hear. They were awaiting their inevitable fate, which was to die slowly and painfully far from home and all alone without friends or family, on the streets of Macao.

He was suddenly seized by the horror of it all; these bodies, these people in their last hours on this earth, lying in a row as though they were awaiting the blast of the first of the Seven Trumpets of the Book of Revelation –

hail and fire and blood cast down upon the earth, if he remembered. He had heard stories – priests going out at night and putting a piece of bread in the mouths of anyone they saw lying on the ground in case they were not dead but asleep and so could eat a little when they awoke; barges in the *Porto Interior* with dead bodies stacked high above the hull; a pit on Taipa Island big enough to hold 10,000 corpses, nearly full even though it was dug just last month. The soldiers from Mozambique – God, their skin was black, just like coal – tossing the bodies into the pit and finding every now and then one who was not quite dead. He had been told that the soldiers stabbed the body with their bayonets, crying "now you are finished" before throwing the body into the pit of death. Reeves thought that he might have a fever, his thoughts twisting around in his head. If it was not for the food and medicine from Wong Kong-kit, bodies of his British refugees might be lying on the street, ready to be picked up and cast into a pit. A horrendous thought of Rhoda and Letitia lying on the street among the dying Chinese came into his head. They were dressed in their summer frocks and their chests were heaving. They were looking at him and Reeves could not hear the words they were mouthing. He gave a little cry but could not stop thinking about it.

He returned to the consulate and went straight to his office without his usual loud and cheery greeting to the staff. He closed its door and sat in his chair staring forward. He sat there for some time – he did not know how long – and then there was a knock from the other door to the outer office and Mr. Gonsalves entered, carrying a file. Reeves did not look at him but continued to stare into the distance. Then he spoke, still looking at a point on some far horizon.

"This is a nasty business, Micao, this dying, and there is no end to it." Mr. Gonsalves sat down in the chair on the other side of the desk. He did not know what to say. The consul was in a different world. Then Mr. Gonsalves spoke in a gentle voice as though he was comforting a child waking up from a nightmare.

"Mr. Reeves, none of this is your doing. God is moving in his mysterious way. Put this out of your mind and remember that you are taking care of your people. This is what you were put here to do." Without thinking about it, he leaned forward and touched Reeves on the arm. He left his hand there for perhaps a little too long to be touching an Englishman and then sat back.

Reeves turned his head around towards Mr. Gonsalves and for a moment seemed to be looking right through him. But then he caught Mr. Gonsalves's eyes, and said nothing for what must have been just a few moments but what for Mr. Gonsalves was a very long time.

"You are right, Micao. We cannot change the world or even a small part of it. There is one tiny corner given to me and I can take care of that. Tell the guards to stay here; I am going for a walk. I will be back." With that, he came round from behind his desk, walked past Mr. Gonsalves and exited, not through the main door to his office but through the one that led to the outer office and eventually to the rear garden of the consulate. He walked back down the narrow alley that ran down a side of the consulate building to the street and crossed the *Praya Grande* to the pedestrian footpath that lay along the seawall of the *Porto Interior*. He did not know where he was going.

There was a long row of banyan trees that lined the *Praya Grande* between the road and the pavement. Their branches and hanging tendrils had been trimmed and hung down on one side of him to surround him in an enveloping canopy with the warm earthy smell of damp foliage and moss. He was sheltered from the world under there. A little in front of him, he could see a Chinese woman in a conical hat moving a broom back and forth rhythmically, like a slow metronome. It had rained recently and the leaves that had fallen from the banyan trees stuck to the pavement like postage stamps on the cobblestones. The Chinese woman did not appear to care that the leaves did not move as she swept back and forth, but she slowly and methodically shuffled with her broom along the pavement. The sea in the *Porto Interior* was a gray pewter in the afternoon light. Reeves thought that you never saw blue water unless you left Macao and got well out to sea, out of sight of land.

He had not walked far when he realized that he was opposite the warehouse he and Mr. Gonsalves had rented from Wong Kong-kit for the British refugees. He had not seen it since that day; he wondered whether he should have inspected it earlier, but he had been assured by Mr. Aycock and Mr. Swemmelaar that the building was proving to be entirely satisfactory. He crossed the street and as he stood in front of the warehouse, he fancied he could hear people talking in British accents that made his heart leap a little, and laughter from somewhere towards the rear of the building. He was gladdened by the sound; it sounded almost like a party and he tried to remember the last party he had been at. He could not, at least one with such laughter.

He walked down the alley alongside the warehouse towards its rear garden and the sound of people laughing. When he got there, he found himself in some sort of outdoor kitchen that Wong Kong-kit's men must have had constructed. There were two brick stoves and a small pile of twigs and wood scraps next to each. Reeves could see a fire lit under one and he could feel its warmth, even where he stood. There was one long table with benches on either side. The table was covered with a white cloth that appeared to be a sheet. He thought he saw several catties of rice that had been emptied onto the table. Sitting around the table were about twenty adults and a number of children. There were several earthenware jugs on the table and Reeves caught the familiar scent of rice wine. Each of the adults had a cup of wine in front of them and everyone, including the children, was leaning forward picking through the rice on the table and throwing what they had found onto the ground in front of them. They were talking loudly among themselves and every so often, someone would say something that caused the rest of them to burst out in laughter, even the children. The adults drank from their cups and refilled them from the jugs.

Reeves watched this for a little while before one of the men sitting around the table saw him. He was sitting there in shirt sleeves, a handkerchief knotted over his head and he raised a florid happy face.

"Hallo," he said, "It's the consul come to pay us a visit." The rest of the people around the table looked up and smiled at Reeves. "If you've come for dinner, you're way too early, mate," said the man with the florid face. "We've got to get all the little stones out of this last lot of rice. Really, I think they got it from a sand and gravel merchant, not a rice merchant." He laughed loudly at his own joke and all the other people around the table laughed too.

Reeves felt happy with these happy people, for the first time in a while. He held up his hand and began in an embarrassed way. "No, no, I have not come for dinner. I was just passing by on my way back to the consulate and I thought I would stop by and see how you are doing."

"Rice and two veg tonight. No meat until Friday," said the florid-faced man wiping his hands on his shirt. "Sit down and join us with a nice cup of Chinese wine. Your head will hurt like billy-oh in the morning but I promise your eyes will still be round." He laughed again as did the rest of the table, especially the children who found the idea of waking up with Chinese eyes very funny. Reeves sat down, a cup was found for him, he took his first drink of the rice wine and the memories of the dying Chinese and his dying wife and daughter under the overhanging tenement roofs began to soften and dissolve.

"What are you doing here?" he asked, looking at the people picking at the rice. The florid man answered. His face was red from the wine but his skin was dark and he looked like he spent time outdoors. He was strong, had a Newcastle accent and Reeves wondered whether he had been a foreman in the Naval Dockyard in Hong Kong.

"A little issue with the rice lately. A lot of little stones in it and we have to pick them out. I was going to complain and send it back, but the Chinaman who brought it round was bigger than me and carried a six-shooter. I didn't fancy his reaction." Again, there was loud laughter. "He could have shot me and taken me to one of those Chinese butcher shops and sold me for a Sunday roast." The people around the table thought that this was the funniest remark he had made and the laughter sustained itself loudly for some time. Reeves, drinking his second cup of wine, joined in the laughter enthusiastically, happy to be laughing.

Reeves stayed perhaps an hour. He had some more wine and even helped pick out the hundreds of small black stones that contaminated the rice. He made some jokes himself that, judging from the enthusiastic laughter, the people around the table enjoyed as much as those from the florid man. At last, conscious somewhere in his mind that he had left the consulate without his guards and that he should return, he stood up and raised his cup.

"I must return to the office," he said more loudly than he had intended and was aware somewhere that he was swaying slightly. ("No!" cried one of the women loudly and everyone laughed again.) "Thank you for your hospitality." ("Take some stones with you," said another woman to loud laughter.) "Next time I would be delighted to stay for dinner." He paused and even though he knew that the wine had affected him more than he intended, he went on. "You are all my family and I will do my best to take care of you." He stopped talking.

The people around the table gave this last statement a loud cheer. Reeves abruptly turned and walked away, down the alley. When he came to the street, he thought he could, or perhaps he imagined he could, still hear the cheering. He would go back to the residence and perhaps he could have tea with Rhoda and Letitia in the garden. He needed to see them. He would tell Rhoda about his day and put Letitia on his lap. Perhaps she would talk to him.

Chapter 11

On one of the first warm days in 1943 after the harsh winter of the previous year, Mr. Gonsalves had come into Reeves's office and said that a Miss Emily Hahn, an American, would be in Macao from Hong Kong the following week and could she see him on Wednesday in the afternoon. Reeves told him to make a note in the diary and did not inquire further. He assumed that she would be seeking assistance or relief and he would add her to the consulate's case load. The Legation in Chungking had objected to his helping Americans and had ordered him to cease, but he ignored the directive. Americans were the allies of the British in this war and as far as he could tell they were doing most of the fighting, at least in Asia. He would take care of them as he took care of the British. Most of the destitute Americans were actually Filipinos, who made a claim to be American because the Philippines was an American colony, now occupied by the Japanese. Reeves found the Filipinos jolly people who worked at the hotels as musicians or waiters and those jobs were scarce now in wartime. Reeves was certainly not going to let them go hungry. Miss Hahn was coming from Hong Kong and her name sounded different, certainly not Filipino. She might be an actual American.

Two days later, he was having a drink at the Melco Club with some of the British refugees who had some independent means and could afford a drink there. Reeves was always slightly taken aback by these little social get-togethers, as though it was 20 years ago and the engulfing war just over the border and all across most of the globe was inconceivable. Or even just outside the Melco Club on the streets, men, women and children were slowly starving to death. It seemed like his world in Macao had many moments like that, where it floated above the bloody turmoil elsewhere.

Many of the British at the Club had brought their wives, but Rhoda preferred to stay at the consulate. The scheme to grow vegetables for the refugees had collapsed when the British women supervising it found that most of the produce was stolen by the Chinese workers and sold on the black market. Then the Chinese children were unable to digest the milk from the cows and nearly all was wasted. Rhoda, who had taken her position as the wife of the most senior British official seriously, had felt responsible somehow for the scheme's failure and was now embarrassed to be around the other women. Reeves assured her in the most comforting way he could that it was not her fault, that she and the other ladies had done their best and no one was blaming her. But Rhoda had bitten her lower lip and without looking at him, had said that she needed to devote her time to Letitia now that she was in school and she did not have time to go to the Club. But you should go, she had urged, it is important that you are seen amongst the British community. She was looking at him when she said that and Reeves believed that she meant it. She wanted him to succeed in his job, he thought, and being seen was part of his job. Especially in wartime, he must do his job.

That evening at the Club, Reeves was standing in a circle with most of the men, while their wives were standing in another circle some distance away. Neither the men nor their wives had asked after Rhoda. He mentioned in an off-hand manner that a Miss Emily Hahn was coming to see him next week. He was taken aback by the reaction. The eyes of the men widened; they began to laugh and one tapped Reeves on the arm saying that he should watch himself, she ate men like him for breakfast, that she was the scarlet woman of Hong Kong. She had seduced Major Boxer who headed all of British intelligence in Hong Kong and who was already married – not only married, but married to the most beautiful woman in Hong Kong, Ursula Churchill-Dawes. Everyone knew Ursula. But Emily could give her a run for her money in the looks department.

The man's eyes widened and he leaned into Reeves. She was quite open about her intrigues with Boxer, did not give a fig what people thought. She had a child by Boxer out of wedlock. The man telling the story poked

Reeves in the chest with his finger. Do you know what she did when the baby was born? The man paused to make sure Reeves was listening. Took out a classified advertisement in the births section of the *South China Morning Post* reading "To Major Charles Boxer and Miss Hahn, a daughter." The men standing in a circle did not laugh, but kept their faces serious, feigning shock that she would have done such a brazen thing.

Then one of the men remembered a story about her and said, "Wait, wait, you must remember the time she came into the Hong Kong Club. Walked right into the Smoking Room cool as a cucumber, even though it is forbidden to ladies, even the wives of members. One of the lads – we all liked Emily and no one wanted to ask her to leave – said to her, 'Emily, I hear that you are putting down a Boxer uprising.' We all laughed and she was a good sort who could take a joke. She just looked back at us and didn't blink an eyelid. You know what she said, we couldn't believe it at the time. 'Don't worry, I have the situation well in hand.' How we all laughed. I told you she's a good egg."

The men in the circle with their glasses of rice wine liquor laughed loudly and the group of wives in the other corner turned with suspicious eyes and wondered what was so funny. Reeves was glad for the moment that Rhoda was not at the Club. She would have looked over from the circle of wives and worried that people were laughing at him.

* * *

Reeves was sitting in his office waiting. Miss Hahn's appointment was for 2:00pm and it was already 3:00pm. There were perhaps other things he should be doing but he was nervous and could not concentrate. He was going to meet some sort of minx, a vixen, a *grande horizontale* of some sort. He had never met anyone like that before. How does one behave? What does one say? Do I even shake hands or is that too forward? He was still frozen in indecision when Mr. Gonsalves came in and announced Miss Emily Hahn. Miss Emily Hahn did not wait but followed Mr. Gonsalves right into the office.

She held out her hand to Reeves. He saw a beautiful woman, with an oval face, very red lips, and shiny black hair parted on one side. She wore a very stylish straw hat and a fitted silk frock in a discreet pattern of small blue flowers on a white background. There was a strand of small pink pearls around her neck that drew Reeves's eye to the V of bare skin between her neck and the top of her frock. He hoped that she had not seen him looking at it. "I'm Emily Hahn," she said with a broad smile and with a charming American accent. "Unless you have been living in a cave the past two years, you will have heard of me. You must be John Reeves, the British consul." They shook hands and she sat down in one of the chairs in front of his desk without being asked. She folded her hands demurely in her lap and continued to smile at Reeves, then said, "I expect you wonder why I am here."

Reeves felt compelled to speak, although thinking back on her visit, he thought the better course of action might have been to remain silent and let her continue. "There was no reason given for your requesting an appointment. However, I am always delighted to meet a citizen of one of our allies. Is there anything I can do to help you or is this purely a social call?" He worried about the impression he was making.

"Let's start with making this a social call and you can give me a drink. Then I will tell you about the business. Do you have any gin?"

Reeves did have some gin, one of his last few bottles. It was in a cabinet in his office and he rang for Mr. Gonsalves to arrange for two glasses and ice.

"Ice?" said Miss Hahn in mock astonishment, "You have ice in this place? There is not a cube to be found in all of Hong Kong. The Japs put a shell right through the ice plant and then they stole all the refrigerators. I find myself envying the Eskimos with all that ice around them, even though I hate blubber." She laughed.

"Our *Fabrico de Gelo* continues to function and supply all our needs, Miss Hahn." Reeves again worried that he sounded stilted and prissy. He was glad when the Number One Boy came in with two glasses and a bucket of ice on a tray. He went over to a cabinet and removed a bottle of gin from it. He poured a measure of gin into each glass and then took the tongs on top of the ice bucket and added two cubes of ice to each glass.

"John," she said, "Don't be such a cheap sumbitch with the ice. Those things are not the crown jewels. Put as many cubes in my glass as it will hold without spilling a drop of that precious liquid." Reeves did as he was told and passed the glass to Miss Hahn. "Well, here's mud in your eye," she said, raising her glass to Reeves and taking a sip. "God, that's cold," she said, "And coming from Wisconsin, the most frozen state in my country, I never expected to be so glad to have something cold." Reeves did not understand her reference to Wisconsin, but raised his glass in response and took a welcome sip of gin.

Emily put down her glass. "I suppose I could stay here all day drinking gin, and I am sorely tempted to do so, but if the word gets out that you are serving gin to any wayward girl that knocks on your door, you will have a line around the block." Reeves was charmed by this easy banter – he could never have pulled it off. Miss Hahn reached into her purse and pulled out an envelope. "I am told that you have a pony express service or something like that and can deliver these papers to the British Embassy in Chungking. From Chungking, although this is not your problem, they will deliver them to Mrs. Ursula Boxer, now employed as a code clerk in the Far East Combined Bureau with SEAC in Colombo, Ceylon." Reeves had seen references in dispatches from the Foreign Office to SEAC – the South East Asia Command – a vast headquarters built by the British to direct the Allied war against the Japanese. Reeves wondered what went on there, since the American Navy was doing nearly all the fighting and he was sure they were not taking orders from Ceylon. At least he had seen actual Japanese soldiers here in Macao, which was more than could be said for the British headquarters staff over 2,000 miles away, quartered safely in Colombo. They may say later that he had a good war, but he was closer to the war than a lot of those soldiers and officers. He wondered whether anyone would ever acknowledge that.

Emily Hahn continued. "Mrs. Ursula Boxer, as you might have guessed, is the woman who is currently the legal wife of Mr. Charles

Boxer. Mr. Boxer is the one I have taken in adultery, if a woman can do such a thing, and he is also the father of my bastard child, my daughter Carola Militia Boxer. Hit me again with one of those." She pushed her glass towards Reeves and paused. He could have listened to her for hours. She had called her daughter a bastard without a blink or a blush. What woman did that? He added a large amount of ice to her glass and filled it with gin. He did the same for himself and looked again at her oval face framed by her black hair. He realized that he should say something.

"These are papers of a confidential nature or containing secrets or classified information that should not fall into the hands of the enemy? If so, we will have to make special arrangements for their safe transmission." Again, he wished he could adopt the buoyant and flippant attitude she affected with such ease.

"Hardly that, Mr. Reeves," she said with a wry expression on her face. "These are going to be filed in open court and then every tabloid from Sydney to Southampton will have the gory details on its front page. These documents," and here she tapped the envelope with a scarlet fingernail that matched the color of her lips, "are the affidavits and other evidence that she needs in support of her petition for divorce from my lover – her husband. There is some pretty racy stuff in there. Her abandonment by Charles, although if one wanted to be strictly accurate, she abandoned him when she headed to Australia when they evacuated all the white women from Hong Kong just before the Japs invaded. Or maybe she is referring to his abandoning her marital bed for the hurly-burly delights of my double bed. I will need to read the papers again more carefully." Reeves was astonished – who was this woman?

Her voice suddenly became a little softer and quieter, even sadder. She looked away for an instant and then back.

"Further acts of adulterous intercourse have become somewhat more difficult lately. I have only seen Charles at a distance of a hundred yards through the barbed wire of Stanley Prison where the Japs have him locked up. I would like Carola to have a little sister or brother, but it looks like that will have to wait until the war's end. When that happens, I would like Major Boxer to be free to marry me so I will no longer be the Whore of Babylon, or rather of Hong Kong." She looked directly at Reeves. "I would count it as a personal favor, John, if you could see that these papers are delivered to your Embassy in Chungking for onward transmission to Colombo. It will mean so much for my future happiness." She gave him a sweet calculated smile.

Reeves stammered at first in his reply. "There is an informal courier service from Macao to Chungking under an irregular unit of the British Army operating behind Japanese lines. It is intended exclusively for official communications, but I cannot see why I cannot make an exception for these documents. I can send a message to its commander, Colonel Ride. I cannot guarantee a date for delivery. Chungking is in northern China, almost 1,000 miles from Macao." He decided to try a little levity. "It all depends on how active the Chinese bandits are." He was pleased to see that she smiled.

"Attaboy Consul, I knew I could depend on you. I was afraid I was going to have to use my feminine wiles." She lowered her eyes to look at Reeves and batted her eyelids in a parody of the vamp manner, although he was not quite sure she was not serious. "And you being a married man. Not that that seems to have been much of an impediment to me in the past." She said this last sentence with a thoughtful expression on her face.

Emily Hahn suddenly spoke in a tired manner. "I have to be on a boat soon. The steamer between here and Hong Kong only runs every four days. If I miss it, I will be in violation of my travel documents and I will miss the English lesson I am giving to the head of Japanese Intelligence in Hong Kong and I need to pay the bills and I need his protection. I do not think you have any idea what I have to do to survive in Hong Kong, find food for my daughter and stay out of a prison camp." She looked down for a minute and then up. Her face looked very weary. "I am a single white woman with a young daughter surrounded by thousands of angry Japanese soldiers. I have to fight for something to eat, I have to fight to prevent myself from being assaulted. I worry that we will be tossed out of our apartment and into the street where we will be beaten, robbed and left to starve. I cannot begin to explain my life right now." She stood up, reached across the desk and squeezed his lower arm tightly and released it. "I will walk down to the docks; luckily it is just along the road. Don't worry, I will see myself out." With that, she came around to his side of the desk and kissed him on his cheek. She left the room, but at the door, she turned, finally smiled, lifted her hand and wiggled her fingers in a little wave of farewell.

He went and closed his office door that Emily had left open and then sat down behind his desk. He had not had much experience with women. There was not an elder sister who might have instructed him in how to relate to a girl like Emily. There were no girls at Haileybury and precious few when he got to Cambridge. There were the sisters of classmates and his boat crew who would visit their brothers at the university on occasion, but when he was introduced to them at social events, they had little apparent interest in him, certainly not as a possible romantic partner. He had Rhoda but she was decidedly nothing like Emily.

What had he wanted out of his own marriage? As an only child, he was used to solitude. He had never felt the need really of a companion or even a partner, he sometimes admitted to himself. What had put him into the arms of Rhoda was that she seemed to need him to take care of things. Or she *had* needed him to take care of things. Lately she was spending a lot of time by herself. Despite the child he had fathered, he and Rhoda seemed no more than acquaintances. She did not mind having him around but seemed to take no real pleasure in his company. And for his part, he would think that perhaps he felt much the same. Again in moments of honesty, he admitted to himself that romance, intimacy, friendship, fun and adventure were not at the forefront of his mind when he married Rhoda. He had met one woman in Peking when he was studying there – Molly Kaye – who might have provided those, or so he would like to imagine. They had gone on picnics in the countryside; he had photographed her smiling and laughing – she had a wonderful smile and laughed a lot – she seemed to find much of life made her laugh. On her last day in Peking, he had presented her with an album of those photos. She had told him he was a sweet man and kissed him again, quite passionately, before taking the car to the train station to return to Simla in India. He imagined then that he had seen something in her eyes when they had met his – he could not tell you what it was, but it was something. That was a decade ago. He realized now how often he thought of what might have been. In any event, she had never answered his letters.

And now there was Emily Hahn who drank his gin and talked of sex and adultery and smiled at him and made sparkling and witty small talk. She could offer so much but would never need him like Rhoda professed to – Emily was living openly by herself in Japanese-occupied Hong Kong and surviving quite nicely. He could not imagine that he would be able to do that. And what would Emily want with him, a mid-level civil servant in an obscure city doing not-very-important work, in conditions of deprivation out of an office furnished with second-hand furniture, most of it battered and chipped. Of course she would go for a glamorous soldier like Boxer, who had fought gallantly in the defense of Hong Kong and even been wounded. Reeves had seen pictures. Boxer was a handsome devil; he did not wear glasses. Reeves finished his gin, and what remained in Emily's glass. He told Mr. Gonsalves that he was done for the day.

To his surprise when he went into the family drawing room at the consulate, Rhoda was waiting there, sitting on the edge of a chair with her hands folded in her lap. She looked fragile, as though she might break if touched. She glanced up at him and gave him a nervous smile. She had been in her room for a few days ("I have such a sick headache" she had told him when he inquired after her) and he thought that she was about to cry. He noticed, again to his surprise, that she had powdered her face and applied lipstick.

"I was hoping you were coming home for dinner tonight. The servants found us a chicken and they are stewing it. They found some garlic to add and I know you like that so much. You told me that you had garlic on your trip to France." Reeves had a memory of his one trip to Paris as a student, making the best of a small allowance from his parents, third class on the boat train, in a week in November when it did nothing but rain. He had found a cheap bistro where the workers in a nearby glass factory used to eat, and he had sat there not understanding their French with only his book for companionship.

"We could not stew it in red wine as I am told the French do it. Red wine is far too precious to use for cooking, But the servants assure the Number One Boy that it is fat and tender." Rhoda's voice was quiet and had a nervous quaver; it was like the first time he had met her in Hankow. "Can I get you a drink? We have that rice liquor you like. We should save the real drink for when we have guests."

Reeves did not know what to say. Rhoda could not stomach liquor with her weak digestion and he often sensed her silent disapproval of his drinking the amount he did. She had never before offered him a drink.

"My dear, that would be very kind of you. The local spirits are fine; you are entirely right to keep the good stuff for our guests. Are you going to have anything? Shall I ring for some tea or lemon water?"

Then, to his astonishment, she replied, "No, I think I will join you in a drink. Not that distilled wine that you like; I am sure that that is too much for me. But I will take a cup of rice wine. At Christmas, I always had a glass of wine. Daddy kept an excellent cellar, I was told." She poured the two drinks, passed Reeves his, then took hers and sat down. "Tell me about your day. I do so worry about the strains you are under." She was looking at him just as she did when they first met.

Reeves did not know what was going on. It had been so long since he had had a conversation with Rhoda, as two normal people, or how he imagined a typical couple might converse. Reeves told her about his day, largely dealing with a particularly knotty issue of proof of nationality with one family. He relegated Emily's visit to a passing comment. She told him about Letitia's day at school, her difficulty with reading and her lack of friends, a problem with a maid that she had taken to the Number One Boy to solve. Soon dinner was announced.

She had somehow known that he was coming home. The dining room table was set for two with china and silver that they had been given by Rhoda's parents as a wedding present. There were candles, not oil lamps, on the table. There were the good glasses; Reeves kept his cup for the rice wine liquor. "I do hope you like the chicken and that it takes you back to your time in France. I know you liked it there so much."

Reeves felt a sudden anguish at her so painfully forced brightness. Rhoda had been talking for a while and stopped. He tried a sally about the Governor, about his having to learn a little Japanese to keep the Nips happy. It wasn't very witty but it was the best he could come up with. Rhoda looked frightened as if he was serious, and then realized that he was not and her lips opened in a suggestion of a smile, then closed again. She went on about the people that were keeping chickens and other fowl in an abandoned brickyard near the Harbormaster's offices. The two turkeys needed a trough to eat from because they could not stretch down to reach their mash on the ground. She looked up nervously to see if her husband was listening.

He was looking at her, but his mind was also grappling elsewhere with questions, the answers to which were elusive. Why was Rhoda making this effort now to extend a hand to him? She had always been nervous – 'high-strung' – her father had said almost apologetically as though he needed to excuse her behavior and temperament. She would close herself off from him and not talk for days, not out of anger, but because of some profound sadness deep within her that he could not fathom or comprehend. At the beginning, he had felt like he was with someone with a wasting disease that no treatment could cure or alleviate, and all he could do was watch helplessly, or, later, indifferently.

Reeves felt that somehow he had disappointed her and that was the cause of her sadness. She must see him as doing minor administrative work while men were dying elsewhere in the defense of Western civilization. His future prospects were uncertain in the China Consular Service – would it even be needed after the war? – and even less certain was his ability to secure a posting close to England, where it was always her dream to go.

She bore this disappointment silently, without ever discussing it with him, and withdrew more into herself.

Tonight, Reeves was thinking, she was trying to connect with him, and he could see the effort it took. He thought about how long it had been since they had been intimate. After they were married, but not before, there had been furtive and fumbling embraces as both struggled with what they thought was required of them. Rhoda had been both terrified and resigned. Then she found herself pregnant, and from the beginning sick and weak and then the months and years followed of her sleeping in a separate room. Reeves found that mostly he did not miss her physical company and thought about it on fewer and fewer occasions as time went by. And now this.

Reeves was suddenly aware that Rhoda was talking to him. She had finished a second glass of wine, something he had never seen her do in the time he had known her. Her eyes had tears in them; she was speaking very quietly and there was a tremor in her words.

"One of the mothers at Letitia's school told me that you were meeting with Emily Hahn today. Her husband had told her – you had said something about it at the Melco Club." Rhoda paused, the tears still in her eyes, but she was not crying yet. Then the words tumbled out. She knew all about this Hahn woman from this mother. She said she could never be a woman like that. She knew she was glamorous and beautiful and did not care for her reputation and that she was a sinner in the eyes of God. Rhoda said she had tried to live a good life but she knew men would always seek out women like that. She had overheard her brother talk about what the sailors from the navy ships did when they docked at Shanghai; there were places to go, where women… There will always be women like that if that is what you are looking for. The Bible teaches us that sin lieth at the door.

She wiped an eye with an otherwise untouched napkin. "But I want you to know, John, that today I resolved to try to be a better wife to you no matter how hard it is. John, I really will try, I really will try." She unfolded her napkin, pushed her face into it, bowed her head and cried quietly. Reeves watched her, not knowing after so many years of the two of them in this marriage what to say. He thought of the awkward interview with Emily Hahn in his office and tried to imagine what Rhoda thought had gone on.

Rhoda raised her head and put down the napkin on the table. She had ceased her crying. "I doubt you understand how difficult this is for me. But please try to understand that I am trying, I am trying." Reeves realized that the tureen of the stewed chicken had not been touched. It smelled wonderful. He suggested that she might feel better after a little dinner. They ate together, she trying but not eating very much. They continued with small talk as though the previous conversation had not happened, Rhoda still leaning forward with a forced eagerness to hear everything Reeves had to say. At the end of dinner she asked Reeves if he would not mind taking her arm and helping her up the stairs. He was happy to do so; this he knew how to do. She dropped his arm and almost pushed him away. She went to her own bedroom, closing the door and leaving him outside on the landing. Reeves thought that she had tried; she must have done it more out of duty than tenderness, but she had tried, then could not carry it further. Somewhere inside the consul, so deep that he may not have been aware, he was relieved that it had gone no further. He went back downstairs for more of the distilled rice wine.

Some months later, Reeves was reading in the *Macau Tribune* the list of the Americans who had been repatriated from Hong Kong to the United States on the *Teia Maru* in an exchange of prisoners. On the list were the names of Emily Hahn and her daughter, Carola. Like Molly Kaye from those picnics in Peking last decade, he knew he would never see her again.

Chapter 12

Several months after Emily Hahn's encounter with Reeves, there was a meeting nearly 800 miles from Macao in Chungking, the capital of that part of China not occupied by the invading Japanese and called by the British and Americans, not always ironically, Free China. The meeting was between Major General G. E. Grimsdale, the senior Military Attache in the British Legation and the Legation's First and Third Secretary from the Foreign Office. Grimsdale was a tallish man, with a slight limp from a wound in the previous war that presumably had kept him far from the more active parts of this war. He was uncertain how the two civilians from the Foreign Office would behave, so he decided, as he might have expressed it if he was on a tactical exercise, to attack and seize the high ground.

"Gentlemen," he said, watching impatiently as the two stirred sugar into tea served in Army mugs, holding them awkwardly as though they had never seen one before. "What I am about to tell you is highly confidential and must be very closely guarded. It should not be repeated outside of this room." He paused to see the effect of his words. The actual effect was that both diplomats were inwardly insulted by the implication that men from the Foreign Office were unfamiliar with confidential material and would not know how to keep it secret. But their faces showed no sign of annoyance, and Grimsdale continued.

"You may have heard of Peter Fleming?" he said.

"The author fellow? The one whose wife is a film actress? In that film about the Navy" asked the Third Secretary, and then was suddenly aware that he had spoken before the First had said anything. He worried briefly about the consequences.

Grimsdale looked exasperated and opened a file on his desk. This was not relevant; the Navy had been annoyingly mentioned, and he resented this slight loss of control. He looked at the file for an instant and took back the conversation in a loud abrupt tone. "Yes, he has written some books about his travels in Asia and South America. I understand they were quite popular. Fleming is now an officer attached to HQ staff under Mountbatten in Colombo."

Mountbatten was the British commander of all allied forces in Asia, including even the Americans, although Grimsdale's opinion was that the Americans did whatever they bloody well wanted, regardless of Mountbatten. The Americans with their limitless money and their people and their aircraft and their weapons ran the show in China. An American general ran the Chinese army and another ran the Chinese air force, without a single British person involved. The best the British could hope for in China is that the Americans might help keep Hong Kong out of the hands of the Chinese when the war was over, if they even remembered who the British were. But he kept these thoughts to himself.

"Fleming commands D Division, running schemes of deception against the Japanese. Fleming and his group have meant more to the war effort than several battalions or even a regiment." He was tempted to add 'more than the entire Foreign Office' but there was something in the way he was speaking and looking at the two diplomats that conveyed that message. "He recently concluded a very successful operation, the details of which are confidential." This was the second time that Grimsdale had implied that the two Foreign Office representatives could not be trusted with confidential information.

The First Secretary felt obliged to say something to avoid the feeling of being lectured to, and also to see if he could begin to bring this conversation to a conclusion. As nicely as he could, he asked "And how could the Foreign Office be helpful to Mr. Fleming?"

"Major Fleming," corrected Grimsdale, scowling at the First Secretary. "He has taken a particular interest in Macao."

"Macao?" said the First Secretary incredulously, "Why on earth Macao?"

"I understand your surprise," said Grimsdale, pleased once again to have the advantage. "Macao would seem to have no relevance to our fight against the Japanese." Both the First and Second Secretary nodded. "But a branch of the Japanese Greater East Asia Ministry has recently moved to Macao from Kwang Chow Wan. That branch has, as part of its remit, espionage and the gathering of intelligence. Though God knows what they expect to find in Macao beyond whores, narcotics and gambling. I suspect they are using Macao as a base to look more broadly in southern China. Fleming has devised an operation to deceive these people."

"But where does the Foreign Office come into this? This is indeed a great story, but I fail to see its relevance to the usual role of the Foreign Office." The First Secretary had intended 'great story' to indicate by subtle irony that he was not really impressed, but Grimsdale seemingly failed to notice.

"Fleming may need the cooperation of your Consul in Macao, to act under his direction." Grimsdale added this last phrase to indicate that this would be an entirely Army operation with the Foreign Office in a decidedly junior role. "You consider the Consul sound and reliable?"

The question surprised them both. The First Secretary barely knew Reeves's name. The Third Secretary, forced to deal with him, glanced at the reports that would occasionally come from Reeves and would either pass them on to someone who might possibly find them more interesting or file them to be forgotten. He knew Reeves had gotten average reviews in his last posts, was married to a woman who was said to be peculiar, reputedly drank too much and had been relegated to Macao, a place of no possible relevance to the war effort or the interests of Britain abroad. He had issued a mild reprimand to Reeves more than once for some minor breach of protocol, but nothing serious. At some stage someone would have to decide what to do with all these British consuls in China. Chiang Kai-shek was insisting on abolishing the Treaty Ports, even before the war was over, and then none of those consuls would have a role.

Britain's presence in China would inevitably be severely reduced, if it wasn't severely reduced already. Reeves was one of the many mediocrities who would become someone else's problem at the end of the war. But the tribal instinct of the civil service attacked by an outside force asserted itself and the First Secretary responded sharply.

"Reeves. Excellent man, very sound. Reeves is your man," said the First Secretary.

"Good," said Grimsdale, "Fleming is in a conference room down the corridor. Please follow me."

The first thing that the two diplomats noticed, indeed it took them aback when they entered the room, was that Fleming was extravagantly handsome. The firm jawline, the very blue eyes, and the full head of hair (left far longer than was usual in an army officer). The second thing that both noticed was his extraordinary uniform. Fleming was wearing an officer's battle-dress tunic, correctly buttoned, brass buttons shining as they should, red beret neatly tucked under one of his shoulder tabs, shirt and tie properly knotted, all very correct. But then he was wearing a pair of light-blue canvas shorts that came to his knees, golf socks, and suede shoes that the First Secretary knew as desert boots. None of what he wore below the waist had ever been seen on a British Army officer, or at least Grimsdale had not seen it.

The man who must have been Peter Fleming came to his feet with a startling alacrity and thrust himself at the First Secretary with an outstretched arm. "You must be Wofford?" he asked "General Grimsdale here has been most helpful in locating you two. As I have frequently mentioned at SEAC in Kandy, my job would be impossible without the deep local knowledge of our senior people on the ground where D Division operates. Tell me, what kind of fellow is your man in Macao?" The First Secretary, taken aback momentarily by the unanticipated compliment, hesitated an instant before replying.

"Excellent fellow. Distinguished record at Cambridge. Speaks several languages. Learned Chinese. Served with distinction in his previous two posts that were of particular importance to the Foreign Office and for our diplomatic efforts in the Far East, Now the senior, indeed the only Allied representative in the only neutral and unoccupied territory in thousands of miles of Japanese-held South East Asia." The Third Secretary knew that what had just been said, while not inaccurate, had nothing to do with the First Secretary's actual opinion of Reeves, which, if he had time to think of it, would verge on the contemptuous.

"Here is what I need," said Fleming, "Tell me whether this Reeves chap can pull this off. For one night, in a public place, he is going to have to appear quite drunk and then talk very indiscreetly. He is going to have to do this where the right sort of Japanese will overhear him and they are going to have to believe that he is actually drunk and spouting off his mouth. Do you think Reeves can pull this off?" The Third Secretary suppressed the thought that from what he had heard of Reeves, this would be all too easy a performance for him.

"It would be out of character," lied the First Secretary, "but even the most competent of us might appear to succumb to the stresses of wartime. I am sure he could put on a credible show."

"Excellent," said Fleming, "Now let me tell you what we have in mind. I have cleared this at the highest levels at SEAC and the top brass are all very encouraging. This operation is intended to make the Japanese Navy think that we are a much more formidable foe than we actually are." He knew the Secretaries would have no idea how the Consul in Macao fitted into all of this, but this was one of the pleasures of being in D Division and doing a briefing where you lifted the veil on a mystery for a marveling audience, tiny fold by tiny fold.

"Like the best deceptions, this one is intertwined with the truth. The Japanese will undoubtedly be aware that the aircraft carrier, the HMS *Indomitable*, is destined for an eastern station of the Royal Navy and will most likely be anchored in Colombo Harbor. That so much is true. What is not true is that it will carry a new kind of naval fighter aircraft, the Sea Dragon. The Sea Dragon comes in both a fighter and a dive bomber version and has been engineered to outperform the Japanese Zero in speed, armament, firepower, and maneuverability."

"The Sea Dragon does not exist?" asked the Third Secretary.

"The Sea Dragon," said Fleming with a satisfied smile, "is the joint product of a long night of pink gin with an officer of the Fleet Air Arm attached to Mountbatten's staff. It was created in the General Staff mess there and has no existence beyond that. Although I suppose it also exists in this office in the minds of the four of us. And soon it will exist in the mind of His Majesty's Consul in Macao."

Fleming suddenly became serious, leaning forward to the two diplomats. "Reeves is going to have to memorize details of this fantastical aircraft. He is going to have to talk about them convincingly and he is going to have to talk about them while pretending to be drunk or being actually drunk. And he is going to have to do this when the right Japanese from their intelligence unit in Macao are around. They will then report to their superiors the new information about Britain's marvelous new airplane." He reached into his battle tunic and pulled out an envelope. "Here are the technical specifications for the Sea Dragon that Lieutenant Commander Simmons of the Fleet Air Arm and I worked out during that night in the bar. There is a second sheet containing specific instructions as to what he is to do and how. It is in the code to which he has the cipher."

The First Secretary took the envelope. "I will draft a cover note so that Reeves knows that this operation is sanctioned by the Foreign Office. He can't be taking his orders from anyone, you know." The First Secretary smiled at Grimsdale. He may be used to command but there were limits. "We will have this delivered to Reeves."

"From what I have heard of Reeves, it is difficult to imagine him conducting espionage," the Third Secretary said delicately to the First as they walked back to their offices.

The First Secretary turned and smiled at the Third, who was unable to gauge the significance of the smile. "Reeves's competency or lack of competency is irrelevant. We will offer Reeves for this role. But he will report back to us. We will determine what to pass on to Grimsdale and Fleming and in what form. In that way, how successful the operation appears will be entirely in our hands. We will shape the story of its success. If it fails, as it well might, we will be the only ones who will know." He turned his head, confident he had imparted to one younger and less experienced a valuable lesson in the art of warfare, at least as fought amongst the departments of the British government.

Grimsdale and Fleming had a similar mistrust of the Foreign Office. Once the two Secretaries left, they began to discuss the involvement of Colonel Ride in the operation. Colonel Ride commanded the British Army Aid Group or BAAG. This was an irregular force of soldiers and officers seconded from the British Army, civilian volunteers who had escaped Hong Kong and Chinese guerillas. Ride had been in the Hong Kong Volunteers at the time of the Japanese invasion, had been captured and then escaped. Grimsdale did not quite approve of Ride and the BAAG because Ride was Australian, and not regular army, but he conceded he had his uses. The BAAG operated largely behind enemy lines in occupied China. It spirited escapees out of Hong Kong and Macao through hostile regions of China to Free China. It ran an espionage operation, with operatives in both Macao and Hong Kong as well as in occupied China. Ride would brief one or two of his trusted people in Macao on the operation. Grimsdale did not know their actual names, but they had code names, Phoenix, Nitram, Cyclone – who thought of those names? Mrs. Wilson on Reeve's staff was a secret liaison to the BAAG and she would see that Reeves executed the operations correctly. Mrs. Wilson and the BAAG agents in Macao would also provide an accurate account of how the operation was carried out. Ride had frequently passed on to Grimsdale rumors about Reeves, his drinking, his talking loudly about secret and confidential matters, his disregard of official regulations. Grimsdale knew that if the operation was a failure, he would ensure that the Foreign Office, and not the Army, would get the blame.

Chapter 13

It was a Saturday afternoon in the spring of 1943 that Reeves received word that the operation would take place that evening. The summer had been lethargic; nothing much had happened and even outside Macao, the Great Powers locked in bloody combat over the entire globe seemed in equipoise, no one combatant having an obvious advantage. And now, after months of silence, Reeves was going to be a central figure in an operation to deceive the enemy with only a few hours' notice. He re-read again the cover sheet transmitting his instructions. The operation had been codenamed Desperado by the First Secretary and Reeves could not help worrying that this was yet another subtle slight from the Foreign Office.

Mrs. Wilson had decoded the instructions and given them to Reeves directly. He had asked where she had got them and she replied that she had been given them from a BAAG agent she knew only as Phoenix. He had asked her who Phoenix was and she had replied that she did not know, even though she knew he was Y.C Liang. Mrs. Wilson was married to the Assistant Hong Kong Police Superintendent, now sadly interned in Hong Kong, and she was used to keeping secrets. Before the war, her husband had asked her on more than one occasion to help out. "Just go over there and listen in," he would say at a drinks party, "You can tell me what they are talking about when we are home." She would stand a little way off from a group of men talking, pretending to be examining a vase or a picture – no one paid attention to a single middle-aged woman anyhow – and listen. Later at home with a final drink before bed, she would recount what she had heard to her husband. Most of the time, he would say something like Oh is that all it was? But occasionally he said that is extremely interesting and then hinted how the conversation she had overheard might fit into a matter he was working on. He knew she could be relied on to keep this confidential.

Mrs. Wilson did not have the same confidence in Reeves. For one thing, he had a sixteen-year-old boy in charge of the Consular archives. His name was Derek Symons and he was the much younger brother of Joyce Symons, a British refugee from Hong Kong. She grudgingly admired Reeves for giving the boy a job, which helped the family out financially, although Joyce's sister was married to a Macao lawyer and lived in quite a nice house, thank you very much. Filing documents and labeling files was not a difficult task and was not beyond a bright schoolboy. But some of the documents were highly confidential, secret even, and was it proper to entrust their care to a mere sixteen-year-old? She wondered whether any of this had even occurred to Reeves. He seemed to have selected Derek for this position because he enjoyed his company and wanted someone to whom he could talk. Or because he wanted him to play for the consulate hockey team, the Valentes. Reeves had single-handedly revived the Macao Hockey Club – he surely had more important things to do. She had gone to watch one of the games and found it very rough and the players much older than Derek. She thought it was really not suitable for a sixteen-year-old boy.

And Reeves talked so much. Her husband, the Assistant Superintendent of the Hong Kong Police, surely would not have approved. Reeves would have a drink in the afternoon with some of the young clerks in the consulate and he would start telling them about things the Governor had said to him when he was last at the *Palacio da Praia Grande,* which she was sure the Governor would not want repeated, or talk about who had managed to slip out of Hong Kong to reach Free China, information that might be of interest to Colonel Sawa and Japanese secret police of the Kempeitai, stationed in Macao in defiance of its neutrality. She regularly reported her concerns and doubts about Reeves to Colonel Ride of the BAAG.

Mrs. Wilson made sure Reeves had memorized the details of the imaginary Sea Dragon. In the evening, when the staff had left the consulate and she could be sure that they were alone, she drilled him in the details of this fictitious aircraft. Engine: 1850hp Rolls-Royce; maximum speed: 390 mph; armament: six .08 automatic cannons; wingspan: 37 feet, 8 inches; operational ceiling: 37,000 feet; bomb racks on the dive-bomber version: two torpedoes on the fuselage and one five-hundred-pound bomb under each wing. Reeves was to add other details on the Sea Dragon's range and maneuverability that, in sum, would tell the informed listener that the Sea Dragon was vastly superior to anything in the Japanese arsenal. To Mrs. Wilson's pleasure (and surprise), Reeves took this very seriously and quickly committed the details to memory. He even practiced saying them while pretending to be inebriated, which amused her no end. In a couple of evenings he was letter-perfect. She still had doubts that Reeves could pull this mission off but she relayed a message to Phoenix that Reeves was ready.

Phoenix and his network had learned just a few hours ago that Colonel Sawa was going to have dinner at the Central Hotel. He was going to be entertaining four officials from Military Intelligence working in Macao at the Japanese Greater East Asia Ministry branch. Phoenix was unsure of what time they were actually going to be there. Colonel Sawa never reserved a table; he would simply show up and expect to be seated. The message from Phoenix to Reeves was that he should go first to the sixth floor of the hotel that evening where there was a dance floor and a band. After lingering there a while, he should then go down to the fifth floor to the Golden City restaurant where he would have dinner. Colonel Sawa and his party would be there at some stage.

At around 8:00pm that evening, Reeves arrived at the Central Hotel on the *Avenida Almeida de Ribeiro*. Reeves thought of his instructions, drafted in Chungking, given to Colonel Ride and the BAAG, passed from unknown person to unknown person and arriving months later after a treacherous journey of a thousand miles in Macao. He was nervous; he had never done anything like this before. He sat in his office and wrote reports. He had no idea whether it would be dangerous. He had often wondered how he would have done in the Navy had they accepted him. On a ship, called on to be brave, to ignore danger, to risk death by burning, drowning, fire or an exploding shell. He imagined the horror and worried that he would be frozen in terror, the object of the contempt of his fellow naval officers. Would he do better today?

And how important was this mission? Would the Japanese really be fooled by some consular official spouting off details about an imaginary war plane? How was he supposed to know about it? Wouldn't their other intelligence sources quickly demonstrate that there was no Sea Dragon? Was this whole operation misconceived? But perhaps there were factors of which he was unaware and this was indeed a small but vital part of our war against Japan. He realized he would never know; he would do his duty and would forever be ignorant of the wider import of his actions, if indeed they even had such a significance.

He decided to bring his pistol with him. It had been sent to him via the BAAG from Chungking, and until today it had remained in his desk drawer in the original yellow and black packaging of the Colt Manufacturing Company, Hartford, Connecticut, together with a second box of 25 cartridges. He had wondered where Connecticut was and how the Foreign Office had decided he would only need 25 cartridges. The barrel of the pistol was only three inches long and the gun appeared very light and very small. It felt now like a toy in the compact leather holster on his hip.

The *Pac Cap Pio* lottery had just been drawn at the Syndicate headquarters near the Central Hotel and the streets were filled with disappointed ticket holders with nowhere to go. They milled around on this hot evening talking to each other and the air smelled of sweat, dust and the fetid smoke of cooking oil that had been used too many times. Reeves's guards led him through the crowds in the street into the hotel towards the lift, pushing their way through the yelling mob of gamblers around the fan-tan tables on the hotel's ground floor, leaving Reeves to follow in the path they had cleared.

The lift door opened on the sixth floor. The music was the first thing Reeves heard. There were six Filipino musicians on a raised platform at one end of the room, each in a white shirt and white pants, with black bow ties. There was a singer, very pretty, who looked like many Macanese as though she had the blood of a dozen races in her. She was dressed in a tight scarlet gown, with a hibiscus in her hair that matched the scarlet of her dress. She was also very young, perhaps barely out of high school, and she swayed gently back and forth to the music, eyes closed in some private rapture, singing softly into a microphone on a stand in front of her.

Reeves was led to a table. He sat down and also closed his eyes. He let the soft captivating music flow over him. The manager brought a bottle of red wine to his table. It had been a long time since he had had any red wine. It had been a long time since any wine had arrived in Macao. This must have been in the Central Hotel's cellar for a few years at least and there would be no more once these bottles are gone until the war was over. He took the first sip of the wine, a second, and then drank half the glass. He began to relax; this was nothing like being on a ship in the middle of a naval battle. He could do this. He still found himself touching the little pistol under his coat in the small holster on his hip.

There were several Chinese taxi girls, sitting in chairs along one wall, hands folded in their laps. One of the taxi girls in particular was leaning forward, smiling and trying to catch Reeves's eye. He had heard about these girls who danced with strangers for tips. He smiled and stood up, making a bow that was a little too deep and held out his hand. She eagerly walked over, took his hand and led him to the center of the dance floor. They were the only people there.

The taxi girl was slender and taller than most Chinese girls. She wore a tight green and white cheongsam and had her coal-black hair hair pulled back with red clips in the form of dragons or lizards. She smelled faintly of cedar or some oil from some tropical plant. She lowered her head just slightly, looking up at him from kohl-rimmed eyes and smiling in what could have been a submissive gesture, but then she put one arm decisively on his shoulder and took Reeve's left hand to place it on the small of her back. She placed her other hand in the same place on Reeves's back and made an abrupt gesture with her head to indicate that Reeves should put his free hand on her shoulder.

Reeves could smell the cedar of her perfume and the rice powder that made her face almost as pale as ivory. He could feel the bone of her spine beneath the thin silk of her dress as his hand rested on her lower back. Her lips were very red, dyed like pomegranates, against the ghostly dead white of her face. They waited for the band to recommence.

Very soon, the band started to play, very slowly and softly, and the Macanese girl singer began, almost whispering the song into the microphone. The clarinet and the saxophone had the lead; the trumpet was muted and the drummer could scarcely be heard. The taxi girl pulled Reeves to her and put both arms around his waist, resting her head easily on his shoulder. Reeves, unconsciously, put his arms around her and pulled her even more tightly towards him. He smelled the cedar wood, her rice powder, soap, her sweat and her skin. They swayed together to the music, scarcely dancing. He was suddenly aware that he could feel her two hands on his back, her front pressing against his shirt through the thin fabric of her dress. What was she wearing underneath? Perhaps she was wearing only the dress and she was naked underneath it.

He suddenly thought of another dance during his last month at Cambridge. Charles Godson, captain of the boat crew, a foot taller than everyone else and very handsome, had been dancing with an equally tall and very beautiful debutante who had come down from London and they seemed to Reeves, standing by himself over by the refreshments table, Charles in his dinner jacket and her in blue silk, to float sublimely above everyone else. Now Goodson was dead, killed in the Western Desert, leading a charge of his men of the Royal Lancers against the Germans, for which he was awarded a posthumous DSO. Reeves thought of himself now, doing his bit for the war effort with a taxi girl on a dance floor in Macao. He continued to press the taxi girl against him until the song was over.

There was long sustained clapping and the Macanese singer laughed delightedly, making a wobbly bow. The taxi girl continued to hold Reeves close throughout the applause, breaking away reluctantly when it finally died down. She stepped back, her hands locked in front of her, and looked up at Reeves with a smile, two drops of sweat making two small gray stains on her forehead through her snow-white powder.

Someone was tapping on his shoulder. He looked up to see the manager standing next to him. "Consul Reeves, Mr. Liang has a table in the restaurant and he is wondering if you would join him for dinner." Reeves was taken aback by the unexpected invitation from Y.C. Liang. He thought the plan was to have dinner by himself and execute the operation. But perhaps there was a change. Y.C. was a friend of the British. It would be good to have him there. He touched the pistol under the cloth of his jacket. The band had started playing a song Reeves recognized from his university days – 'The Sheik of Araby.' He thought he should tip the taxi girl, it must be expected; she was probably supporting her whole family. He pulled out his billfold and gave her a banknote. He had no idea how much he had given.

One floor down at the Golden City restaurant, there was the loud harsh chatter from the mostly Chinese patrons, talking to their tablemates at a high volume as though they were sitting across the other side of the room. The first thing Reeves noticed was not the noise but the smell of food – fish, spices, sauces, roast pork, stewed and baked chicken, the steam from bowls of rice. Reeves marveled at how the rich and the well-connected in Macao were unaffected by the war. Only the poor and the refugees suffered. The manager led the way to a table for four at which Y.C Liang was sitting alone. Reeves noticed that Colonel Sawa and three Japanese soldiers – officers – were sitting one table away. Reeves tensed slightly as he realized that the operation would actually occur.

Reeves approached the table. "Mr. Liang, thank you for your generous offer. I am honored to join you for dinner." The manager bowed and melted back into the noise of the restaurant. A waiter appeared almost instantly with the half-finished bottle of Portuguese red from his table at the dance floor and Reeves's glass, which was still a quarter full.

Y.C. Liang stood up to greet his guest. "Consul Reeves, it is an honor to have you at my table. Please sit down and we can talk. We will need to be quiet with the Japanese soldiers so close. You have been well?" The two chatted pleasantly, about the war, about the refugees Reeves was caring for, the Governor's staff, the price of rice, poverty, food shortages, how many fishing junks the Japanese would let leave the harbor and fish out in the South China Sea. There was a whole fish, pigeon, vegetables, round beans and the whitest fluffiest rice Reeves had seen in a long time. It was, Reeves thought again, as though the war was not happening for these people. He ate a little; he was enjoying the Portuguese red, and when he had finished that bottle, another quickly appeared in its place.

There was a sudden noise at the table with the Japanese officers. Reeves looked over to see what had happened. Y.C. Liang had stopped smiling and was looking intently at Reeves. Colonel Sawa was standing up looking at Reeves, rocking back and forth on his feet and holding a glass containing a clear liquid. He appeared quite drunk. The other Japanese officers were sitting down around the table grinning at Reeves. They were dressed in a more formal dark khaki dress jacket with a red-tabbed stand-up collar surrounding the neck and buttoned at it. Colonel Sawa was in his field uniform of rough khaki. He wore no jacket and his shirt, as it was every time Reeves had seen him, was open to the third button, exposing a white, flabby chest. There were sweat stains under his arms. He alone of the four officers wore his sword, which moved to and fro from a strap on his belt as he swayed back and forth. He saw that Reeves had seen him and he jerked the glass in his hand upwards, spilling a little. He shouted four words, pronouncing each one distinctly and then drained his glass. All four officers laughed very loudly and then drank. Reeves did not understand what had been said.

"Did you understand that?" he asked Y.C. Liang.

Y.C. Liang looked Reeves directly in the eye and said "He said the *Prince of Wales* and the *Repulse.*" Reeves looked back at Mr. Liang, shocked a little at being reminded. These were two British battleships that had been sunk by the Japanese off the coast of Malaya during the early days of the war in a bad defeat for Britain and the British Navy. Reeves looked back at Colonel Sawa, who had refilled his glass and was waiting for Reeves. Colonel Sawa raised his glass again and shouted several sentences. The sweat stains under his arms were growing larger. The other Japanese officers shouted a word in agreement and all four drained their glasses.

Reeves turned to Mr. Liang and asked him what he had said. Mr. Liang said quietly that Colonel Sawa was trying to speak English and that he was saying that the Japanese bombers that had sunk the two British battleships would sink all the British ships, and the American ones too. Reeves knew that his moment had come. Over the hours he had been here at the Central Hotel, he had drunk one bottle of wine and had started on a second, but he knew how to talk when he had drunk a lot. It was, he reflected as he stood up, one of his party tricks. Y.C. Liang was watching him intently.

Reeves was holding his glass as he stood up and turned at the same time. A little of the red wine spilled onto his linen pants. Well, he thought, that was a nice piece of stage business. I hope the audience appreciates it. He walked over towards Colonel Sawa, who by this time had sat down to enjoy the congratulations of his fellow officers for his toast. Reeves unintentionally stumbled and more wine spilled, but this time on the floor.

"Colonel Sawa,' he said and he realized that he was slurring his words a little without meaning to. "It is good of you to mention your early victories in what will be a long war. Soon, I am looking forward to you being here when we are drinking to all the British victories. Very soon, I will have a lot of toasts to propose and I will want you to listen to them." He let out a belch that was also unintentional, but he thought that it too was another excellent piece of stage business. One of the officers snorted contemptuously. That's good, thought Reeves, at least one of them is paying attention. He paused for what he thought was a dramatic effect.

"We have," and here he made another pause for the same reason, and then raised his voice, "the Sea Dragon, the most powerful and fastest aircraft in the air." The Japanese officer who had snorted, laughed and said something in Japanese to the rest of the table. They laughed too.

"You may laugh now,' said Reeves, "but soon you won't be laughing." He thought that he sounded like one of his old school masters. "This plane, this plane is fast. Faster than the Zero, faster than the Mitsubishi, faster than the Nakajima" – he couldn't remember the letters and numbers after each plane but he thought they would get the idea. "It goes," (pause and then louder), "390 miles per hour, even faster when diving down from 37,000 feet to destroy your aircraft from a height they can never reach." He pronounced '390' and '37,000' slowly and distinctly, albeit with a slur, so there could be no question as to what he was saying. The Japanese officer who apparently understood English looked at him without expression. "They will dive down from this great height and destroy your aircraft with their six cannons – six cannons. Your planes will be powerless against them."

He paused and took a sip of wine from his glass , mostly because he felt a little thirsty. He smiled at the impassive Japanese officers. This is like being in one of those revues back in 'varsity. "Oh gentlemen," he went on, "that is not all. Not all by a long shot." Another sip, more of a gulp really, of his wine. "Once the Sea Dragon has shot down every Japanese plane, then the second wave of Sea Dragons will come. They will be carrying torpedoes and 500 hundred pound bombs. Not one, but two 500 pound bombs. Down, down, down they will come, bombing your fleet and all your warships sunk." He imitated with his hand the planes diving down to destroy the Japanese fleet. The hand was holding his wine glass and the wine spilled on the floor. The officers laughed again.

"Go ahead and laugh," said Reeves, but soon the whole Japanese Navy will be on the bottom of the ocean and all your planes scrap metal. You will not be laughing when you have to fight the Sea Dragon." He hiccupped. "Sea Dragon, Sea Dragon, Sea Dragon," he taunted and raised his glass. "To the Sea Dragon," he shouted and took a sip. But his glass was empty. The Japanese officer who apparently spoke English turned and talked to the other three. It appeared he was telling them what Reeves had said.

Reeves hoped that they were absorbing all the details of the fictitious Sea Dragon.

Colonel Sawa stood up suddenly and took a step towards Reeves, so that he was at a far closer distance than Reeves was comfortable with. He was leaning forward so that his face was even closer to Reeves's. He could smell some sort of liquor on Colonel Sawa's breath and when he began to shout, Reeves felt a fleck of warm wet spittle on his face. Colonel Sawa shouted for what seemed like a long time, his face, red from drink, turned even redder. Throughout the tirade, Reeves stood there impassively, watching the Colonel and noticing, despite the amount he had drunk, small unrelated details – that one of his teeth was black, that there was a small white scar on his chin, that there was a small red birthmark lower on his chest, that there had been a tear in his shirt and that it had been repaired with a khaki thread that not had not yet faded to the same shade as the rest of the shirt. Long after this encounter in the Central Hotel, Reeves could still remember these details about Colonel Sawa. He wondered why he had noticed them in the first place.

Then Reeves saw that the Colonel's hand had come to rest on his holster on his belt on his right hand side. The holster had a closed flap over its top, so Colonel Sawa was just resting his hand there, rather than preparing to withdraw his pistol. But Reeves was reminded that he too was carrying a pistol. He unconsciously reached down, parting his unbuttoned jacket, touching the handle of his small revolver and exposing its existence to much of the dining room.

There was a shout from two of the Japanese officers and all three stood up, opening the flaps on their holsters and this time grasping the handles of their sidearms. Colonel Sawa took a step back and grinned at Reeves. It took Reeves a few seconds to realize what was happening, that his hand was resting on the top of his revolver, and the Japanese officers had reacted. This was very much like one of those scenes in a Western film where the sheriff was in a standoff with some villains. How would this scene end? Would Colonel Sawa actually kill a consul? This was not part of the plan. Why was this happening?

Reeves heard the scrape of a chair as Mr. Liang stood up, two of Reeves's guards appeared, shimmering out of nowhere to stand on either side and slightly to the front of him. They too had their jackets open and their hands on their pistols. His third guard came up behind him, put his hand on Reeves's shoulder, gently turned him around, pushing him forward out of the restaurant, and all four left towards the lift on the far wall of the room. One guard was leading and two were close behind so that Reeves's back was protected. Just before they entered through the open lift doors, Reeves turned around, pushing through the two guards that had been behind him. He faced towards the four Japanese officers in the restaurant, who were still standing but with their hands no longer on their revolvers, and yelled as loudly as he could, "Sea Dragon!" He had done it; he had done it, although it was nothing like being on the bridge of a destroyer in battle or leading a charge in the Western Desert, he had still done it.

The next morning when Reeves came into the consulate, the young men working on all the paperwork for the relief of the refugees looked up at him expectantly. Mrs. Wilson could hear Reeves in the large room outside his office where all the young men had, or shared, desks. She could hear him even though she was sitting with Mr. Gonsalves in the outer office of the Consul's, far from where the young men were sitting. He was talking about his night last night, about drinking wine, about dancing with a very tall Chinese girl, about his dinner with his good friend, Mr. Y.C. Liang.

Mrs. Wilson came out through the outer office and through Reeves's own office and stood at the door that opened out on the room where the young men sat. They were looking up enthralled as Reeves got to the part of the evening where, as he put it, there was nearly a gun battle between him, his guards and six Japanese officers. Mrs. Wilson coughed loudly and said something urgent had just come in for the Consul. Later lads, he told the young men as he went into his office. Mrs. Wilson shut the door behind him.

"I really must insist on your being more discreet," she said, "There is no need for those men to know anything about what you did last night."

"Mrs. Wilson, Mrs. Wilson, Mrs. Wilson." Reeves was exultant. "It was an absolute triumph." He got more emphatic. "An absolute triumph." He was quite loud.

"Mr. Reeves," she said urgently, "I must insist you keep your voice down. You can be heard all over the consulate. Secrets must be kept secret."

But nothing was to spoil this moment for Reeves. He continued even more loudly. "You would have been so proud of me, Mrs. Wilson, so proud. I remembered every single imaginary fact about that bloody Sea Dragon, every single made-up number, despite working my way through two bottles of excellent Portuguese red. From the Douro, Mrs. Wilson, all the way from the Douro. I even showed them how the Sea Dragon would pounce down on all their bloody battleships. Like a tiger on some poor Indian peasant." He made a downward swoop with one hand, making a loud noise like a dive bomber might have made and then imitating a bomb exploding.

"Sssh," said Mrs. Wilson despairingly, wondering if he was still drunk from last night, "Ssh."

Some days later, Mr. Gonsalves told Reeves that Mrs. Wilson was ill and was going to stay in bed for a week or so. Reeves made occasional inquiries to Mr. Gonsalves who told him that he had heard Mrs. Wilson was still sick. Then a month later, Reeves picked up a copy of a newspaper lying on Mr. Gonsalves's desk. It was the *Diario de Noticias* and under the headline 'Refugiados que se escapan de Macau' was the account of Mrs. Wilson's arrival in Chungking. She had been smuggled out of Macao and through China to Chungking by Colonel Ride and the BAAG. Reeves did not really miss her; Mr. Gonsalves was far more easy-going. He was not to know that the assessment Mrs. Wilson gave of Reeves and his behavior to Colonel Ride was not very flattering. It could even have been described as harsh. Colonel Ride had a long conversation with the First

Secretary in which he said that Reeves was indiscreet and could not be trusted.

Reeves cabled a lengthy report on Operation Desperado to the First Secretary in Chungking. He spent a long time on the draft, working late into the night over several evenings. He tried to keep his tone modest – any suggestion of self-promotion was frowned on in the Consular Service, but he included all the facts so that the reader could conclude that Reeves had done all that had been asked of him and that he had done it well. Someone in the Foreign Office would have at least glanced at it but it was unclear whether Fleming ever saw it. Fleming had been briefed by Colonel Ride that Reeves had done what he had been asked to. But decryptions of intercepted Japanese communications over the next week had no mention of the Sea Dragon aircraft and Fleming concluded that the Japanese had not taken the bait. He did not blame Reeves; these things did not always work out, although it would have been great if it had worked. You tried scores of things hoping one would succeed. He left Chungking shortly to return to HQ without giving it further thought.

Reeves never heard back from the First Secretary on his report. He took pleasure in thinking of the role – a critical role he told himself – he had played in the operation. He often imagined himself at a family gathering back in England telling his parents, his uncles, the Admirals, and all his other uncles, aunts, cousins and nieces how he had led an operation to deceive actual Japanese intelligence officers where he was almost in a gun battle in a crowded restaurant. He was sure his parents would be proud of him. He was a part of the war effort.

Chapter 14

It was nearly midnight when Reeves returned to the residence after Operation Desperado. He was excited, even exalted, about what he had done. He so wanted to share his triumph with Rhoda; she would see him in a different light; she would understand he had abilities and talents that she was hitherto unaware of; she would perhaps draw closer to him. There might be respect. He entered a silent and empty house; the servant who had opened the door disappeared, and Reeves found himself alone. He went upstairs and tentatively pushed Rhoda's bedroom door open to see if she was willing to talk, but she was asleep, curled up tightly on one side of the bed facing the wall. She did not move when the door opened. Letitia was lying next to her mother in the bed. He saw by the moonlight from the window that she was awake and staring at the ceiling. She was unaware of his presence in the room. He had an urge to reach out and touch her, hold her even. She was his daughter; there was so much he could tell her. He wanted to see her look up at him with a smile, ask him questions, call him 'Father' or even 'Daddy' – she was young – to hold his hand and squeeze it slightly. He had never taken her to her school. Perhaps there would be a day soon he could do it. He decided against disturbing her; she might cry out and wake Rhoda.

The next morning Rhoda and Letitia came down to join Reeves at breakfast. Rhoda, who had been impressed when Reeves had told her that he was spending last night on a special assignment for Chungking, asked with genuine enthusiasm how it had gone. Reeves brightened; he had waited for this moment, and started with a sprightly account of the whole evening, beginning with his guards pushing through the crowds in the lobby of the Central Hotel. But when he reached the part about his dancing with a taxi girl, Rhoda's eyes had watered, her lips tightened and she looked away. Reeves tried to explain that this was part of the character he was assuming, that it was just one dance for a few minutes, and it was critical for the success of the mission that people saw him like that. But Rhoda left the room before finishing her meal, saying that she needed to get Letitia ready for school. Reeves tried a few more times over the next several days to tell her about his success at the Central Hotel, but each time it was clear that the subject caused her pain. He should not have mentioned dancing with another woman. Somehow he thought, as with Emily Hahn, Rhoda had concluded that Reeves did not really need her. Lately he had not given her much cause to think otherwise.

After what would be the final attempt to tell the story of how he had triumphed at the Central Hotel, he had gone to work as usual but there was only the routine paperwork of the consulate to occupy him. He felt disturbed and out of sorts. When would the next opportunity arise to show what he was really capable of? By the afternoon, he was still restless sitting in his office; he could not bear to look at another document for his signature and he decided to take a walk.

Reeves had no particular plan or route in mind, turning haphazardly one way or another at street corners, but, when he thought about it later, he should not have been surprised that he ended up on Macao's street of brothels, the *Rua da Felicidade*. Why shouldn't a man feeling as he did – a little lonely and disaffected – find himself on the Street of Happiness? Isn't that what he was seeking, even though the happiness on offer there would be momentary and would almost immediately fade? The old melancholy would then surge back, like a stern wave breaking on a shore after the one before had flowed back into the sea.

He walked without aim down the street, then stopped, halted by the faint melancholy wail of Chinese singing, in front of a tall ragged bamboo fence in front of an empty lot between two houses. He could see, through the gaps and tears in the dried bamboo, a sort of Cantonese opera in mid-performance on a small makeshift stage of old wooden pallets.

Only a few people had paid to be admitted behind the fence to see the opera. Reeves, looking through the fence, could see about seven performers, seemingly from one family. There was no one playing an instrument. The performers were all dressed in the ragged black pajamas that the poor Chinese wore every day, although the teenage daughter nervously singing center-stage had draped a piece of cloth that once may have been white over her shoulders by way of signifying a costume. She kept glancing back as she sang at the woman behind her who looked like her mother, as though she was afraid of being scolded or slapped for making a mistake. The father of the family had tried to smear a mustache with a piece of charcoal on his lip and down his face to show his character, but he really only looked dirty. Two small children, a boy and a girl, no more than six or seven, stood rigid and terrified on the stage. They did not know what to do but they knew they were not to move. The grandmother who seemed too frail to stand was sitting down on a box or crate and her singing could hardly be heard. The children began to cry.

Reeves saw the little lean-to at the back of the lot. That's where this family must live, all crammed into a shack that would offer little protection from the rain or wind or cold. They must be refugees from Canton, doing the only thing they knew how to do to survive. They would have arrived in Macao with little beyond what they were dressed in and now were probably just this side of starvation. He remembered all the food in the Golden City Restaurant of the Central Hotel, his own comfortable residence. Only the poor were suffering in Macao during this war.

The people on the street were looking at Reeves as though they knew why he was walking down a street of brothels. How do they know why I am on this street? he thought to himself. I just happened to end up here. Nothing more than that. He walked on.

He stopped again and glanced down an alley between two of the gray-brick houses. It was already early evening and the alley was deep in gloomy shadows. But light was coming out an open door on the side of a house halfway down the alley. It fell on a girl in a green silk cheongsam, with very long black hair almost to her waist, perhaps Chinese or part-Macanese, sitting on a stool. She was illuminated in the darkness as though in a religious painting from the Renaissance and she was talking to someone whom Reeves could not see inside the house. When the long-haired girl in the alley realized that Reeves was looking at her, she turned and smiled expectantly. She made a gesture with her hand that could have been beckoning Reeves to approach or it could have been a shy wave. Reeves looked at her and then realized that some people had stopped and were standing near him to see what he would do. Whatever he wanted to do, he would not do it before an audience. He continued down the street.

He eventually came to the Central Hotel. He had not been here since the Sea Dragon episode and he stopped to look at it. It stood twelve stories high, the tallest building in Macao. Someone had intended it to be quite imposing, but now it just loomed bulky and ungraceful, the dull gray of its cement stained with black mildew from the humidity. It had been built to show that Macao could be part of the modern world, but the building was just ugly and out of place. The true Macao was a city of pastel-colored buildings, eternally in the past. Reeves could not see that changing.

There was a tap on his shoulder and he turned around to see Y.C. Liang, with that same smile, the same jade cufflinks on the sleeves of his white shirt. The friend of the British, appearing unexpectedly in his life once again. He had never once mentioned the money he lent for the refugees. Reeves was glad to see him; they could relive Operation Desperado.

"Come with me," said Y.C. Liang, "No man comes to the Central Hotel by himself except to cast off his troubles. I can help you." They went into the hotel and crossed to the lift. The lift boy pushed down on the lever and the car began to ascend. Reeves paid no attention, expecting to be taken to the bar on the roof. Instead, the car opened on a dark floor with just a few electric light bulbs dribbling a watery light through the dark. Y.C. Liang led the way down a corridor and opened a door on the right.

The only light in the windowless room came from two oil lamps with smoky orange flames casting flickering shadows on the wall. A man was sitting on a stool. He was old, perhaps over seventy, dressed in a long black robe and a small black cap. He stood up and bowed. A wooden platform about two feet high and covered with a loosely woven rush matting took up most of the room. There were two porcelain pillows down one end, in blue and white with a slight curve in each where a head could rest. Save for a small gap at the near end, wide enough for one man to pass through, the platform was surrounded on all sides by an intricately carved wooden grill, three foot high. Seen in the wavering orange flames of the lamp, the space seemed sheltered and intimate. Reeves stopped abruptly. He actually twitched.

"You have brought me into an opium den, a real opium den. I can't be seen here."

Y.C. Liang laughed. "Consul Reeves, years from now you will be an old man back in your little house in the English countryside. And you will have your friends over for sherry or port or whatever you drink and they will ask what you did during the war when you were His Majesty's Consul in the wickedest city in the East. I think that is what they call Macao. And after today, you will be able to gather them around, tell them to pull their chairs closer and recount the story of the night you went to an opium den. What a good way to spend the war. No Englishman has ever been to the East without returning with at least one story of depravity." Y.C. Liang had his hand on Reeves's shoulder and pulled him round to face him. He had the gentlest smile on his face.

"Consul Reeves, I am worried about you. I can look at you and see that you are troubled. Just like the British working man likes his mug of bitter beer at the end of the day, a Chinaman likes his pipe of opium. It soothes his soul, he forgets his worries, he has a glimpse of the heavens. What can be wrong with that?" Without Reeves quite knowing how, Y.C. Liang had guided him through the gap in the wooden grill, onto the platform and laid him down on the mat, lying on his side, propped up on one elbow, with his head over the hard blue and white porcelain pillow. Y.C. Liang lay down in the same position opposite him, propped on his elbow and looking at Reeves. The two men's faces were no more than two feet apart. The servant in the robe and slippers went to a tall chest against one wall and removed a small tin box and a small pipe with a long thin stem. Reeves thought that it was too late to protest. Besides he did not want to protest, he wanted to be soothed by opium. He smiled back at Y.C. Liang.

"Consul Reeves, do not worry, you are not doing anything untoward. Opium is part of Macao. A Government monopoly. They license the opium dens, tax the opium and ensure it can be only sold in regulated and licensed opium shops. How could they disapprove of any of us taking a pipe now and then? And if it gives our poorer citizens a brief respite from pain, hunger, poverty, the grip of disease, how can anyone object?" He kept his gentle smile on his lips and did not take his eyes off Reeves.

At the far end of the rush-mat covered platform, the old man in the robe and slippers was kneeling in front of the lamp and was holding a needle in its flame. When it was sufficiently hot, he took the opened tin that he had taken from the cupboard before, and scraped at its contents with the heated needle.

"Kam Shi Yi opium. Some of the younger people call it California opium, even though it is from Persia. $16 a tael. Have you met Mr. Namazee, the Macao agent of the Persian Opium Export Monopoly Company? A most charming and educated man." Reeves allowed that he had not had the pleasure.

The old man had extracted a small quantity of black opium from the tin with the needle and was rolling it into a small ball between his thumb and forefinger. He pierced the ball with the needle and held it over the flame. After a moment it hissed faintly and wisps of vapor floated up and were gone. Reeves caught the perfume of unseen flowers. The servant put the ball of opium in the bowl of the pipe and passed the pipe to Y.C. Liang. He held the bowl of the pipe over the flame of the nearest lamp. The opium in the bowl hissed and crackled almost imperceptibly and then the faint sound stopped and the perfume of those mysterious flowers became stronger. Y.C. Liang put the end of the pipe's stem in his mouth and sucked deeply. He held his breath and passed the pipe to Reeves.

Reeves put the stem of the pipe in his mouth; it was still damp from when Y.C. Liang had sucked on it. He drew deeply on the pipe, following the example of Y.C. Liang, held his breath to keep the vapors in his lungs. He did it until he felt he could hold his breath no longer, expelling it in a long low whistle. Y.C. Liang did the same again, then took the pipe from Reeves and put it down on the matting between them. The servant, on his knees, leaned forward and picked it up. He began preparing another pipe.

Y.C. Liang lay back, his head on the porcelain pillow and Reeves did the same. Neither talked and Reeves closed his eyes. He had expected the porcelain pillow to be hard and uncomfortable, but it cradled his head gently. He smelled the burnt floral sweetness from the opium fumes that lingered in the closed room. There was some heat he could feel on his face from the flame on the lamp. He heard the occasional creak from the wooden platform as the servant shifted on his knees while preparing the second pipe. He saw what he thought were stars then realized he was in a closed room with his eyes closed. He felt a calmness rise within him like a mist in the morning. He had not felt this untroubled since he was a small boy alone in the garden of his parents' house on a summer afternoon, watching a stream flow by to places unknown.

Y.C. Liang tapped him on the shoulder. He opened his eyes to see him with that same smile as he passed the pipe. Reeves took the pipe and sucked in the sweet fumes of opium, holding his breath before expelling it slowly.

In a few moments, he thought he could feel every inch of his skin brushed with tiny caresses as if from butterfly wings. He was swaddled in the calmness he had felt before. He was in a walled garden with shadows playing on flower beds of tulips of every possible color. Anything bad was on the other side of that wall and could not reach him. His body rose and floated above the rush mat, and then drifted down to sink within its embrace. He had left this vale of tears, as the psalm called it. He would never return.

He was aware of the soft stroking on his cheek for some time before he opened his eyes. He opened them to find Y.C. Liang brushing his face softly with the backs of the fingers of one hand. He was very close to the consul.

"Come on, Mr. Consul, it is time to leave. Two bowls is enough. My worries have vanished, which would indicate how insubstantial they were to begin with. How do you feel?"

Reeves did not say anything at first. He was aware of a rush of warmth, affection or even love for Y.C. Liang. Then he was aware of something much more than calmness; it was a serenity; it was an inner peace. The troubles of this world meant nothing to him; his mind was a secluded pond, still, deep, without a ripple, polished silver on its surface.

"I feel very well, Y.C., refreshed, as though I had had a good night's sleep, which I have not had in God knows how long." He sat up, looking forward – the servant had vanished – then at Y.C. Liang. "Thank you," he said.

Y.C. Liang stood up, bent over him, and took him tenderly by the arm.

"I'll take you up to the roof bar. You can sit there and have a cold drink and enjoy the peace before you head home." He left Reeves once they reached the roof.

There were tables set out on the roof of the Central Hotel; some were shaded by awnings although that was of less concern now that the sun had set. Reeves chose a table for four close to the wall. The bar made a sweet cocktail with fruit juices, predominantly lychee and sugar cane, and the local rice wine liquor. There was plenty of ice and Reeves sipped the cocktail, tapping his foot in time to the beat of music from his opium dream that only he could hear.

The manager came over to him, a thin Chinese man with a pencil mustache, a white shirt and bow tie This time of the evening, he did not wear a jacket. He stood next to Reeves with his head turned away as though he was not really talking to him and said "You want a girl?" It was as though he was doing nothing more than casually inquiring whether he wanted a second drink.

"I beg your pardon," said Reeves, not in indignation but in astonishment at the question. He had never been asked that before. Later, when looking back on this evening late at night, he would, cradling his second or third drink, admit that deep within him he was hoping for this question. He wanted that same touch on his skin he had felt when he had smoked that second opium pipe. He wanted warmth; he wanted to feel affection; he knew somehow he wanted to connect.

"Five patacas for the girl, five patacas for the room, 40 avos for the maid. She wash you and clean room afterwards. You pay me." He was now looking at Reeves. To the only other guest on the rooftop, it looked like a casual conversation.

"I am not sure," Reeves said.

"Very wide eyes," said the manager in that same matter-of-fact manner, still looking away, "very young, her first time, you take care of her."

Not looking at the manager, Reeves said, "I have been working hard lately. Perhaps if she could massage my back a little, I would feel better when I went back to the office later this evening. I am enervated." He emphasized the word 'am' and realized too late how absurd 'enervated' sounded. Would he ever fit in, he suddenly thought? In the Consular Service? Amongst the Portuguese and British? Even in a bordello in Macao?

"Sure boss,' said the manager. "You pay me. Follow." The two left the rooftop and rather than take the lift, went down the stairs. The air in the staircase was hot and close, the paint on the walls was peeling and flakes of it had fallen onto the scuffed wood of the stairs. There was the muffled sound of wastewater in hidden drain pipes. They went down three flights and then through a door into a gloomy corridor. It was stale and dusty. There was a single electric light bulb in the ceiling down at the end of the corridor. It was like a single star seen in the desert.

Reeves could see four doors in the corridor into which they had stepped, set not very far apart. The rooms behind the doors could not be very large, he thought. The manager opened one of the doors and the two stepped inside. The manager pushed by him to open the window and the noise of people in the street below came into the room.

"You pay me," said the manager and Reeves reached into his pocket and picked out a handful of patacas. He gave these to the manager and he left.

"Wait here," he said at the door, before leaving and closing it, "A girl come soon."

It was not only the noise of the streets that was coming in the window, but the smell of heat, dust, dirt, cooking, and the dampness that always seemed to be present in the Chinese quarter. It was night, no light came through the window, but several surprisingly bright light fixtures in the ceiling lit the room. Reeves saw the gray walls that had once been white, patched and scuffed in places for reasons that he could not guess at. A badly made wooden stand in the corner held a jug and wash basin, but they were dry and dusty and Reeves thought that it had been a long time since they had held water for washing. There was a wicker waste basket next to the wooden stand. It was empty; nothing was ever discarded in wartime Macao. Pushed against one wall was a narrow bed frame. On it was an innerspring made of wide strips of bamboo woven diagonally in a lattice pattern. The bamboo innerspring was covered with a single sheet, more gray like the walls than white. It was ripped in parts and the bamboo could be seen through the tears. Reeves sat down on the bed to wait. It gave some but not much. He thought it would be hard to lie on.

The door opened without anyone knocking and a stern-faced man came in. Reeves stood up, startled. The man looked around at every corner. Reeves could not think of what he was looking for. The man stepped back into the corridor and left. A girl in a thin cotton robe came in, followed by a maid with a rag over her arm and carrying a chipped enamel bowl of water. The door closed and Reeves thought that the room was awfully small. The maid was in the usual black pajamas and had bare feet. She pushed back tight against a wall, her head lowered, staring at the bowl of water, not wanting to look at Reeves. The girl opened her robe, pulled her arms out of its sleeves and dropped it to the floor. She was entirely naked.

Reeves could not help glancing up and down her, then he pulled his head up and tried only to look her in the eyes. He thought she was very young. He had caught a smudge of pubic hair; she was very thin, her legs more like brittle sticks, and he had clearly seen her rib bones underneath her stretched white skin with its scattered brown freckles. He could not even tell in his quick glance whether her breasts were developed; her chest and nipples seemed more like a boy's than those of a girl. For one moment, he thought she might have tuberculosis or some other disease wasting her slowly.

She was looking at him and Reeves could not imagine what she was thinking. He thought he saw momentary fear in her face, then a stoic resignation to whatever was going to happen. She stepped back and said something in Cantonese to the maid. The maid put the bowl of water on the washstand next to the empty jug and washbasin. She took the rag off her forearm, dipped it in the water and wrung it out. She held it out in front of her, her head still lowered to avert her eyes. The thin naked girl pointed down and Reeves realized that she was indicating his groin.

He suddenly realized that he was expected to remove his trousers so the maid could wash his genitals. His mind was suddenly a swirling jumble of memories of the times he had been naked, the changing rooms at school, his wedding night, a medical examination, showering after a hard match last week with the Macao Hockey Club at the *Caixa Escola* playing fields, lying in bed by himself at night in his room at the consulate when the heat did not break from the day to the evening, the damp steaming air pressing down upon him brutally.

He stepped back, the backs of his legs hitting the bedframe and he almost fell back, but didn't. "I cannot do this," he said out loud but really to himself. "I must go." He did not consider why he could not do it. It could have been cowardice, decency or a deep-seated fear of intimacy. He never asked himself later what was the real reason he suddenly decided to leave. The thin naked girl looked frightened for a moment, but then Reeves reached into his pocket and pulled out some more coins and a banknote – Reeves saw it was the lowest denomination issued – and placed them on the washstand. The girl and the maid both turned to look at what he had left there. Reeves took one step to the door, opened it and left. Before leaving, Reeves looked back one final time into the room. The maid had put down the bowl of water and was smoothing out the sheet where Reeves had sat on the bed. The thin girl was pulling her robe back on, still looking at the money on the washstand, but not touching it.

Reeves walked down the corridor to the lift and pushed the button to call it. The lift came, its lift boy standing impassively at his lever staring at the door a foot in front of him. The lift doors opened and Reeves stepped out into the lobby of the hotel. Nothing had changed; the noise of people was overwhelming; the large fan-tan table in the middle was as crowded as ever. The shouts and cries from the gamblers filled Reeves's ears. The clerk behind the lobby desk was reading a newspaper. No one paid any attention as Reeves left to walk back to the consulate; no one knew where he had just been.

In the months to come from time to time, the same familiar melancholy would wash over him. But he never again tried to seek out a woman, even inadvertently. He thought that whatever the relationship he had with Rhoda and he really did not know what they was, that would be the best he could do. An opium pipe was a different matter and every now and then, he and Y.C. Liang would come to the Central Hotel to share one. He always felt better afterwards; no one would find out. He was not going to deny himself this little pleasure.

Chapter 15

In 1943, a murderous unremitting war that raged across two thirds of the globe still had scarcely touched Macao. In cables from Chungking, Reeves read about the first victories of the American Navy against the Japanese in the southern Pacific, thousands of miles away, and their ships Americans a dogged push north, perhaps to Japan itself. But that would be a long, slow, slog over years. In China, just over the border, one million Japanese soldiers fought Chinese armies in brutal indecisive battles, marked by indiscriminate slaughter on both sides and neither side with a claim to victory or defeat. The war would last a long time; life in Macao would go on regardless. Reeves sometimes thought about why fate had put him on this small sheltered peninsular, rather than among the millions now under arms fighting the Japanese and the Germans.

But in early summer, Reeves began to get reports out of China from Colonel Ride and the BAAG. They had picked up information from the various Chinese factions – the Nationalists, the Communists, the war-lords, and the many bandit gangs – who, when they were not fighting among themselves, were fighting the Japanese. The reports were, despite their different sources, consistent: that Japanese troops were leaving their garrison in Canton and were moving south towards Macao. They were not just patrolling the countryside, the reports concluded, they were preparing to invade Macao itself. Reeves passed these reports along to the Governor. He wondered whether this was the end of Macao as he knew it, the end of this magical kingdom by the sea; he wondered how he would behave if there was an actual invasion? Would he acquit himself well? Would people think well of him? He hoped he would not find out; he preferred to leave it as a question.

Reeves's reports reinforced the Governor's own impressions. He had been told of disturbances on the northern border of Macao at the *Portas do Cerco*: Japanese soldiers taunting the Portuguese troops on guard duty and once beating a Mozambique soldier who inadvertently strayed a little far north over the border. There were more Japanese troops on the streets of Macao. They had always come across the border with impunity, passing the guards with hardly a sideways glance, but usually singly or in pairs, and then disappearing into the gambling halls, bars and brothels. But now they came in larger numbers, six, seven or even a dozen together, in full uniform, swords at their sides, and they would swagger down the street in a wide row, forcing people to get out of their way, stopping traffic until they had passed. It was as though, thought the Governor, they had already conquered Macao.

Sitting in his suite of offices in the pink *Palácio da Praia Grande,* the Governor could not help feeling that there was a noose around Macao and it was tightening every day. Dr. P.J. Lobo had told him that Macao had just a two-week supply of rice for its swollen population. There was little rice to be had in neighboring Canton Province for purchase or barter. Last year, there were torrential rains during the crucial month after the rice seedlings had been planted, and much of the crop had been destroyed before it had even been ready for harvest. This year, there was a drought and the paddies were now dusty sun-baked beds of dried mud without a green shoot to be seen. The Governor had sent the little Macao tramp steamer, the *Wing Wah*, to Amoy in French Indochina to fetch rice, but on its return, just out of the Gulf of Tonkin, it had been sunk by an American submarine which had mistaken it for a Japanese vessel. In Macao, Japanese naval officials permitted only a few of the fishing junks to leave the harbor and then patrol vessels would often bar them from their best fishing grounds or chase them right back into the *Porto Interior* before they had even had time to lower their nets. The few fish brought back to Macao went to the rich and well-connected. It was nearly impossible to find any meat in the markets – a few scrawny chickens and ducks, some pigeons, at exorbitant prices. Vegetables were scarce. There were more dead in the streets for the black soldiers from Mozambique to collect and bury.

The noose may be tightening, thought the Governor, but I will speak to the Bishop of Macao. Portugal is a Christian country and Macao has been part of Portugal for over 400 years. If a foreign power should seize Macao, it would be in violation of the laws of God. The people of Macao will be better able to face whatever may happen if they feel they have God on their side. The Bishop can help.

The Governor requested lunch with the Bishop. The request, when it had arrived from the Governor's Chief of Staff, had been very politely phrased: Would it be convenient for the Bishop to have luncheon with the Governor on Wednesday so that the Governor might discuss some matters with him, and that the Governor would be pleased to come to the Bishop's palace so as not to inconvenience him.

Precisely at one o'clock on Wednesday, the Governor arrived at the Bishop's palace, a modest two-story house facing the *Largo da Se*, next to the Cathedral. The Bishop's secretary, a recent graduate of the seminary, opened the door of the residence before the Governor was half-way across the courtyard. The Governor nodded at him, brusquely handed over his hat as though the secretary (who also bore the title of Diocesan Chancellor) was some sort of manservant, and was shown into the dining room. The Bishop was waiting, standing by a side table.

Bishop João de Deus Ramalho, calmly watching the Governor through his rimless glasses, wore a small silver cross over his maroon silk shirt. The cross had been fashioned in the seventeenth century by Japanese Christian artisans who found sanctuary in Macao after fleeing persecution in their home country. Almost all of his predecessors in Macao over hundreds of years had worn that cross. The Bishop continued to look at the Governor. Before coming to Macao, he had been Vicar General in a part of Canton Province fought over for decades in bloody wars by warlords and bandits, and ravaged regularly by typhoons and famine. Macao was an island of peace in the midst of horror. Whatever the Governor wanted, it would not trouble him much.

The Governor shook hands with the Bishop and immediately took a place at the side of the table, leaving its head for the Bishop. By this gesture, the Bishop knew that the Governor was coming to ask for something, rather than to tell him what he wanted done. No matter, he was used to supplicants. The Bishop poured him a small glass of white wine from a decanter on the table; the Governor asked about the Bishop's ministry to the refugees, the work of the *Santa Casa de Misericordia* amongst the poor and hungry, his project to build a new convent. A nun in a floor-length habit and a full wimple opened the door and brought in two plates of greens fried with garlic in peanut oil. She put them down with a nervous quickness and left the room. The Governor talked about what the government of Macao was doing about the poor and destitute.

The Bishop looked at the Governor and put his fork down on his plate and began to speak. "When the first bishop of Macao arrived here in 1566, his first act was to found the Holy House of Mercy, the *Santa Casa de Misericordia* to take care of the poor. It is good to remember that for nearly 400 years the bishops of Macao have kept foremost in their minds the admonition in the Gospels of our Lord Jesus to take care of the sick, the poor and the troubled." Whatever the Governor was doing to help the poor now, thought the Bishop, it was fitting to remind him that the Church had been helping far longer.

The Governor was about to say something but the Bishop continued talking. "Did you know that the first bishop of Macao had been Bishop of Nicaea?" The Governor replied, a little tersely, that he did not know this. The Bishop settled back a little in this chair and looked up. "I often wonder about his lonely little house and the modest church in Nicaea in the middle of the Ottoman Empire."

"Bishop Ramalho," began the Governor, but the Bishop continued to talk, leaning back in his chair and looking up and past the Governor. The Governor wondered if he should try to interrupt him again, but the Bishop was well into his story.

"Imagine the knock on the door one night; a servant lighting a lamp, the exhausted messenger from the Holy Father in Rome summoning him to his new post in Macao, a place at the end of the known earth. There would have been the hasty packing of a few possessions, the journey of months through the dusty provinces of the Middle East on the back of a donkey with only a single friar walking by your side for a companion, the worry about bandits and highwaymen, nights on beds of filthy straw in barns or country inns, all around you the heathens, across the desert that burns in the day and freezes at night, the howling of unseen jackals, you would be almost dead with thirst, hunger and exhaustion, and finally the ocean, the Arab dhow to the Portuguese fort at the mouth of the Red Sea, and then the long wait for the first ship that would take you to Goa."

The Governor tried to interject again with another "Bishop Ramalho" but the Bishop simply looked at him and smiled. He continued.

"You have been journeying for months by now and there are months still to go. Sea voyages, storms, pirates, disease, hunger. At last you are in Macao on the coast of Cathay and you know that this is the end of your life, that here you will die and you will never again see the land of your birth, your family, your brothers and sisters, and the first thing that you think about is those less fortunate than yourself. You order a building constructed for the *Santa Casa da Misericordia* to take care of the downtrodden. This is why God sent him here; this is why God sent me here." Bishop Ramalho stopped and smiled at the Governor. The Governor thought that that may all be very well, but the Church is going to have to do something for me.

The nun came back into the room holding two plates with an omelet on each. There were mushrooms but otherwise the omelets were plain, pale yellow on a plain white plate. There was salt, no pepper.

"Bishop," the Governor said quickly to forestall any further digression. He leaned forward towards the Bishop. "I need your help. All of what we love about Macao is in peril. The threats against Macao are growing each day. The Japanese may seize us; we all may die of hunger. We have never been in a more fragile situation than we are now. Macao may not survive as a part of Catholic Portugal." The Governor knew he was being a little more dramatic than the facts warranted, but he wanted the Bishop's attention.

The Bishop looked at him. Both his and the Governor's glasses of wine were untouched. He said mildly "I am sure our Lord looks down kindly on our city. It was the first Christian city in all of China."

The Governor raised an eyebrow. "If He is looking down kindly on Macao right now, I can only conclude that he is inordinately fond of leprosy and starvation." He paused, realizing that he should not have said that. The frank and blunt habits of the wardroom of a naval ship were hard to break. But the calm expression on Bishop Ramalho's face did not change. He was waiting with patience. The Governor continued.

"I want you to place the City of Macao under the special protection of God. In particular, I want to take the statue of *Nossa Senhora de Fátima,* the statue of the Blessed Virgin, our Lady of Fatima, that is so special to Portugal. I want to remove it from St Dominic's, parade it through the City in front of the people and place it in the Cathedral." He gestured with a broad sweep of his left arm, as though the Bishop might not know where the Cathedral was. "This is the mother church for all of Macao; in that way all of the City will know that we are under her protection. We will celebrate Mass in thanks." He waited to see what the Bishop would say. The Bishop was quiet for a while, then simply said:

"The congregation of St Dominic's has worshiped Our Lady of the Holy Rosary of Fatima since I came to Macao. They may not welcome her image being removed and taken to the Cathedral."

The Governor met this argument with impatience. "You are their spiritual father. The priests have taken a vow of obedience to you. They will do what you say. And if there is a problem with the parishioners, tell them it is something that I want and that, should they have questions, they are welcome to talk to me." He knew that this would not happen.

The Bishop looked at the Governor and continued in the same mild tone. "We do not know God's plans for Macao. I do not presume to tell Him what His course of action should be."

The door opened and the nun entered again, her long habit brushing the floor of the dining room. She was holding two plates of pineapple slices and lychees. She put them down and left with the two plates that had held the omelets. The Governor began to speak but the Bishop held up his hand. The nun re-entered holding a silver pot with a curved handle like a squirrel's tail. The Governor realized that the Bishop was serving some of his precious stock of coffee. Perhaps Doctor Lobo had given him some. The Governor talked in a calmer tone of voice although he was conscious of the effort to control his impatience.

"Bishop Ramalho, I think that in this as in many things we can discern the will of God. You yourself said that we were the first Christian city in all of Asia. He will want to save this tiny island of believers in a sea of unbelievers." The Governor appeared to relax his posture and smiled. "It won't be the first time that the Blessed Virgin has protected Macao. I am told that when the Dutch tried to take Macao all those years ago, as they had taken Malacca, that the statue of the Blessed Virgin left the Chapel of Our Lady of Guia and spread her cloak to catch the enemies' bullets before they could do harm."

There was silence for a while. The Bishop appeared to be thinking and then he began to speak. "When would you like to do this?" There was no change of expression on his face to indicate that he had stopped weighing what the Governor had asked him and had made up his mind to comply. The Governor looked at the Bishop and said abruptly.

"We will do this on May 13th, the feast day of the Virgin of Fatima. There will be a procession with the statue from St Dominic's to the Cathedral. You will find a niche high in a wall in the Cathedral for the statue so that she can be seen by all. I think we will need an inscription. I will let you know what that should be."

The Bishop ignored the peremptory tone of the Governor and said calmly "It would be good for the people to see the Blessed Virgin and be reminded at the time of their greatest trouble to turn to our Lord. I will speak to the priests at St Dominic's."

The sky on the morning of May 13th that the Governor had fixed for the procession was almost azure, and by 10:00am, the sun had just come over the hills from the east, tinting the roofs and spires of Macao with its golden glow. The senior officials of Macao were assembling outside St. Dominic's The Governor was in the summer uniform of a naval captain; there was his *Chefe de Gabinete*, Jose Joaquim Costa e Silva, in a dark suit; Bishop Ramalho in scarlet robes; the Police Chief, Captain Alberto Carlos Rodrigues da Cunha, in his blue dress uniform; Dr P.J. Lobo in a khaki suit; the two consuls from Great Britain and Japan, each in their diplomatic uniform. Reeves's uniform of white drill with simple narrow silver piping looked quite ordinary compared to the Japanese consul's of dark royal blue with elaborate arabesques of gold cord on its sleeves and all over its front. Reeves thought of the Japanese consul solemnly taking part in a parade intended to ask God to protect Macao against the Japanese. If asked, Reeves suspected Mr. Fukui would say that he was simply a guest in a ceremony in a neutral country that Japan had no designs on. Reeves thought that he would have done the same if he had been in Mr. Fukui's position.

There was already a crowd outside St Dominic's when the official party assembled: the priests from the church, the cathedral and elsewhere, some of the congregation of St Dominic's and their families who had come to farewell the statue, lesser government officials not in the official party. All were in uniform or the dresses and suits saved for special occasions. Even the little boys were in dark jackets, white shirts and ties, although they were wearing shorts, not trousers. The little girls wore white dresses with bright colored ribbons. The Governor was pleased with the large crowd. In truth, the Governor really did not believe that God would intercede to save Macao. But if Macao was truly threatened, he needed to do something to rally and unite its people. This religious ceremony would serve. And then, it was hard to shake off a Catholic upbringing. Perhaps God would help after all.

There was no breeze on the *Largo do Senado* which St. Dominic's faced, and it was very hot; summer had already begun. Upon the arrival of the official party, the long line of the procession started to form. First came the Bishop, then the Governor, the senior military officers, the other senior government officials, the two consuls, the priests in black robes, and then everyone else in no particular order.

The procession had barely formed when out of the double center doors of St Dominic came four young seminarians in long black robes carrying the statue of Our Lady of Fatima on two long poles. The statue was painted plaster, not stone, and the seminarians were having no trouble carrying it. She was about four-foot tall with a gold and cream cloak over an undergarment of a delicate light blue. The two palms of her hands, coming out of the broad sleeves of both garments, had been brought together and were raised quite high in prayer or a blessing. Her head was tilted slightly to one side, looking up, her face blank. She seemed to be unaware of her new role as the protector of Macao. On her head was a very tall crown in a gold lattice-work that seemed to float by itself. Perhaps it was a miracle that the crown rested on her head without tumbling to the ground. The black-robed seminarians carrying the statue moved to the front of the procession. It began to move across the square towards the narrow street that led up the hill to the cathedral.

As the procession moved up the hill, Reeves felt the spectators lining the street crowding in from both sides. It would be so easy for someone to toss a bomb or fire a pistol into the procession then disappear in the crowd and the tangle of alleys behind it. He could die here in the middle of a procession shuffling up a hill towards a small cathedral. He would have red blood stains on his white consular uniform and his name would be added to a brass plaque in the Foreign Office in London commemorating its officers and employees who had died while in service. There would be a notice in the next issue of his university magazine alongside the obituaries of its graduates who had been killed that quarter, in far more noble circumstances, while serving in the Armed Forces. Would people remember him? The procession soon reached the safety of the cathedral. Reeves concluded that he really was never in danger.

The four seminarians took the statue of the Virgin of Fatima inside. The doors closed for several minutes and then opened. The official party entered and those from the procession who could fit inside the Cathedral. There was no sign of the statue; Reeves thought that it would have been prominently displayed. The rest of the procession waited outside, watching through the open doors. The mass was long: there was a sermon by the Bishop that Reeves could not follow, hymns led by a choir, several bible readings, prayers and then the communion. Despite the open doors, the air inside soon was stale and hot. Reeves began to sweat inside his uniform; it wrinkled and the crease in the trousers that his valet had so carefully produced that morning with a hot iron disappeared in the damp fabric.

The last congregant in a long line had taken the wafer and drunk from the communion cup; the mass ended. But there was no benediction and recessional from the organ. The Bishop and the Governor came around instead to the side of the Cathedral, quite close to where Reeves was sitting. The two stopped in front of a small pair of closed curtains hanging from a brass rod high in the wall, as though they were waiting for a puppet show to begin. The Bishop and the Governor knelt before it, the Bishop on both knees, the Governor on one. The Bishop said a short prayer and then both got up. They stood on either side of the closed curtains facing the wall and then the Bishop, with an air of a magician at the climax of a complicated illusion, reached up and with a small cord, pulled open the two curtains.

There in a niche was the gold, cream and blue plaster statue of Our Lady of the Holy Rosary of Fatima; her tall lattice crown still precariously on her tilted head with her upturned eyes and expressionless face. Behind her in two-inch-high letters of bronze were the words ``*Rainha do Mundo, Mae Portugal, Amparai Macau"* which Reeves mentally translated as "Queen of the World, Mother of Portugal, Protect Macao." Well, he thought, it cannot do any harm. And it might do some good. As the congregants and the official party filed out of the church and onto the square in front of it, Reeves could see Mr. Fukui at the front of the crowd talking earnestly to the Governor.

* * *

That night, Mr. Fukui asked his secretary, Mr. Taki, to stay late, together with Mr. Matsumoto, the consular code clerk. He was going to send a cable on Macao to the head of the Japanese Consular Service for Asia. He knew the Army wanted to seize Macao; he hoped that in some small way he could stiffen the resolve of the Foreign Ministry to oppose it.

The heat of the day continued into the night and the usual evening breezes off the sea were absent. Even then, Mr. Fukui insisted on the windows being closed and the heavy curtains drawn so that they might work in secrecy. The electric light would flicker on and off; Mr. Fukui had had several oil lamps lit and soon the room was oppressively hot. The flames from the burning wicks in the lamps cast dark dancing shadows on the ceiling, like thunderclouds racing in an approaching storm. Despite the heat, Mr. Fukui kept his jacket on and the other two men did the same, not wanting to remove them if Mr. Fukui did not.

He started to dictate his cable. He did not spend much time on the importance of keeping good relations with Portugal. The Foreign Office had over one hundred diplomats in Lisbon, some of whom were valuable spies, and knew that already. They did not want to risk their expulsion by Portugal in retaliation for a Japanese invasion of Macao. He went almost immediately to talk about Macao itself.

He attempted to make the case that Macao had benefits for Japan. It is a transit point for the trade in wolfram, which Japan's ally Germany finds useful. It is a source of candlenut oil, which he was told, has certain uses in lubricating our industrial machinery. It is also a source for fibrous matting which is used by our Army and Navy. He knew that this did not sound like much.

He went on to argue that neither Japan or our enemies would gain militarily by occupying Macao – it had no use as a base for the armed forces of either side. Instead, a neutral Macao could be a valuable source of information and intelligence. He knew that this was not true; the great events of the world that might have interested the government in Japan bypassed Macao. Little could be learned here.

He ended with asking the head of the Asian Consular Service to, should he agree, to use his influence in the right ministries to convince the Prime Minister and the Cabinet of the wisdom of leaving Macao alone. Mr. Fukui would rely on his secretary to add the usual salutations, pleasantries, the right measure of humility and the appropriate amount of praise and deference he owed those of a higher rank to whom the cable was addressed.

Mr. Taki and Mr. Matsumoto bowed and left the oven-like room, the sweat on their faces looking orange and gold in the light from the flame in the oil lamps. Mr. Taki would produce a draft of the cable, which Mr. Fukui knew that it would be excellent and that he would have few changes. Mr. Matsumoto had already begun work to encrypt it.

He walked to the windows facing the street, drew the curtains and raised the window frames up to finally let in some air. He stood, his hands behind his back, his jacket still on and buttoned, but with a light, almost imperceptible, breeze cooling his damp face. With the electricity cuts, none of the street lamps was illuminated and he could see little of Macao beyond vague shapes in the shadows that could have been anything. He knew that the Army who wanted to seize Macao would find out about his cable and he would have more enemies. Colonel Sawa would undoubtedly come around to berate him. He was giving Colonel Sawa one more reason to hate him. He thought of the parade and the service that morning. He thought of that strange little figure of the girl that they had carried into the cathedral and hidden behind a curtain until the end. She was nothing more than a large doll. Did they really think she could help Macao? How was she going to do it? He was the only one who could help Macao now.

Chapter 16

In the weeks following the procession from St. Dominic's to the cathedral to install the Virgin of Fatima to watch over Macao, the threat that had loomed so large before faded and then seemed to vanish. Colonel Ride reported that the Japanese troops that had been seen moving south to Macao had withdrawn to Canton and that some had been sent west and north to reinforce the troops fighting the Chinese armies in central China. Dr. P.J. Lobo was able to barter scrap iron, the little Portuguese gunboat the *Patria*, parts of the dismantled Navy squadron of six biplanes and free passage for wolfram to Germany, for new supplies of rice and oil. There was rain later that summer and vegetables in quantity appeared in the markets. The war again was something that was happening elsewhere. Macao was once again at peace.

Reeves was relieved. He gave less thought to the war. If it was his destiny to be fighting in it, fate, or the British Government, would have arranged it. He would have a good war as they say and he became more comfortable with that. He would do his duty in Macao.

He spent more time now with his friends Pat Heenan and Ed Redden in the old Pan American hangar. Pat Heenan of the Royal Life Insurance Company was living there with Ed Redden. Both men had little to do: Pat was not underwriting any life insurance and the last plane Pan American had flown to Macao – the little Sikorsky S 42 up from Manila – had been attacked by Japanese aircraft and sunk in Hong Kong harbor when war broke out nearly two years ago. Nevertheless, both men continued to receive a salary and were enjoying life in a way Reeves envied.

They were jolly men, free from the cares of the world. When Reeves was with them, he too felt happy and free of care. He would take the consulate's Studebaker and drive it down to the hangar. Redden would close the enormous double doors of the hangar on the side that faced the city so you would not have to see or even think about Macao. Then he would throw open the doors at the other end of the hangar – the ones that faced the harbor and the South China Sea – and the cool breezes would come in while they sat with their drinks and their meals in the shade.

Redden would sometimes take them out in the Pan American launch. All three of them would be in shorts, no shirts, and they would go out of the harbor and into the sea. When out of sight of land, or when it was just a distant line of green and black shadow on the horizon, Redden would cut the engine, let the launch drift, so that it rocked to and fro in the silence, the small waves gently slapping the hull, and talk about what they would all do after the war. Heenan would lie back on the cushions in the stern of the boat and talk about getting out of the insurance industry. He would go live in Spain – he had lived there after he left school and spoke excellent Spanish, or perhaps somewhere in Latin America. Somewhere he said he could keep his beard. If the District Manager of the Royal Life Insurance Company could see him now, he would be sacked, or at least made to shave it off, and he had grown to like it. Redden talked about getting out of Macao and joining the Navy. He had been in the Naval Reserve before the war and the Navy could use men like him who knew how to fly. After that, he didn't know. Back to Colorado and ranch. Get married. Find another post with Pan American. Perhaps in Europe. There was cold beer in an ice chest and it tasted good.

Reeves thought about what to say. His was a life, so far, of being told what to do. When the war was over, it would be hard to see what would happen to the China Consular Service, or what was left of it, now that it had been subsumed within the regular consular service. The war would sweep away the old China with its treaty ports and gated settlements and the merchants, consuls and officials from the legations who ruled there would be swept away along with it. He wanted to stay in the Consular Service, with a posting in New York or Paris or Valparaiso or anywhere. He thought that his extraordinary service in Macao, which was really part of Portugal, would cause him to be noticed and he would be posted out of Asia. They would need to build a new world after the war was over and he wanted to be part of it. It was hard to imagine the war would actually end but surely it must someday.

Rhoda had asked Reeves to try to move close to England after the war and he had agreed. Rhoda was two generations away from England; she and both parents had been born and grown up in Shanghai. England was a mythic place; a place they called home, but with their friends and relatives and their lives all in China. Rhoda clung to an idea of England that existed only in her head, composed of snatches of conversations, old novels, some from the last century, and bound volumes of equally old illustrated magazines on her parents' bookshelves; an England of the imagination that would solve all her problems she believed.

Reeves had not discussed with her what he wanted to do when he got to Europe. They rarely talked anymore. But if he was to raise this issue, he was afraid that she would not understand how his job in Europe fitted into her vision of the mythical England, and when she did not understand, she turned inwards, away from him. But with Redden and Heenan, he talked freely of his ambitions and they paid him the courtesy of listening with solemn attention.

Later, when they were back at the hangar, if it was not too hot, they would drag a couch outside and sit there. If it was very hot, they would drag it to the open door so that they could just stay in the shade, the three of them sitting in a row, still without their shirts while the sun went down on the other side of Macao. Redden would serve what he called a Pan American cocktail. He had a large collection of liquor bottles, some from a supply used to resupply aircraft, and some gifts from stewards who knew that they could account for them as consumed by the passengers. Redden would take an empty bottle and randomly selecting a full or partially full bottle from the shelves would pour a shot into the empty one. He would then repeat the process with other bottles until the empty bottle had been filled. It would be borne triumphantly out on a tray, together with three glasses. An inch of the mixture would be poured into each glass and the tradition was that Redden would say one, two, three and then the three men would drain their glasses in a single gulp. There was often coughing and spluttering, but the second part of the tradition was, once that was over and their eyes had finished watering, Redden would say "Damn, that was good." No matter how many times he said it, they always laughed.

Then Redden and Heenan would bring out a spirit stove and put it on the pavement in front of the couch. Redden would light it and put a large pot on top of the stand. In would go whatever one of the Chinese servants had found in the market: pork hocks but rarely, fish, fish guts, chicken, chicken guts, root vegetables, greens, some fruit, especially pineapple and lychees, black beans, rice wine, rice, ginger, *balichao* – a particularly pungent fermented local fish sauce, soy sauce, *chili vinagre,* dried blood from God knows what animal. It would boil for a while and then Redden would produce a ladle, three bowls and spoons. "Ladies and Gentlemen," he would say, his voice booming out in imitation of a circus ringmaster before bowing elaborately, "Children of all ages, presenting in the center ring, the one, the only, the toast of all of Europe and North America, the world renowned Pan American stew." Again, they laughed every time. Reeves was surprised by how often it tasted good, but maybe that was just the hot spices. Or just sharing a meal with good friends. Or just the drink.

When the sun went down and dusk settled down over the harbor, they would pull the couch back in the hangar. There in the soft light from the oil lamps Redden would bring out, they would continue to talk, this time a little more quietly. They would talk of family, of friends whom they had not seen, things they regretted, first loves, what they missed from back home. Reeves did not talk about Rhoda and Letitia – here they seemed far from his mind, but would talk about things he never discussed at home – his parents, now elderly, growing up in the English countryside, his life at University, Molly Kaye, the woman he had spent two weeks with in Peking when he was a student-interpreter there and who never wrote back when Reeves wrote to her at her home in Simla.

They would finish one bottle of the Pan American cocktail mixture and Redden would pull another bottle off the shelf and they would start into that. Later in the evening, quite drunk, Reeves would get into his car. It knows its way home, he would say to himself, it's like an old brewery horse that finds its way back to its stable with the carter asleep on the wagon. Redden and Heenan are my best friends.

Then one day they were gone. Reeves drove down to the hangar, unlocked the doors with the keys Redden had given him, and walked in. He knew they would not be there; he had helped them escape out of Macao. The Portuguese authorities in Macao did not care who came and went but the Japanese prohibited anyone leaving Macao without their permission. Reeves had gotten a certificate of Spanish nationality for Heenan from a sympathetic Portuguese official – Heenan spoke the language after all and the Japs were never going to hear the distinct Liverpudlian accent in some of his pronunciations. Spain was an ally of Germany and Germany was an ally of Japan in its fight against Americans and the Japanese gave him permission, as a Spanish national, to book passage on the little ship that still ran between Macao and the French treaty port of Kwang Chow Wan, still run by French administrators, on the far west of the southern coast of China. Once there, he simply had to cross a bridge to be in Free China and it was really just a walk and a train ride over a few days to Kunming and Chungking where the British Embassy would help him. Wong Kong-kit at Reeves's request had smuggled Redden and Earl Stubbs, the manager of the Pan American radio station, out of Macao on a junk one night and delivered them to agents of the BAAG working under Colonel Ride on the mainland who in their turn had guided them over the long land journey to Chungking.

Reeves liked to imagine that Redden and Heenan had just walked around the corner and would be back any moment. The pin-ups from the American magazines were still on the walls, smiling near-naked girls dressed only in a few wisps of fabric. There were the travel posters from places he could only dream of; there was the smell of Redden's and Heenan's sweat on the couch; there was the faint smell of the last Pan

American stew that they had shared together; there were the few liquor bottles left on the shelves. He took one down, found a glass – it was dirty but he did not care – and poured a drink – of what? It did not matter. They were really good friends, he thought.

One day Reeves went down to the hangar, but did not go in. He went around it and along to the small stubby wharf, where the Pan American launch was still tied. Reeves knew where Redden had a key to the motor hidden and he knew that there was still petrol in the tank. He untied the lines, fore and aft, and jumped aboard, afraid it might drift out from the wharf before he had gotten in. He turned the key and the motor started immediately.

That morning he had gotten an encrypted message from the British Embassy in Chungking from someone he had never heard of, no one from the Foreign Office, ordering him to seize the launch and "arrange for it to be delivered to the authorities in Free China." How on earth was he going to do that? Have Wong Kong-kit's pirates motor it up the West River to Samfou and then take it in pieces overland to Chungking ? Besides, it did not belong to the British. It belonged to his friends Ed Redden and Pat Heenan, and he was going to save it for them until they got back, when the three of them could once again take it out into the South China Sea, cut the engine, drift in the gentle summer waves and sit in the stern together to tell stories. He knew what he was going to do. He would do it in a way that he would never be reprimanded, no one important would find out. He owed that to Ed Redden.

He put the engines into reverse and backed it out away from the little wharf, just as he had seen Redden do it. He had always had a hard time making it go astern. But then Reeves was in the middle of the *Porto Exterior* and heading to a gap in the breakwater. Soon he was out in the South China Sea, the motor of the launch throbbing beneath his feet, the bow tilted up slightly as the launch picked up speed, the rhythmic bumps over the small waves, the wind in his hair and the flashing silver glint of the warm sun on the rippling sea, He swung the launch around the southern tip of the Macao peninsula and headed north past the *Porto*

Interior to the Portuguese Navy Yard. They were waiting for him there. He pulled next to a long pier; a cradle made out of thick canvas straps was lowered into the water by a crane, and Reeves slowly maneuvered the launch into it, like a horse slipping into a carriage harness. The launch was lifted out of the water and put on a trailer to be stored in a corner of the boat yard. Neutral Portugal would never release the launch until the war was over and then only to its rightful owner, Ed Redden. He cabled Chungking and told them that he no longer had possession of the launch and that their request should be addressed to the Portuguese authorities. He never heard back.

Sometime later, Reeves heard that Redden had left China on an aeroplane; Reeves had never been on an aeroplane, Redden flying from Chungking over the highest mountains in the world blanketed with thick snow even in the hottest days of the summer when the sun scorched you in Macao, over the jungles of Burma, on to India with elephants, and rajahs dressed in white silks stitched together with gold thread, through to Egypt where he flew over the pyramids, through French Africa, with the mud forts where Beau Geste of Reeves's boyhood fought the marauding Bedouins, and onto Brazil with parrots and emeralds, San Juan – on a tropical island – and finally Miami, where there were palm trees, everyone drove a new convertible car, and there were beautiful girls in bathing suits. Reeves slowly realized that Redden would never return to Macao.

In the end, Reeves wanted to put the memories of Redden and Heenan behind him and he stopped going to the Pan American hangar. Instead, when he wanted to be by himself, he would walk through the parish of Saint Anthony to the Protestant Cemetery. The cemetery, with its small painfully plain chapel in one corner, was surrounded on all sides with a high wall, high enough that none of the surrounding buildings or any of the city could be seen. The wall also shut out the noise of the city; all Reeves could hear was the faint rustle of distant leaves in the tall trees that bent over the graveyard like priests pronouncing a blessing, the shading branches held out over the gravestones in benediction. There was peace for him here too.

Tall weeds grew thick and dense on what had been the paths between the gravestones. Someone before him had pushed through to create a narrow track through the center of the graveyard. A tree growing in one corner had blown down, actually snapped like a pencil – it must have happened in a typhoon – and crushed several gravestones. Some others had fallen down completely, flat on the ground like soldiers slain in a long-forgotten battle, or the gravestones were leaning against each other like grieving mourners. Nearly every stone was covered with vines, creepers and thick moss, covering the inscriptions.

Reeves visited the cemetery often. He would bring with him a small pair of garden secateurs and a wide putty knife, clear the vines and creepers away from some of the stones and scrape off the moss and fungus so that he could make out some of the inscriptions. What Chinese stonecutters incised these words on stones, not knowing the letters or what the words meant? Here the dead of a century ago slept side by side undisturbed: The four sailors from the American ship *Marion*; Mrs. Seth with half her tombstone covered with writing in Armenian; a commander of a ship called the *Futty Mombarruck*; a woman with the first name of Euphemia; the man who brought the telegraph to Japan; the babies on this earth but a few days; a man "who sleeps under the shadow of the cross;" Sarah Anne, the wife of Captain George Balls, who had died at the age of 28, buried with the inscription 'The Lord gave and the Lord hath taken away. Blessed be the name of the Lord;" the Malacca coroner, a man who, after 23 years in the East, drowned 'on the eve of his return home.' Disease, drowning, murder by pirates, a plunge from a ship's rigging, a fatal surrender to a hostile climate, unfamiliar food, sharks, cholera, dysentery, sunstroke, wounds, foul water, fever. They were all here, the dead men, women, children, infants, forgotten by their descendants still living. Sometimes Reeves found scarlet poinsettia flowers pushing through the dank green weeds and rising next to a stone tombstone. *Media vita in morte sumus.* In the midst of life, we are in death, he thought.

But if the dead could sleep peacefully for all those years until the last trump when they will be raised incorruptible, then the quick could also be at peace. Reeves would come to the rough wall, push open the door and close it behind him. He would find the sarcophagus that he had cleared and cleaned, so that it was like a small stone island close to the middle of the graveyard. He would lie down on the flat tombstone that surmounted it, stretch out and look up. It was summer. He had brought wind chimes to hang in the lower branches of the trees and he would close his eyes to listen to their faint tinkling. The frangipani trees were in full leaf and flower, enveloping the graveyard with shade except where shafts of sunlight shot through the branches to pick out gravestones to mark with beams. A brief breeze blew above and a small shower of petals from the pink and yellow flowers on the tall swaying trees fluttered down like a snowfall of butterfly wings on him, the green undergrowth and the fallen trees. *Media vita in morte sumus.* In the midst of life, we are in death, all of us, him, his wife and daughter, everyone in Macao. His ambitions, such as they were, seemed small. Soon, we would soon be as forgotten as the people who were laid under these stones a hundred years ago. Reeves was, for the moment, at peace.

Chapter 17

Throughout 1943, Reeves helped many of the people who had fled to Macao or been trapped in Macao to escape to Free China and then on to India and England or America. By now the number was approaching one hundred and he had arranged for each one of them to leave. He was the one, using a special imprest account he had been given just for this purpose, who gave them the cash needed for the journey – a bundle of American, Macanese, Hong Kong and Chinese National bills, plus some Japanese military scrip that no one managed to spend and everyone threw away at the end of the journey. He was the one who paid the pirates to smuggle them out of Macao by sea under the very noses of the Japanese – "my good friend Wong Kong-kit will take care of your ocean voyage" he had said on more than one occasion trying to be jocular in very tense times. He was the liaison to Colonel Ride's BAAG which would oversee the long land journey to Chungking from the little bay on the mainland where Wong Kong-kit's pirates would land them. It was 750 miles to Chungking if you drew a straight line on a map, but since they would be walking, or bicycling or in sampans, trucks or trains, on paths, tracks, streams and rivers that twisted, turned, and sometimes doubled back, they were told to expect a journey of nearly 1,200 miles.

Reeves wondered sometimes whether he and Rhoda should try to leave Macao. He doubted Rhoda could put up with the long grueling journey to Chungking. They would be sleeping in huts and barns; there would be cold, hunger, and miles of hard walking. How would Letitia even cope? Although Mrs. Fletcher had escaped: she was the wife of the Chairman of Macao's electric company whose husband had been caught in England at the start of the war and was unable to return to Macao. And she took her two boys, aged six and eight with her. They had reached Kunming after seven weeks and then they all had been flown to India and on to England to rejoin Mr. Fletcher. But she was a hearty determined woman and her two boys were full of life. Rhoda and Letitia were nothing like them. He decided they would never be able to make the journey. He took comfort in his thoughts that England during the war was a place of grim privation, food and fuel rationed, and the constant threat of German bombing. He could convince himself if he could not convince Rhoda that they were far better off in Macao.

Could Reeves even leave if he wanted to? He was here because the Foreign Office wanted a consul in Macao. He would need to get permission to leave; he would have to give an acceptable reason that was not mere restlessness and even then permission would inevitably be denied. If he left without permission, he would be summarily dismissed from the Consular Service and then what would he do? Drift through war-torn China with a wife and daughter in tow? He knew he could not leave Macao until the war ended and the Foreign Office decided what to do with him. He envied each group he saw depart. I am a bird in a gilded cage, he thought.

He would often think of seven in particular who escaped Macao, just after Redden and Heenan, at the end of summer in 1943. Six had been in the British Army in Hong Kong and had escaped from the Shamshuipo camp where they had been imprisoned after the colony's surrender. They had been guided through the New Territories of Hong Kong, dodging Japanese patrols, by the East River Guerrillas (who were communists but the six escapees did not mind) to a deserted bay, and then taken by Wong Kong-kit's men in a junk to Macao, hidden below decks in the hold. The seventh was a civilian, Mr. Williamson, a senior engineer with the Hong Kong Telephone Company, who had an Irish identity card and had made this first part of the journey as a citizen of a neutral nation simply by buying a ferry ticket from Hong Kong to Macao and showing his identity card to the Japanese guards on the docks. The only officer of the seven was Captain Hadley of the Royal Scots and he was to command the group on its journey to Chungking. Captain Hadley looked very young –

he had a mustache that struggled to grow – but the group looked to him as their leader. Captain Hadley seemed unsure about assuming this role.

They had spent a lot of time at the consulate with Reeves, coming by his office or even the residence and drinking his rice wine liquor. Rhoda did not like it when they came round to the consulate. She thought the men were 'licentious,' and Reeves wondered who used a word like that anymore. But Rhoda had grown up in an isolated English community in China who had not seen England in some cases for generations, and it really should not surprise him that she was closer to the idioms of her Victorian forebears than those of her contemporaries.

Hadley would often stay after the men had left to drunkenly stumble back to their accommodation. He told Reeves stories of the fall of Hong Kong, the hopeless bloody battles, the deaths of friends, the shambles of the retreat to the far side of Hong Kong Island, the surrender and their imprisonment in Shamshuipo. The camp was a nightmare. Little food, men reduced to skeletons, no medicines, rags for clothing, scores dying each day from dysentery – "sitting on the crapper and shitting your life away" as one said. Reeves wondered how he would do in battle and in the horrors of a Japanese prison. Reeves loved these conversations; he felt somehow honored that Hadley would share these memories with him. Reeves imagined Hadley and his men would all ride out the war with him in Macao together. He could take care of them.

But Macao had gradually worn on them. After several weeks, they chafed at the enforced idleness. A twenty-year soldier who had spent his entire service in Hong Kong in various clerical capacities in the Quartermaster's Corps wanted to join a regiment in India, far from the fighting, where he could find a dark-skinned woman to keep as a wife in a little flat, and pay someone to sweep the barracks so he would not have to do it, just as he had done in Hong Kong. That's how you have a good war, he had said, more than once. When the fighting was over, he was going to take his pension and retire from the Army, not in England, but somewhere in the East with that same dark-skinned girl, a little cottage by the sea, the sound of the bells of temples and incense drifting in the air like the poem says. Someone else could fight for King, Country and Empire, if there still was an empire. Others were eager to rejoin the fighting for a bit of excitement. Mr. Williamson of the Hong Kong Telephone Company was tired of working for the Japanese in Hong Kong. He could join the Posts and Telegraph Department in India and have a bungalow there with servants and a garden. Captain Hadley believed that, if he could get to India, he would be posted to a regiment, and the exigencies of wartime would increase his chance of the promotion that had so far eluded him. Reeves listened to this and thought that outside of Macao there was nothing for him.

Reeves as he got to know Captain Hadley had the impression that he was a little adrift in the Army. Captain Hadley had a mild manner and his orders to the men seemed more in the nature of polite requests. The habit of command did not seem to come naturally. He had not gone to Sandhurst but had joined the Officers Training Corps at his not very good university. He had joined up right after his graduation – 'anyone could see that the war was coming" – and had been posted to the Royal Scots in Hong Kong. He never quite fitted in the officers' mess and he thought his colonel disapproved of him, which is why he was still waiting for his next promotion. "Never liked my haircut, the Colonel, as far as I could tell; told me that with a haircut like that I would spend twenty years in the Army and still be a captain." He talked about the bloody chaos of the Japanese onslaught on Hong Kong, the deaths of so many of the officers and men of his regiment, his survival purely by chance (he had been sent back from the front lines on some sort of an errand), the donkey-like stupidity of some of his superior officers. After the war, he would like to stay in the Army if they could find a place for him. Hard to think of what else he would do. He was sure he would be needed in his small way to keep the peace in the world that would emerge. Reeves thought that he had a lot in common with Captain Hadley. He was a friend.

The night before they were to leave Macao, Reeves came down to the filthy little godown where the escapees were waiting. He brought two gallons of rice wine liquor in a big gray stone jar and they had all gotten drunk together, Reeves sitting on some empty packing crate just like the others, not caring about getting his trousers dirty. The escapees were dressed in a motley selection of clothes: some were in shorts, others wore parts of their old uniform, combined with Chinese singlets, pajamas and jackets. Nearly all wore the locally made canvas trainers with rubber soles made from old automobile tires. Only Mr. Williamson looked like he was properly prepared for a lengthy trek, dressed in the heavy boots and khaki drill pants and jacket he wore when he had been inspecting telephone lines in the countryside deep in the New Territories. Each had a large haversack made of a rough canvas worn on a strap over a shoulder. Captain Hadley had a British Army-issue Webley pistol and fifty rounds of ammunition that he had gotten from Reeves, who in turn had gotten it from the BAAG's Macao agents. One pistol amongst seven of them, thought Captain Hadley, wouldn't make much of a difference against bandits or guerrillas or the Japanese army.

Reeves had brought down to the warehouse such food for the journey that he was able to procure and they had divided it up between them – bottles of sugar, tins of British Army-issue bully beef that had made its way to Macao's black market, several large rusty tins of American Quaker oats, tins of loose tea, tins of sardines, tins of Chinese curried chicken, tinned pineapple, tins of condensed milk, boxes of hard biscuits and two waterproof tins of matches. It all went in the haversacks along with a few spare pieces of clothing, a blanket, an enamel plate and mug, and an empty water canteen for each man. Captain Hadley shook hands with Reeves as Reeves prepared to leave. We will get together after the war, he said with a laugh, we will be a splendid team, you can run the Foreign Office and I can be Field Marshal of the whole army. Then we will show them. Reeves drove back to the consulate. He would miss Captain Hadley. All his friends had left Macao.

* * *

It was around 4:00am and still dark when a Chinese man came into the warehouse where the men were lying on the floor sleeping off Reeves's rice wine liquor, even Captain Hadley. The man shouted something in Cantonese and gestured for them to follow, turning abruptly to leave the warehouse. They all stepped out in a very dark street; the street lamps were not lit and there was not another person they could see. They walked single-file down the street towards the docks; the only sound was the occasional clank of the tins of food banging together in their haversacks.

When they crossed the *Praya Grande*, also deserted, they came to a wood and tin shed at the head of one of the wharves. The Chinese guide gestured for them to wait in its shadows and then walked down the wharf. He was gone for what seemed like a long time and then returned, waving an arm for them to follow. Captain Hadley was in the lead, his hand resting on the haversack with the Webley pistol, although it would have taken too much time to remove it from there if he had actually had need of it. A large Japanese coastal freighter was tied alongside the wharf. They could see no guards on it, but all assumed they had to be there.

At the end of the wharf, the Chinese man halted and pointed down at the water at the side of the wharf. Through the darkness, they could see two sampans, low in the water and tied at the bow and stern. A bare-footed man stood in the stern of each sampan holding a sweep oar. The men instinctively walked hunched over, fearing a shot from the unseen guards on the freighter.

They climbed down a ladder onto the platform and the men divided themselves between the two sampans. When they were all in the two boats, they floated barely a few inches above the water. The Chinese guide untied the two boats, the men at the stern of the sampans leaned into the sweep oars and the two boats glided between the anchored junks on which whole families were still sleeping silently. A brief breeze brought the harbor smells of garbage, human waste, rot, mud and salt. There was not a sound except the very faint splash from the sweep oars.

In a few minutes in that gray wet greasy light that comes before dawn, they came to a junk lying at a single anchor away from the tightly packed junks closer to the seawall. The men hauled themselves aboard by the ropes that hung over the side and were motioned to sit down on the deck against the stern cabin and against the railings. The anchor was quickly pulled up and the sail was raised – it unfurled up the mast like a lady's fan being unfolded. The seven men sat tensely on the deck, each expecting at any moment Japanese soldiers to appear on the docks and start shooting at them. In each of their minds was their forcible return to the miseries of the prison camp at Shamshuipo.

The wind came up out of nowhere, the junk began to move forward, slowly heading west. Captain Hadley stood up and looked over the stern east to Macao, where its hills, spires and city walls could be seen low on the horizon in a black silhouette, with the first golden light of sunrise in a frayed glowing fringe on the city's upper edge. Many-towered Camelot, he thought to himself but did not say anything. The men looked back with him; they all felt a sudden regret at leaving the city that had sheltered them. Each turned over in their mind the decision to leave.

Shortly, an unrelenting rain was pelting down, blown right across the deck by a strong northerly wind. A fog soon mixed with the rain and there was no visibility beyond a few yards in any direction. If there were Japanese patrols out there, they could not see them and they could not see the junk. The men, shaking with cold, moved into the little stern cabin but there was no warmth there.

After ten hours with the men fitfully dozing, the junk slowed and a crew member took a bamboo pole from the deck and pushed an end down over the side. He yelled something to the captain; the seven escapees came out of the stern cabin. The wind caused the mist to drift a little and the men saw they were in a small bay, about fifty feet offshore. There was a beach of pebbles rather than sand, a fringe of tall grasses and then thick woods. The captain came over and talked to the twenty-year soldier who had learned some Cantonese in Hong Kong. He came over and told the other six that they were all getting off the junk ('disembarking' was the word he used, intending it to be amusing). They were to lower themselves down the ropes, the water would be only waist-high – it did not matter since they were soaked by the rain – and they were to spend the night. Someone would come for them in the morning. Above the beach, after a struggle, they were able to get a fire going to heat some of their food and dry their clothes.

They all must have slept much more soundly than they thought because they were awakened when it was quite light by sounds of people speaking Chinese. The seven men stood up, straightening themselves up awkwardly and stiffly, blinking in the strong morning sun, unconsciously scratching and rubbing themselves, but very much aware that they were dirty, unshaven, unwashed, smelly and hungry.

Standing in a wide semicircle several yards away from the huts were a few small boys, no more than eight or nine years old and a dozen or so armed men and women. Captain Hadley looked at them again and saw that they were really boys and girls, barely teenagers. Then he realized they were guerrillas. They were dressed in some sort of a uniform: each wore a felt hat or cap with a red star in the center of the the crown; a blue tunic or blouse, all faded; black pajamas tied tight at the ankle with canvas strips in imitation of puttees, and a red scarf knotted around their neck. All had rifles, not all of the same make, and some seemed as big as the teenage boy or girl carrying them. What Captain Hadley as a professional soldier noticed was that all of their weapons had their metal work and wooden stock polished and gleaming. They were actually real soldiers, cradling their weapons like real soldiers, a children's crusade just over the border with Macao and no one seemed aware of it there. Reeves had not warned them if he ever even knew, but the guerrillas were expecting them. Colonel Ride's men must have arranged it.

A girl who had been standing to one side with the look of disdain stepped forward. She did not change the expression on her face nor did she unfold her arms. She was not carrying a weapon.

"I am Comrade Li. I am the political commissar for this district. My orders are to escort you north and give to another group who will eventually see that you are delivered to the British Embassy. It is expected that you will rejoin the fight against the imperialist Japanese army that has invaded China." Captain Hadley thought that the communists had gotten him out of the prisoner of war camp at Shamshuipo and they are now going to deliver me out of Macao to Chungking to serve once again in the British army, where I might end up in battle against them. I live in a rummy world.

Comrade Li grunted another order and one of the teenage boys yelled something. He must be the leader, thought Captain Hadley, although he was really just a schoolboy who ought to have been in class. The little boys scampered off ahead like rabbits and soon were out of sight. The rest formed a column, with a large break in its middle for the seven men to step in to fill. The men slung their haversacks over their shoulder and the column set off. Comrade Li stood to the side watching it walk off down the track towards the woods and then joined it at the very end, walking a few yards behind the last guerrilla, separate, by herself.

After a few hours, the column emerged from the woods and the men realized that they had been climbing up one of the hills that form the low range that fronts the China coast that they had seen from Macao. The hills were taller and more rugged than they seemed from a distance.

They were now on the crest of a hill above the timberline looking down into a valley. Behind them was the South China Sea but, to all their disappointment, they could not see Macao. Somewhere to the north was Chungking. They walked down the hill between terraced rice paddies into the valley. They had finally left Macao behind, for better or for worse. Every one of the men wondered whether they had made the right choice. Captain Hadley thought of Reeves back there, the lonely Union Jack flying over the consulate, Reeves by himself in his office.

They stayed with the guerrillas the next twenty days. They usually ate with them, cooking their own food or eating the few scraps that the villagers or farmers had left out in baskets where the guerrillas could find them. They slept away from the villages or farms, out in the open or in empty farm houses, barns or granaries. They went to sleep to the sounds of rats and woke up with fleas and lice in their clothes that they never could quite get rid of. They rarely saw other people as they trudged towards the northwest; the little boys scampered ahead to scout for bandits, the Japanese, the Kuomintang, the followers of whatever warlord held sway in this part of the province, or whoever else thought the guerrillas would be better dead. When the boys saw anyone, the men and the guerillas hid in ditches or in the woods. They were always hungry.

They found themselves talking about the first meal they had had when they arrived in Macao. The sailors on the junk – later they were told they were pirates led by someone named Wong Kong-kit – had hidden them in a godown near the harbor. Reeves had found them there – such a nice man, they all agreed – and had taken them to a small eating house nearby in the Chinese *barrio,* away from prying eyes he had said. The eating house was really just a few chairs and tables in an alley with a single wok over a wood fire. Each of the men had been given two bowls, one of steamed rice into which a sliced plum and one fresh lychee had been mixed; the other bowl was filled with fried shredded cabbage with black fungus. In that bowl, they could smell the peanut oil used in the frying and the rice vinegar and wine that seasoned it. They would talk about that meal as one of the most delicious they had ever had – the sweetness of the pieces of fruit against the neutral flavor of the rice, the way the fungus or mushrooms had picked up the flavors of the wine and vinegar, how the cabbage managed to be both crisp and moist. It was now how they remembered Macao, it was the paradise after the hell of the prison camp. Paradise seemed a long time ago and far away.

At the end of what they thought was the third week of their walking, they came over a rise and halted on a grassy field overlooking a large village by the side of a broad river. Captain Hadley waited until the men had gathered around him. He was really more like a scoutmaster than an Army officer. He pointed at the river. "You know what that is," he said, "That's the Yangtze."

It looked more like a lake than a river. It stretched across a considerable distance to the river bank on the other side. Comrade Li pointed to a junk tied to a small makeshift wharf and told Captain Hadley that it would take them up the river. The guerrillas were in a line behind them and the small boys had reappeared, hopping nervously around, eager to be moving again. Captain Hadley looked at the river some more and then turned to the guerrillas who had brought them this far. But they were already twenty yards off, heading back to where they had come. Comrade Li never looked back.

The men walked down to the river bank to the wharf where the junk was tied. A benevolent eye with a purple iris had been painted high up on its bow; the soldiers thought there had to be another eye in the same place on the other side. Dozens of strips of red cloth with white characters had been tied to the single mast. The twenty-year soldier said they were prayer flags and he hoped the gods were reading them. They climbed up a rope accommodation ladder that hung down the hull and scrambled onto the deck, their haversacks bumping clumsily.

On a shout from someone, perhaps the captain, one sailor leaped over the side to untie the junk from the wharf, and the sail was unfurled. Twelve of the crew, six on each side, took up oars that had been lying on the deck and lowered them into the water. They were very long and looked very heavy. The junk drifted back a little in an unseen current and the crew on the river bank side pushed it out further into the river with their oars. The junk moved slowly up the Yangtze.

The sun sank lower in the west, it grew dark but the oarsmen kept rowing. Late at night, the junk halted and an oarsman leaped onto the river bank with a rope, one end tied to the mast, to secure the vessel to a large pointed rock. They were all given a little rice and cabbage to eat. The crew brought out their opium pipes and then wrapped themselves in quilted blankets and lay down on the deck. The men slept in the stern cabin. All night, through the cracks in the walls of the cabin, they could see the flicker like fireflies of the pale orange lights of the crews' opium lamps and could smell the sickly sweet smell of the opium itself.

They were woken very early the next morning just after dawn by the cook banging on the walls of the stern cabin. When they came out on deck, they saw a plain bowl of rice with a little shredded cabbage for each of them waiting on the deck. The eyes of the crew were bloodshot, from alcohol or opium or both, and they stared at the ground before raising the sail and letting the junk proceed up the Yangtze.

For seven days, they sailed up the river; it rained nearly constantly and the clouds were low in the sky, pushing down damply on the junk. They ate their two bowls of rice each day and some of the tinned food from their haversacks. During the eighth day by the time the junk anchored for the night, the rain had stopped and the sky was a broad plum-purple velvet expanse with jewel-like glistening points of light from the stars. The moored junk gently and soothingly swayed; the breeze that drifted over the junk was warm.

When they awoke the next morning, they could see that they were on what also looked like a lake although they knew it too had to be part of the Yangtze. There was not a ripple on the broad stretch of the river here; evanescent mists, the early morning light tentatively shining through, shimmered a few feet off the river; a flock of white-headed ducks floated on its tranquil surface. Far away on either side were ranges of tall mountains, still mostly in shade and painted in dark purple shadow against the soft pale sky, Stretching in front of them on either side of the river was a wide plain, a checkerboard of black, yellow and green fields and, like stretched silver foil in the sun, fish ponds and rice paddies. They caught the fragrances of turned earth, growth and fecundity.

There was a cry from the low river bank where the junk was tied to several stout bamboo trunks. A man on the river bank in a Chinese army tunic and a round straw hat was shouting something. The captain high on the roof of the stern cabin shouted back and pointed at the seven men at the deck. He came down a sort of rope Jacob's ladder to the deck and began hitting some of the men urgently on the shoulder and pointing to the man on the river bank.

"I think our little cruise is over,' said Captain Hadley, "I think we will be strolling through Arcadia with this young man. What don't we get our bags, thank our hosts and let's get on with it." They did so and Captain Hadley gave some of his small store of money and some of the tins from their supplies to the captain. The crew paid no attention; they lay on the deck tightly wrapped in their blankets, insensate, immobile.

The man in the army tunic could not have been more than twenty and surprised them all by talking to them in English with a distinct American accent over his Chinese intonations. He said he was studying at Kweilin University. He talked about it enthusiastically. American missionaries had founded it; many of its professors had studied in the United States and there were actual Americans teaching there. He had read Mr. Ernest Hemingway and liked him very much. He had taken Ernest as his English name, but his American professor called him Ernie. One day he wanted to study at the Kansas State University in Kansas, America, where his professor had studied, but right now he was a guide for Colonel Ride's BAAG. He was to take them to Kweilin where army trucks would take them over the mountains to where, on the other side, they would find the train line to Chungking.

"OK, guys, ready to roll?" He smiled happily and proudly at his use of this idiom he had learned from his professor from the Kansas State University. He had no difficulty in pronouncing 'r.' They walked along a road, clay and dirt, but wider and smoother and straighter than they had seen in the southern part of China from where they had come. A ditch ran along both sides of the road, which was raised a little so that they could look over the fields. Captain Hadley and Ernie took the lead; the others followed in two rows of three each. They all, except for Ernie and the civilian from the Hong Kong Telephone Company, reverted to their army days and fell into step, and their pace in the morning sun had a certain happy bounce to it. There were a patchwork of fields on either side where rape seed was planted, and their flowers as they trembled in the slow wind and sun were every variety of yellow – egg yolk, custard, canary, lemon, butter. They came across a small red-clay wayside shrine in which sticks of incense, lit by a person or people unknown, were still smoldering and the afternoon air carried the sweetness of the incense, bringing the blessings of the local gods to all who sensed it.

They marched in silence, the mesmerizing rhythm of their footprints on the road lulling them into inward contemplation, each man with his own thoughts. Once, they were startled by a cluster of dragonflies that suddenly swarmed out of the ditch by the side of the road, their wings making a brief rainbow as they caught the sun. They saw white and peach roses growing wild, much bigger and more profuse than the ones Captain Hadley remembered in England.

It was later afternoon when Ernie, pointing ahead, told them that this was where they were going to spend the night. As they came closer, they saw a compound of buildings surrounded by a tall wall, so that all that was really visible were glazed green-tiled roofs with the ends of their eaves turned up like the tips of Alibaba's slippers. Tall cypresses grew near the walls and cast shade.

Ernie led them off the road towards the walled compound on a little path that wound round one side, through the cedars and to the side that faced away from the road. There through an opening in the wall, they saw a mud-brick and timber house, a granary, and barns. There was a little lake with a high arched stone bridge over it and a small stone pagoda at one end. A boy was fishing from it and in the afternoon light they could see the silver fishes he was after, close to the surface, turning, diving, flashing silver. "We are in the middle of a Willow Pattern plate," said the medical orderly. They caught the smell of food cooking over fires.

That evening they ate with the farmer, his wife, his sons, daughters and all his relatives. It was a long time since they had eaten in such abundance. There was chicken, fish, bean curd, tea in tiny cups, cooked pears and apples, rice, pork with layers of fat, eggs, thin dry sausages, marrows, noodles, jams, buns, cakes and the flavors of wine, arrowroot, vinegar, pepper, cloves and cinnamon. They drank rice wine and toasted the farmer and his family and sang old songs from their boyhood in England. They slept in the loft of a barn on piled sheaves of dry stalks of rice straw. It was a deep, untroubled sleep.

The next morning the women of the farm served rice, eggs and steamed green vegetables. Everyone lined up to bow as they left. The men formed a solemn line and bowed back. Ernie told them it would be five more days of walking before they reached the trucks that would take them over the mountains.

They walked down the path to the road through the cypresses and set along it. They had enjoyed singing songs of their boyhood the night before even though more than one of them had had thoughts of family in England whom they had not seen for years. But now they were happy in the sun and they sang 'The British Grenadiers', 'The Eton Boating Song','It's a Long Way to Tipperary' and 'The Man Who Broke the Bank of Monte Carlo." Then the twenty-year soldier sang 'The Fatal Wedding' which they had never heard before. When he reached the part where he sang, drawing out the main phrase in each line, 'But the bride, she died at the altar,/The bridegroom died the next day,/The parson dropped dead in the churchyard,/As he was about to pray' they all laughed so hard that they stopped marching for a few moments. Captain Hadley thought that Reeves would have loved singing along with them. He thought that he probably had few occasions to sing with other people. He had a lonely job.

On the last morning before they were to cross the mountains they had a simple breakfast of rice and tea in the farm house in which they were staying. Lunch at noon along the road was a basket of breads by a field of poppies. They were carmine, purple, pink, white, white with pink fringes, blue, scarlet and violet, and shook and shimmered in the moving air. They were planted right up to the walls of the temple and farm buildings, breaking against them like small ripples in some fantastic sea and then flowing around them to lap against some other building. The men ate their bread and looked at them, saying nothing, not standing up to continue their journey.

"There was a poem we had in school," said the twenty-year soldier finally, "About some blokes on a journey who come to an enchanted island and decide to stay amongst the flowers rather than go back home. It went on for a while if I remember."

"I think you are thinking of 'The Lotos-Eaters'," said Captain Hadley. He looked around and thought to himself that we are on Tennyson's island where it always seemed afternoon; we are in Coleridge's Xanadu, Marco Polo's Middle Kingdom, Shangri-La, some dream of Cathay that exists separate from the world they had hitherto known. He wondered whether they could stay and never leave. He felt obliged to say something. "If we wanted to lie amongst flowers and smoke opium, we could have stayed in Macao," he said.

"Why didn't we stay in Macao?" asked one of the soldiers.

"You will recollect," said Captain Hadley, "that you were bored out of your mind in Macao. You wanted to leave so that you could fight the Japs again. You wanted a little stimulus in your life. When your so-far unborn child asks you 'What did you do in the war, Daddy?' you did not want to reply that you sat it out getting blotto on rice wine liquor with the British consul on the China coast, thousands of miles from where the action and excitement was."

"I am thinking," said the soldier, "that I placed a great deal too much importance on action and excitement. Perhaps we can bivouac here until our lords and masters find out how to end the war. It may be years but that is fine with me. This would be a good place to spend the war." He plucked one of the poppies and pulled it through a shirt button on his chest. He lay back on the grass, his eyes closed.

Captain Hadley looked around and was seized by the thought that they could all stay here; they could be farmers. All seven of them would live together in a farm house with a tiled roof and a fish pond. They would plant fields of wheat that would start with brilliant emerald shoots of green each spring – 'the wheat that springeth green' as the Easter hymn has it. He would send food – fruits, vegetables, grains and meats, the whole cornucopia – back to the consul in Macao. He could give what he did not need to the British refugees. It would be our contribution to the war effort. Perhaps I could even travel back to see him again. It would be good to see how he was doing. Or he could come and visit me here.

The reality of his situation intruded rudely. He stood up and addressed the men in his usual mild way: "Why don't we move on, gentleman. You know we have to." He waited a minute and they eventually rose, but Captain Hadley could see they were reluctant.

After they had walked most of the day. Ernie came to where the trucks were lined up – eight of them – by the side of the road. The trucks, the Dodge nameplate plate still above the radiator, seemed to be mostly dirt and rust. The headlamps had been removed and you could see the screw holes on the mudguards where they had been bolted. The windshields were also gone and the seats in the cab had been replaced by a wooden plank. Ernie spoke to an officer in battle dress watching over the trucks. Ernie pointed to the first two in line.

"You ride in these two," Ernie said, "On the back. The driver and his assistant are in the cab at the front. Take these baskets of food for the trip." Ernie signaled to several men standing by the trucks and they gave each of the men a basket with packages wrapped in large leaves. They also gave them each a padded jacket and a pair of padded pants that Chinese soldiers wore. When they put them on, they were too small and Ernie smiled despite his politeness otherwise.

The travelers looked at the trays of the two trucks they would ride in. There was a sheet of thin worn canvas pulled over a number of sacks stacked two high, and roped down with several lengths of fraying hemp cord.

"What are we riding on?" asked Captain Hadley.

"Bags of salt, all the way from the ocean. The general has the monopoly on supplying this region with salt. It is hard to find around here," said Ernie, "He has become a rich man and has three wives. Americans only have one wife. Please climb on the trucks before they leave."

Each of the men came and shook Ernie's hand. Captain Hadley thanked him for all he had done and wished him luck and hoped he would get to go to university in America when the war was over. Ernie told him that there were no mountains in Kansas and that he was looking forward to seeing it.

The men divided into two groups and climbed up onto the canvas-covered sacks of salt at the back of the truck. There was another shout, a horrible crashing of gears from each of the eight trucks, a series of small explosions from the engines, one loud bang and the convoy jerked forward, black exhaust blowing back over the men on the back of the trucks.

Soon the rain came, light at first, then the sky darkened and the rain beat down furiously so that you could not see ten yards ahead. The jackets and trousers the men wore offered little protection, soaking up the rain, rather than repelling it, and quickly becoming cold and sodden. The road turned from dirt and dust to a thick sucking mud through which the trucks slithered as much side to side as forward to the grinding of gears as the drivers attempted to keep moving onward.

They spent five days winding through high mountain passes, their trucks constantly at risk of tumbling into a ravine and falling down hundreds of feet to the rocks and the river below. They were soaked through and cold most of the time, shivering at night in the wind that seemed to blow from both directions cutting through the padded jackets and pants and the thin clothes that they had worn since Macao. The basket of food each and the remainder of what they had in their haversacks was not much and they felt the hard pangs of hunger.

On the morning of the sixth day, they saw that they had come down out of the mountains and were on a dry dusty plain that stretched in front of them until there were foothills and more mountains in the far distance. They could see the line of frail spindles of telephone or telegraph poles stretching out in either direction and the level black line of a railway track seen from the side, as though it had been drawn in India ink with a thick nib and ruler.

They were dropped off at a railway platform, nothing more than a long mound of clay, four or five feet high and leveled for thirty or forty feet. There was a signal on a pole near it with a single light showing green in both directions. The wind blew from the mountains in the north, cold and constant. Captain Hadley gave some money to the soldiers on the trucks they had ridden on. He now had nothing left from what Reeves had given him.

At one end of the platform, a young girl of ten or eleven lay on her side looking blankly off, her face gaunt and her stomach distended from hunger. The men stood on the other end of the platform. They knew that she would die there, perhaps very soon.

Hours later, close to midnight, there was the distant sound of a train whistle, a small light bobbing in the blackness of the horizon, which gradually became larger, and then a steam locomotive, hissing and clanking. The train rumbled into the station with steam spitting from the boiler, coming to a stop with a piercing screech as the wheels locked and scraped on the rails. The men climbed up a small metal ladder into one of the passenger cars.

The carriage was full of Chinese soldiers, thin, exhausted, and their uniforms torn and threadbare. Almost all were injured or wounded in some way. Those who were not asleep smoked foul-smelling cigarettes. The windows were closed, if they had ever opened at all. The carriage was very hot; it smelled of sweat, dirt, decay, and filth. The men squeezed themselves onto a bench, and, leaning against each other, fell asleep. The men were aware of the lurching of the train as it left the station, their hunger, the undressed suppurating wounds of the Chinese soldiers, pus and yellow and brown fluids staining their uniforms and dripping onto the benches and floor of the carriage. Twelve hours later, they were in a dormitory, on a far corner of the grounds of the British Embassy in Chungking. Captain Hadley had his own room in a separate building. They had been given dinner, they were safe at last.

They all stayed in Chungking for several weeks, waiting for a space on a flight out of Chungking. Somehow someone else always had priority and they found themselves waiting at the little airstrip day after day expecting to board the C 47, only to be sent back to their accommodation.

Captain Hadley was the first to be finally flown out on that long flight over the Himalayas to Calcutta from Chungking. He spent the first two weeks there in an Army guest house. It was a two story building with deep verandahs, white, set in large gardens with flower beds, tall shady trees and peacocks that strutted across the close-clipped lawns. He had a large room, with a very tall Sikh in a turban and scarlet jacket to look after him. In the morning, he brought him tea with milk and sugar, eggs with bacon, toast made with white bread and butter to spread on it, jams and jellies. If he wanted more, he could have it. Sometimes Captain Hadley would just sit there and look at all of it on the lacquered tray arranged prettily on top of a white napkin. The sheets on his bed were bleached a snowy white and then starched. Other servants cleaned his room, really polished it, bringing everything to a high gloss. He could sit against the cushions on the rattan sofa on the verandah under a punkah in the afternoon. He had new uniforms made at Ranken and Company. They were of a beautiful material and fit him perfectly.

In the evening, he would take a tonga pulled by a little pony to the Bengal Club, where he was given a temporary membership. His escape from the prisoner of war camp at Shamshuipo to Macao and then to China and on to India had been the subject of articles in both the *Times of India* and Calcutta's *The Statesman*. He was described as leading a band of 'other ranks and a civilian' across a thousand miles of hostile Japanese-occupied China. Captain Hadley reflected that after Macao, they had not seen a single Japanese soldier. He could have worn his dress uniform with decorations and been preceded by a brass band for all the Japanese noticed. Was he really a leader or did they all just stroll through China, guided by seen and unseen hands? Nevertheless he found himself a celebrity; people bought him stengahs in the main bar, slapped his back, and invited him to join their tables for dinner.

He was notified that he was to be promoted to Major and seconded to the 20th Indian Division. He never saw the six other men who had come all that way with him again. He wrote to Reeves and thanked him for his help. He told him about the delights of the guest house he was given in which to recuperate – you could have a good war here, he had written – and his promotion and his secondment. He expected his orders to report to its headquarters in northern India would come in a week or so. In the meantime, he intended to take full advantage of the comforts of the guest house and the cold beer at the Bengal Club. He ended with a reminder. "Don't forget," he wrote, "It is going to be just as we discussed. After the war, you are going to run the Foreign Office and I will be Field Marshal of the entire Army."

* * *

Captain Hadley's letter had gone from Calcutta to Delhi and then slowly on to the British Embassy in Lisbon. It was some months before it finally arrived in Macao, the envelope covered with the smudged black and red stamps affixed by the various post offices it had passed through on its way to the consul. Reeves wrote back to now Major Hadley at his headquarters in Northern India, telling him about life in Macao and, in particular, a concert that the British in Macao had got up to raise money for war relief, which had been so much fun for everyone.

Reeves's letter was returned almost nine months later with a note from the Division Adjutant. "We regret to inform you that Major William Hawkins Hadley was killed during the battle of Imphal. He was a gallant officer, much beloved by the Indian troops he commanded."

Reeves thought of that vicious and bloody battle to repel a Japanese invasion of India itself. Did Captain Hadley die a hero? Was it a random shot when his luck ran out? Did his jeep overturn, killing him? He would often wonder what might have happened if Captain Hadley had stayed in Macao. He had a beautiful voice. He would have been so good in the concert. We could have stayed friends.

Chapter 18

Throughout 1944, the news on the war increasingly favored the West. The Allies had landed in France and Italy and began the long struggle to liberate Europe. The American Navy had victory after victory over the Japanese and every week came closer to the Japanese homeland. Reeves followed the news in the long stretches of the day when he had little to do. His work with the refugees was now routine and largely taken care of by the consulate's clerks. Portugal, although ostensibly still neutral, increasingly favored the Allies, culminating with their lease of naval and air bases in the Azores to the British and the Americans. With Portugal more friendly, the Foreign Office paid even less attention to its vice-consul in Macao. He was irrelevant now, if he ever was relevant, to the conduct of Anglo-Portuguese relations. Often weeks or even a month would go by when Reeves did not receive a single communication from the Legation in Chungking beyond the routine bulletins directed to all consular outposts. His reports were either ignored, or they were acknowledged in a single terse sentence that they had been received. Reeves thought more than once that eventually he would have to find his place in the world outside Macao.

In these quiet times during the day, Reeves liked to leave the consulate and would often come down to the *Porto Interior*. He had brought Letitia down once when her school was closed for a holiday. He thought she might enjoy seeing the junks and the sampans, the seabirds scavenging. She had loved the short ride in the Studebaker, especially when the driver sounded the klaxon at an errant pedestrian. *"Joi jou yat"* she said delightedly in Cantonese, "do it again." Rhoda discouraged her from speaking Cantonese, but she had picked up some phrases from her amah and seemed often more comfortable in Cantonese than English. With her parents, there were long silences between her short sentences, but Reeves had once heard her talking in Cantonese with her amah, tentatively but happily, when it was just the two of them.

Rhoda spent most evenings helping Letitia with her school work and trying to coax her into a conversation. Rhoda often took her meals upstairs in the bedroom where Letitia slept and she did her homework. If Rhoda saw Reeves at all, her voice was full of a sad weariness. She did not know what was the matter with Letitia. She did not seem to be getting better despite what the doctors said. She needed to get to an English-speaking country, although Rhoda had no explanation as to how this move might ameliorate Letitia's condition.

Once at the *Porto Interior*, Reeves and Letitia had walked along the seawall, Letitia a little nervous amongst the other people walking there, and gripping her father's hand tightly. A small girl on a junk had waved at her and Letitia had shyly waved back, which led the girl on the junk to wave even harder, and then all her family had joined in waving. Letitia laughed out loud and released her hand from Reeves's and waved back energetically with both arms. She could hear the laughter of the girl and her family on the junk and this led Letitia to laugh even louder. She took her father's hand again and asked to find another junk with children they could wave at. They walked on; Letitia said it was so much fun to come here to see the boats. Reeves hoped there would be more moments like this.

But then a truck backfired on the street with a sharp loud explosion and a cloud of foul-smelling dirty smoke. Letitia had screamed loudly, thrust her head tightly against Reeves and, sobbing, asked to be taken home. She never again allowed Reeves to take her to the *Porto Interior* and during every car trip with her father subsequently – not that there were many – there was a nervous discussion by Letitia about whether there would be another loud bang. Rhoda would look angrily at her husband every time Letitia mentioned the truck backfiring as though it was somehow his fault and she was increasingly reluctant to leave the two of them alone together. As a result, Reeves saw even less of his daughter.

Most of the time Reeves came down to the *Porto Interior*, it was by himself to see the *Sai An*, still tied up at the same pier where Reeves had prevented it from sailing to Hong Kong over two years ago at the outbreak of the war. This was the ship that had brought him to Macao; it was the ship from which he had first seen Macao's spires, its castles and its improbable pastel houses; it was the ship he had dreamed of taking around the islands of the South Pacific. What would be the best word to describe it? Sturdy? Staunch? The ship was nearly two hundred feet long but you would not say it had 'fast lines' as Reeves remembered some people describing ships. It was very wide, there was a downward curve along its length – 'sway-backed' someone had unkindly said – but Reeves loved the line of that curve, the two decks that did not quite join, the enclosed bridge and the large Union Jack painted on both sides of the upper hull.

Reeves flew the Union Jack from the consulate and the Japanese in their consulate next door had to look at it each day. Every Japanese ship and patrol boat that came into the *Porto Interior* would also have to look at the Union Jack on the side of the *Sai An*. This was the flag of his country, a country he had not seen in over ten years, the only British flag to be seen for thousands of miles in any direction. He wished his parents, and his university classmates now under arms could see him cocking a snook like this to England's enemies. He was sure they would cheer him on.

Reeves's excuse to come down to the *Porto Interior*, not that he really needed one, was that he was the custodian of British property in wartime and had charge of the vessel. It was owned by a Chinese company with a Chinese board of directors, but it was registered in Hong Kong and thus was British. He had also used his authority over the *Sai An* to house British refugees on it. There were only 70 refugees on board and, at least compared to the other accommodations available for displaced British subjects in Macao, they had both space and comfort. Captain McDougal, now sitting out the war in a flat with a view of the harbor and the ship, insisted on the engineers running the ship's engines for an hour each day so there was hot water during that time, a luxury elsewhere.

In the warm weather, there was the forward deck at the bow, shaded by a square of canvas on poles and Reeves would sometimes sit there with a sundowner of rice wine liquor and talk with some of the more agreeable refugees in the evening. Reeves had also commandeered Captain McDougal's day cabin, a small room just behind the bridge, as an auxiliary office. It had a small desk, a brass lamp above it on gimbals, a bed that could double as a couch and that would fold up against the wall should Reeves feel the need of more room. He would take papers from the consulate down to the day cabin to review, often leaving them on the desk in neat stacks for days or weeks, and draft memoranda and letters, again working on these over weeks and leaving the drafts on the desk in the same neat stacks. There was a Chinese-Macanese office boy in the consulate named Ah Chui who would bring documents back and forth when Reeves was working down there. Mrs. Wilson, when she was still at the consulate, was horrified at consular papers being left in the open on the ship overnight or longer, but Reeves dismissed her concerns, saying the ship was watched over by loyal British subjects. He told her that the consulate was sometimes too frantic, which both knew was patently untrue, and he needed a place where he could get away and think. He felt very much at peace on the *Sai An.*

Around 11:00 one evening, the telephone rang in Reeves's bedroom. He had not returned to his residence – Rhoda would never notice – but was staying upstairs in his room in the consular offices on the *Praya Grande.* He was not asleep when the phone rang. It was hot, the window was open and he had been awakened a short while ago by shouts, the sounds of a few cars and trucks and then gunfire, at first what sounded like pistol shots and then the jack-hammer staccato of machine-gun fire. Perhaps the police were fighting the triads, but then the police and the triads rarely bothered each other. He picked up the telephone on his nightstand.

Before he could even give his name, there was an exasperated voice from the receiver. Reeves immediately recognized the Scots accent of the captain of the *Sai An*.

"Reeves, it's McDougal here. I have had the Devil's own time getting through to you. Something is the matter with the telephone exchange. The bastards are stealing the ship."

"You mean the *Sai An?*"

"What other bloody ship would I be calling about? Some fishing junk? It's the only bloody ship in the *Porto Interior*. They are getting up a head of steam, laying tugs alongside and taking her God knows where. It's Jap-controlled seas and harbors for thousands of miles in all directions."

"Who is stealing her? The Jap Navy? They can't do that, Macao is the territory of a neutral country."

"Some Chinese hooligans armed to the teeth swarmed up the gangway. They offloaded all the refugees staying there and my officers on duty. One of them came to my flat and warned me. I tried to get down there but someone had thrown up a barricade of shipping crates at the entrance to the ferry wharf with some pretty nasty looking machine guns poking over the top. The police have moved that truck with the armor plating on it near and one hell of a shootout has begun. You take your life in your hands if you get within a hundred yards of the wharf."

"Do you think it could be pirates?"

"I don't know who the hell they are. What would the pirates want with an empty ship? They want the rich people on it to rob. Pirates can't use the *Sai An*, where the bloody hell would they get bunker oil to fuel it?"

The gun fire through the open window was getting louder.

"Reeves," McDougal had raised his voice by now, "I didn't bloody call you to have a chit-chat. Right now I don't give a good Goddamn who is stealing my ship. It could be the bloody forest pixies for all I care." Reeves, amused for a moment with McDougal's fury, wondered whether all of his sentences would be punctuated with a 'bloody.'

McDougal's fury was at its height. He was shouting so that Reeves had to hold the receiver away from his ear. "All I want to do is to stop it from leaving the *Porto Interior*. And it won't get very far unless it has tugs to guide it down the channel. And this, if you don't mind, brings me to my point unless you want to make further polite conversation, there are two harbor tugs taking the *Sai An* out of the harbor. I don't know who is stealing my ship, but they have help from the Portuguese authorities who have laid on two tugs to make their life so much easier. Telephone the bloody Governor in his bloody pink palace and make him stop this." There was a bang as Captain McDougal hung up the receiver; Reeves imagined that he had slammed it down heavily.

In the silence that followed, the full import of what McDougal had said struck Reeves. Someone was stealing his beloved *Sai An*. He needed to stop it. It could not fall into enemy hands. How was he going to reach the Governor at this time of night? Mr. Gonsalves generally arranged these sorts of things. Then he remembered he had some telephone numbers in a lovely small leather notebook from Liberty's that Rhoda had given him for Christmas when they were first married. He put on a dressing gown, walked down the stairs, glad that the electricity was still on so that he could see, and went into his office. There on the desk, neatly in one corner, was the little leather notebook. He switched on his desk lamp and opened it to the right page. There was the Governor's private number that went right through to his office. But he would not be there at this time of night. Perhaps there was a night guard who answered it and he could pass on an urgent message. This was his only option. He called the exchange and asked to be put through to the number. They succeeded on their fourth attempt.

A man immediately answered in a string of Portuguese of which Reeves recognized only the word 'Teixeira,' the Governor's surname. Reeves explained slowly in English, assuming like so many Englishmen in the East that he would be understood when he spoke English, that this was John Reeves, the British Consul in Macao, and he needed to talk to the Governor on a matter of utmost urgency. There was a moment's silence, some clicks, and then the Governor came on the line.

"John, I assume that you are calling about the *Sai An*." No small talk, just right to the point. Reeves had forgotten how direct the Governor could be. All those years in the Navy. Just like his own brusque uncles, the admirals.

"Governor, I apologize for calling so late." Reeves could not help himself; he could not just plunge into a conversation. "But I just heard some disturbing news: that the *Sai An* is leaving the harbor under the control of an illegal crew who have no authorization to be on it or operate it."

The Governor came back in a calm measured tone. "From what I understand, that is the case. I have gathered a small group of senior officials here in my offices to review the situation and ascertain what steps can be taken and when."

Reeves breathed in sharply, stood up, and pulled himself up to his full height, despite his being alone in the office where no one could see. "Governor Teixeira," he said stiffly, "The information I have is that there are two tugboats of Portuguese registration that are assisting the illegal removal of a British vessel under my conservatorship from neutral waters. You must stop this." Reeves could not understand why this was happening. The Japanese recently were paying less attention to the city, preoccupied as they were with the fighting far to the north. There was an odd normality in life in Macao right now. He had been to see some American cartoon films at the *Teatro Vitória* on the *Rua dos Mercadores*, every seat occupied, and the audience howling with laughter at the pratfalls of Donald Duck and Bugs Bunny, as though they had never heard of the war. He had seen Jamaican rum for sale in a store. He assumed that Wong Kong-kit was smuggling, unimpeded, films and liquor into Macao stolen from the Americans in Free China.

"Thank you for passing that on." The Governor's voice was soft and calm. You would not think, Reeves thought, that the Governor was dealing with a crisis that at the very least called into question Macao's status as a sovereign province of a neutral nation. "We had heard rumors. We are at this very moment trying to reach the Harbormaster, but so far have been unsuccessful. He lives a very private life in the evening. The police have gone around to his house but he is not there."

Reeves felt like saying that he did not give a damn about what the Harbormaster did in his off-hours. But his politeness asserted itself. "Governor, there must be something you can do. Can the Marine police send a launch? Can the Navy send its gunboat? We cannot allow the *Sai An* to leave Macao territorial waters." Reeves found himself talking quite loudly and then stopping abruptly, breathing heavily, as though he was winded from climbing several flights of stairs.

"John." The Governor's voice was quiet as though he was trying to calm an agitated person. "You will recollect that we sold our gunboat, the *Patria,* when we needed to buy rice and oil to feed our people. A harbor police launch is shadowing the vessel, but is limited in its ability to interfere. This is a two-hundred-foot steel-hulled vessel with dozens of heavily armed men on board. The police launch is wood-hulled, 30 foot long, and has six men on board. They are reporting to us by radio."

"Have the police tell the tugboats to stop and pull away." Reeves thought that he could be just as terse as the Governor.

"The police do not yet have an effective line of communication into the tugboats, but they are endeavoring to establish one." Reeves realized that the Governor knew all about the tugboats; that his previous equivocation had been a pretense. Was he behind the theft of the *Sai An* or was he merely condoning it? What was his game? Reeves continued in that same tone of terse indignation.

"They are cutting out the *Sai An.* You have artillery on Barra Fort. You can order them to fire and prevent this from happening. Governor, it is imperative to act now." He wondered from what book of naval history did the phrase 'cutting out' come from? One that an admiral uncle must have given him?

"'Cutting out?'" There was a chuckle from the Governor. "You are remembering the Hornblower stories of your youth. I loved them too. I think I learned some English from them. Mr. Consul, you cannot expect me to order that artillery shells be dropped on a British vessel. I cannot be responsible for it coming to harm."

"But you could disable a tugboat. Without a tugboat, the ship can never make it down the channel and we can ensure it stays in port."

"The tugboats are the property of the Portuguese Government and there is a Portuguese captain and a Portuguese engineer on each one. I cannot order the *artilharia* to fire on their own vessels and their own countrymen."

Reeves paused, standing in his office in his dressing gown and pajamas. He put the receiver down on his desk but did not replace it on the telephone. He thought for a moment. There was no sound from the receiver; the Governor seemed willing to let Reeves have this moment of quiet to himself. He picked up the receiver again.

"Governor, I am sorry that you are unable to help. But I cannot stand idly by while British property for which I am responsible is purloined so blatantly in this manner. I intend to go down to the ferry wharf and do my best to put a stop to this." He had no idea how he was going to do this. He could take the Chungking boys on the night shift guarding the consulate, and he had his little American pistol with the three-inch barrel and his 25 cartridges. He could hear the intermittent clatter of the machine guns and knew that this would not be enough. But he had read, again as a schoolboy, about British soldiers achieving victory against overwhelming odds, and he would try. The honor of the consular service, which was something somewhere he still believed in, was at stake. The Governor started talking quietly in that same soothing tone.

"John, I urge you to stay in the consulate building. It is very dangerous out there. Our police and soldiers right now are in the middle of a gun battle with triads or bandits from Canton down at the wharves and on the ship. It will be extremely dangerous for you to go outside and I cannot be responsible for your safety." Then he spoke with an urgency and forcefulness. "Please John, I am begging you. Stay indoors. You will be killed if you go outside. You are my friend and I am telling you this."

"Governor Teixeira, thank you for your concern and I have taken your advice on board. I do have my duty to do however." Reeves replaced the receiver on the phone and almost immediately regretted severing the conversation. The Governor sounded genuinely concerned about him and he had brushed him aside peremptorily. He could not blame the Governor for what is happening after all. He could not think of the *Sai An* with the same affection that Reeves did. The Governor was in a long weary struggle to keep Macao intact and unscathed by the war. If he chose not to intervene right now, he must have a motive to avoid a larger conflict and serve a larger purpose. Reeves thought the Governor had a nearly impossible job. He was a good person. But he had to try; he could not confess failure now.

He went upstairs, dressed in some old clothes as though he was going for a Sunday ramble, and walked downstairs, stopping in the office to get the keys to the Studebaker. He crossed the consulate to the front door that opened up onto the *Praya Grande*. Two of the Chungking boys were lounging in the anteroom by the front door, chattering to each other, presumably speculating on the gunfire outside. When they saw him walking towards the door, they sprang up and stood in front of it, waving their hands and shouting something urgent in a Chinese dialect Reeves did not recognize. He pushed them aside, opened the door, and stood on the stone steps.

For seconds, it was all quiet. All that could be heard was the rustle of the leaves in the banyan trees over the path by the seawall and the slight slapping of the waves against it. The breeze was warm and felt good against his face. There was no moon and the street lights were out; the banyan trees were dark silhouettes against an even darker sky.

Then there was the rhythmic regular series of small explosions as two machine guns began firing on either side of him from somewhere in the darkness. He saw tiny points of burning light, one after the other, like blazing beads on a string, immobile, hovering stationary in the air momentarily, and then suddenly gaining immense speed and hurling towards him, only to flash over his head above the roof of the consulate.

The two Chungking men grabbed him from behind and pulled him roughly back into the consulate, slamming and locking the door. They are firing tracer bullets, Reeves thought, at the consulate, from both sides. The next time he appeared on the front steps they would aim directly at him or that was what they wanted him to believe. Rhoda, safe at the residence, would not survive as a widow. He was needed to take care of her. Getting gunned down on the street would not be seen as an heroic gesture, just as an unfortunate accident all too common in wartime. All he would gain would be a fleeting sympathy, never respect.

He took a pair of field glasses from his office and went upstairs to where there was a ladder on the wall that led to the roof. He came up the ladder, through the hatch, and immediately lay down on the roof, crawling on his stomach like some hunter stalking a stag, towards the balustrade. He peered through two of the balusters.

From this position on the roof, he thought it would be difficult to spot him in the darkness. He could see the whole sweep of the *Porto Interior*, the tightly packed rows of sampans and junks and then out to the South China Sea. To his left were the wharves and the ferry pier. It was on these that he trained the field glasses.

He saw the *Sai An*, black smoke coming from her single stack, lights on in the bridge and on the outside, spotlights shining on the Union Jack. The ship was still alongside the wharf but no longer secured by hawsers. There was a tug alongside her and another ahead. Behind lay a junk with a diesel engine.

He could hear all the engines of the ships distinctly; the low bass rumble of the *Sai An,* the cough of the diesel engine of the junk; the rumble of the tug engines at a slightly higher pitch. There was a fault or a leak in the engine of the nearest tug and every half minute it gave a jaunty whistle as steam escaped through a hole or a crack in a pipe. It seemed to be taunting him. *We are leaving and there is nothing you can do about it.*

Then the *Sai An* shuddered, the rumble of her engine was louder and the waters behind her churned like rapids in a mountain river. The *Sai An* and the tug next to her slowly began to move forward away from the ferry wharf and out towards the South China Sea. The tug in front of her took up a position closer to the bow and the motor junk at the stern. The launch belonging to the harbor police was keeping a distance of about 100 yards on the starboard bow, safe from pistol shot or shots from the ferry

Then there was a sudden eruption of machine-gun fire. A stream of tracer bullets from somewhere on land could be seen directed at the *Sai An* and an answering stream came from the vessel towards the shore. There were other guns being fired, he could see the orange flashes from unseen barrels in the darkness, he could hear the clang of bullets striking the *Sai An*'s hull ineffectually; spent bullets from returned fire sounded like hail as they fell on the iron roofs of the godowns close to the wharf. The tracer bullets flashed back and forth beneath him like angry fireflies streaking through the darkness. Every now and then he heard the whistle from the leak in the engine of the tugboat on the port side. This is theater thought Reeves. They know they cannot prevent the *Sai An* from leaving. It has a thick steel hull, bullets fall off it like rain on a roof. They are going through the motions, I have lost the *Sai An*.

Reeves watched the *Sai An* and the three boats accompanying it recede in front of him. The harbor police launch was still politely keeping its distance. The gun fire died down and stopped. Reeves was breathing fast in small frustrated gasps. The last thing he saw before he put down the field glasses was the *Sai An* turned broadside to him as it headed out into the South China sea. Even without the field glasses, the Union Jack, still illuminated in a ship's spotlights against the bright white paintwork of the hull, could be seen clearly. The ship and its flag slowly faded into the darkness of the sea.

Then it was quiet on the *Praya Grande,* just the sound of the waves and their soft lapping on the seawall. Reeves came down from the roof and went to his room, but did not sleep. The *Sai An* was of little importance to the war, but it was a ship under his protection and he had failed to protect it.

That morning, he drafted a cable to Chungking about the incident, describing the inaction (he was tempted to use the word 'complicity') of the Portuguese authorities in failing to prevent the hijacking of a British-registered vessel. He suggested our Ambassador in Lisbon transmit to the appropriate high-level authorities a *demarche* – he thought that was the correct term for an angry diplomatic letter; consuls were never allowed to send one – expressing outrage at the Portuguese Government's failure to protect British property from the predations of pirates, bandits and Japanese sympathizers.

Two weeks later, which seemed to Reeves an extraordinary delay, he received a brief reply. He was told that this was more a local matter, rather than one for senior officials in Lisbon. The ship was Chinese-owned and no British citizen was facing a loss. He was to meet with the colonial administration in Macao, not at the Governor's level, to express the British Government's 'concern.' He was not to follow up. One meeting would suffice.

'Concern' thought Reeves was the weakest word the Legation could find. Nothing must upset Portugal now they were favoring the Allies. Sometimes I wonder why I am here, he thought. Then he thought that there were wheels within wheels of which he was unaware and probably never would be. The *Sai An* and he were tiny specks on a vast machinery of state that would rumble inexorably on and forward with him or without him. He would never know its purpose, he would never know its direction; he would never make a difference in either; it was presumptuous of him to think he could. He was a vice-consul, the lowest rank of an inferior service, in a distant colony of a not very important country.

Chapter 19

It is 4:00am, January 16th, 1945, several months after the loss of the *Sai An*. Reeves is asleep in his bed as are nearly all of the inhabitants of the peaceful little city of Macao. Both Reeves and Macao are unaware that they are about to be touched by the great war raging outside its borders which hitherto has paid it little attention. Sixty miles southwest of Macao, ships of the American Navy have gathered. At that time, it is still very dark; there is no sign of dawn. There was a storm the day before, and even today the clouds are low and the sea is rough, waves ten to fifteen feet high and strong winds blowing out of the north, soaked with the last of yesterday's rain. The USS *Hancock*, an Essex-class aircraft carrier, wallows and rolls in the rough seas like a drunk prizefighter. She is an unsightly and ungainly ship, all its bulk and weight high up in its long flat flight deck, which seems too large and heavy for the narrow hull on which the deck is precariously balanced. On that long flat deck, the superstructure has been piled up and pushed over to one side without any regard to harmony or proportion. The *Hancock* is shoving, barging and bullying its way through the rough seas, unlike the battleships, cruisers and destroyers that surround it, which slice smoothly through the waves on their sharp-edged hulls like ice skaters.

The American Navy in the past two years had slowly ground out a stunning series of victories in six great battles at sea against the Japanese Navy in the Pacific, slowly moving north, until its Third Fleet, under the command of Admiral William Halsey, was off the southern coast of China, a few days' sail from where they would be in a position to attack the Japanese homeland itself and perhaps finally bring an end to this war. There was not a man among the tens of thousands of sailors and officers in the entire Third Fleet who was not impatient for that day to arrive when the Navy could finally have its revenge for the attack on Pearl Harbor. But first, there would be a delay of a day for a routine attack, code-named Operation Gratitude. It would only require a small part of the Third Fleet; the necessary ships were selected, collected together and labeled as Task Force 38.2, with the *Hancock* at its center. Operation Gratitude was a plan for an attack on minor Japanese installations in Hong Kong, Canton, Sanchow and wherever else they might be found in and near the Pearl River Delta. There was no plan to attack Macao, which lay nearly in the center of these targets that surrounded it.

On the *Hancock*, the armorers had been working since before midnight fitting the aircraft in its hangars and on its sprawling deck with belts of bullets, rockets, bombs and torpedoes. The pilots of these aircraft were awake too. At this time, in the dark before dawn, they were in the ready rooms and, in particular, Ready Room Four, where they would be briefed on Operation Gratitude. They have had coffee and breakfast.

Some of the pilots were given specific targets with coordinates and map references and they now had their heads down studying them. Others were told to blanket the entire area in the Pearl River Delta. There was no specific definition of 'blanket,' but every pilot thought he knew what it meant: fly over an area and destroy any enemy aircraft on the ground that could threaten you and your fellow flyers. And most pilots knew that blanketing included destroying the hangars used to conceal aircraft, the warehouses with supplies, the runways used for takeoffs and landings, and the revetments on the edges of airfields. The Japs, as the pilots told each other, were famous for hiding warplanes on the edges of airfields in revetments.

Many of the pilots were to fly over or near Macao on their blanketing missions and there was a lot of information about Macao passed on, but in contradictory fragments, at different times, to different people, and not to all the pilots. Orders were given that Macao was neutral and pilots were not to come within two miles of it; other orders told the pilots they were to inspect the Macao peninsula and the adjacent waters for aircraft and seaplanes and only attack aircraft and air installations; still other orders said that Macao was occupied by the Japs and they were using its aviation facilities – there was a Jap seaplane base there; and some orders even told the pilots to stay away from the old town of Macao, but everything else was fair game. What would be fair to say is that few in the Third Fleet had even heard of Macao; there was not a single person who appreciated that Macao was the territory of a neutral country 10,000 miles to the west, and certainly no one had accurate intelligence as to what was actually happening in Macao. What every pilot, however, knew in his heart was that he was not going to ignore any air base or anything anywhere that looked like one that might threaten them or Halsey's Third Fleet, soon to steam north to finish off Tokyo and end this war. Macao would be blanketed.

At the last minute a message about Macao came over the speaker in Ready Room Four. But there was static and crackling; the words were mostly incomprehensible, like those announcements you heard in bus terminals or train stations. The pilots were concentrating on their orders or talking loudly and excitedly to one another and later, during the inquest on why neutral Macao was bombed, not one pilot could even remember the announcement, let alone what was said. It was never ascertained who had made the announcement or what was his message about Macao.

At 7:00am, the pilots went up to the long flat flight deck where dozens of the aircraft were parked, clustered like huddled seabirds on a stormy beach. There was still rain and low cloud cover and a cold winter wind blew over the deck. The light was gray and watery. There was no sign of land or the destroyers ahead on picket duty. The *Hancock,* despite its forward speed, still swayed. The pilots had to be careful walking across the wet tilting deck to their planes.

The engines were started on the planes and then everyone waited as the *Hancock* turned into the wind, leaving a long ugly ragged arc of a foaming wake behind it. The ship picked up speed to nearly thirty five knots; the wind blowing directly into the face of the aircraft was an additional fifteen knots. Dozens of aircraft were on the deck, shaking as their engines reached full power. The noise, even in the open and in a howling wind, was piercing.

The first of the aircraft to take off was towed out of the pack of planes at the stern of the carrier by a little boxy tractor. Its wings, which had been folded against the fuselage like a bird at rest, were straightened. The crew on the deck pressed themselves against the tall superstructure rising clumsily at the side of the carrier. The small stolid aircraft sat shuddering for a moment, its engine screaming; the crew chief on the deck swung both arms around at chest height and pointed them towards the end of the deck, as though the pilots needed to be told where to go. The plane dashed forward on the pitching deck for a few seconds and then sprung upwards in almost a leap and flew away. The second plane followed seconds later and then the next. It was like hornets leaving a hive.

The planes were Hellcats and there were twelve blanketing the southwestern part of the Pearl River Delta. They started in formation but then split into two groups. Around 9:00am, Lt. George Kemper, leading a group of five Hellcats on their way to a possible Japanese airbase in Sanchow passed over Macao and saw the Naval Aviation Seaplane hangar and the Pan American office and warehouse. He led his formation down in a nosedive and they strafed all three buildings, each Hellcat firing its six .50 caliber machine guns at the rate of a thousand bullets per minute.

Thirty minutes later, Lt. Lloyd Newcomber leading a squadron of five Hellcats saw the same buildings and led his squadron into that same strafing dive. This time as they pulled away, they saw flames and thick sooty black smoke billow out of the Pan American warehouse. "It was," he told the three admirals and one judge advocate who had convened on the battleship USS *South Dakota* in a court of inquiry the following week to examine this violation of Portugal's neutrality after an angry protest from the Portuguese Government had arrived on Admiral Halsey's flagship, "consistent with burning aviation fuel."

At 3:00pm, Lt. H.W. Neibling, commanding a squadron of four Hellcats passed over the hangar and the Pan American buildings. He led each one of the Hellcats in a nosedive and strafed the buildings again. Lt.

Neibling thought he saw revetments on the far side of the field, where the Japanese might have hidden planes and war material, and all four aircraft shot at them. In fact, they had strafed the thick lichen-covered stone walls of the *Fortaleza de S. Francisco,* an ancient fortress dating from the early seventeenth century and now under attack for the first time in its long and hitherto somnolent and peaceful history. The massive stone blocks making up the walls were chipped but otherwise undamaged.

All the pilots of the aircraft that had attacked Macao were able to return safely to the *Hancock.* They gave little thought to what they had done. The attacks were routine, were unopposed, had lasted only a few minutes and did not compare to the terrifying air battles of the past two years and the combat they expected when they attacked Japan itself.

The next day, the *Hancock,* the ships that accompanied it, the rest of the task force, and all of Admiral Halsey's mighty Third Fleet steamed north, every hour bringing them closer to Japan. Macao was forgotten.

* * *

Reeves had received a call that morning that the Pan American buildings were under attack from American aircraft. The aide in the Governor's office who had called him said excitedly that stars in circles could be clearly seen on the wings of the planes; they were definitely not Japanese. Japanese planes had the red rising sun on their wings and these markings looked very different. The planes had shot at the Naval Air Station, but none of the fragile little Osprey seaplanes were there; they had been broken into parts and sold to the Japanese for rice and oil. They had hit the *armazem,* the Pan American warehouse next to the passenger terminal, and the drums of aviation fuel stored in the warehouse were burning. The trucks of the *bombeiros municipais* were down there and as soon as the fire department said it was safe, the Governor was going to go down and inspect the damage, probably after lunch. Would Consul Reeves care to join him?

Reeves was eager to go. This was by far the most interesting thing to happen for him in Macao for months. He continued to supervise the aid given to the British refugees and their dependents, who by now numbered over 5,000, but there were few surprises or challenges in that. Reeves felt his life had become routine and ordinary; others, among whom were men with whom he had been at university, were part of Eisenhower's 73 divisions poised to invade and defeat Germany itself, or with the air, sea and land forces gathering for the final decisive invasion of the Japanese mainland. Reeves was drafting memoranda and initialing invoices for payment.

But Reeves still thought he could be useful. He had started a project to plan for an administration for Hong Kong after the war. He had not been authorized or asked to do this, but he was, after all, the closest senior British official – just 35 miles away, with the most detailed and up to date on conditions there. He had talked to many Macanese who had relatives still in Hong Kong and they had passed on information about what was happening there. He had talked to the business community about what Hong Kong would need to recover from the Japanese occupation. He thought it made sense to use the people and resources of Macao, which would have survived the war unscathed, to help rebuild Hong Kong, which he assumed would revert to being a British colony, with life very much as it was before the war. He was developing a comprehensive organization chart of the new government and a map of the principal infrastructure that would be needed. He already had a thick file of supporting documents, which gave him both pleasure and a feeling of pride when he saw it on his desk. He was not to be a prisoner of the limitations put on other consular officials. He was sure Whitehall would appreciate his initiative. "Initiative" was something the Foreign Office encouraged in its staff, although he had to admit he had seen very little of it in his career.

He had also conceived of a project to identify all the people in the region who had worked for or collaborated with the Japanese. They would need to be isolated after the war, kept away from positions of responsibility, their gains from war-profiting confiscated. He could give the Special Branch and the other security services a head start in making the post-war world safe. He talked to the Police Chief, Y.C. Leung, the Governor's staff, his Macanese friends and even Wong Kong-Kit and soon he had over 2,000 names. He could not vouch for all of them, but then that was the job of the security services to make the final determination. But this list would undoubtedly help them. He was sure no other consul had taken such a project. He was eager to continue it; it would distinguish him in the Consular Service.

But first there was the burning warehouse. He had some responsibility for it; after all, he was the guardian of the all American property in Macao and the warehouse was leased by Pan American. He had been told that the airline made the lease payments promptly each month, even in wartime. But Reeves had let the Macao government use it for storage; he could not see his friend Redden minding.

The aviation fuel in the warehouse was now the property of the Macao government. Reeves remembered the barrels of fuel. There were 30 of them, each holding 55 gallons. There was a fuss when Redden had sold it to the Macao Government. He had wanted the retail price of $10 a gallon; they had wanted to pay the wholesale price of $5. In the end, Dr Lobo, who was doing the negotiating, prevailed. As Redden had said to Reeves, what are we going to do? Take it with us to Chungking on the backs of coolies?

Dr. Lobo had stored other miscellaneous goods in the warehouse – stacks of wire coils, metal bed frames, odd pieces of scrap metal, two old church bells, boxes of nails, an axle from some car, three 17th-century moss- and verdigris-covered bronze cannons from the *Pousada de S. Tiago*, six feet of rusty wrought-iron fencing, all of which could be valuable to someone somewhere sometime.

Dr Lobo was waiting to trade the fuel for rice and food. He thought as the year progressed that the Japanese, as the American submarines continued to sink their coastal shipping, would find themselves increasingly short of aviation fuel and that he could do a very advantageous trade for supplies Macao needed. And now all that fuel was burning.

Reeves drove his Studebaker down to the warehouse just after lunch, arriving around 2:30 in the afternoon. He parked a little away from the warehouse. The fire trucks were gone. Two Macao policemen were leaning on their motorbikes but they made no move to approach or stop him. There was a smell of smoke, fumes, and rotting damp from the water the firemen used to douse the flames. The warehouse was a shell of what it had once been. The corrugated metal roof was gone and part of one brick wall had collapsed to expose the blackened scrap metal within. The glass in the windows had been shattered in the fire; the charred remnants of the window frames hung at odd angles.

It was quite a mess. But Reeves was not really concerned; the warehouse was leased, not owned by Pan American. He would file a report with the British Legation in Chungking and it would be passed on to the American Embassy. He could not imagine the Americans even caring about this minor incident given all the death, devastation and destruction of the war.

Reeves heard two cars approaching and there was Dr Lobo's Packard and the Governor's dark green Dodge, quite new when the consul had arrived in Macao, and now waxed and polished, the afternoon sun coming through the rain clouds to catch the brightwork and glint on the fenders and bonnet. In showroom condition, as the advertisements put it. The Governor's and Dr Lobo's drivers – Dr Lobo's driver was the enormous butler Reeves recognized from his visits to Dr Lobo's house – opened the rear doors of the two cars and Dr Lobo and the Governor came out. They both shook hands with Reeves. For a minute, they looked at the burned and scorched shell of the warehouse in silence. Dr. Lobo spoke first.

"It is a pity about the fuel. Two days later, I would have delivered it to the Japanese. 1,650 US gallons. We had secured a very advantageous swap for large quantities of rice, grains and cooking oil. It cannot be helped." He pulled out a handkerchief and wiped his glasses of the damp from the north wind.

"I have cabled Lisbon and I expect they will protest to the American Embassy there. That part is out of my hands," said the Governor. He had his hands in his pockets and was looking at the wreckage. He did not seem concerned or worried. He stopped for a moment and looked amused. "For four years, I have fought to keep Macao safe and out of the war. All that time, I was worried about the Japanese, and for four years, they have sometimes threatened us, crossed our borders with impunity, but have never attacked us. Two days ago, I started to breathe a little more easily when I received reports that many of the troops over the border in Canton were being withdrawn to Japan to form part of the defense of the homeland. I thought Macao was further out of danger, and here we are, attacked by our friends, the Americans – allies of Great Britain I understand." He smiled at Reeves to let him know this was a mere pleasantry and then became serious as he talked.

The Governor continued. "These things happen in wartime. We are lucky no one was killed or wounded. Someone who did not want the Japanese to have the petrol gave the Americans good information." Reeves wondered who were the spies. Did he know them?

Dr. P.J. Lobo looked at the smoldering warehouse. "I will have the scrap metal moved elsewhere. I think I can still trade that for rice. Governor, if I can trouble you to have the police stay until my men have arranged that. Unattended, this will be a great temptation to many of our poorer citizens. Goodbye Mr. Reeves and thank you again for coming." He and the Governor walked to their cars and stood by them for a moment talking in low voices that Reeves could not hear. He assumed that they would be talking in Portuguese and he could not participate in the conversation even if he had been invited to. He stood watching them for a while, staying where he was, a little distant, alone.

There was a whine from somewhere, loud and insistent. Reeves, the Governor, Dr Lobo, the enormous butler, the Governor's driver, the two Macao policemen, all looked around. The sound was echoing off the cliffs of Guia Hill and it was difficult to hear where it was coming from. Then the whine became much louder and seemed to be coming from the sky. Everyone looked up and each saw at the same time seven black shapes high against the rain clouds. The whine was now piercing and the seven shapes moved rapidly away from the warehouse and hangar to the west, but just for a moment. But then as they turned back, the shapes rolled, and suddenly there were the silhouettes of seven stubby aircraft, still black against the dirty gray rain clouds. Then there was the thunderous roar of engines and a single line of planes dove towards the five men standing near the cars.

"They are coming to attack," shouted the Governor and ran towards the ditch lying alongside the road. The enormous butler grabbed Dr Lobo as though he were picking up a small child. He took five strides to the side of the road, pushed him down into the ditch and leaped in beside him. The Governor was already crouching in the ditch, his clothes wet and muddy. He peered over the edge and yelled.

"Reeves, my friend, get down," the Governor was yelling. Reeves had frozen for an instant, then he ran to the ditch, tripping at the edge and fell in. He barely missed the Governor's driver lying terrified in a pool of filthy water. Not a good sign if he actually had had to fight in a war, he thought.

Almost at the moment Reeves reached the ditch, the whine became a tremendous deafening roar and there were a series of sharp explosions, so close together they were almost a single sound, and then the seven aircraft, no longer stubby silhouettes, but huge powerful armored fighter planes, thundered overheard, all brute force and blind strength, deafening the seven men for a moment. Reeves thought he saw the flashes of the machine guns in their wings, firing. There was a second bang close by, the smell of petrol fumes and then the heat of a fire.

The seven Hellcats pulled up and climbed into the sky and the high-pitched roar of their engines faded slowly into silence. The Governor got up and kneeled in the ditch. He did not attempt to get out of it. He shaded his eyes, even though the sun was in the west behind clouds now. The two Macao policemen who had been several yards away by their motorbikes had not leaped into the ditch but had taken their pistols and were firing into the air at the departing aircraft. The pistols made small ineffectual popping sounds.

"They are leaving, I think." The Governor turned to his left. "The Americans have hit my car. It is on fire. Let's get away from it in case it explodes." The five men scrambled out of the ditch, the enormous butler pushing Dr Lobo, and ran to stand against the soot-covered wall of the Pan American warehouse. They stood in their clothes, soaked and filthy with ditch water, and watched the Governor's car burn; the petrol tank did not explode.

In the distance, the whine of the planes could be heard again, although they could not be seen until the last minute; they raced over the roof of the Bela Vista Hotel, fired some more, and then in an instant, the planes climbed and vanished into the clouds. Nothing could be heard, except the crackling of the Governor's car burning. There was the odor of burnt rubber and cloth, and the fainter exhaust fumes from the departed Hellcats.

The Governor was the first to speak. His face had a smear of mud on it and there was dirt and grass in his hair. But he was smiling, he was almost exhilarated. "They shot at us, but they missed. We live to fight another day." He put his arm around Reeves. "You know, we sit here in this little city behind those walls and we think the world with its problems will pass us by, that our Lady of Guia and the City of the Name of God will protect us and keep us safe. We now see we were mistaken; we thought we could hide here while the war raged around us. But the world will always find us to make its mischief." The Governor pulled Reeves closer to him. "Do not think, Consul Reeves, that Macao can protect you from whatever fate has in store for you." He released his grip and patted Reeves on the back. He was breathing hard; he was grinning. The Governor was exultant being this close to the war. Reeves felt an exhausted relief at having survived.

Dr. Lobo and Reeves both offered to drive the Governor back to his residence; they assumed he would want to change out of his mud-covered clothes. Both of their cars were untouched by the bullets and they both commented on the bad luck of the Americans hitting the Governor's car. The Governor chose to ride with Dr Lobo, saying there was some business with the food supply he wanted to discuss. He and Dr Lobo left after a warm farewell to Reeves. The Governor's Dodge was a charred and smoking shell; the tires melted and dark green paintwork blackened and peeling.

Reeves watched Dr Lobo's car pull away. He could see through the rear window of the Packard, Dr Lobo's and the Governor's heads close together, faces close, in the intimacy of a discussion. He thought about what just happened. There was no glory or fame in being shot at with friendly fire. People would have the usual concern that they would have for anyone in an accident or near-accident, but not admiration. Or else there would be the suspicion that he had brought it upon himself, through carelessness, putting himself in the wrong place.

Reeves walked over to the old Pan American hangar, just beyond the burnt-out warehouse and let himself in with the key he had brought with him. He had not been in the hangar for some time, now that Heenan and Redden were gone. They were his two great friends, who gave him drinks, had parties, joked and slapped him on the back, treating him like one of them. They had escaped to China and Redden was living in Miami, a city Reeves knew only in his imagination and knew he would never visit.

The air inside was damp and musty. The doors and windows had not been opened in months. Some light came through the windows on the side. Reeves tried the electric light but nothing happened. He assumed that the wires had been severed in the attack by the American aircraft.

Then he looked up into the darkness of the ceiling and at first he thought he was seeing stars. Then he realized that not only the roof, but the walls, were punctured with ragged holes through which the outside light was coming, hundreds of holes he thought, some close together, some randomly scattered. They are from the machine guns that the planes were firing; they have shot up a place where Redden and Heenan and I drank cocktails and ate stew. He grew accustomed to the light and saw that the poster of the beautiful brown-skinned native girl with the scarlet hibiscus in her hair watching the Pan American seaplane landing in a tropical lagoon was untouched. The roll-top desk where Redden had kept the bottles of liquor was splintered in several places. He thought that Ed Redden would find it funny that the Pan American offices had been machine-gunned by the United States Navy and thought he would write and tell him, before realizing that he did not even have an address.

He drove himself home to change out of his muddy clothes. He wanted to tell Rhoda about the American planes attacking the Governor's car and the warehouse and how he had been right there when it happened and how they had all had to dive into a ditch to avoid being killed. But at this time in the afternoon, she would be behind closed doors with Letitia, if she even wanted to hear about it, which he doubted. When they spoke now, she was uninterested in his work. Besides he was eager to get back to the consulate to continue work on his two projects for Hong Kong after the war. They were ambitious projects; some people might accuse him of overreaching, but he was not concerned. Better that my reach exceed my grasp, he thought; ambition will be admired and taken into consideration. The projects were important for his career. He would have a role. Or what's a heaven for.

Chapter 20

"The subject," said the First Secretary in the British Legation in Chungking even before the Third Secretary entering his office had been offered a chair, "is Reeves, our man in Macao. I used to think the most annoying thing he did was to spell Hong Kong as one word."

"Was Hong Kong ever one word?" said the Third Secretary, taking one of the two chairs in the First Secretary's office without waiting for an invitation, fearing one might never come.

The First Secretary looked at the Third. "Mr. Johnson, there is much you have not learned during your time in the Middle Kingdom." He put on his reading glasses and picked up a sheet of paper on which he had made some notes. "In 1843, the Foreign Office decided that Hong Kong should be written as a single word. On September 23rd, 1926, they in their wisdom changed their mind and decreed, to be specific in Gazette Notice Number 246, that Hong Kong should henceforth appear as two words." He put down the paper and looked up. "The Diplomatic Service and the Consular Service have followed this edict ever since. Except of course for our friend Reeves, who persists with a single word when he has to name our Crown Colony on the southern coast of China, the solitary consul in what was formerly the China Consular Service to do so. If that was the worst of his sins, I could still be quite fond of him. But it is not, regrettably."

The Third Secretary noted to himself that the First Secretary was hearing before him of issues around Reeves, which would indicate that those were quite serious. "What sins would those be, Sir?" he asked with what he hoped was appropriate politeness.

"Sins of commission it would seem, although if you have further evidence he is neglecting his consular duties, we can also list sins of omission. For most of Reeves's tenure, we have not had to worry about him. He has done a commendable job playing nursemaid to the British displaced persons in Macao although those duties are not in the normal purview of a consul. We have had reports from him about the situation there and the activities of the Japanese, at least those he could observe. He has described the Macao economy in painful detail. There has been nothing in those reports to give offense. But in the past months, as though waking from a deep sleep, he has been very active. Do you know what this is?" The First Secretary picked up a bundle of papers held together by three brass fasteners and waved them at the Third Secretary as though he was trying to signal him.

"No sir."

"This arrived a week ago and is a product of Vice-Consul Reeves's newly found enthusiasm for work. It consists of a list of nearly three thousand people whom he alleges have been overly friendly with the Japanese during the war – Wang Ching-wei men, Chinese merchants, Hong Kong civil servants, Indian policemen. Of particular interest is that few of them actually reside in Macao. Most are in Hong Kong or Canton Province, where, I believe, Mr. Reeves has no jurisdiction. I suppose we should commend him for his initiative and zeal."

"Gosh," said the Third Secretary and then wished he had not. "Are you going to give it to the police or the intelligence people? They might find it useful once the war is over."

"Of course not." The First Secretary was almost contemptuous in the way he said this. "We have no idea whether this list is the product of dogged detective work worthy of a Bulldog Drummond or the product of a fevered mind corrupted by drink, opium and loose women. For me to pass on these would mean the Diplomatic Service was somehow vouching for the reliability of this list and I have no idea how reliable it is. It could be a list of cut-throat villains or it could be a list of some of our more upstanding citizens in southern China. We simply do not know and that is not enough to risk the reputation of the Diplomatic Service."

The First Secretary tossed the bound bundle of papers onto the far edge of the desk where the Third Secretary had to stretch to pick them. "Please cause this document to be taken to the Registry and filed appropriately. You might like to make sure it is cross-referenced with the other documents on Reeves. No one need see it."

"I will see to it, sir. But that cannot be all that concerns you about Reeves. The list seems harmless enough."

"I have now made it harmless, so, yes, I take your point. But no, that is not all that Reeves has done in the frenzy of the past month, not by a long shot and that brings us to our present conversation." He picked up a large folded piece of paper on his desk, which he then unfolded until it was the size of a double sheet of newspaper.

"This document," said the First Secretary, "is a diagram purporting to propose a structure for the government of Hong Kong following the defeat of the Japanese and the resumption of British rule in the Colony." He held it up for the Third Secretary to see, like an auctioneer displaying a painting for sale, and then laid it down again on the table. He continued to look down on the chart, as though he was studying it.

"When you examine it closely, you will have to admire its detail. Reeves must have spent weeks preparing it. There are over eighty pages of supporting documents. It envisions departments dealing with Chinese affairs, claims for war damage, schools, the fire brigade, health, the drains, planning for the use of land, the buses and trams, the law officers, the supply of electricity and potable water, the police, coastal shipping, a Treasury department and a police service, to name a few. There are maps to show where the ditches for the drains are to be dug, maps of the routes for the buses. There is even a design for a new identity card for British subjects resident in Hong Kong and another for the Chinese residents. I have to commend the attention to detail and thought that went into this."

The Third Secretary was looking at the paper. He did not say anything for a while; it was quite beyond his comprehension that a consul would think of putting this together. Then he spoke. "When did he draw this up? Who authorized him? This is really astounding."

The First Secretary stood, walked over to the nearest window, and, turning his back on the Third Secretary, looked through one of the two remaining panes of glass; the rest of the window frames were covered with oiled paper where the glass had once been. Then he turned around and faced the Third Secretary. His face was set in anger, or perhaps it was just frustration.

"If this exercise had been simply sent to us in Chungking, we could perhaps treat it as some sort of schoolboy escapade and have a good laugh about it. Reeves would simply be one in a long line of consuls in China who have gone loopy. Madness is the only explanation for Reeves's imagining that it was within his remit to design a post-war Hong Kong." His face formed some sort of a smile. "I have always believed that consuls should be seen and not heard. They should know their place." Then he resumed his former expression of frustration and anger.

"Our issue is that Whitehall is now aware of Reeves's proposal. They have seen the plan, the diagram, the supporting documents and Reeves's explanatory notes, how I don't know. Whitehall has its own committees for post-war Hong Kong and they will brook no interference. They are sending me urgent queries as to what is going on. They cannot believe some obscure vice consul has taken this upon himself." The First Secretary walked to his desk and sat down. He picked up another document.

"By way of example, here is J.C. Sterndale-Bennett, Esq. CMG, MC, our own beloved head of the Far Eastern Division of the Foreign Office pestering me to find out what is going on with Reeves and Hong Kong." He picked up another document. "Here is our very own Colonel Ride to General Grimsdale saying that the Reeves Committee is causing consternation with the Japanese and the Macao government. Ride, you will remember, has been very harsh in his assessment of Reeves."

His voice now was audibly angry and was loud in the office with just the two of them. "You are to instruct Reeves as clearly as you can so that there can be no misunderstanding that he is to cease this committee work forthwith. Second, I know I cannot fire Reeves, but I intend to remove him from Macao as soon as it can be arranged and then make his life so miserable he will resign from the Consular Service. He clearly does not have the temperament, judgment or intelligence to work there." He stopped speaking harshly, smiled and said, sounding almost tranquil "Perhaps he could be transferred to Chungking where he could work closely under our direction."

"How are we going to remove him from Macao?" asked the Third Secretary. The suggestion had startled him. Consuls could not be fired and, no matter how incompetent, were simply left in place. After all, what harm could they really do? He continued. "We can hardly expect him, his wife and his young daughter to make the overland journey to Chungking. Then there is the problem of how his replacement will get to Macao. We are planning on replacing him, aren't we? We cannot have the Japanese with the only consular mission in Macao as long as the war is going on."

The First Secretary responded as though the answer was obvious. "Of course we are planning on replacing him. Someone compliant and obedient; I have a search on. As for the rest of the details on how to exfiltrate Reeves and infiltrate his successor, I expect you to find solutions, then come back and report to me." The meeting was at an end; the Third Secretary left.

* * *

Reeves was unaware of the displeasure he had caused in the Legation in Chungking. But it was the afternoon of the assassination of the Japanese consul that morning and that preoccupied him. Mr. Fukui had been gunned down on his morning walk on a busy street in Macao just a few hundred yards from the consulate to which he had been returning.

The city was tense. It was warm but few people were in the street. On the *Avenida de Almeida Ribeiro*, there would normally have been scores of people on the street, looking in at the stores and what the street vendors might have to sell, even if there was little for sale and even less money to make purchases. This time there was no one on the street and the stores had their shutters tightly fastened. Reeves saw a single body lying face down on the sidewalk, but he had no idea why. Below the high arches of the *Banco Nacional Ultramarino* there was a squad of the black soldiers from Mozambique, their rifles cradled in their arms where they could be easily raised to fire. They stared at Reeves in the car with unsmiling faces as he was driven by. Reeves felt a sense of unease; he did not know what the assassination meant for him. The Allies seemed to be winning the war; who would want to shoot him? He would start carrying his little pistol every time he went outside. He again imagined himself in a gun battle and the report of it appearing in his university newsletter.

Four days later, Mr. Fukui's body was returned to Japan for his funeral rites and internment. The Governor had decided to give him what honors he could. The body was taken from the mortuary of the *San Januario* hospital, placed in a coffin and loaded onto an army truck, freshly polished for the occasion. At the Governor's offices on the *Praya Grande*, the coffin was covered with a Japanese flag, on which were laid floral arrangements and wreaths from the Governor, the military, the police and various Chinese merchants. At 11:00am precisely, the truck pulled very slowly out of the forecourt of the *Palacio da Praia Grande* and drove at a crawl to the docks. Following on foot were the Governor in full naval uniform, Colonel Sawa, still in his field uniform, shirt unbuttoned, the staff of the Japanese consulate in black ties and dark suits, the Police Chief and senior military officers. Reeves was unsure of whether to attend the funeral of an official of a country with which Great Britain was at war. He finally decided that he would attend – this was an issue about the inviolability of the consular service – and he wore his white consular uniform with the silver piping.

At the docks, the flower- and flag-draped coffin was hoisted about the *Isuki Maru* that would leave for Tokyo that evening. It would cling close to the coast, hoping to avoid American submarines. An honor guard of Portuguese soldiers in full dress uniform, their faces damp with sweat, fired a six-gun salute as the coffin was lifted high in the air. Reeves saluted along with the other officials. Reeves did not know what to make of Mr. Fukui's murder. He was a decent man, doing his best. In the end, watching the coffin lowered into the hold, he decided that this minor tragedy was one of those inexplicable random pieces of bad luck. He could think of no other explanation.

The procession broke into small groups to talk while the participants waited for their cars. Reeves went over to the Police Chief and asked him whether there had been any progress in discovering Consul Fukui's assassin. There had been none, the Police Chief reported, but then he had turned to stare at Colonel Sawa, who was smiling to himself, but standing alone and talking to no one. Colonel Sawa did not return the Police Chief's stare. The Police Chief also mentioned that the new Japanese consul was not to arrive for four more months.

Reeves reported on the funeral procession and passed the news on the delay in the arrival of the new Japanese consul to Chungking. The Third Secretary, reflecting Chungking's continued dissatisfaction with Reeves, reprimanded him for participating in the funeral cortege without his permission, something he previously would not have bothered to do.

Within ten days of the death of the Japanese consul, there was a second assassination. The Wong brothers had been delivering rice, smuggled in sampans from Canton, directly to a Macanese rice merchant, Fernando de Senna Fernandes Rodrigues. Rodrigues had refused to pay the percentage of its selling price that Wong Kong-kit had demanded and, as a result, Wong Kong-kit had him shot. Wong Kong-kit had a monopoly on the smuggled rice trade.

The Police Chief made a special trip to see Reeves to tell him of Rodrigues's assassination. Rodrigues was also the chair of the Macao Red Cross and the Police Chief was aware that Reeves knew him. He sat sadly in a chair in Reeves's office looking away. He had not waited for Reeves to offer him a drink, but had helped himself to the gin in the decanter on the sideboard. He began to talk slowly.

"Mr. Rodriguez was walking with his two daughters down the *Rua do Cemiterio*. The daughters are beautiful girls, eleven and thirteen, Alina and Norma." The Police Chief was still looking away and Reeves was sure that he ran a finger around one eye to remove a tear. "The three of them had just arrived at the corner where there is the high school on *Tap-Seac* square, when out steps a gunman from behind the arches and opens fire, bang bang, at just a few feet. Do you know what those beautiful girls did? Alina is the first to see the gunman and she makes a big leap, even though she is a little girl and throws herself between her father and the gunman. The gunman keeps shooting and she takes three bullets right in her stomach." The Police Chief patted his stomach to show where he meant. "Alina is lying there right on the stones of the square and the gunman shoots more bullets into Mr. Rodrigues. So Norma, she is older and taller; she jumps up and holds the collar of the gunman's coat and tries to pull him to the ground. He empties the last bullets in his gun into her. The gunman runs but some of the children in the school see him and later tell my men who he is – Wong Kau, one of Wong Kong-kit's men. They had seen him around the school."

Tears were now coming from the Police Chief's eyes openly and he made no attempt to wipe them away. "Fernando Rodrigues was taken to *San Januario*, but he was already dead when they got there. Norma had time for Father Teixeira to administer extreme unction before she died. Alina went in another ambulance to *San Rafael*. Father Teixeira went there and heard her last confession. But she is still with us, right between living and dying. Every minute I pray for her."

Reeves did not know what to say. He walked over to the side table and poured himself an inch of gin. He put the decanter down on his desk where the Police Chief could reach it easily without standing up.

"I am so sorry to hear about Mr. Rodrigues and his daughters. I too will pray for Alina." The Police Chief looked at Reeves. From what he had heard, the consul did not go to church, unless you counted that little yellow building with the Chinese lady priest where some of the

Protestants went. Where would he pray for Alina where it would do any good? The tears came back into his eyes again, but his voice was level.

"They are beautiful girls. Everyone in Macao knows and loves them."

"Have you had any luck catching Wong Kau yet?" Reeves realized that he was awkwardly changing the subject.

The Police Chief's face returned to an expression of professional composure. "Wong Kong-kit knows he has gone too far this time. Colonel Sawa cannot save him. Wong Kong-kit and his triad has been in the pay of Colonel Sawa for years and thinks that he can get away with anything because Colonel Sawa will protect him. Wong Kong-kit is hiding in his house on the *Avenida do Coronel Mesquita*. He has sandbags around the windows and machine guns on the balcony. I have men watching the front door. Wong Kau will not stay away forever. He is hungry and needs to be paid for what he did. When he comes up the *Avenida do Coronel Mesquita* to visit the house of Wong Kong-kit, my men will seize him. Then all of Macao will know Wong Kong-kit is powerless to protect his men. Even Colonel Sawa will know that."

Reeves, when he thought about it later, was not surprised to learn that Wong Kong-kit was doing business with the Japanese as well. How else was he going to smuggle food and medicines into Macao through Japanese-occupied China? This was wartime and you did what you needed to do to survive and prosper. It, in Reeves's mind, did not detract from all the favors Wong Kong-kit had done for him and the British. He had found medicines and food for the British refugees; he had found housing for all of them; he had smuggled nearly 300 of them out of Macao to freedom without a single loss. Reeves could not have done his job without Wong Kong-kit. He had grown quite fond of that old unscrupulous pirate over the years. "I am so sad to hear all of this." He did not know what else to say.

The Police Chief looked thoughtful. "These are crazy times, Consul Reeves. One of my men heard that it was Colonel Sawa who paid a triad gunman to kill Mr. Fukui. I do not know if that is true. Mr. Fukui was always asking the Governor to intercede with the Japanese Embassy in

Lisbon to get them to remove him and his soldiers. Perhaps Colonel Sawa did not like that and took his revenge. He is a stupid man and only understands brute violence."

Reeves thought about this. Mr. Fukui was killed by one of his own men? He was horrified by the thought.

The Police Chief stopped for a moment, his thoughts briefly his own. Then he continued in a quite abstracted way. "The funeral is tomorrow for Mr. Rodrigues and his daughter Norma. A mass at *San Agostinho* and then the burial at *S. Miguel Arcanjo.*" He crossed himself.

Reeves thought he should at least say something. "Of course, I will come to the funeral and I will send a wreath. Mr. Rodrigues was very well thought of in the British community and did much fine work as the head of the Red Cross in Macao."

The Police Chief was standing up, his big German Luger pistol pulling his belt lower. His face showed no sign of his previous emotion. He hitched on his belt to pull it up but it fell to where it was before. He came forward to Reeves's desk and leaned forward and put both hands on it.

"Don't go to the funeral." He then reached over to touch Reeves on one arm and continued in an almost delighted tone, as though it was the funniest thing in the world. "My men heard that you were on a list to be killed at the funeral or shortly after that. Not by Wong Kong-kit's triad, another triad. Wong Kong-kit loves the British – he would not harm a hair on your head. And one of my men, a Chinese detective, heard that your Mr. Aycock was on that same list. That's crazy, who would want to shoot you and Mr. Aycock? I don't believe a word of it. Those guys in the triads get drunk and then they start saying anything. You know Macao; we are a peaceful city. But better not to go to the funeral. Stay inside for a few days until my men beat some sense into the triads. Then they will go back to killing each other and leave the rest of us alone. You have a nice house; enjoy it." He came around the desk and kissed Reeves on both cheeks before leaving.

Reeves wrote up a brief report on the assassination of Mr. Rodrigues, merely referring to him as the head of the Portuguese Red Cross in

Macao. It seemed unnecessary to describe in detail his connection with rice smuggling and Wong Kong-kit. He was unsure how much the Foreign Office knew of Wong Kong-kit and how much he had done for British subjects in Macao. Reeves had never mentioned him in his reports knowing that the Foreign Office would prohibit his having any dealings with him and he needed him to accomplish his mission of taking care of the refugees. Pragmatism was a virtue not always rewarded in the Civil Service. He reported on the rumor that Mr. Fukui's assassination was the work of Colonel Sawa and the Japanese Kempeitai, working with a local triad. He was sure this story of internecine strife within the Japanese Government would fascinate the Foreign Office and he would get credit for reporting it. Finally he wrote that the Police Chief had warned him that he and Mr. Aycock ('a senior clerk in the consulate' he added by way of explanation, quite certain that the Legation had no idea of the names of anyone in the consulate) had been placed on a list for assassination. He did not mention that the Police Chief did not give it any credence and he himself found it hard to believe, knowing what he did about Macao. Reeves thought that his being on a list for assassination had a nice ring to it and wondered what the reaction would be in Chungking. He thought wryly they might see him in a different light, as someone important enough to be on a list to be assassinated. There was a nice irony in building a career in this manner. He took comfort in the Police Chief's assurance that he had nothing to worry about. That seemed right to him.

* * *

Shortly after the second of these two cables arrived in Chungking, the First Secretary had the Third Secretary called to his office. When he knocked and entered the office, the First Secretary was sitting behind the desk, his elbows on it and his fingers coming together in a suggestion of a steeply pitched roof. He did not get up.

"I want you to cease your efforts to devise a plan to remove Reeves from Macao. I need to apprise you of a change of plans."

"A change of plans?" said the Third Secretary unnecessarily.

"We have had a report from Reeves, which I meant to forward to you, that the head of the Macao Red Cross has been shot. An event of little interest, except that Reeves has reported in the same document that he was informed by the Chief of Police that Reeves and one of his half-caste clerks might also have been marked for assassination." He paused for a moment and smiled. "If Reeves were shot, it would solve one of our problems. The precedent it sets however could be troubling." The Third Secretary never knew when the First was saying these things in jest.

The First Secretary continued. "I brought this to the attention of the Ambassador. Sir Horace has sent a note to our Ambassador in Lisbon asking him to express our regret to Dr Salazar's government and his hope that the current troubled situation in Macao does not cause anxiety for the safety of British subjects. One could have, perhaps, desired that this message about safeguarding British subjects might have been conveyed in slightly stronger terms. But be that as it may, I am sure you see the larger problem."

The First Secretary paused for a moment, confident that his junior colleague did not grasp what he called the 'larger problem.' Without waiting for a reply, he continued.

"It is an elementary point. Having asked the Portuguese to ensure the safety of British subjects in Macao, to withdraw the senior British representative will be tantamount to a declaration that the Portuguese are incapable of doing so. We cannot insult our oldest ally in this manner. Reeves must remain, even though his life might be in danger. There are larger issues involved."

"Then I will close this particular file, sir. I am glad this is resolved, even in this manner." The Third Secretary was starting to stand, when the First Secretary began to speak.

"Please stay seated. There is one other aspect to this Reeves business. He is to be promoted." The First Secretary enjoyed the look of astonishment on the Third Secretary's face.

"Promoted? You mean to be a full consul?

"Yes," said the First Secretary, "That is exactly what I mean. He is to be promoted from vice consul to consul."

"But sir, that is highly irregular. He is not yet forty. He should have another seven to ten years in service before even being considered. And what about his record of service to date? This will cause uncomfortable questions to be raised amongst the other vice consuls who are still waiting for their expected promotions. And it was my understanding that the Foreign Office has placed a moratorium on all promotions in the Consular Service whilst we are at war."

"You might give me a little credit for being aware of these issues," said the First Secretary, his smile gone, so that his last statement would have the force of a mild reprimand. "But these are unusual times. Reeves has also informed us that the new Japanese consul will not arrive for some months. He will have the rank of a full consul. If we promote Reeves now, he will have seniority over the Japanese consul. If we fail to promote him, the new Japanese consul will outrank him and will have precedence. Distasteful as this action *vis à vis* Reeves is, we cannot have Great Britain be seen in an inferior position to our enemies, even in a place as unimportant as Macao. Please draw up the necessary documents to make this so. If it is any consolation to you, I will ensure that Sir Horace does not send a telegram of congratulations." Again the meeting was over. The Third Secretary left.

* * *

Thirteen days later, without prior notice, one of Colonel Ride's BAAG couriers brought Reeves an engraved certificate in a black leather case with the royal coat of arms stamped on it in gold leaf, informing that he was "trusty and well beloved" and that an unnamed 'we' was resposing "especial trust and confidence" in him. The certificate then went on to say that he had been promoted to the rank of Consul in His Majesty's Consular Service. There were some supporting documents giving the effective date of his promotion and spelling out his increases in pay and allowances. There was a transmittal note ('dictated but not read') signed by the Third Secretary.

Reeves sat in his office and a tear came into his eye. He could not believe it. He had been promoted, perhaps ten years before he had any right to expect it. The news was so sudden and unexpected: it was clearly the result of his work compiling the list of Japanese sympathizers and assisting in the planning for post-war Hong Kong. No other consul would have taken that initiative. He was being recognized at last. Where would they send him now after Macao? Somewhere grand and of significance? His career was looking up; the war would surely end soon and the Foreign Office would be able to move him. He could tell the people in the office, but they would have no idea of what this meant to him and their congratulatory wishes would be confused. He would think about how to tell his parents later; it would be by letter and he wanted very much for them to have the context so that they could see how important this was. But he could tell Rhoda now. He hoped that she might be interested; little about him these days seemed to interest her.

When he arrived home, he asked The Number One Boy who had opened the door to tell his wife that he was home and that he wished to see her. He would be in the living room. Reeves went into the living room, sitting on the couch with the leather case with his new commission as a full consul on his lap, as though it was a present for someone. He was looking at the door expectantly when it opened.

Rhoda entered, holding Letitia's hand who was reluctantly following, her head turning from side to side so that she was not looking at her father. They did not sit down at first.

"Is everything alright?" she asked. "I have been reading to Letitia. We found some English children's books in the library in that old building."

"The *Leal Senado*?" asked Reeves. "The old Macao Senate?"

"I suppose so." Rhoda did not seem to care. "There was one copy of Beatrix Potter's 'Tale of Peter Rabbit.' I have been reading it slowly to Letitia." Reeves thought that Rhoda too only knew those animals from books. Rhoda stopped suddenly and sat down abruptly on the couch opposite Reeves, pulling her daughter down with her. Letitia pushed herself closer to her mother and buried her head in her mother's chest. Reeves realized how tall she was getting even though she had just turned eight.

"She is making progress. I can really see it. She is sounding out some of the words and she is looking at the pictures." Reeves saw that Rhoda's eyes were wet but did not know what to do quite at that instant. Rhoda looked up at him. "I think she is really trying, but it is hard when you have never seen a rabbit or a squirrel or even an owl. She doesn't know what they are. She may never."

Rhoda was looking at Reeves sadly and he realized that this may lead to another discussion of when they might leave China for England or Europe. Now was the time to tell her his good news.

"My dear," he said, holding the black leather case on his lap in two hands, "I have good news. Perhaps Letitia would like to come over here and sit next to me." He looked expectantly over towards his daughter, but she twisted even more firmly against her mother, her head pushed against Rhoda's chest and one arm tightly wrapped around her mother's neck. Reeves felt a small pang; he really wished his daughter wanted to sit with him.

"Perhaps it is better to leave her alone," said Rhoda, "She has had a trying day with her reading and we have several more pages to go before bedtime. Tell me your news." Rhoda could not keep the nervousness out of her voice for this last sentence.

"My dear," he repeated and thought briefly that this was a phrase that he had not used very much. He opened the leather case, turned it around and displayed it to her. She looked at it without understanding what it was and then looked up at Reeves, her face tired with the efforts she was expending with Letitia, and not saying anything.

"This is my commission as a consul," said Reeves, smiling towards his wife in a way he had not done for a long time. "Rhoda," he said and paused before delivering the news "I have been promoted to full consul, years before my time. I do not know, but I have to believe my work here has been recognized."

Rhoda's eyes narrowed. She looked at him suspiciously then looked away and began to talking, apparently to no one in particular. "There was such a nice consul in Shanghai when I was a girl. He was a knight and when he came to dinner, my father would call him Sir Sidney. Perhaps they will make you a knight?" She asked this question without looking at him.

Reeves was somewhat taken aback. Why was Rhoda drifting back into memories of her childhood? Did she really think he might be up for a knighthood? As gently as he could, he tried to bring her back to the present. "No, my dear. He was undoubtedly a consul-general in a very large and important city and I will have a long wait until I am promoted again. It may never happen and we should not certainly expect that I will be knighted."

"Such a nice man, he wore bow ties." Rhoda was now looking out the windows to the garden.

"They will not tell me our next posting until the war is over," said Reeves, not wanting to talk about the Consul General in Shanghai, "But this promotion is a very good sign that we are in line for a city outside of China. Perhaps there will be owls and rabbits and squirrels." He addressed this last sentence to Letitia with a brightness he hoped was not forced. Reeves put his commission to one side and stood. He hoped this sentence also did not sound forced. "Let us have a glass of bubbly to celebrate. We still have a bottle left from what we shipped from Mukden."

Rhoda stood too, dragging Letitia upright with her. She finally looked at him and was smiling; a weak smile to be sure, but still a smile. "John," she said, "I hope this is good news for us, it has been very hard for me here." Reeves thought of her struggles with Letitia, her inability to form friendships with the other British women, the worries about her parents and brother interned in Shanghai. But others had gone through worse. This was a good place to spend the war. Rhoda had paused and then continued. "Let me finish reading to Letitia and then I will try come down and join you."

Rhoda never did come downstairs for the celebratory glass of champagne. Reeves ate dinner by himself and drank rice wine liquor. When he went upstairs to his room, he could hear Letitia's quiet crying and Rhoda's strained words of comfort. He thought that his daughter must have somehow been frightened when she was taken downstairs to the living room. He could not help feeling guilty. He knew she would not understand, but his promotion was also good news for her. He hoped she would understand some day.

* * *

A week later, Reeves received a brief telegram of congratulations on his promotion from Sir Ronald Hugh Campbell, the British Ambassador in Lisbon, a man he had never heard of before. He never did receive a telegram from Sir Horace Seymour in Chungking.

Chapter 21

By the late spring of 1945, the rains, damp chills, and winds of winter were finally past. Reeves again could not help thinking that the war would soon be over. Perhaps it was the weather – glorious long days of sunshine with cool breezes from the south west. The hibiscus and bougainvillea came out in full bloom with bursts of pink and scarlet flowers and their scent drifted in the air in certain streets even when the flowers were hidden behind walls in back gardens. The sky was almost always cloudless, a rich translucent blue canopy over the small town. The bells of the Angelus from the many churches were precise and clear in the evening air.

Reeves liked during this weather to work out of the original consulate building on the *Calcada do Gaio*. He had kept his office at the back of the ground floor facing the little walled garden, with the lemon trees and the scent of blossom and flowers in the spring warmth. On one such perfect afternoon, Mr. Gonsalves brought in a telegram and a letter, which Reeves could see from the writing, was from his mother. He opened the letter first and was surprised to see that it was dated only three weeks ago. The mails were faster now at the end of the war. His mother told him of the sudden death of his father; he had died unexpectedly in the chair by the fire one evening. He did not appear to suffer or be in pain; he had been looking forward to the reopening of much of his business now that the war in Europe seemed to be winding down. His mother told him of the funeral arrangements, the burial in the family plot not far from the house. She hoped that he would get home leave soon and they could put flowers on his grave together. She was sorry his father did not meet Rhoda and his granddaughter. His mother included the paid obituary from the local paper; a photograph of his father as a much younger man, perhaps the same age as Reeves now, and the bare facts of his father's life, which bore no relation to Reeves's memories of him. He would now only have those memories; he would never see him again.

His breathing shallow, Reeves opened the telegram. It was from an uncle on his mother's side, another Navy man, now retired. In that stark language of the telegram which excluded any compassion, nuance or sympathy it told Reeves that his mother had taken a turn for the worst and told him to apply for compassionate leave to come immediately. Reeves rose, stunned by these two coincidental communications, closed the door to his office and locked it, and then sat down in his chair, swiveling it to face the sun-dappled garden.

His father and mother had never learned of his promotion, his triumph, his reward for his work in Macao, and now they would never know about it. He had not written to them on the subject. He thought that it would be better if they found out about it when it was published in the quarterly edition of the Foreign Office *Gazette*. Many of his father's friends in business followed the *Gazette* and they would surely see it and telephone or write their congratulations to his parents. In that way his parents would find out and perhaps really appreciate the significance of the promotion, which, he worried, they might not have accepted from him. It would be such an unexpected and pleasant surprise. But he had been too clever, "too clever by half" as his father used to say, and now they would never know.

He thought about being an only child, a late-in-life baby whom he often wondered whether his parents really wanted. He wondered whether he had disappointed them, not going into business like his father, moving all the way to China, not being part of the Diplomatic Service. Then, just as he had after seeing them for the last time before boarding the ship for China in Southampton, he remembered their many clumsy kindnesses; his father rising early to make a fire on a cold winter's morning so he could toast bread on a long fork to have with melted butter before the walk to the little village school; their taking him to the village fair even though he realized later they hated the noise and the crowds; his mother's rubbing his chest with the camphor compound when he was in bed with a cold. And now he could never thank them, tell them how much these little gestures, these offices of parenthood, meant to him. They would never tell him how proud they were of his service in the Consular Service. He quietly wept as he sat, the French windows open, so the garden and all its flowers appeared almost ready to flow into his office.

When he felt composed, some several minutes later, he wrote out a telegram on an official form to his uncle: "Deeply regret compassionate leave impossible exigencies of wartime." He was astounded by his uncle even to think it was possible he could leave Macao and travel all the way back to England. He must be dotty, he thought. He handed the form and told Mr. Gonsalves to take it down to the General Post Office for transmittal. He resolved to occupy himself with the business of the consulate and try not to think about his parents.

He would have to tell Rhoda but he worried that it would cause her only to think more of her parents interned in Shanghai. When he did tell her, she put her arms around him for the first time in a long time and said how sorry she was and how terrible it was that he could not be there. She did not mention her parents, for which Reeves was relieved. She had not touched him in a long time.

Two weeks later, a telegram came from the same uncle tersely telling him of the death of his mother, with no detail but the date and the single word 'regrets.' Reeves was anticipating the news in this telegram and he took it with far more equanimity; he still thought of them and there still was some grief, but his parents were now in his past, and he continued with the business of the consulate.

He found much to occupy himself. He led a memorial service at the Protestant Chapel for the American President, Franklin Roosevelt, when he unexpectedly died and, when Germany surrendered the next month, Reeves led a Victory in Europe Thanksgiving service, again in the Protestant Chapel. The congregation sang Kipling's *Recessional* with its gloomy warnings about the decay of empires, and Reeves stood at the front of the chapel and read out loud Psalm 136 with its odd ideas of mercy

('Who smote Egypt with their first-born: For His mercy endureth for ever' – who kills children as a demonstration of mercy? Reeves thought.) The British community, crowded into that small chapel, looked at him as he presided. Reeves thought that they seemed to see him as their leader. Perhaps he was.

After the surrender of Germany and the further American victories in the Pacific, Colonel Sawa could be often seen walking in the streets, his sword dragging in the dust. He was usually drunk. Reeves had heard that he had even stormed into the offices of the *O Renascimento* newspaper, yelling and screaming and stinking of rice wine liquor, and demanded that they stop publishing lies about American victories and Japanese defeats. He had tried to get his sword out of its scabbard to threaten them, but failed. When the staff had laughed, he left the office, swaying and staggering, almost falling over. He had become a figure of fun. Reeves had seen him asleep on a park bench on more than one occasion and almost felt sorry for him. Whatever form Japan took after the war, there would be no place for him. Macao was his last post.

Reeves heard the news of the surrender of Japan the evening of August 15th. He was sitting in the family reception room at Skyline listening to the BBC. He shouted loudly and urgently for Rhoda, and then poured himself a drink. She came into the room, her face both set and anxious.

Reeves stood and walked over the side table and poured her a small whiskey, adding a large amount of soda water. He did not say a thing. Her worried eyes followed him, her husband knew that she did not like to drink, especially whiskey. He passed the glass to her. She held it a little away from her. She stayed close to the doorway.

"Sit down, my dear, I have some news for you."

She moved warily to the sofa opposite the armchair where he had sat down and perched herself nervously on its edge, a slight shiver flickering across her frail body, like a sparrow in winter, her glass held with both hands in her lap. She looked at him. She was pale.

He smiled at her. "Please raise your glass, my dear, and drink to peace. The BBC has just announced that Japan has surrendered. The war is finally over." He took a large draft from his glass and looked at her, wanting to see how she would react. She did not touch hers.

For what seemed like a long time, she said nothing but simply stared at him, her face unchanged from when she had come in. Then her shoulders slumped, her eyes filled with tears and she gave a sort of a smile. She stood up and was still for a minute; then she walked towards Reeves. Surprised, he put down his glass and stood up. She was now crying and embraced him, still holding her glass, so that some of the whiskey spilled down Reeves's shirt back. She pulled him tight against her.

"Oh John, she said and sobbed, "Oh John, now we can get out of here. We can find proper doctors for Letitia. You will hear soon about your next posting. Promise that we will be somewhere close to Europe. Daddy and my brother can leave Shanghai. They can come and visit us. Letitia will be better and she will be able to read. Thank you for telling me, thank you." Reeves thought of all these hopes she had stored up over the years of what she thought of as her long exile in Macao now spilling out. He wished he could say something to comfort her and give her hope. She sobbed some more, released Reeves, put down her glass and left the room as she had done so many times before. Reeves was conscious of the damp on the back of his shirt and the smell of whiskey in the air from the spilled drink.

The morning after the surrender of Japan, Reeves went to a cupboard in his office and found, wrapped in brown paper, the new Union Jack that Colonel Ride's BAAG had smuggled to him from Chungking, to be raised only when peace was declared. He walked up the stairs and then climbed the ladder through the hatch onto the roof, the brown paper parcel under his arm. He unwrapped the parcel and the sheet of brown paper, caught in a gust, blew away and fluttered over Macao for a few moments before disappearing from his sight. He unfolded the flag on the roof, conscious somewhere that you were not meant to lay a flag on the ground. It was much larger than he expected and he wondered for a moment how he was to attach it to the stout halyard that ran down the short flagpole fixed to the balustrade on the roof of the consulate. But then he saw the clips on the halyard, adjusted the distance between them, fastened them through the two brass grommets on the flag and hoisted it up the mast. There was a stiff burst of wind suddenly from out of the northwest and the flag unfurled with a snap, flapping slightly. Reeves was alone; no one from the consular staff had accompanied him. He stepped back, brought his feet together, squared his shoulders, and saluted in what he thought might be the correct manner. One part of his life was about to end, and a new part, now unknown, was about to begin.

Rhoda started joining him for meals. She asked at almost every dinner if he had heard anything about his next posting and could not disguise her disappointment when Reeves said he had no news. She asked her husband repeatedly to give his understanding of what might happen. Reeves would explain each time that the China Consular Service had been disbanded and merged into the overall consular service some ten years ago. There were no more British settlements for consuls to administer and, after the surrender of Japan, the Communists and the Nationalists had turned on each other and China was now engulfed by a civil war. There would still be some need for British consuls in China, but only a few of them in a much diminished role. Much of Europe and Asia was in ruins and the desirable posts in North and South America would go to men with more seniority and political favor than he had. He thought he believed to a certainty that his performance in Macao would advance his cause – he had been promoted after all at a time when all promotions were in abeyance – and he spoke some European languages, so Europe remained a possibility. He hoped – he really hoped – that he could play his role in whatever new world would rise, phoenix-like, out of the smoking embers of the old. Rhoda would watch him with wide sad eyes every time he would recount these thoughts and say nothing. She was, he thought, deciding whether to believe him.

On August 19th, Reeves was to officiate at the World Peace Thanksgiving Day service at the Protestant chapel. The Reverend Florence Lim had organized it for the Anglican community; he wondered who had chosen the title for the service; so much of the world was still at war.

Rhoda agreed, to his surprise, to accompany him to the Protestant chapel for the peace service and for a brief moment, he wondered whether she now saw herself as having a future as the wife of a British consul. He did not know how to think of that. Because it was summer, she wore a dark-navy cotton frock, white gloves and a little straw hat that she had had since her last year of school in Shanghai. The driver parked near the house that had once been the residence of the President of the Select Committee for Macao of the British East India Company. Reeves had the same thought then that he had had every time he saw the house: that in another life, two centuries ago, he might have been living there in splendor as the East India Company's chief representative, presiding over all of Britain's trade with China.

It was very hot as they approached the Protestant chapel and even though it was on a hill, one of the highest points in Macao, there was not a trace of a breeze. The leaves of the frangipani trees that rose over the cemetery lay flat and still on the branches and there was no cool in their shade. The tiny chapel stood by itself in the full sun, the yellow stucco almost shimmering in the bright light.

The people who were to attend the service were waiting outside, unwilling to enter the hot, oppressive chapel until they absolutely had to. There must have been close to seventy and Reeves thought how closely packed they would be inside. There were a fair number of Chinese whom he did not recognize and he thought he knew little or nothing of the congregation to whom the Reverend Florence Lim ministered. He recognized most of the British. The men had found jackets and ties and even suits; the women had all found the one nice frock they had. There were some children, again in their one nice set of clothes. They were talking happily to each other about when they could return to Canton, Shanghai and other cities in China. They seemed willfully oblivious to the abolition of the treaty ports and the civil war engulfing China. The women were fanning themselves with their hands or an actual fan; most of the men had taken their hats off and were doing the same. They greeted Reeves warmly and seemed surprised to see Rhoda. The Reverend

Florence Lim came out in the white surplice and robes of an Anglican priest and motioned for the crowd to enter the chapel. Reeves could not get used to seeing a woman dressed as a priest, let alone a Chinese woman.

He and Rhoda entered the chapel first, the crowd standing back until they had gone in, and were the first to take their seats in the front row of folded chairs right in front of the pulpit. The British community had not always been so deferential to Reeves during the war; he had been a visible symbol of their impoverished exile in Macao and they resented having to rely on the charity of the British Government. But now he was the representative of Great Britain, which had won a great victory. A fan stood in one corner of the front of the chapel slowly turning from one side to the other, blowing the hot air around, but doing little to alleviate the heat inside.

Reeves looked at the program and found that half of it was in Chinese. He wondered what it would be like to be a member of the Church of England and not know English. He had been asked to read Psalm 148, which was full of praise for the Lord but had nothing to say about world peace. Reeves also read an extract from the Book of Zephaniah, a book he had never heard of before. It did talk about the Lord casting out your enemy and returning your captives to you, so that was more *a propos* he thought. The Reverend Lim read from scripture and said some of the responsive prayers in Cantonese and Reeves could see some of the British looking at each other. They were hearing Cantonese spoken for the first time in an Anglican church and did not not know whether to approve or not. Peering earnestly out at the congregation from behind her round black-rimmed glasses, Reverend Lim also preached a short sermon on peace in that staccato clipped intonation that Cantonese speakers of English often had.

At last there was the recessional hymn, which turned out to be the sprightly "My Eyes Have Seen the Glory" and Miss McKinney, a spinster school teacher from Hong Kong, lent over the small scratched upright piano and gave it her all. The congregation repeated the blessing and filed gratefully out of the chapel in search of relief from the heat. Outside the chapel, the British stood on one side and the Chinese on the other. The British, quite sincerely, thanked the Reverend Lim for the service but most were looking forward, now that the war was over, to having a real vicar for their Sunday services.

Some of the British came up to Reeves and Rhoda. One of the women asked Rhoda if she knew what her next posting might be and Rhoda seemed to withdraw into herself at the question. There was more chatter about returning to where they had all come from. Reeves and Rhoda took their leave.

* * *

In the afternoon, Y.C. Liang came around to the consulate without an appointment. He was beautifully dressed as always. He handed over a sweat- and dirt-stained water-proof canvas pouch tied with two narrow frayed leather straps. It was about the size of a lady's evening purse.

"I do not know what is in that, but I understand that your Legation in Chungking wanted you to have it as soon as possible. They even used a Kuomintang messenger for part of the way instead of our fine upstanding smugglers and pirates. I got this about an hour ago." He glanced at the battered and stained pouch. "The documents inside I think are undamaged." Reeves wondered how Y.C. Liang knew it contained documents and then went on to think that of course Y.C. Liang would know exactly what was in the packet. Y.C. Liang got up and put his hand out to shake Reeves's.

"I will leave you with the pouch," he said and, putting his straw hat on and, squaring it with a single gesture, turned to leave the office. Then he stopped, turned back to Reeves, his eyes in shadow from the hat, and said enigmatically, "If, once you have read the contents, you need my help, please telephone me immediately. I will await your call." He left the office.

Reeves sat down at his desk and undid the straps to open the pouch. In it was a smaller pouch, also made out of water-proof waxed canvas, in almost pristine condition. The clasp was tied together with wire that passed through a lead seal with the royal coat of arms in miniature pressed into it. He found a pair of pliers in his middle desk drawer and cut the wire.

In it were two envelopes, both bearing the address of the British Legation in Chungking. One was addressed to the Consul; the other to "The Honorable Franklin Gimson, Colonial Secretary, Hong Kong." That one was stamped Top Secret in red ink and with a further admonition in a spidery handwriting in black ink that it was to be opened by the addressee only.

The envelope addressed to Reeves contained a long message over several pages, all in code. Mr. Gonsalves was out with his family today and it took Reeves nearly two hours to decode it using the Consular Code book, carefully copying each letter onto a lined sheet of paper with his neat handwriting in blue-black ink, always faintly surprised when what had started as a random series of letters resolved themselves into a word.

He finally finished. Once he had read through the document again, he could finally make sense of it in its entirety. He was quite astounded; the message was from the Permanent Secretary of the Foreign Office, its most senior civil servant, and Reeves could not conceive of how many levels above him. It was not just the usual brusque order from the Third Secretary in Chungking. There were instructions, but the document did him the courtesy and respect of explaining the background and facts that made them necessary. He was being treated like a responsible adult and not just some aging messenger boy.

The cable was a long and complicated document and Reeves found himself skimming it. It began with a description of the precarious status of Hong Kong. Japan had surrendered but the fleet under the command of Admiral Harcourt that would bring British troops to restore order to the Colony was still some way away. The Hong Kong and Kowloon Brigade of the communist East River Guerrillas was preparing to enter

Hong Kong from its bases. This might cause the Nationalists to move troops to occupy Hong Kong to counter the communists. Chiang Kai-shek has made no secret of his desire to take Hong Kong from the British and this could provide the perfect excuse. Intelligence reported that Nationalist flags could already be seen from several buildings.

Reeves was to arrange for the delivery of the enclosed letter to the Honorable Franklin Gimson, the last Colonial Secretary of Hong Kong and its most senior civil servant, who had been interned by the Japanese and who now was presumably released. The letter would authorize him to assert British sovereignty over Hong Kong before either the Nationalists or the Communists seized it. He was instructed to locate Franklin Gimson wherever he might be and deliver the enclosed letter to him "with the utmost dispatch." The cable ended with the admonition that he was to take personal charge of this assignment and make it his highest priority. He was to report on the results of his efforts directly to Sir Horace Seymour, the Ambassador in Chungking – not the Third Secretary who normally supervised him – and Sir Horace would relay them immediately to Whitehall.

Reeves made a drink and sat back. He had been taken into an inner circle, perhaps the most innermost circle, for the first time in his career. He was to play a part, even a small part, but still a part, in the reestablishment of the British presence in China. He would uphold the honor of the Chinese Consular Service, even though it no longer existed. His telephone rang. It was Y.C. Liang, saying he would come by shortly to offer his assistance. Right then, Reeves was too preoccupied with his own thoughts to wonder how he knew his help might be wanted.

Y.C. Liang entered his office after a single knock, unannounced by any of the clerks in the outer offices. He was dressed as neatly as before and rested his broad-brimmed straw hat on the side table next to the decanters of gin and whiskey before sitting down.

"How can I help?" he said simply.

Reeves sat forward, both hands holding the secret letter for the Colonial Secretary for Hong Kong. He was nervous. "I have been asked to play postman. I am required to deliver this letter with some urgency to Hong Kong and place it in the hands of a particular person."

Y.C. Liang did not ask any questions as to what the letter contained and to whom it was addressed. Instead he began analyzing the task that lay before Reeves. "There are no steamers to Hong Kong any more. The Americans have laid too many mines in the harbors and waterways of the Pearl River Delta. I hear over one hundred mines. Any big ship with a steel hull will be blown up for sure. In the past few months before the surrender, even the Japanese patrol boats did not leave their bases."

"But," said Reeves, "I have seen the fishing boats out – at least a dozen out my window leaving the *Porto Interior* and going right out in the South China Sea."

"The wooden hulls of a small junk will not make a 1,000-pound mine explode. The Americans set them up that way."

"Then let's get a junk and pay them to take us to Hong Kong."

"The word will get out that the British consul has rented a boat to Hong Kong. Someone will sell that information to the pirates and the boat will be captured, sunk and we will be robbed of everything before being drowned. You and I cannot make the journey."

Reeves looked at Y.C. Liang. "You perhaps have a solution to our problem?" He knew full well that Y.C. Liang would have a solution.

"Let me take care of it," said Y.C. Liang. He took the letter from Reeves and left.

Reeves realized, too late to do anything about it, that he had decided to execute the most important assignment of his career, the delivery of a vital document, by handing it over to a Chinese man without any idea of how the delivery was to be accomplished, when it would be done, and how he would know it was done. He sat there in genuine fear of what he was going to say to Whitehall if asked.

* * *

Colonel Ride was proud of the British Army Aid Group. It had provided valuable intelligence to the United States Air Force. It had helped rescue their downed flyers. The BAAG had moved more than 300 refugees, escaped POWs and others across hundreds of miles of bandit-infested Japanese-occupied China and into that part of China still held by the Nationalists without the loss of a single person. The BAAG was the only source of accurate political, economic and military intelligence on occupied Hong Kong. Some of its agents, ignored and unacknowledged by the British command, had been betrayed, cruelly and savagely tortured, and then brutally executed.

Now that the war was over, the British authorities had shut down the BAAG and tossed it onto the scrap heap, its men were scattered and its headquarters, mess halls, and outposts abandoned. Colonel Ride was dismissed. He and his men had been tolerated only when they were useful; no one ever liked an irregular unit outside the chain of command.

Nevertheless, Colonel Ride wanted at least to be part of the liberation of Hong Kong. He deserved that. It was the fitting coda to the last four years. He had lived in Hong Kong, fought with the Hong Kong Volunteers in its defense. He had been the only one who had watched over it during the occupation, helped its people, arranged the escapes of those poor sods who had been thrown into its hopeless defense and imprisoned in atrocious conditions. He had done his duty. General Grimsdale told him that there was no transport available to Hong Kong for him. There were others with higher priorities.

But he knew how to do this; he had done it scores of times. The trains, the sampans and junks, the bicycles, and days of walking along muddy paths through paddy fields to the croaking of frogs. It took him ten days to reach Poseh and then down the West River on some sort of sampan to an old forward base at Yanping where the BAAG men had not yet been disbanded or recalled. There Lt. Colonel E.D.G. Cooper – why did the British have so many first names? – had found a motorized junk and enough petrol to get them down the Pearl River to Hong Kong.

He was not sure what he would do when he reached Hong Kong. Would the British welcome him, ignore him or lock him up? Probably ignore him if precedent was anything to go on. The junk passed Macao, quite close, before it was due to make the sharp turn to the east to follow the invisible path to Hong Kong that ran between the mines that the Americans had laid. Just my bloody luck, thought Colonel Ride, to be blown up by the Americans a few weeks after V.J. day.

Colonel Ride could see the hills of Macao, the steeples of the churches, the solitary facade of St. Paul's church, the houses, as though painted in watercolors, coming down to the *Praya Grande* with its lines of banyan trees. He thought of Reeves. He had been harsh in his evaluations of Reeves to the Legation in Chungking and now he regretted it. He shouldn't have said all those things about him. Not a bad chap really, a little off his rocker, but who can blame him. A bit like me, sent off to do a job no one else wanted to do, given no instructions, second guessed at every opportunity when they weren't ragging on you for something you supposedly did or didn't do. He would buy him a drink when all this was over. Reeves would probably be out of a job like him; he will probably need a drink.

He moved to the prow of the junk by himself. There was a decent crosswind but it was sunny and warm. There was only a slight roll from the waves in the sea. He began to sing, softly at first as though to himself, then loudly as though to an unseen audience. He had always loved singing; he was a founding member of the Hong Kong Singers. He sang rugby songs, hymns from the Presbyterian hymn book and some great old Australian ballads by Banjo Patterson. He adjusted his red beret that he had adopted as part of his uniform although it was nowhere authorized by any Indian or British Army regulation. Who was going to bloody well tell him to take it off? Lt. Colonel Cooper thought it was better to stand well back at the stern of the junk.

Much later Colonel Ride would be asked about the BAAG and what it had done in the war. We had a good war, he would say, right up until the very end. And what happened at the end, someone would ask.

"Oh," he would say, enunciating the final list of nouns slowly and distinctly, "I should have expected it. There was malice, indifference, ignorance, jealousy and empire building." And then he would change the subject. He never saw Reeves again; he would have liked to have seen him and had his perspective. He undoubtedly would have agreed.

* * *

Y.C. Liang's agents had found Gimson in Hong Kong, living in an abandoned and looted house with a few other survivors of Stanley Prison. The agents handed over the letter that had come to Reeves in the battered and stained canvas pouch that had been entrusted to him alone by the most senior civil servant in the Foreign Office. Gimson had read it and then had given to Y.C. Liang's agents a note to be delivered to Reeves for transmittal to Chungking and thence to Whitehall. It read simply "Hong Kong is free/Gimson." Reeves had it transmitted to Chungking *en clair*. He wanted the whole world to know it, to see Gimson's name in the text of the cable and Reeves's name at its bottom. Everyone would know the implications of Gimson's simple four words and the significance of his name: the British had freed Hong Kong from the Japanese and had reasserted their authority over their colony. The world would see that Reeves had played a part in it.

* * *

Admiral Harcourt's fleet of carriers, destroyers, cruisers, minesweepers and submarines reached Hong Kong at the end of August but it wasn't until the middle of September that Japanese in Hong Kong formally surrendered and the British were finally in charge. In the days that followed, Reeves heard nothing from either Hong Kong or Chungking. Reeves had little to do; the allowances to the refugees had ceased shortly after the surrender, most of the clerks had been dismissed and those remaining busied themselves preparing a final accounting of the enormous sums of money disbursed during the war. Reeves watched their activities and would take long walks.

One day, he was sitting at his desk in his office in the consular building on the *Praya Grande* when he saw a warship anchoring far out in the channel off the *Porto Interior*. He picked up his field glasses and there was the British White Ensign whipping back and forth in the wind at its stern.

The Governor and Reeves were invited to dinner that evening on the HMS *Plym,* the warship Reeves had seen. The Governor wore his summer dress naval uniform together with his medals, Reeves a white linen suit. In the wardroom, Reeves was quiet, listening to all the English accents, trying to place them. It was as though he was back home finally, sixteen years after he had set sail from England. Although what did England mean to him now? His parents were dead; there were relatives he had not seen in over a decade. He had no home to return to and he realized how comfortable and at home he had been in Macao. If he were to return to England, where would he and Rhoda live? What would he do? If he was a consul in Europe, would Letitia go to boarding school in England? Would Rhoda be comfortable with that? Would she want to stay close to her or live with her husband in whatever city he was assigned to? He put these thoughts out of his mind.

Then later as they all continued to drink pink gin, Reeves told the story of being the sole Allied representative in this part of southeast Asia, all four years of the war, surrounded by thousands of miles of hostile Japanese territory. He stood up in that crowded wardroom, his head almost touching the low gray steel ceiling and reached his peroration. He may have been drunk; he did not care. He waved his glass in a wide circle, a little of the drink spilled.

"To see another British flag you would have to travel north and west 700 miles to Chungking, or travel directly north 1,800 miles to Vladivostok, sail 4,000 miles to Hawaii, continue southeast 3,000 miles to Port Moresby or finally end up 2,700 miles from here, in Darwin, Australia. We kept the flag flying. It was the only one." He sat down clumsily and suddenly, his chair tilting back a little before righting itself. The officers in the room, the Governor included, applauded tumultuously and then sang a rowdy discordant chorus of "For he's a jolly good fellow." Reeves's eyes dampened; at last someone appeared to understand what he had gone through. He was the one who had done it.

In the weeks to come, more ships of the British navy would visit Macao, anchoring well out beyond the breakwater, and Reeves would find himself entertaining their young ratings and officers. Some of these men were just boys; they had joined the Navy just a year or so ago when the fighting was largely done and had had a good war. Here they were in the Far East. They were going to buy something ceramic or silk for their mothers, get drunk and consort with whores. Reeves was happy to help them. They would often come back to the consulate and there were often twenty or thirty officers, men, and some of women whom they had befriended at the Central or Riviera Hotel, or at one of the many bars on the *Rua do Campo*. They would play dice or cards, drink Reeves's liquor, sing, put music on the radio and dance with the women and end up in tight embraces with them in dark corners of the garden. They finally would then wander down to the docks for a sampan to get them back to their ships before morning. Reeves stayed up with them all until the last one had left; Rhoda stayed in her room.

The Royal Air Force even sent a seaplane over to fetch Reeves to a party at their new mess in Hong Kong. He had never been taken flying and here he was, the only passenger, the guest of honor, being taken by two pilots to Hong Kong to a party. Once the plane was airborne, the pilots flew in a circle over Macao. It lay below with the sea on both sides splashed with sunshine, the church spires pointing upwards. It looked very old, as though it had always been there, and very small.

The *Lourenco Marques* arrived with provisions from Portugal. There was wine, white and red, olives, olive oil, cheese, *bacalhau*. He had great meals with friends on terraces in the shade of trees. Reeves knew that this would not last, but he hoped it would. He was very happy. There was no news from Chungking as to his next assignment, or any real contact at all, but he did not mind. This was as good as a holiday.

* * *

Perhaps a month later, he came back to Skyline from the office around noon – his duties were still minimal – and found Rhoda and Letitia waiting for him in the formal reception room. He suddenly noticed how grown up his daughter looked. She was nearly 11 and was, he thought, tall for her age, although he wished she was not as gangly. She was speaking more, almost always to her mother, and was even reading, spending hours in her room with, as Rhoda would say proudly, "with her nose in a book." Reeves knew that the books were a little elementary for someone her age, but Rhoda had worked hard to get her to this level. He still tried to read to her on occasions but she did not like to sit near him.

"John" she said, breathing in sharply, "Is there any news from those people in Chungking about your next assignment? I would so love to know." Reeves noticed when she stopped talking that she had pushed her lips together tightly as though she was afraid of what she might say next.

"No news, my dear. It is very slow given the difficulties of recovering from the war. The last *Gazette* had only movements of a few personnel between the major cities in Europe. It may be some time before they get to the consuls in the secondary cities. And there has been no decision on what to do about home leave. Too many consuls are eligible and they cannot all take leave at the same time. We need to be patient."

Then it came out all in a rush. Rhoda stayed seated on the sofa, her hands so tightly clasped in front of her that Reeves could see the white marks where her fingers pressed hard against her skin. Letitia was sprawled clumsily next to her, her long skinny arms and legs in every which direction, and looking everywhere except at her father.

"John," she said and then she started crying but she still kept talking rapidly through her sobbing. "I need to get Letitia back to England. She is showing such promise and I know there are specialists there who can help her. Look at her, she is growing up so fast. And Mummy and Daddy are going to be repatriated to England, I heard just last week. A Chinaman is going to buy the family business. They are going to stay with Daddy's sister in Tunbridge Wells. She has a big house in the country near there with room for me and Letitia." Reeves had a sudden thought about his now dead parents and the house in the New Forest. It had been sold. He wondered who lived there now.

"John." The word came out in a strangled gasp and then she continued. "We cannot wait any longer. It may be a year or more until you hear. And what if they deny you home leave as they did the last time and try to tell you that some new post is just as good as home leave." She stopped and a sob came out. "You know they lied to you the last time; Macao is not England and could never be England. I have no home in Shanghai any more. It is going to be just for the Chinese. I need to get to England." There was this England again. This place of hopes and dreams that Reeves suspected was a country exhausted and near bankrupt from the war, a place of cold and privation, food and fuel still rationed. He could only imagine her eventual disappointment. The war destroyed so much of the world they knew or thought they knew. Better to wait in Macao.

Her eyes widened and she paused ever so briefly before continuing. Her eyes would look at her husband, then to the side and then back again. Her next words came out all in a rush while she looked to the side. "We are leaving this afternoon. One of the wives put me in touch with a Navy officer in Hong Kong and he helped me book a passage to England. We are taking an Australian ship to Manila and then an American ship. We need to be on the afternoon sailing of the *Sai An* so that we do not miss our ship. It sails from Hong Kong."

Reeves first thought was how had she managed to book a ticket? She never seemed to be particularly close to the other wives and now one had introduced her to some Navy officer – had he entertained him in the consulate? Had he drunk his liquor and snogged a girl in his garden? And now he had helped separate his wife from him? And from what part of

Rhoda did this newly found ability to book a passage to London come from? He really did not know his wife.

Before he could even speak, Rhoda continued in the same rush of words, now staring at him. "I am so sorry. But that lieutenant from the Navy told me he did not know when the next berth might open up. All the ships are being used to move returning soldiers and essential workers. He was lucky to find this one. Letitia and I will be sharing a cabin. I do not know what the food will be like and whether it will agree with us." She started crying in panting little sobs, as her mother would have done, as though that was what she was expected to do. Letitia did the same.

"I know this is sudden, but I will always be married to you. When you get your home leave, you will come and join us won't you? Then if I have found a nice school for Letitia and you are not too far away in your new post, I can come and be with you. That is my duty to you as a wife." But there was something in her tone. There wasn't emotion; there wasn't affection; it was something that she thought she ought to say. He could not put his finger on it. She came over and held him loosely with one arm around him, one hand grasping her daughter, pulling her behind her, her head lightly on his chest. The embrace was clumsy, but Reeves was reminded of how tightly she had clutched him close that morning over four years ago on the steps of the consulate when the smugglers had delivered her to Macao from the prison camp in Hong Kong. This clumsy clutch had little in common with that embrace on the consulate steps.

"Rhoda," he started, "I am sure I will hear soon and we can travel together." But as soon as he had spoken these words he could feel her head shaking in frantic negation against his chest. She no longer believed, if she ever had, that he would ever get out of Macao in time for her to do for Letitia what she thought she needed to do for her. He wondered whether she believed he would ever leave Macao. He continued, now in a different vein.

"I understand that you have to do what is best for our daughter." The word 'our' stuck for a fraction and he thought of how little he had had to do with her. But he had tried or he thought he had. She wanted little to do with him and Rhoda had taken on the responsibility for taking care of her, to the exclusion of all else. And he had his duties to attend to.

"I will join you as soon as I am able. I will continue to urge the Legation to take cognisance of our situation." He thought again of what he had done in Macao; he thought of his marriage; they had conceived a child together. He could have been a better husband, but Rhoda spent so much time by herself.

Rhoda took a step back from him and let go of Letitia's hand. She was crying intermittently but looking at him. "Thank you for understanding. I will always be married to you and I will try to write when we are in England." It was that same flat tone that Reeves was trying to understand. She turned and Reeves could hear her suddenly breathing in and out in short sharp breaths. "There is so much to do before we leave. Please excuse us." She started towards the door, still exhaling in short anguished pants.

Letitia stood up, hip to one side, slightly twisted. She actually looked at her father for a second – it was more like a glance; she was squinting her eyes and still wrinkling her face. Then she turned and, nearly tripping, stumbled out of the room after her mother.

Reeves sat down hard on the couch as the door closed. He had always tried to do the right thing by Rhoda; he had left her alone because that seemed to be what she wanted and he was trying to please her. He would have liked to help her with Letitia but Letitia had resisted that and there didn't seem anything he could do. He was alone again, but then he was used to that. Even his friends had left. He thought of Redden in Miami in America and then was quickly ashamed for thinking of him at a time like this.

Three days later, he was sitting comfortably by himself one afternoon when the Number One Boy brought in a copy of the *South China Morning Post*, which had come across from Hong Kong on the morning run of the *Sai An*. There was a short mention on Rhoda's departure for England from Macao. She was described as "a friend to all and a source of comfort." Reeves wondered why the journalist had chosen that hoary old expression. He was in Hong Kong. He did not know Rhoda or people that knew her. It made little sense to him. He turned to other sections of the paper.

* * *

Reeves got word that Fletch, the head of the Macao Electric Company, and his wife Marjorie would be returning to Macao from England and would want to move back into their house, which he had occupied for nearly five years.. He had his possessions packed and moved into his room upstairs at the consulate on the *Praya Grande*. "My bachelor quarters," he called it jokingly to anyone who ever asked. Few did.

It was the beginning of early autumn, still the warm sun, and the sea rippled with small waves tipped with silver. Reeves remembered the Pan American launch laid up at the naval shipyard. He called the Governor to ask about it and the Governor had said, without Reeves having to say anything further, that he would have the hull, deck and trim painted, the brightwork polished, the awnings replaced, the engine tuned, and the launch delivered within ten days.

Mr. Gonsalves had brought down from Shanghai a dog-eared copy of 'The British Consul's Manual' from 1856 and in it they found the correct badge for a 'Consular officer afloat' – the royal coat of arms on a white circle. Mr. Gonsalves knew a Chinese sign painter who could duplicate it perfectly in colored enamel paints and he would arrange for him to go around to the shipyard to paint it on both sides of the launch's hull.

Reeves also wanted the launch to fly the flag of a British consul. He had never seen one; he had only flown the Union Jack over his posts. But he knew that there must be one. After all, diplomats had theirs – a Union Jack with the royal coat of arms on a white shield in its center. At last Mr. Gonsalves found in a different set of instructions from the Foreign Office a description of the diplomatic flag and a note that "consuls and consular officers shall be limited to the use of the Blue Ensign with the

Royal Arms in the fly thereof." The citation was to an Order in Council of August 7th, 1869. Reeves decided to fly the Blue Ensign at the aft; the Consular flag would fly at the fore.

Even the grudging words "shall be limited to" did not upset Reeves. He set off to Mlle. Lebron, the dressmaker, at her shop, 'Au Paradis des Dames,' on the *Praya Grande*. Mlle. Lebron, her French accent and form of address unaffected by a Portuguese husband and a forty-year residence in Macao, was able to have the two flags made to the exact specifications with the small pieces of cloth that she still had in stock and the skills of her two Chinese embroiderers. When they were ready, Reeves walked down to Au Paradis des Dames himself and picked them up. He unfolded them on the side table of his office and left them there where he could look at them. He was a consul and these were part in some way of who he was.

The launch was delivered to the old Pan American wharf. It lay in the sun, its paint – white and blue enamel – glinting and shining, rocking back and forth in a gentle swell coming in from the south. Mr. Gonsalves had had the two flags delivered to the Naval Dockyard the day before and they hung fore and aft, moving slightly in the breeze. Reeves untied the two lines tethering the launch to the wharf and leapt aboard. The launch drifted a few feet out into the *Porto Exterior*. Reeves went forward, the key was in the ignition, he turned it and the Kohler engine started the very first time. As he pulled out, he could see the consular flag ahead of him unfold in the wind. No matter what happened to his career or his marriage, no one would be able to deny his service as the British consul in wartime Macao. He suddenly felt proud.

Once beyond the breakwater, he pulled back on the throttle evenly and firmly, just as he had seen Redden do. The launch began to move faster, its bow rising in the air and a long frothy wake trailing behind it. Reeves, despite the protective glass shield, felt the wind blow hard on his face. Once out in the South China Sea, he turned the boat one way and then the other, until he was far out at sea, Macao distant behind him.

* * *

A year after the surrender, Colonel Sawa was still in Macao. The police had taken his pistol and his sword from him, but otherwise left him alone. Japanese troops were never meant to be in Macao; the police were awaiting instructions from Lisbon as to what to do about him now.

Once the most feared man in Macao; a man who directed several of the powerful triad gangs, a man rumored to have ordered the assassinations of several Chinese thought to be Nationalist sympathizers, and even the assassination of the former Japanese consul, Colonel Sawa of the Japanese Military Police, the hated and feared Kempeitai, was still wandering the streets, still often drunk, still in his field uniform now very stained and dirty, his head down, talking intently to himself. Some of the Chinese openly derided him; most paid him no mind. Then one day he was gone.

He was taken at night across the border by the Nationalist Chinese intelligence service, then by train to Shanghai and imprisoned along with other former Kempeitai officers. Forty of them had been pushed into one large cell in the basement of the old stone prison in the former British settlement. There they stood or crouched; there was not enough room in the damp cell for even some of them to lie down. They were given a little rice and some broth twice a day, enough to ward off starvation but not much more. Dysentery and other diseases spread quickly. These men were not in the records of the Allied Army of Occupation in Japan; it is doubtful anyone beyond a few people in the Nationalist intelligence service knew of their existence. They were among the hundreds of thousands of the missing, far too many to care about.

Colonel Sawa was pulled out of the cell by four soldiers at about six in the morning on a Monday. It had been raining all night and at the time he was fetched, a wind was blowing the rain into the cell through a barred opening high on one wall. The prisoners' coughs and hacks were loud against the damp stone walls of the cell. When the soldiers called his name, he tried to stand up at first, but could not. Two soldiers pushed their way into the fetid cell, grabbed him under the arms and pulled him out towards the cell door.

At the door, one pulled him to his feet and tried to march him forward. Colonel Sawa reached down and took hold of the top of his pants. His belt had been taken from him, he had lost nearly half of his previous weight in prison and his one concern was that his pants, now baggy and loose, not fall down around his ankles. He shuffled down the corridor to the outside courtyard, pushed by the soldiers, clutching his pants. He had no shoes and he would sometimes stumble forward because of a pants cuff that had fallen down over the front of his foot and caught.

The courtyard was surrounded by a high wall of large dressed stones. It was protected from the wind but the rain came down steadily and it was cold. The soldiers had their padded jackets and hats; Colonel Sawa was still in his worn and threadbare summer field uniform. It was quickly soaked in the rain and Colonel Sawa began to shake with cold. The soldiers turned him round and pushed him against a wall. He stood there, squeezing his eyes against the rain and the first full daylight he had seen in seven weeks. His soaked shirt, far too big for his starved body, stuck to his sunken chest as though wrapping a small misshapen package. They had not bothered to bind his hands and he stood against the wall, both hands holding the front of his pants in his fingertips almost daintily as though he was afraid of soiling or wrinkling them, tugging them upwards, his only thought that this trousers should not fall down and shame him. He was squeezing his eyes open and shut against the rain and wind. The four soldiers went over to a rack, picked up rifles, formed a line perhaps fifteen feet back and shot him in two quick volleys. When he collapsed to the ground, he was still holding the top of his pants between his fingers. His pants had not fallen.

* * *

It was late in the morning when Mr. Gonsalves came into the office and told Reeves that a Major Hall-Caine was telephoning, all the way from Hong Kong he emphasized excitedly as though the call came from London itself.

"Did he say what he wanted?" asked Reeves. It was another slow morning and he was curious.

"No, Mr. Reeves, but he was most insistent that he talk to you straight away."

Reeves picked up the receiver of the telephone and announced his name and position.

"Major Hall-Caine, British Military Intelligence, GHQ, Hong Kong. Mr. Reeves, I have a situation of some delicacy for which we may need your help." His voice was smooth but Reeves heard a tiredness in it.

"How may I help you, Major?" he said, trying to sound helpful.

"You have heard of a pirate named Wong Kong-kit?" said the Major. Reeves had wondered about Wong Kong-kit. He had not seen him since the end of the war. Mr. Gonsalves said he was hiding from everyone – the Chinese, the Portuguese and the British. The last time Reeves had been past his house on the *Avenida do Coronel Mesquita*, the house looked vacant, the windows dark, the sandbags gone from the front of the house, the machine guns removed from the second-story terrace. There were no guards lounging against the two black Fords still parked in front of the house. They were dirty and the rain had washed twigs, leaves and litter under the wheels, indicating the cars had not been moved in a while. No one had touched them however.

"I know him well. I have not seen him in a while. He was quite useful to the consulate and our mission during the war." Reeves hoped that this might calm the Major, but it did not. He replied tiredly.

"Whatever he may have done for you, he is still a thief, pirate, murderer, traitor, accomplice of the Japs and was mixed up with their secret services. We need to have him in Hong Kong and then we can talk to him at length." Reeves knew that the British authorities were, like every victor in every war, rounding up those whom they thought of as war criminals, collaborators and traitors. The British were planning trials; everyone knew that some would end in hangings. Reeves realized that he had deliberately put out of his mind all that he did not know about Wong Kong-kit. He had preferred not to find out what else Wong Kong-kit had been up to during the war. Was this a fault on his part? He needed to take what he needed to do his job where he could find it; beggars can't be choosers, he thought. And the British under his care in Hong Kong would have fared far worse if it had not been for Wong Kong-kit. The Major paused and then continued. "Here is the issue. The Portuguese have him. And he belongs to us."

"Belongs to you?" Reeves did not understand.

"Yes, belongs to us. He attempted an act of piracy in the waters off Hong Kong. If there was one good thing the Japs did during the war was to keep the pirates off the South China Sea. Now they are back. He had five pirate junks near Hong Kong, just off Castle Peak. He opened fire on what he thought was a soft picking, just a couple of junks drifting. But they were one of our disguised patrols and they returned the fire with everything they had. His junk, however, made it to Macao. Naturally, we have lodged a request for extradition. But that is in the hands of the diplomats. And they are in Lisbon." The Major stopped and Reeves felt obliged to say something.

"How is the best way I can help?"

When the Major replied he was almost conciliatory. "There must be an informal way of solving this outside official channels. Could you talk to the right people in Macao? If they quietly give him back to us, then we can resolve this whole matter." And the Major added almost unctuously, "I am sure a successful resolution of this problem on your part would not go unnoticed in the Foreign Office." Reeves thought he had accumulated enough good deeds at the Foreign Office but he took the Major's point.

The next morning, Reeves made an appointment to see the Police Chief, Captain da Cunha, around at the police headquarters on *Rua Central*. Captain da Cunha, dressed in a starched and pressed khaki uniform, the brass of his buttons and the insignia of his Captain's rank on his epaulets at a high polish, greeted him with a warm smile and ordered a Chinese woman to bring coffee. There was a couch and armchairs at one end of his large office and he gestured for Reeves to take a seat.

"We have coffee at last and I can return some of your hospitality I have enjoyed during the dark days of the war. It is excellent, from Brazil and came on the ship last week from Lisbon. It has traveled a long way." The Captain smiled hospitably. "But you have not interrupted your important day with all your business to talk to me about where I get my coffee. I am sure you have a lot of important things to say." Was this sarcastic or simply his extravagant way of talking? Reeves decided it did not matter.

A Chinese policeman in uniform brought in coffee, two small espresso cups, and a sugar container on a black lacquered tray. He placed them on a side table and left. The Police Chief walked over, poured two cups and passed one to Reeves. He returned to an armchair and sat down with an expectant look on his face, which Reeves later realized was contrived. The Police Chief knew why Reeves had come.

"I have come on official business. My government understands that you are holding the pirate Wong Kong-kit. A formal request for extradition was filed with the Ministry of Justice in Lisbon, but there will be delays while that is under consideration. In view of the long tradition of excellent relations between our countries, we would count it as a great favor if you would voluntarily release him to the British authorities. They in turn, once their proceedings are finished, will return him to the Macao authorities." Reeves stopped; he wished he was having gin in his office with the Police Chief as he normally would have. The strained language of diplomacy was no way to speak to his friend, the Police Chief.

"Your friend Wong Kong-kit," said the Police Chief, taking a sip of coffee, "I can see why you became so fond of him. He is a most interesting man. I have had very entertaining conversations with him." Reeves's request to hand over Wong Kong-kit went unaddressed.

"Then you do have him?" said Reeves.

"Oh, he has been here since last week when his junk landed. My men brought him in so we could talk." He took another sip of coffee and looked innocently at Reeves.

Reeves suddenly did not care for his assignment. Wong Kong-kit had helped provide medicines to his family of refugees and had ensured that hundreds could escape safely. He had been vital to Reeves's mission of keeping thousands of refugees fed, sheltered and healthy. He knew that Captain da Cunha hated Wong Kong-kit – his men had shot Fernando de Senna Fernandes Rodrigues and his two daughters in cold blood – and would not want to let go of him now he had him. Perhaps that was for the best. Why should he inveigle the Police Chief to hand him over to the British who would undoubtedly hang him? Reeves sat back, holding his espresso cup by its saucer and smiled at the Police Chief.

"How is Wong Kong-kit? He was most helpful to me in my work in Macao. I understand that you have had your difficulties but I would not have been able to take care of my refugee family without him. He arranged accommodation, the supply of food and medicines, and facilitated the escape of many of our people to Free China and then on to India and Britain."

Captain da Cunha smiled back and then stood, turning his back and stooped to reach into a cupboard behind him. He brought up a bottle.

"Come, Mr. Reeves, if we are to reminisce about our pirate friend, let us have a little brandy to go with our coffee. It is against police regulations to have alcohol in the building, but you have diplomatic immunity and perhaps I can shelter beneath it." He gave a short laugh and filled the two empty espresso cups with brandy, leaving the bottle on the desk.

"He is quite well, in fact considering his circumstances, remarkably well." The Captain drained his cup of the brandy and, noticing that Reeves had done the same, refilled both cups. "Did you know he refused interrogation at first, saying all that he had to say he had written in this manuscript." The Captain held up a sheaf of papers that had been lying on his desk. "It is all in Chinese, which I do not read, but one of my Chinese sergeants tells me it is a quite remarkable account of his life, from his childhood to the present. I will get it translated and give you a copy."

The consul looked at the papers. Somehow he had not conceived of Wong Kong-kit as an author. Captain da Cunha was talking again.

"But that is not the most remarkable thing. Look here at the end." The Captain shuffled through the manuscript and from the bottom of the pile pulled up two sheets of music. "He finished his account of his life with a song of his own composition, in English, no less. It is called 'A Farewell to Life.' Many of my officers are good singers and play the piano. I took this sheet down to the canteen where there is a piano and I had one of them play the tune and sing the words. It is a mournful sad song from a man who sees the end of his life. It is very good. Perhaps he was inspired by our *fado* music." He suddenly put down the paper and stood up.

"Would you like to see him? We unfortunately have to move him from the holding cells at police headquarters here to the central jail. He can have a cell of his own, he will not be disturbed, and he will face fewer temptations to try to escape. We are putting him in a van very soon. Come down to the courtyard where the van is waiting and you can have a few words before he is taken to the jail." Reeves thought that it was perhaps then that his request that the British be given custody of Wong Kong-kit would be addressed.

They walked out of the office and along the corridor to the stairs to the courtyard of the central police station. A large police van was waiting, its rear doors open and two unusually large Macanese police officers were standing on either side of them, arms folded across their chests. They nodded at Captain da Cunha but did not say anything.

From the other side of the courtyard came the sound of a heavy door opening and then closing. Four Sikh policemen, wearing turbans but otherwise in the uniforms of the Macanese police, came out with Wong Kong-kit. Two were gripping his arms and were pushing him forward. Wong Kong-kit's ankles were shackled as well as his wrists and he could only shuffle forward, the leg-iron chains dragging and banging on the flagstones of the courtyard.

They brought him to within a few yards of the rear of the police van with its open doors. The four Sikh policemen stood back, leaving Wong

Kong-kit standing by himself staring stoically ahead. Reeves, warmed by the two cups of brandy, stood off with the Captain, wondering when he was to be permitted to speak to him. One of the two barrel-chested policemen standing by the van doors stepped towards Wong Kong-kit, put both hands on his shoulders and roughly forced him to his knees. He then put one large hand on Wong Kong-kit's head, twisted it as though he was turning a door knob and turned it to face Reeves and the Police Chief.

For a moment Wong Kong-kit's expression of stoic resignation did not change. This was simply another indignity that he must suffer. Then he saw Reeves and his face was lit with a smile. This was the help he had been hoping for. He looked up imploringly as if to remind Reeves of all he had done for him and could Reeves now return the favor. He did not take his eyes, with their silent plea, off Reeves. Reeves was about to step forward, when the Captain put his arm in front of him and said in a gentle soft voice "Wait a moment."

Reeves knew in some part of his mind what was going to happen even before he was fully conscious of it. Wong Kong-kit was kneeling on the stone pavers of the courtyard, his wrists straining against the iron shackles, his body twisted round towards Reeves, his face still looking at him with that pleading smile. The police officer who had pushed him to his knees pulled out his Mauser from a holster on his belt and, placing it against the back of Wong Kong-kit's skull, shot him once. He fell forward, his head face down on the pavers, part of his skull shattered, a pool of blood spreading slowly on the ground, the shot echoing off the stone walls.

The Sikh policemen stepped forward and all four picked up the body and slid it into the police van, closing its doors with a tinny thud. The two other policemen got in the van and started it.

Reeves closed his eyes, but his last sight of the face of Wong Kong-kit who had done so much for him stayed with him, looking up, his eyes begging for Reeves to help, to do something, anything. Did none of the past four years mean anything? What use was Reeves if he could not save the life of this man? What really was the good of a consul or anyone like him if the events of the world flooded past him and he was unable to turn the tide, even slightly? He had the brief thought of himself on his knees with that same pleading look.

Reeves started to sway, his eyes still closed. Then he felt Captain da Cunha's arm around his waist.

"Come, my friend, he was shot while trying to escape. It is better this way."

Reeves reported Captain da Cunha's statement to Major Hall-Caine and said he had no further details. He told nothing of what he had seen. The Major sighed and said he would make a notation and close the file.

Chapter 22

Almost immediately after the Japanese surrender, China was engulfed in a great civil war between the Communist forces and those of Chiang Kai-shek's nationalists. The British Government stayed loyal to the Nationalists, keeping its embassy in Chungking. The Legation followed the fortunes of war closely and watched with increasing concern the steady advances of the Communist armies over the next year, which threatened all of Britain's interests in China, such as they still were. They worried about the future of Hong Kong. Despite the calamitous urgency of the Communist insurgency, the Legation still found the time to deal with Reeves. In October of 1946, there was a meeting between the First Secretary and the Third in the First Secretary's office.

"I assume that you are unaware of what Reeves has been up to." The First Secretary got straight to the point even before the Third had sat down. He lifted a small sheet of paper from the table by its corner with the ends of two fingers as though the paper might be soiled and he did not wish to dirty his hands. "Do you know what this is?"

The Third Secretary took it, put on his glasses, which he always hated to do in the presence of the First Secretary, and read the document.

"It appears to be some sort of invoice. Is it in Spanish?" He stopped, stared at it further, and then looked up. "No, it is in Portuguese. There are the words '*Marinha de Guerra Portuguesa*' at the head of the paper." He handed the paper back, removing his glasses.

"You are correct," said the First Secretary, "It is an invoice from the Portuguese Navy. It was presented some months ago to our Naval Attache in Lisbon who in his turn forwarded it to our Ambassador there, thence to Whitehall, and, after a subsequent long journey, to Sir Horace Seymour here in Chungking and finally to me. The invoice is for the expenses of the refurbishment of a motor launch at a Portuguese naval shipyard."

"I am still confused, sir."

The First Secretary put the invoice back in a file and rested his folded hands on his desk. "The naval dockyard is in Macao. The repair and restoration of this launch was apparently ordered by Reeves. He has abrogated to himself the use of a consular launch. Are you aware of any official duties that Reeves has that would require the use of a motor launch? Macao is not a treaty port. He is not required to inspect ships, collect customs duties and attend to the welfare of British sailors in distress, if I am correct?"

"That is a correct summary, sir."

"Reeves has committed an *ultra vires* act without authority or even bothering to notify us. My understanding is that it has some sort of an ensign on both its bow and stern and the consular badge on either side. He uses it to ferry drunken sailors back and forth, and to attend parties on British naval vessels, where he enjoys naval rum and gin. Did you instruct him to minister to members of our Senior Service?"

"No sir, his duties explicitly are circumscribed by the borders of Macao."

"Despite the number of celebrations in Macao, he is still not satisfied. He has also boarded an RAF Otter, which I gather is a type of seaplane, and has been flown to Hong Kong for a drinks party at the RAF mess there. Presumably you did not instruct him that his duties as His Majesty's Consul in the Portuguese territory of Macao also include attending to the RAF airbase in Hong Kong?" The Third Secretary did not respond.

"But even with his traveling from party to party all over the coast of southern China, this has not been sufficient for our man Reeves. He has been throwing his own shindigs. He held a party in honor of the birthday of King George. To conserve funds, consular offices were prohibited from holding a King's Birthday celebration. Only the diplomatic missions were permitted to do so."

The Third Secretary felt that he should say something. "I assume Sir that you are suggesting, even by the standards of the Consular Service, we now have sufficient grounds to dismiss Reeves. I can certainly cable Whitehall to begin the process."

The First Secretary lowered his head for an instant and then looked up. He sighed. "We are not going to sack Reeves. There are other considerations. Reeves has done an excellent job of ingratiating himself with the Portuguese. They have feted him at banquets, presented him with illuminated scrolls extolling his worth, and wreaths of laurel for all I know. The Portuguese Government has notified us that they intend to present him with their Cross of Merit. Whitehall does not want to call into question the judgment of our old ally by dismissing someone they consider a friend. But there are larger problems beyond the Portuguese. Read this." He passed over a creased and ragged newspaper clipping to the Third Secretary. He reluctantly put his glasses on again.

"'The Consul Who Defied the Japs'?" said the Third Secretary incredulously. He read on. "This makes him look like a hero. Where is this from?" He held up the clipping distastefully.

"The *Daily Sketch*. The article continues for several paragraphs in a very adulatory tone about Reeves's activities in Macao. No one that we know would read this paper. But it is popular amongst a certain segment of Tory voters. The journalist is a favorite. No, we cannot fire Reeves. We risk an idle, mischievous and malicious press raising a hue and cry over our shabby treatment of one who so loyally and bravely served the Crown. They will make him a folk hero and the Opposition will ask questions in Parliament. No, we must handle this differently and achieve the same result."

"What do you propose, sir?"

The First Secretary smiled. "First, we will square the next Honours List. We will recommend Reeves for an OBE."

"An OBE," exclaimed the Third Secretary. He was quite indignant. "After all he has done – or hasn't done."

"Here is my thinking," said the First Secretary and the Third noticed that he was smiling. "First, to give him nothing will cause his tame friends in the press to bleat that he is being unfairly treated. Second, I am not going to establish the precedent that any member of our service, no matter how much we despise him, can be foisted off with a lesser MBE. If he was our friend and given what he has been through, we might recommend a CBE, just one below a knighthood. But he is not our friend, so an OBE, right between those two medals in terms of importance, is appropriate. The public will be unable to complain and Reeves will have a vague sense of disappointment without ever quite being able to put his finger on why he might have deserved better."

"I see, sir."

"We need to get him out of Macao before he is proposed for sainthood and that brings us to the issue of his next posting. This does present some challenges given the austerity in which we now find ourselves. There is little in China that is even left now for any consul, let alone Reeves. We no longer have our treaty ports, as you are aware."

"What are you thinking of, sir?"

The First Secretary looked directly at the Third so as not to miss his reaction. "I was thinking of Rome." He let that last word linger in the air.

"Rome?" Again the Third Secretary was indignant. "That is surely a prime posting. Reeves has done nothing to indicate he deserves this. I do not understand your reasoning."

"My dear fellow, there is Rome and there is the rest of Italy. There will soon be a vacancy for a consular officer to look after British interests in the *compartimenti* of the Abruzzi, Molise, Sardinia and the Sardinian Islands. He will be nominally resident in Rome. But he will be required to travel extensively in these impoverished and war-torn regions. These are areas that have not changed since medieval times. The *quattrocento* bypassed them. There will be village inns with only straw for bedding. The straw will have fleas. The wine will taste of tar. The local trains will only have third-class carriages with hard wooden benches. Their windows will not open during the heat of summer and will not close during the cold of winter. The food will be meager and insufficient. If this does not cause Reeves to think of careers outside of the consular service, we will, long after the public has forgotten who he is, transfer him to someplace truly dreadful."

The Third Secretary thought for a minute about the plan for Reeves. He could see no reason to comment on it or challenge it in any way. "When do we notify Reeves, sir?"

"Oh, we can take our time, quite a lot of time. He will be expecting news. Subjecting him to prolonged uncertainty is part of our plan, isn't it?"

* * *

There were few messages from Chungking any more and they were almost always routine notifications that were sent to all consular posts. Reeves was anticipating the news on his next posting. He wanted to tell Rhoda, although she had not written since her arrival in England. His duties continued to be minimal; there were no longer refugees under his care. The British whom he had sheltered and succored in Macao during the war returned to Hong Kong or Canton or Shanghai or England, where they hoped to resume their former lives. Few, if any, had stopped by to thank him or even say goodbye. To them, Reeves was a reminder of the time when they were impoverished, beholden and without stature. They preferred to put that behind them and ignoring Reeves was part of that. With the end of the war, Macao seemed to resume its accustomed obscurity. The British Government was forever worried that the Chinese, either the Nationalists or the Communists, might seize Hong Kong; there was no evidence that either side was even interested in Macao. Reeves occupied himself with closing the accounts of his disbursements during the war. Still it would be nice to know where he might be posted next. He thought of Falstaff waiting for the invitation that never came to the coronation of his old friend: *"I shall be sent for in private...I shall be sent for soon at night."* There were months of near silence while he waited.

But then suddenly came the letter from Chungking, signed by the Ambassador no less, and delivered by the King's Messenger, that he would be awarded the OBE when the next Honours List was published and that he was to be appointed as a consul in Italy, based in Rome. He sat back in his office and thought of the medal around his neck against the white of his tropical consular uniform. It would push ever so slightly against the cloth. Then he remembered his parents, both deceased for nearly two years now. This would be another thing they would never know about him. They both would have been so proud. Both of them read the Honours List when the newspapers published and talked about who had been mentioned and who had been omitted. He could imagine their surprise and then pleasure when they saw their son's name. There would be phone calls, and neighbors knocking on the door, with their congratulations. Their son had made something of himself.

He held that melancholy thought for several minutes, picturing his parents, before he remembered the second part of the message, his posting to Rome. His service in Macao was finally recognized. What other consul had done what he had done? He was getting an important post in a country he supposed (he did not know) was critical to the postwar reconstruction of Europe. They must have been impressed with his proposals for Hong Kong after the war. And they must need him in Rome, because they were denying him home leave for the time being and they were ordering him to travel to Europe in just a few weeks on the HMS *Ranee,* an aircraft carrier converted to passenger transport. He would have preferred to wait for an actual ocean liner with a room of a certain class on an upper deck facing the ocean, to which his rank and years in service, even as a consul, entitled him. But he understood the demands of service and their desire to secure his services rapidly. He would write to Rhoda when he knew the exact date of his departure. He would tell her about his OBE and he wondered how she would react. Would she have already read about it in the papers and if so, what would have been her thoughts. He would tell her that he did not know when he could take leave from his new duties to travel to England to see her and his daughter, but he was looking forward to doing so. He preferred to think that the reason he had not heard from Rhoda was the difficulty with the mails between Macao and England.

He threw himself into completing his reports for the war years. Mr. da Silva had produced an accounting of the expenditures of nearly two million pounds, with a discrepancy of only three pennies. When the final ledger was presented, Reeves had clapped Mr. da Silva on the back and the two of them had had a celebratory drink and Mr. da Silva hardly ever drank. Reeves had started preparing graphs of the rates and amounts of his expenditures, the increase in the numbers of people he took care of from year to year, the numbers of them who suffered from illness and disease and at what time of the year they contracted those maladies, the people whom he employed and in what function. He thought the Foreign Office would find these useful and they would provide an invaluable guide to future consular officials in analogous situations. He could be a mentor to them. HMS *Ranee* was due to sail in August; he would need at least until September to complete his work. Regardless of how much they needed him in Rome, he would ask for an extension. It was important to have a complete account of his accomplishments here. He was sure he would receive a favorable answer. Mr. Ronald Ascot Hall, the Consul-General in Canton to whom Reeves now reported, was coming to inspect the consulate. He would understand the importance of wrapping things up tidily, and let Reeves stay on.

Reeves was notified by telegram of the date, and by which steamer, Mr. Hall would arrive from Canton. He drove down in his beloved Studebaker to the ferry wharf on the morning of Mr. Hall's arrival in time to see the small dirty steamer, streaked with rust and the faded paint chipped and flaking, enter the *Porto Interior*. He stood on the wharf while the dock hands made the lines secure to the bollards and the crew lowered the gangway. He was suddenly struck by the thought that he now reported to this man for the brief time that he remained in Macao. He had spent five years in this City essentially a free agent, not really reporting to anyone directly.

The first man down the gangway was a small slight man with a severe face, who, despite the heat, was dressed in a dark three-piece suit, a shirt with a stand-up wing collar, and a gold watch and chain across his waistcoat. His Homburg hat was precisely set on his head. Reeves had not seen anyone in a stand-up collar since, well he could not remember when; it must have been fifteen years ago in another time in Peking. There was a Chinese man, also in a dark suit, following, carrying a briefcase and an umbrella. Reeves suddenly realized that the man in the stand-up wing-collar shirt was Mr. Hall, and the Chinese man following was some sort of clerk brought along to carry Mr. Hall's briefcase and umbrella. As Reeves stepped forward to introduce himself, he remembered that he was in a white linen suit and a colorful green tie. One look at the severe face of Mr. Hall told Reeves that Mr. Hall would find his dress unacceptably frivolous.

Reeves greeted Mr. Hall, who merely nodded in reply, and the two of them walked silently up the wharf, the Chinese clerk following with the umbrella and briefcase. When they reached the Studebaker, Reeves remembered that he had driven it down himself. He had not even thought to use his driver. He walked to the back of the car and opened the rear left door for Mr. Hall. He stopped and looked at him.

"Where is your driver?" he said tartly.

"He is back at the consulate. Macao is a small place and I typically drive myself. He has other duties," he added. Mr. Hall looked at him.

"From now on, please avail yourself of your driver at all times. A British consul has a certain status in China, even now, and it is important that the Asiatic be aware of it." Mr. Hall climbed into the car and closed the door himself, sufficiently hard that Reeves wondered whether he had deliberately slammed it. The car ride up to the consulate was awkward, with Mr. Hall in the back, Reeves in the front driving, and the Chinese clerk sitting next to him. There was silence until Mr. Hall, looking out the window, suddenly began to speak.

"Did you know, Reeves, that my predecessor in Canton, right up until he was evacuated with the onset of war, and when all the senior Chinese officials were driven in their cars, was carried around Canton in a sedan chair borne by eight coolies in livery. That showed the natives." It was as though the Chinese clerk was not there. Reeves nodded but did not say anything.

The two walked into the main registry of the consulate. All the young men had gone, as had Mr. Aycock and Mr. Swemmelaar. There were no more of Reeves's extended family of refugees to account for. There was only Mr. da Silva and Mr. Gonsalves. They bowed and greeted Mr. Hall with a deference that clearly pleased him. They also had on dark suits. Mr. Hall had taken off his hat and there was a red ring around his bald head where the hat had pressed against the skull. Reeves thought that he would start with the crown jewel of his work: Mr. da Silva and the ledgers that showed a discrepancy of only three pennies out of 1,750,000 pounds. An astounding feat of accounting for disbursements.

"Mr. da Silva," said Reeves, "I believe you have something to show our guest." Bursting with pride, Mr. da Silva opened the main ledger, which he had ready on a desk and opened it to its final page. The ledger had been newly bound in leather with gold embossing, and the two pages to which Mr. da Silva had opened it had pale green lines and thick red margins. Both pages were filled with Mr. da Silva's immaculate numbers in dark black ink. Mr. da Silva's smile threatened to explode, he was beaming so hard. Even before Reeves spoke, Mr. da Silva had his finger on the final sum in the columns of neat black figures.

"Sir, I think that you will find this interesting," said Reeves to Mr. Hall. Mr. Hall took a pair of gold-rimmed spectacles from a leather case in the inside pocket of his jacket. He put them on in a fussy manner, leaned over the ledger, peered quickly at the pages, and, looking up, turned to Reeves.

"These are your accounts?" he said sharply.

"Yes sir, I thought you would find them interesting." Reeves was about to explain the threepenny discrepancy in over two million pounds – an amazing accomplishment – when Mr. Hall continued:

"They are not in the format prescribed by the Foreign Office for consular offices. They are of no use to me. This man is your bookkeeper?" he said harshly, indicating Mr. da Silva who by now was looking frightened. Mr. Hall did not wait for a reply. "He should have known better. In any event, we will have no further need of him. This consulate will have very limited expenditures from now on. Mr. Gonsalves here can keep whatever books are necessary." Mr. da Silva left the room, his face shocked. Reeves wondered whether he might cry.

Mr. Hall turned away from the ledger and stared around the room.

"What is all this?" he said, with a wave of his arm. Reeves looked around the room as if for the first time. It did look shabby, he thought. Shelves made of whatever planks could be found with the wartime shortages, mismatched and unpainted, and lined with wooden boxes of different shapes and sizes, nailed crudely together from the scraps of wood, packing cases and boxes. It was all that could be found with the war on. Any sort of new timber was nearly impossible to find.

Reeves lifted his chin and spoke proudly. "These contain the records of the over 5,000 refugees whom we took care of during the war."

Mr. Hall moved over to the wall and looked at the boxes more closely. He could see the envelopes, pieces of paper and scraps of cards that made up the records. He did not try to pick any up. Reeves decided now was the right moment.

"There are a lot of useful data here, sir. I am working on compiling a summary of it and also proceeding on getting all my records in final form for the Foreign Office. The consulate here had a unique role during the war. I am sure it will be an object lesson for some time to come and will be a useful case study for our newer consular officers as to what our service is capable of. I am requesting that I be permitted to stay at my current post another six weeks to complete my work."

Mr. Hall spun round. "Quite impossible. We have already named your successor, Mr. Hugh Cecil Rabbetts." Reeves had not heard that his successor had been named. His advice had not been sought. He had never heard of him; he had not been asked to brief him. But he said nothing as Mr. Hall continued.

"Mr. Rabbetts will be here in under three weeks. Very sound man, Mr. Rabbetts. You must be gone when he arrives. It is always best that the old consul is not present when the new man arrives. Makes things less awkward." He turned to the shelves with their shabby crude boxes. He waved his arms at them again. "All of this…" He stopped, searching for a word, "…paper is of no earthly use to us. Pack it up and send it to the Colonial Office. It was their money you spent, not ours. They can decide what to do with it in London." He turned to Reeves. "No, I understand that the Foreign Office has booked your passage on the *Ranee* in two weeks time. You must be on it."

Reeves only half heard him. He was looking at the crude little boxes on the rough shelves on the wall. Those were his boxes. He had helped round up the scraps of wood out of which they were constructed – they came from timber merchants, warehouses, shops, cellars in friends' houses. And they may have looked like rough scraps of paper to Mr. Hall, but he had had to find each one, cutting up used envelopes, the backs of calendars and brochures, the last unused pages of school exercise books, brown wrapping paper cut into squares and then smoothed. On those miscellaneous paper fragments, the names and details of British subjects had been written and the amounts of money he had caused to be disbursed to keep them from penury and starvation. Their faces passed through his mind in a random cavalcade. They were his family. And this man, this Mr. Hall, wanted to simply wash his hands of four long years of Reeves's work and send the boxes off to some damp cellar in London. He couldn't possibly do that. He paused.

"Very well, sir," said Reeves.

* * *

The night before Reeves was due to depart Macao, there was a farewell dinner for him in the *Clube Militar,* the old officers' mess near the public gardens and the *Fortaleza de San Francisco*, the lichen-covered walls of which American aircraft had machine-gunned at the end of the war. That seemed a long time ago now. The Governor himself had chosen the location.

The club, built in the last century, had a deep shaded verandah and was painted in a mixture of peach and ochre, its Doric columns in white enamel. It stood just off the southern end of the *Praya Grande* and as Reeves came up the steps to the front doors, he stopped and looked back over the banyan trees to the *Porto Interior*. An orange sun was setting and the thought that this would be the last sunset he would see in Macao for a long time filled his mind for a moment to the exclusion of all other thoughts. This was not sadness. He thought of the Portuguese word that Mr. Gonsalves had told him about: *saudade.* Mr. Gonsalves insisted that it could not really be translated, but he said it was the melancholy that came when a man ached for something he had once possessed and knew he would never have again. In a day, Reeves would no longer have Macao. Perhaps he felt *saudade.*

But he forgot all about his mood as he approached the door. He heard the sound of boisterous laughter, loud conversation that tipped over into almost shouting, music and singing. He had on his dinner jacket – he could not remember the last time he had worn it. He was wearing for the first time his new OBE on a scarlet ribbon around his neck. It felt heavy and he was very aware of it. The Number One Boy had knotted his tie for him and Reeves unconsciously straightened it as he walked into the lobby of the club and turned into the large dining room.

It was very crowded, even packed. As many tables as possible had been pushed into the room so that in order to move between them, you had to turn sideways. They were covered with white cloths and the tables glinted with shiny silver and polished glasses. The men were also in dinner jackets, the women in long evening gowns and jewelry. All of Macao seemed to be there, Portuguese officials, Chinese and Macanese businessmen, priests, the now small British community, a stray naval officer from Hong Kong. Everyone seemed to be already drinking and talking excitedly to each other. When a group standing near the door of the dining room saw Reeves enter, they began to cheer and clap. The *tuna* band at the far end of the dining room, sensing that something was about to happen, began to play something that promised a crescendo; the Starlettes, an all-girl singing group, standing next to the *tuna* band, stopped singing and stood on tip-toes, craning to see over the heads of the guests who had just come in, Almost instantly, the rest of the crowd realized who had entered and they too began to applaud and cheer. As Reeves pushed his way through the throng of people to the front of the dining room, men would grasp one or other of his hands to shake them or clap him hard on the back; women who were nearby leaned in and tried to kiss him on the cheek. The band played even louder. The noise was overwhelming.

There was a long head table at the end of the room, placed on a platform so it could be seen more easily by the rest of the people. There was a lectern with a microphone to the side and the people at the head table were seated only on one side of it to face the rest of the room. "Like the Last Supper," thought Reeves as he approached the table. He saw the Governor in a naval dress mess jacket, the Governor's wife, Dr Lobo, his son, Roger, Dr Gosano, Captain da Cunha, Y.C. Liang – in a white dinner jacket no less – Bishop Ramalho in a suit, clerical collar and a scarlet waistcoat with the silver pectoral cross made by Japanese Christians all those centuries ago, Father P.J. McCarthy, the jolly Jesuit from the Seminary of St. Joseph, Mr. Jack Braga. Sitting uncomfortably at one end was the Reverend Florence Lim, her hair held to one side with a simple clip. She was wearing a severe black dress and jacket as well as her clerical collar. She blinked at Reeves but did not smile.

The people at the head table all stood up as Reeves approached and they too joined in the clapping. The Governor gestured to a vacant chair between him and his wife. Everyone sat down once Reeves had sat down.

The applause had already started to diminish when Bishop Ramalho stood and raised his hand for silence. The crowd quieted and bowed their heads because they all knew, even the Chinese, what was coming. The Bishop intoned a long grace for the meal. As Reeves bowed his head so as not to be conspicuous he saw the menu between his place setting. It was in color, with crossed Portuguese and British flags at the top. Reeves felt the raised printing and wondered if it had actually been engraved. Large letters under the crossed flags read, 'Farewell Dinner for the Honourable John Pownall Reeves, British Consul, Macao." Then it listed the dishes they were going to have – Soup *à la Portugaise*, Fillet of Fish, Chicken with Partridge Sauce, – where did they find partridges in Macao? were they from a can? – pudding, fruits, tea, coffee, the red and white wines – all from Portugal – and brandy. It was all in English and the organizers seemed to have chosen a meal that they thought an Englishman might like. Reeves felt flattered in some way and wondered what Portuguese-style soup tasted like. The Bishop finally finished his grace and the Chinese waiters in white jackets immediately entered from the swinging doors at the side, holding trays of the soup *à la Portugaise* high in the air.

The people sitting at the tables started talking to each other, eating their soup, commenting on it, trying the bread rolls on the table. Even after a year since the end of the war, good bread was still a novelty. The *tuna* band started to play an American tune that must have been featured in one of the latest movies at the *Vitoria*. Many people must have seen that film, because they began to clap, congratulating themselves for having recognized it. Then the four girls who made up the Starlettes began to sing in harmony, moving to the music, snapping their fingers in the right places, all making the same turn to the left or the right at the same time, dressed in the same pink and yellow floral dresses, their hair done the same way with the same pink barrettes holding it in place. At the end of the song, they turned and smiled at Reeves. A small girl came out and shyly placed floral leis around the necks of the Governor and Reeves.

The music and the singing continued; Reeves conversed with the Governor and then turned and talked a little with his wife, but not for long as she did not have much English. He enjoyed both the red and white wines. The meal continued. Then it was time for the speeches. Y.C. Liang thanked him on behalf of the Chinese community of Macao and hoped that the services the Chinese people of Macao had given the British was the beginning of a closer and more harmonious relationship between the British and the Chinese of all of southern China. Mr. Braga gave a long account of the British presence in Macao over the decades and said that the consul was part of this glorious tradition. The Reverend Florence Lim, reading from notes, her round, black-rimmed spectacles at the end of her nose, thanked him for his support of the Protestant Chapel and the Anglican congregation. Bishop Ramalho did not look up once while she spoke. The Governor's speech was less than four minutes. He talked about his friendship with Reeves, how he could always call on him, that Portugal's neutrality prevented him from saying it at the time but he was always on the side of the Allies. He ended with the observation to remember that the war in the Pacific had been won with naval power. There was tumultuous applause, everyone liked the Governor. Reeves had the brief thought that he could have had a good friend in the Governor had he gotten to know him a little more. He was always afraid of bothering him.

Then Father McCarthy got up to speak. Reeves wondered why the Governor, as the most senior person at the dinner, was not the last to speak. He would realize later that Father McCarthy had been asked to speak last because he was judged the most elegant speaker of English in Macao. The priest, Reeves noticed, had eschewed the wine at dinner for whiskey and had drunk it the entire evening without ice or water.

He was a big florid man with a shock of white hair and a smile that rarely left his face. He pulled a large sheaf of papers out of his coat pocket, put on his reading glasses and began "Dearly beloved." He stopped, looked quizzically at the notes and then hastily pushed them back into a pocket. "Sorry," he said in the unmistakable accent of his native Shannon, "That was meant for Sunday." The audience realized it was a joke, even though not all could comprehend his Irish accent, and laughed uproariously. Father McCarthy joined in the laughter, looking at Reeves, as though the joke was somehow on him.

Then he raised his hand for silence and began. "We are here," he began in a somber tone almost as if he was delivering a eulogy, "to celebrate the presence in Macao of John Pownall Reeves and to mourn his impending departure. You may know him as His Majesty's Consul in Macao, but he was more than that, oh yes, more than that." Like an old stage actor who knew how to hold his audience in the palm of his hand, he paused and looked around the room. It was completely silent as they waited. "He was.." – another pause – "an almoner." The room broke into wild sustained clapping, although Reeves thinking about this later surmised that there would not have been more than a handful of people in that room who knew what an almoner was. Even he had to think for a moment.

Father McCarthy returned to this theme of almonry. He talked about the consul as director of social services, a director of medical services – "at one stage he had six doctors in his employ at the clinic" even though Reeves knew it was only three; "he was our Minister of Education" and went on to speak of Reeves's support of the schools run by the Irish Jesuit fathers and the Canossian and Franciscan sisters. Father McCarthy's voice rose; he said the consul was the Minister of Sport, played a gallant game of hockey as the center-forward; he was the Postmaster-General communicating for all us with the outside world, he was a travel agent "but just one-way tickets and only to Chungking" and a thousand other things at the same time. Reeves was only half paying attention, conscious that he would have to speak next and not sure what he would say. He had drunk wine and brandy but that would not stop him.

At one stage he was forced out of his thoughts by the realization that Father McCarthy was addressing him directly. "Mr. Reeves, you took under your care over thirty different nationalities. Do you think Mr. Reeves that if a Chaldean had presented himself at your door, he might have had a claim on your services?" Father McCarthy mopped his face and head with a handkerchief and waited expectantly for an answer. He had elongated the word 'Reeves' in his most distinct brogue when he pronounced it.

Reeves stood up, his chair scraping and almost falling over backwards, but he reached behind and grabbed it just before it did. "Father McCarthy, if a Chaldean had knocked on my door, I would have abided by the traditions of hospitality of Macao and welcomed him with open arms." The people at the tables clapped and laughed although Reeves doubted whether anyone apart from him and Father McCarthy had heard of the ancient Mesopotamian kingdom of Chaldea.

Then Father McCarthy became serious. His subject was no longer Reeves. He talked about Macao, the years of privation it had been subject to, the people who had flooded into the city and how the city had risen as one to take care of them. He ended with "Macao was a refuge where one could find peace, shelter, food, Christian charity in the midst of a world of paganism and cruelty... This is the story of a great city." Reeves thought that he was now going to that world of paganism and cruelty, leaving behind this land of the lotos eaters, this island of peace in a troubled world, this Shangri-La. But that was his destiny and he would be one of those who made it a better world, perhaps more like Macao. The audience was respectful and silent as they thought about the past four years.

When Reeves stood up behind the lectern to address the guests, he still did not know what he was going to say. He was only conscious of the floral lei scratching and tickling the back of his neck and his medal, the gold glinting in the light that had been shined on him. Thinking about it the next day as the *Ranee* steamed west and Macao faded out of sight behind him, he could not recollect what he had said. He must have talked about the beauty of the city, the friends he had made, the splendid leadership of the Governor. Whatever he said, he reflected, at least met with the audience's approval because they clapped long and hard after almost every sentence.

What he did remember was that at the very end, he felt he might begin to cry. He did remember the last sentence of his address as a few tears trickled down his cheeks.

"We have received the inestimable blessings of liberty."

He was returning to his chair when he noticed the Governor rising and motioning for him to remain standing. An aide in an army uniform came from somewhere behind holding a long leather case on two outstretched hands. The Governor took the case, stepped to the microphone and said, while turning in a twist and looking at Reeves "Please accept this as a symbol of the friendship of the people of Macao and the high esteem in which they hold you."

Reeves took the case, opened it and there lay, nestled in blue velvet, a silver and gold diplomatic sword in its scabbard. He put the case down on the lectern, pulled the sword out of his scabbard and looked at it. There were ruby and green stones set into the glistening steel of the blade and an intricately engraved pattern ran along it; the grip was chased with gold thread. He suddenly noted that the silver guard had his monogram worked into it. He felt the tears begin to well in his eyes again.

Then he realized that the audience was on its feet clapping and cheering. They were clapping and cheering for him. He turned, grinned at the crowd and, taking a firm grip on the sword, waved it back and forth over his head as though he was signaling a great victory to an army he had commanded. For a moment he imagined his parents down there smiling proudly at him, his admiral uncles, his classmates at University and the schoolboys at Haileybury, the members of his boat crew, the crew captain, Charles Godson, heroically killed in the Western Desert, that very tall and beautiful girl whom he had brought to the dance that night, the crew member who had sat in front of him on the boat, drowned when his corvette was torpedoed, all looking up at him with a respect they had never evinced before.

The clapping and shouting grew tumultuous, men rushed forward and pushed him into a chair. Four strong men took hold of a chair leg each and hoisted Reeves high into the air. They carried him around the room while he continued to wave the sword from side to side. Everyone in the room began to sing 'For he's a jolly good fellow.' Reeves waved the sword in time.

* * *

Reeves did not remember what time he got home, but it must have been very late, early in the morning the next day. He had gone right to bed. Sometime later – he had not looked at the little travel clock beside the bed that had been a gift from his father, he was awakened by a howling outside his window. Then the entire window began to rattle in its frame and the glass was struck by something, as though someone had thrown a stone and it had hit the pane with a sharp report.

Reeves sat up in bed suddenly, still feeling the pleasant glow of the wines and spirits he had had at the dinner. Then the howling became even louder and the window frame rattled even more as though someone was trying to shake it loose from the wall. The consulate itself was creaking. He looked out the window. There was no sky or no horizon. An inky blackness had descended over the *Porto Interior*. From the few street lamps illuminated on the *Praya Grande*, he saw rolling, barrel-shaped waves pushed and shoved by a powerful wind – that was the origin of the howling – break against the seawall and pour over the footpath and flood the roadway, swirling past the allee of banyan trees. The furious sea was a sickly gray. The branches of the banyan trees were pushed back as though they were going to be pinioned to one side; leaves were torn off and blown away almost instantly. One tree was suddenly ripped out of where it had been planted and lay on its side, tossed violently from side to side, its roots waving in the air. The wind continued to howl and moan. Objects it had picked up – stones, shells, twigs, shafts of bamboo, were thrown against the consulate and Reeves's bedroom window, as if by an angry mob intent on revenge. It was a late summer typhoon.

Reeves lay in his bed in the darkness listening to the typhoon, wondering whether his window would be smashed and the now torrential rain, driven at a slant by the wind, pour into his bedroom. He thought he could actually see the window shake in its frame and feel the consulate building tilt and move as its timbers creaked. He must have, despite the howling destruction outside, fallen asleep, because the next thing he remembered was the silence and the morning light outside his window.

He got up and looked out. There was mud and debris and broken branches on the roadway, but the rolling waves of the South China Sea were once again contained by the seawall. The light was clear and pure, as if all impurities in it had been swept away in the fury of the storm leaving nothing but the essence of the morning.

Then Reeves heard a tapping and a snapping, and he realized that it was coming from the Union Jack on the flagstaff on the roof. It had been flying all night, throughout the typhoon. He quickly dressed and climbed the ladder to the roof .The Union Jack was still attached to the lanyard by two of the four grommets, but the flag itself was in tatters. The shreds flapped and snapped in the wind. Reeves hauled down what was left of the flag he had so proudly raised on the day of victory, detached it and rolled the remnants up tightly. They will come with me to Rome to remind me of my last day in Macao; they are of no use to anyone here. When he came down the ladder back to the second floor, the Number One Boy was waiting for him. "Mr. Gonsalves is here to see you."

Mr. Gonsalves was waiting in the front hall. He was not expected. He was dressed in what Reeves remembered his mother would call 'his Sunday best.' Mr. Gonsalves came forward and embraced the consul, pulling him hard against him. He then pushed Reeves away by his shoulders, holding him at arms' length for an instance while looking affectionately at him. "Come," he said, "We are going for a short walk." Reeves could offer no objection.

They walked out of the consulate and down the *Praya Grande*, Mr. Gonsalves taking Reeves by the arm as if they were two lovers taking in the air. They turned up the *Rua da Barra*, past the Moorish Barracks where Reeves had spent time with the Harbormaster and into a European part of Macao, a residential section of small apartments and townhouses that lay in a narrow band of land between the two harbors.

"Where are we going?" said Reeves.

"You will see," said Mr. Gonsalves, still holding tightly onto Reeves's arm. Then he steered Reeves abruptly to the right and he found himself in a square that he had never seen during his time in Macao. He was in Europe but a Europe of the imagination and of dreams. There were three and four story townhouses with dark forest-green shutters, thrown open now that the storm had passed. The houses were pink, yellow, blue, burnt umber, and pale green. They had polished varnish on the front doors and intricately woven wrought iron balconies. This was some ideal of Europe that did not exist in Europe itself. Two banyan trees in opposite corners of the square shaded the square and there were seats and benches under them on which you could sit. There was a well in the middle and three maids were there drawing water to pour into earthenware jugs to take back to their houses. The wooden bucket at the well clattered noisily against the brick sides of the well as it was lowered. The maids giggled happily.

"This is the *Largo do Lilau* – Lilau Square," said Mr. Gonsalves, "Come with me." He walked Reeves over to one side of the square where there was a large curved granite basin set into a wall of dressed blocks of stone. Above the basin was the carved head of a lion. A stream of water flowed out of its mouth into the basin.

"The *Fonte do Lilau*, Lilau Fountain. Most Englishmen do not know about it." He reached into an outer pocket of his jacket and pulled out a small silver tankard. He leaned forward and filled it with the water that flowed out of the lion's mouth.

"Come, John," he said, passing the tankard of water to Reeves. He had never called Reeves by his first name before. "Drink this. We Macanese believe that anyone who drinks from the Lilau fountain will never forget Macao." Reeves took the small tankard and drank.

* * *

No more than two hours later, Reeves was on a wharf in the *Porto Interior*. He saw his beloved *Sai An* nuzzled against the ferry wharf. Out in the roads, the great hulk of the HMS *Ranee* loomed, black and bulky against the horizon. The consular launch lay rocking gently on one side, a Portuguese sailor at the helm and another next to him, both in their uniforms. The consular flag was in the fore and the Red Ensign at the aft. The launch had been freshly washed and polished and it shone in the morning sun. Reeves's suitcases for his journey to Europe had been stowed.

Reeves walked down the wharf and shook hands formally with each person who had come to say goodbye to him. He shook hands with the Governor, the Chief of Police, Y.C. Liang, the Harbormaster, Mr. Aycock, Mr. Swemmelaar, Mr. Gonsalves, the Reverend Florence Lim, Bishop Ramalho, Dr Gosano, Dr Lobo and his son, his Number One Boy. There may have been others, he did not see them. He felt he dare not say anything beyond 'Thank you for coming.' He climbed into the launch, a sailor untied it from the pier. As it pulled away, there came the boom from artillery firing. Reeves moved to the stern of the launch and prepared to hear the six guns that a consul was entitled to as a salute. But then there was a seventh and then more, until the guns had fired twenty-one times. The Governor had given him a twenty-one gun salute. Only a reigning monarch or a head of state was entitled to twenty-one guns. He stood up, a little unsteadily in the moving boat, waved both arms to his friends on the wharf, now distant figures, and fancied he could see them wave back.

"Farewell, Macao," he cried, "Farewell."

Epilogue

In 1949, after barely three years in Italy, John Pownall Reeves was suddenly appointed British Consul for the Province of East Java in Indonesia, a few months after that country had wrested its independence from the Dutch. His residence was in Surabaya. That city was the scene of a brutal battle in November 1945, when British troops, acting on behalf of the Dutch, had crushed an uprising of Indonesian soldiers and guerrillas fighting for independence, with a great loss of life amongst both civilians and the local soldiers. Even today, the date of the battle is celebrated as Heroes Day in Indonesia. It was an almost impossible posting for a representative of the British Government given the acrimony in which the British were held, and his position there might be seen as a further sign of the disfavor in which Reeves found himself.

Reeves abruptly resigned from the Consular Service not long after arriving in Indonesia, turning his back on England and emigrating to South Africa. He brought with him as his companion and partner his former secretary from the Surabaya consulate. Rhoda had never responded to his letters from either Macao or Rome and he made no other effort to reconnect. His friends in South Africa described him as an eccentric figure, sitting in his library, surrounded by his beloved collection of Chinese artifacts, his hair, now grown very long, tied with a ribbon or let loose to his shoulders, and the nails of both little fingers long and curling in the style of the then elderly mandarins he must have met when he first arrived in Peking. The Foreign Office denied him permission to publish a book about his time during the war, saying "it would serve no useful purpose."

John Pownall Reeves died in 1978, without ever returning to Macao. His daughter had died some years before. Rhoda, from whom he was never formally divorced, renounced any interest that she might have had in his estate.

A Note on the Sources

There is surprisingly little written on Macao during the Second World War. Upon the death of the British consul, a draft manuscript was found among his possessions recounting his time in Macao during the war. In 2014, a version of it entitled *The Lone Flag* was published by the Royal Asiatic Society and the Hong Kong University Press, and ably edited (and footnoted) by Colin Day and Richard Garrett. It is very much a first draft and the average reader might find it somewhat hard going.

Hong Kong University Press also published in 2016 *Wartime Macau*, a series of essays largely by academics and intended for a more academic audience although some of the papers have a broader appeal. The book was superbly edited by Geoffrey Dunn, who also contributed some of its more vivid articles.

If you follow the footnotes and bibliographies in both books, they will lead you to documents in archives around the world, articles in various journals and publications, and books, some of which were self-published and exist only in single copies in one library in the world. In the end, I looked at documents and books in archives and libraries in New York, Washington, Miami (where the archives of Pan American Airlines are housed), Macao, Hong Kong, London and Canberra, where J.M. Braga's extensive collection of documents, clippings, papers and ephemera on Macao from the 1920s to the 1950s can be found in the National Library of Australia.

And finally there is the one book on Macao by Jason Wordie, the preeminent historian of the Hong Kong-Macao region. His *Macao: People and Places. Past and Present* is a magisterial (and definitive) account of Macao's history and present-day geography and architecture, beautifully written, with equally beautiful photographs. I consulted it frequently and I cannot recommend it more highly.

The Good War of Consul Reeves is a work of historical fiction although I tried to hew as close to the facts as I could. The definitive work on Macao during the War has yet to be written. There must be accounts within the Japanese and Portuguese archives (just the documents from Portuguese intelligence and the Macao police would be enthralling) which would round out and amplify the picture we now have of this fascinating period. I hope someone undertakes this task.

Acknowledgments

First and foremost I want to thank my wife Alicia who believed I could accomplish this project and encouraged me to undertake it, when there was little or no evidence to support her faith that it could be done. Jane Rosenman was my editor and her astute comments and questions over several drafts immeasurably transformed the final draft. Pete Spurrier, the publisher of Blacksmith Books, was willing to take a chance on a first-time author and for that I will be always grateful. Bethany McLean and Joe Nocera, two incomparable journalists, encouraged me right from the beginning. Pattie Sellers, another great journalist, took the first chapter and showed me how much good editing could improve a draft. Steve Schwarzman, the founder of Blackstone, gave a magnificently generous gift to the New York Public Library to ensure it remained at the forefront of the world's preeminent research libraries. Melanie Locay, the manager of the Library's Center for Research in the Humanities, patiently guided me during the three years I spent in the Wertheim Room of the Library researching the book. Jason Wordie, the preeminent historian of Hong Kong and Macao, was generous with his time, advice and encouragement from the outset. Tina Hampson was critical in locating key documents in the UK National Archives and Grace Sixsmith was of huge assistance in the National Library of Australia. Eduardo Adam-Rabel was similarly helpful with the Pan American archives at the University of Miami. Emma Bilney spent hours in the archives of the Macao Central Library procuring documents. Professor Steven Kenneth Bailey was generous in sharing his research for his forthcoming book on the bombing of Macao by the American Navy at the end of 1945.

To all these people, my heartfelt thanks. The book would not have been possible without you.

EXPLORE ASIA WITH BLACKSMITH BOOKS

From booksellers around the world or from *www.blacksmithbooks.com*

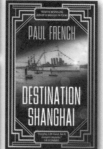